Praise for Robert Crais
and the Elvis Cole Novels

"The dialogue's clever, and the action's lean and pictorial, with gunshots pinging like mad pinballs."
—*Voice Literary Supplement*

"Cole delivers the goods in the kind of bravura performance only a pro can give." —*Kirkus Reviews*

"This novel shows why the Elvis Cole series has become one of crime fiction's best."
—*Detroit Free Press*

"Sue Grafton's Kinsey Milhone has become a fixture in the genre [and] Robert Crais's Elvis Cole ought to become one, too. Cole is fast replacing Spenser as the best of the intelligent but sensitive tough guys." —*Detroit Free Press*

"Elvis Cole is lean, mean and completely lovable."
—*People*

"Crais . . . flips a quick, cutting wit at Hollywood hucksters, and shows a keen ear for their inane industry prattle."
—*The New York Times Book Review*

"The ghostly influence is Robert B. Parker, including the wisecracks and the incessant attention to food. . . . But once Crais gets past the mandatory wise-mouthing and sets his story in motion, forget influences; he is his own man."
—*Los Angeles Times Book Review*

"Cole noshes like Spenser . . . and he views the world through the same darkly moral shades as Marlowe and Archer." —*Chicago Tribune*

"Elvis is the greatest . . . [He's] perhaps the best detective to come along since Travis McGee."
—*San Diego Tribune*

"Crais is in a class by himself—he is quite simply the best." —Eric Van Lustbader

THE LAST DETECTIVE

BY ROBERT CRAIS

The Monkey's Raincoat
Stalking the Angel
Lullaby Town
Free Fall
Voodoo River
Sunset Express
Indigo Slam
L.A. Requiem
Demolition Angel
Hostage
The Last Detective
The Forgotten Man
The Two Minute Rule
The Watchman
Chasing Darkness
The First Rule
The Sentry
Taken
Suspect
The Promise
The Wanted
A Dangerous Man

THE LAST DETECTIVE

AN ELVIS COLE AND JOE PIKE NOVEL

...

ROBERT CRAIS

BALLANTINE BOOKS
NEW YORK

2020 Ballantine Books Mass Market Edition

Copyright © 2003 by Robert Crais
Excerpt from *A Dangerous Man* by Robert Crais
copyright © 2019 by Robert Crais

Published in the United States by Ballantine Books,
an imprint of Random House, a division of
Penguin Random House LLC, New York.

BALLANTINE and the HOUSE colophon are registered trademarks of
Penguin Random House LLC.

Originally published in hardcover in the United States by Doubleday,
an imprint of the Knopf Doubleday Publishing Group,
a division of Penguin Random House LLC, in 2003.

ISBN 978-0-593-15717-6
Ebook ISBN 978-0-385-50427-0

Cover design: Kaitlin Hall
Cover image: René Morales/EyeEm/Getty Images

Printed in the United States of America

randomhousebooks.com

2 4 6 8 9 7 5 3

Ballantine Books mass market edition: January 2020

For Wayne Warga
who maintained his post
under intense enemy fire
and did not waver
even as he was overrun.

ACKNOWLEDGMENTS
• • •

The author would like to thank the following people for their contributions:

Eli and Tara Lucas, masters of *Emydon* out of Petersburg, Alaska, provided information about commercial fishing and the Alaskan brown bear; more important, they allowed me to share in the richness of their lives.

Kregg P.J. Jorgenson and Kenn Miller provided insight and detail about U.S. Army Rangers, Ranger operations, and LRRP (lurp) missions conducted during the Vietnam war. Gary Linderer provided additional information. The liberties taken with reality (i.e., use of the term *hoo*) are my responsibility, as are all errors of fact.

Randy Sherman, MD, Professor and Chief of the

Division of Plastic and Reconstructive Surgery at the USC School of Medicine, provided information, illustrations, and early-morning counsel on wounds, wound trauma, and recovery; Joe Pike could not have a finer surgeon.

Elyse Dinh-McCrillis provided Vietnamese translations.

Detective-3 John Petievich, LAPD-retired, opened doors to Missing Persons operations within the Los Angeles Police Department.

Additional thanks go to Aaron Priest. Jason Kaufman, Steve Rubin, and Gina Centrello made it better, and demonstrated patience beyond any that could reasonably be expected. Thank you.

THE LAST DETECTIVE

THE CHURCH OF PIKE
ANGOON, ALASKA

The cold Alaskan water pulled at the fishing boats that lined the dock, the boats straining against their moorings to run free with the tide. The water here in the small harbor at Angoon, a fishing village on the western shore of Admiralty Island off southeast Alaska, was steel-black beneath the clouds and dimpled by rain, but was clear even with that, a window beneath the weathered pilings to a world of sunburst starfish as wide as garbage cans, jellyfish the size of basketballs, and barnacles as heavy as a longshoreman's fist. Alaska was like that, so vigorous with life that it could fill a man and lift him and maybe even bring him back from the dead.

A Tlingit Indian named Elliot MacArthur watched as Joe Pike stowed his duffel in a fourteen-foot fiberglass skiff. Pike had rented the skiff from MacArthur, who now nervously toed Pike's rifle case.

"You didn't tell me you were goin' after those bears up there. It ain't so smart goin' in those woods by yourself. I don't wanna lose my boat."

Pike secured his duffel between the skiff's bench seats, then took hold of the gun case. Pike's weapon of choice that day was a stainless-steel Remington Model 700 chambered in .375 Holland & Holland Magnum. It was a powerful gun, built heavy to dampen the .375's hard recoil. Pike lifted the case with his bad arm, but the arm failed with a sharp pain that left his shoulder burning. He shifted its weight to his good arm.

MacArthur didn't like this business with the arm.

"Now you listen. Goin' after that bear with a bad arm ain't the brightest idea, either. You're gonna have my boat, and you're gonna be alone, and that's a big bear up there. Has to be big, what he did to those people."

Pike strapped the rifle case across the duffel, then checked the fuel. It was going to be a long trip, getting from Angoon up to Chaik Bay where the killings had taken place.

"You better be thinkin' about this. Don't matter what kinda bounty the families put up, it ain't worth gettin' killed for."

"I won't lose your boat."

MacArthur wasn't sure if Pike had insulted him or not.

Pike finished with his gear, then stepped back onto the dock. He took ten one-hundred-dollar bills from his wallet and held out the money.

"Here. Now you won't have to worry about it."

MacArthur looked embarrassed and put his hands in his pocket.

"Let's just forget it. You rented it, it's yours. You're makin' me feel like a miser and I don't appreciate that."

Pike put the money away and stepped down into the skiff, keeping his weight low. He cast off the lines.

"You bank the boat when you get up Chaik, use that orange tape to flag a tree so I can find ya if I have to come looking."

Pike nodded.

"Anyone you want me to call, you know, if you need me to call someone?"

"No."

"You sure?"

Pike nosed away from the dock without answering and set off for deeper water, holding his bad arm close.

The light rain became fat drops, then a low foggy mist. Pike zipped his parka. A family of seals watched him pass from their perch on a promontory of rocks. Humpback whales spouted further out in the channel, one great tail tipping into the sky as a whale sounded, Pike's only thought to wonder at the perfect quiet that waited in the waters below.

Pike rubbed his bad shoulder. He had been shot twice high in the back almost eight months ago. The bullets shattered his shoulder blade, spraying bone fragments like shrapnel through his left lung and the surrounding muscles and nerves. Pike had almost died, but didn't, and had come north to heal. He worked king crab boats out of Dutch Harbor and fishing boats out of Petersburg. He long-lined for black cod and halibut, and if the crews on the boats he worked saw the scars that laced his chest and back, no one asked of their nature. That was Alaska, too.

Pike steered north for four hours at a steady six knots until he reached a circular bay with two small islands at its mouth. Pike checked his chart, then double-checked his position on a handheld GPS. This was the place, all right. Chaik Bay.

The pounding chop of the channel gave way to water as flat as glass, undisturbed except for the head of a single white seal. The bottom rose as Pike eased toward shore, and soon the first of the carcasses appeared; dead salmon as long as a man's arm drifted with the current as they washed out of the creek, their bodies mottled and broken with the effort to spawn. Hundreds of seagulls picked through the fish that had washed onto shore; scores of bald eagles perched in the treetops, a single eagle at the peak of each tree, watching the gulls with envious eyes. The smell of rotten fish grew sharp.

Pike shut the engine, let the skiff glide into the rocky beach, then stepped out into ankle-deep water. He pulled the boat high above the tide line, then tied it to a hemlock limb. He flagged the limb with orange tape as Elliot MacArthur had asked.

Alder, spruce, and hemlock trees lined the shore like an impenetrable green wall. Pike made camp beneath the soft boughs, then ate a supper of peanut butter and carrot sticks. Later, he smoothed a place on the beach where he stretched until his muscles were warm, then did push-ups and sit-ups on pebbles that clawed at his flesh. He worked hard. His spine arched and his legs lifted in the most strenuous asanas of hatha yoga. He spun through the strict choreography of a tae kwon do *kata*, kicking and windmilling his arms as he blended the Korean form into the Chinese forms of kung fu and wing chun in a regimen he had practiced every day since he was a child. Sweat leaked from his short brown hair. His hands and feet snapped with a violence that frightened the eagles. Pike pushed himself faster, spinning and twisting through the air, falling within himself in a frenzy of effort as he tried to outrace his pain.

It was not good enough. His shoulder was slow. His movements were awkward. He was less than he had been.

Pike sat at the water's edge with a sense of emptiness. He told himself that he would work harder, that he would heal the damage that had been done, and recreate himself as he had recreated himself when he was a child. Effort was prayer; commitment was faith; trust in himself his only creed. Pike had learned these catechisms when he was a child. He had nothing else.

That night he slept beneath a plastic sheet and listened to rain leak through the trees as he considered the bear.

The next morning, Pike began.

The Alaskan brown bear is the largest predator living on land. It is larger than the African lion or Bengal tiger. It is not named Smokey or Pooh, nor does it live a happy-go-lucky life at Disneyland playing the banjo. The male bear, called a boar, can weigh a thousand pounds, yet slip through the wilderness in absolute silence. The bear appears fat with its barrel-shaped body, but it can accelerate faster than a thoroughbred racehorse to chase down a running deer. Its claws reach a length of six inches and are as sharp as plank spikes; its jaws can crush a moose's spine or rip a car door from its hinges. When the brown bear charges, it does not lumber forward on its hind legs as portrayed in movies; it crouches low to the ground with its head down, lips pulled high in a snarl as it powers forward with the speed of an attacking lion. It kills by crushing the neck or biting through the braincase. If you protect your neck and head, the bear will strip the flesh from your back and legs even as you scream, swallowing whole chunks without chewing until it reaches your entrails. The ancient Romans staged fights in their blood pits between Ural Mountain grizzly bears and African lions. The Romans would set two lions against a single bear. The bear usually won. Like the great white shark that glides without fear through the depths, the brown bear has no peer on land.

Pike heard what happened up Chaik Creek from a boat captain he met in Petersburg: Three Department of Fish and Game biologists had ventured up Chaik Creek to conduct a population count of spawning salmon. On their first day, the biologists reported a high number of brown bears, which was typical for the spawning season and not unexpected. The biologists were not heard from again until a garbled plea was received by a passing boat four days later. Officials from F&G working with local Tlingit trappers determined that a mature boar stalked the three biologists for some distance along the creek, then attacked when the trio stopped to build a fish trap. Though armed with high-power rifles, the ferocity of the attack prevented the team from using their weapons. Two of the team members—Dr. Abigail Martin, the senior biologist, and Clark Aimes, a wildlife supervisor—were killed immediately. The third biologist, a graduate student from Seattle named Jacob Gottman, fled. The boar—estimated by the depth and breadth of its track at weighing better than eleven hundred pounds—pursued Gottman to a gravel bar downstream where it disemboweled the young man, tore off his right arm at the elbow, and pushed his body beneath the uprooted base of a fallen alder tree. Gottman was still alive. When the bear returned to the original attack site to devour Martin and Aimes, Gottman made his way downstream to Chaik Bay where he called for help on a small walkie-talkie. One of his last pleas was heard by the fifty-foot salmon boat, *Emydon*. Gottman bled to death before he was reached.

"It had to be a mercy." The captain stared into his coffee. "No doubt, it had to be a mercy. They said his guts trailed behind him like a garden hose."

Pike nodded without comment. He had seen worse done to men by other men, but he did not say that.

The captain explained that tests on their remains indicated that the bear was rabid. Fish and Game sent two teams of trackers to hunt it down, but neither team was successful. Jacob Gottman's parents put up a bounty. A Tlingit trapper from Angoon went

in to find the bear, but didn't come back. The Gott-
mans doubled their bounty. The trapper's brother
and father-in-law spent two weeks along the creek,
but had found only one sign: the single largest print
that either had ever seen, with claw marks the size of
hunting knives. They had felt him in there, they said;
felt the dark deadly weight of him like a shadow in
the trees, but they never saw the bear. It was as if he
were hanging back. Waiting.

Pike said, "Waiting."

"That's what they said, yeah."

That evening Pike phoned a man in Los Angeles.
Two days later Pike's rifle arrived. He set out for Angoon.

Wilderness swallowed him. Trees as old as the land
pushed from the earth to vanish into a canopy of
green. Rain leaked through their leaves in an unwav-
ering drizzle that left Pike wet to the bone. The steep
sides of the creek were so tangled with ferns, saplings, and the clawed stalks of devilclub that he
slipped into the water and waded. Pike loved this
wild place.

The others had come earlier in the spawning cycle
when the creek was filled with fish. Now, dead salmon
littered the gravel bars and hung from roots like rotten drapes. Easy meals weren't so easy. Pike reasoned
that the mad boar would have driven away the cubs,
sows, and smaller boars to keep the remaining fish
for himself.

Pike hiked for the rest of the day but found nothing. That night he returned to his camp. Pike hunted

like that for five days, each day working farther up-stream. He paused often to rest. The scars in his lungs made breathing painful.

On the sixth day, he found the blood.

Pike slipped around the uprooted base of a fallen alder and saw streamers of crimson like spilled paint splashed on a gravel bar. A dozen dog salmon had been scooped from the water, their torn flesh bright with fresh blood. Some were bitten in half, others were absent their braincase. Pike froze, absolutely still. He searched the devilclub for eyes that stared into his own, but found nothing. He took a butane lighter from his pocket and watched the flame. The wind blew downstream. Anything upstream could not smell him coming.

Pike crept to the gravel bar. Tracks as wide as dinner plates were pressed into the mud showing claw marks as long as daggers.

Pike hefted his rifle to settle his grip. If the boar charged, Pike would have to bring the rifle up fast or eleven hundred pounds of furious insanity would be on him. A year ago he would have had no doubts about his ability to do it. Pike released the safety. The world was not certain; the only certainty was within you.

Pike waded upstream.

The creek turned sharply. Pike's view ahead was blocked by a fallen hemlock, its great ball of roots spread like a towering lace fan. Pike heard a heavy splash beyond the deadfall. The splash came again; not the quick slap of a jumping fish, but something large pushing through water.

Pike strained to see through breaks in the deadfall, but the tangle of roots and leaves and limbs was too thick.

More splashes came from only a few feet away. Red flesh swirled around him and bounced off his legs.

Pike edged around the deadfall with glacial silence, careful of every step, soundless in the wild water. A dying salmon flopped on a knobby bank, its entrails exposed, but the boar was gone. Eleven hundred pounds, and it had slipped from the water into a thicket of alder and devilclub without making a sound. A single huge paw print showed large at the edge of a trail.

Pike stood motionless in the swirling water for a very long time. The boar could be lying in wait only ten feet away or it could be long gone. Pike climbed onto the bank. The boar's trail was littered with bones and the slime of rotting fish. Pike looked at the dying salmon again, but now it was dead.

Pike eased into the thicket. A shroud of ferns, devilclub, and saplings closed around him. Something large but unseeable moved ahead and to his right.

Huff!

Pike raised the gun, but the devilclub clawed at the barrel and was stronger than his bad arm.

Huff!

The boar blew air through its mouth to taste Pike's smell. It knew that something else was in the thicket, but it didn't know what. Pike wrestled the gun to his shoulder, but could not see where to aim.

SNAP!

The boar snapped its jaws in warning. It was setting itself to charge.

SNAPSNAP!

It could split this brush like tissue; its attack might come from anywhere. Pike braced himself. He would not retreat; he would not turn away. That was the single immutable law of Joe Pike's faith—he would always meet the charge.

SNAPSNAPSNAP!

Pike's strength failed. His shoulder quivered, then lost feeling. His arm trembled. He willed himself to hold firm, but the rifle grew heavy and the brush pulled it down.

SNAP!

Pike crept backwards out of the thicket and into the water. The snapping of steel jaws faded into the patter of rain.

Pike did not stop until he reached the bay. He pressed his back to a towering spruce and worked to bury his feelings, but he could not hide from his shame or his pain, or the certainty that he was lost.

Two days later he returned to Los Angeles.

PART ONE

. . .

THE
FIRST DETECTIVE

The headstone anchors me in the dream with a weight I cannot escape. It is a small black rectangle let into the earth, kissed red by the setting sun. I stare down at the hard marble, burning with a hunger to know who lies within the earth, but the headstone is blank. No name marks this resting place. My only clue is this: The grave is small. I am standing over a child.

I have the dream often now, almost every night, some nights more than once. I sleep little on those nights; instead, I rise to sit in the darkness of my empty home. Even then, I am a prisoner of the dream.

Here is what happens: The sky darkens as a mist settles across the cemetery. The twisted limbs of an ancient oak drip with moss, swaying in the night breeze. I do not know where this place is, or how I got there. I am alone, and I am scared. Shadows flicker at the edge of light; voices whisper, but I cannot understand. One shade might be my mother, another the father I never knew. I want to ask them who lies in this grave, but when I turn for their help I find only darkness. No one remains to ask, no one to help. I am on my own.

The nameless headstone waits for me.

What lies here?

Who has left this child alone?

I am desperate to escape this place. I want to beat feet, boogie, truck, book, haul ass, motor, shred, jet, jam, split, cut out, blow, roll, abandon, get away, get gone, scram, RUN . . . but in the strange way of dreams a shovel appears in my hands. My feet will not move, my body will not obey. A voice in my head tells me to throw the blade aside, but a power I cannot resist forces my hand: If I dig, I will find; if I find, I will know. The voice pleads with me to stop, but I am possessed. The voice warns that I will not want to see the secrets that lie below, but I dig deep and true to expose the grave.

The black earth opens.

The casket is revealed.

The voice shrieks for me to stop, to look away, to save myself, and so I clench my eyes. I have recognized the voice. It is my own.

I fear what lies at my feet, but I have no choice. I must see the truth.

My eyes open.

I look.

1

· · ·

A silence filled the canyon below my house that fall; no hawks floated overhead, the coyotes did not sing, the owl that lived in the tall pine outside my door no longer asked my name. A smarter person would have taken these things as a warning, but the air was chill and clear in that magnified way it can be in the winter, letting me see beyond the houses sprinkled on the hillsides below and out into the great basin city of Los Angeles. On days like those when you can see so far, you often forget to look at what is right in front of you, what is next to you, what is so close that it is part of you. I should have seen the silence as a warning, but I did not.

"How many people has she killed?"

Grunts, curses, and the snap of punches came from the next room.

Ben Chenier shouted, *"What?"*

"How many people has she killed?"

We were twenty feet apart, me in the kitchen and Ben in the living room, shouting at the tops of our lungs; Ben Chenier, also known as my girlfriend's ten-year-old son, and me, also known as Elvis Cole, the World's Greatest Detective and Ben's caretaker while his mother, Lucy Chenier, was away on business. This was our fifth and final day together.

I went to the door.

"Is there a volume control on that thing?"

Ben was so involved with something called a Game Freak that he did not look up. You held the Game Freak like a pistol with one hand and worked the controls with the other while the action unfolded on a built-in computer screen. The salesman told me that it was a hot seller with boys ages ten to fourteen. He hadn't told me that it was louder than a shoot-out at rush hour.

Ben had been playing the game since I had given it to him the day before, but I knew he wasn't enjoying himself, and that bothered me. He had hiked with me in the hills and let me teach him some of the things I knew about martial arts and had come with me to my office because he thought private investigators did more than phone deadbeat clients and clean pigeon crap off balcony rails. I had brought him to school in the mornings and home in the afternoons, and between those times we had cooked Thai food, watched Bruce Willis movies, and laughed a lot together. But now he used the game to hide from me with an absolute lack of joy. I knew why, and seeing him like that left me feeling badly, not only for him, but for my part in it. Fighting it out with Yakuza spree killers was easier than talking to boys.

I went over and dropped onto the couch next to him.

"We could go for a hike up on Mulholland."

He ignored me.

"You want to work out? I could show you another tae kwon do *kata* before your mom gets home."

"Uh-uh."

I said, "You want to talk about me and your mom?"

I am a private investigator. My work brings me into contact with dangerous people, and early last summer that danger rolled over my shores when a murderer named Laurence Sobek threatened Lucy and Ben. Lucy was having a tough time with that, and Ben had heard our words. Lucy and Ben's father had divorced when Ben was six, and now he worried that it was happening again. We had tried to talk to him, Lucy and I, but boys—like men—find it hard to open their hearts.

Instead of answering me, Ben thumbed the game harder and nodded toward the action on the screen.

"Check it out. This is the Queen of Blame."

Perfect.

A young Asian woman with spiky hair, breasts the size of casaba melons, and an angry snarl jumped over a Dumpster to face three musclebound steroid-juicers in what appeared to be a devastated urban landscape. A tiny halter barely covered her breasts, sprayed-on shorts showed her butt cheeks, and her voice growled electronically from the Game Freak's little speaker.

"*You're my toilet!*"

She let loose with a martial arts sidekick that spun the first attacker into the air.

I said, "Some woman."

"Uh-huh. A bad guy named Modus sold her sister into slavery, and now the Queen is going to make him pay the ultimate price."

The Queen of Blame punched a man three times her size with left and rights so fast that her hands blurred. Blood and teeth flew everywhere.

"*Eat fist, scum!*"

I spotted a pause button on the controls, and stopped the game. Adults always wonder what to say and how to say it when they're talking with a child. You want to be wise, but all you are is a child yourself in a larger body. Nothing is ever what it seems. The things that you think you know are never certain. I know that, now. I wish that I didn't, but I do.

I said, "I know that what's going on between me and your mom is scary. I just want you to know that we're going to get through this. Your mom and I love each other. We're going to be fine."

"I know."

"She loves you. I love you, too."

Ben stared at the frozen screen for a little while longer, and then he looked up at me. His little-boy face was smooth and thoughtful. He wasn't stupid; his mom and dad loved him, too, but that hadn't stopped them from getting divorced.

"Elvis?"

"What?"

"I had a really good time staying with you. I wish I didn't have to leave."

"Me, too, pal. I'm glad you were here."

Ben smiled, and I smiled back. Funny, how a moment like that could fill a man with hope. I patted his leg.

"Here's the plan: Mom's going to get back soon. We should clean the place so she doesn't think we're pigs, then we should get the grill ready so we're good to go with dinner when she gets home. Burgers okay?"

"Can I finish the game first? The Queen of Blame is about to find Modus."

"Sure. How about you take her out onto the deck? She's pretty loud."

"Okay."

I went back into the kitchen, and Ben took the Queen and her breasts outside. Even that far away, I heard her clearly. *"Your face is pizza!"* Then her victim shrieked in pain.

I should have heard more. I should have listened even harder.

Less than three minutes later, Lucy called from her car. It was twenty-two minutes after four. I had just taken the hamburger meat from my refrigerator.

I said, "Hey. Where are you?"

"Long Beach. Traffic's good, so I'm making great time. How are you guys holding up?"

Lucy Chenier was a legal commentator for a local television station. Before that, she had practiced civil law in Baton Rouge, which is what she was doing when we met. Her voice still held the hint of a French-

Louisiana accent, but you had to listen closely to hear it. She had been in San Diego covering a trial.

"We're good. I'm getting hamburgers together for when you get here."

"How's Ben?"

"He was feeling low today, but we talked. He's better now. He misses you."

We fell into a silence that lasted too long. Lucy had phoned every night, and we laughed well enough, but our exchanges felt incomplete though we tried to pretend they weren't. It wasn't easy being hooked up with the World's Greatest Detective.

Finally, I said, "I missed you."

"I missed you, too. It's been a long week. Hamburgers sound really good. Cheeseburgers. With lots of pickles."

She sounded tired. But she also sounded as if she was smiling.

"I think we can manage that. I got your pickle for ya right here."

Lucy laughed. I'm the World's Funniest Detective, too.

She said, "How can I pass up an offer like that?"

"You want to speak with Ben? He just went outside."

"That's all right. Tell him that I'm on my way and that I love him, and then you can tell yourself that I love you, too."

We hung up and I went out onto the deck to pass along the good word, but the deck was empty. I went to the rail. Ben liked to play on the slope below my house and climb in the black walnut trees that grow further down the hill. More houses were nestled beyond the trees on the streets that web along the hill-sides. The deepest cuts in the canyon were just beginning to purple, but the light was still good. I didn't see him.

"Ben?"

He didn't answer.

"Hey, buddy! Mom called!"

He still didn't answer.

I checked the side of the house, then went back inside and called him again, thinking maybe he had gone to the guest room where he sleeps or the bathroom.

"Yo, Ben! Where are you?"

Nothing.

I looked in the guest room and the downstairs bathroom, then went out the front door into the street. I live on a narrow private road that winds along the top of the canyon. Cars rarely pass except when my neighbors go to and from work, so it's a safe street, and great for skateboarding.

"Ben?"

I didn't see him. I went back inside the house. "Ben! That was Mom on the phone!"

I thought that might get an answer. The Mom Threat.

"If you're hiding, this is a problem. It's not funny."

I went upstairs to my loft, but didn't find him. I went downstairs again to the deck.

"BEN!"

My nearest neighbor had two little boys, but Ben never went over without first telling me. He never went down the slope or out into the street or even into the carport without first letting me know, either.

It wasn't his way. It also wasn't his way to pull a David Copperfield and disappear.

I went back inside and phoned next door. I could see Grace Gonzalez's house from my kitchen window.

"Grace? It's Elvis next door."

Like there might be another Elvis further up the block.

"Hey, bud. How's it going?"

Grace calls me bud. She used to be a stuntwoman until she married a stuntman she met falling off a twelve-story building and retired to have two boys.

"Is Ben over there?"

"Nope. Was he supposed to be?"

"He was here a few minutes ago, but now he's not. I thought he might have gone to see the boys."

Grace hesitated, and her voice lost its easygoing familiarity for something more concerned.

"Let me ask Andrew. They could have gone downstairs without me seeing."

Andrew was her oldest, who was eight. His younger brother, Clark, was six. Ben told me that Clark liked to eat his own snot.

I checked the time again. Lucy had called at four twenty-two; it was now four thirty-eight. I brought the phone out onto my deck, hoping to see Ben trudging up the hill, but the hill was empty.

Grace came back on the line.

"Elvis?"

"I'm here."

"My guys haven't seen him. Let me look out front. Maybe he's in the street."

"Thanks, Grace."

Her voice carried clearly across the bend in the canyon that separated our homes when she called him, and then she came back on the line.

"I can see pretty far both ways, but I don't see him. You want me to come over there and help you look?"

"You've got your hands full with Andrew and Clark. If he shows up, will you keep him there and call me?"

"Right away."

I turned off the phone, and stared down into the canyon. The slope was not steep, but he could have taken a tumble or fallen from a tree. I left the phone on the deck and worked my way down the slope. My feet sank into the loose soil, and footing was poor.

"Ben! Where in hell are you?"

Walnut trees twisted from the hillside like gnarled fingers, their trunks gray and rough. A lone yucca tree grew in a corkscrew among the walnuts with spiky leaves like green-black starbursts. The rusted remains of a chain-link fence were partially buried by years of soil movement. The largest walnut tree pushed out of the ground beyond the fence with five heavy trunks that spread like an opening hand. I had twice climbed in the tree with Ben, and we had talked about building a tree house between the spreading trunks.

"Ben!"

I listened hard. I took a deep breath, exhaled, then held my breath. I heard a faraway voice.

"BEN!"

I imagined him further down the slope with a broken leg. Or worse.

"I'm coming."

I hurried.

I followed the voice through the trees and around a bulge in the finger, certain that I would find him, but as I went over the hump I heard the voice more clearly and knew that it wasn't his. The Game Freak was waiting for me in a nest of stringy autumn grass. Ben was gone.

I called as loudly as I could.

"BEN!!!"

No answer came except for the sound of my own thundering heart and the Queen's tinny voice. She had finally found Modus, a great fat giant of a man with a bullet head and pencil-point eyes. She launched kick after kick, punch after punch, screaming her vow of vengeance as the two of them fought in an endless loop through a blood-drenched room.

"Now you die! Now you die! Now you die!"

I held the Queen of Blame close, and hurried back up the hill.

2
...

The sun was dropping. Shadows pooled in the deep cuts between the ridges as if the canyon was filling with ink. I left a note in the middle of the kitchen floor: STAY HERE—I'M LOOKING FOR U, then drove down through the canyon, trying to find him.

If Ben had sprained an ankle or twisted a knee, he might have hobbled downhill instead of making the steep climb back to my house; he might have knocked on someone's door for help; he might be limping home on his own. I told myself, sure, that had to be it. Ten-year-old boys don't simply vanish.

When I reached the street that follows the drainage below my house, I parked and got out. The light was fading faster and the murk made it difficult to see. I called for him.

"Ben?"

If Ben had come downhill, he would have passed beside one of three houses. No one was home at the first two, but a housekeeper answered at the third. She let me look in their backyard, but watched me from the windows as if I might steal the pool toys. Nothing. I boosted myself to see over a cinder-block wall into the neighboring yards, but he wasn't there, either. I called him again.

"Ben!"

I went back to my car. It was all too easy and way too likely that we would miss each other; as I drove along one street, Ben might turn down another. By the time I was on that street, he could reappear behind me, but I didn't know what else to do.

Twice I waved down passing security patrols to ask if they had seen a boy matching Ben's description. Neither had, but they took my name and number, and offered to call if they found him.

I drove faster, trying to cover as much ground as possible before the sun set. I crossed and recrossed the same streets, winding through the canyon as if it was me who was lost and not Ben. The streets were brighter the higher I climbed, but a chill haunted the shadows. Ben was wearing a sweatshirt over jeans. It didn't seem enough.

When I reached home, I called out again as I let myself in, but still got no answer. The note that I left was untouched, and the message counter read zero.

I phoned the dispatch offices of the private security firms that service the canyon, including the company that owned the two cars I had already spoken to. Their cars prowled the canyons every day around the clock, and the companies' signs were posted as a warning to burglars in front of almost every house. Welcome to life in the city. I explained that a child was missing in the area and gave them Ben's description. Even though I wasn't a subscriber, they were happy to help.

When I put down the phone, I heard the front door open and felt a spike of relief so sharp that it was painful.

"*Ben!*"

"It's me."

Lucy came into the living room. She was wearing a black business suit over a cream top, but she was carrying the suit jacket; her pants were wrinkled from so long in the car. She was clearly tired, but she made a weak smile.

"Hey. I don't smell hamburgers."

It was two minutes after six. Ben had been missing for exactly one hundred minutes. It had taken Lucy exactly one hundred minutes to get home after we last spoke. It had taken me one hundred minutes to lose her son.

Lucy saw the fear in my face. Her smile dropped.

"What's wrong?"

"Ben's missing."

She glanced around as if Ben might be hiding behind the couch, giggling at the joke. She knew it wasn't a joke. She could see that I was serious.

"What do you mean, missing?"

Explaining felt lame, as if I was making excuses.

"He went outside around the time you called, and now I can't find him. I called, but he didn't answer. I drove all over the canyon, looking for him, but I didn't see him. He isn't next door. I don't know where he is."

She shook her head as if I had made a frustrating mistake, and was getting the story wrong.

"He just *left*?"

I showed her the Game Freak as if it was evidence.

"I don't know. He was playing with this when he went out. I found it on the slope."

Lucy stalked past me and went outside onto the deck.

"Ben! Benjamin, you answer me! *Ben*!"

"Luce, I've been calling him."

She stalked back into the house and disappeared down the hall.

"Ben!"

"He's not here. I called the security patrols. I was just going to call the police."

She came back and went right back onto the deck.

"Damnit, Ben, you'd better answer me!"

I stepped out behind her and took her arms. She was shaking. She turned into me, and we held each other. Her voice was small and guilty against my chest.

"Do you think he ran away?"

"No. No, he was fine, Luce. He was okay after we talked. He was laughing at this stupid game."

I told her that I thought he had probably hurt himself when he was playing on the slope, then gotten lost trying to find his way back.

"Those streets are confusing down there, the way they snake and twist. He probably just got turned around, and now he's too scared to ask someone for help; he's been warned about strangers enough. If he got on the wrong street and kept walking, he probably got farther away, and more lost. He's probably so scared right now that he hides whenever a car passes, but we'll find him. We should call the police."

Lucy nodded against me, wanting to believe, and then she looked at the canyon. Lights from the houses were beginning to sparkle.

She said, "It's getting dark."

That single word: Dark. It summoned every parent's greatest dread.

I said, "Let's call. The cops will light up every house in the canyon until we find him."

As Lucy and I stepped back into the house, the phone rang. Lucy jumped even more than me.

"That's Ben."

I answered the phone, but the voice on the other end didn't belong to Ben or Grace Gonzalez or the security patrols.

A man said, "Is this Elvis Cole?"

"Yes. Who's this?"

The voice was cold and low.

He said, "Five-two."

"Who is this?"

"Five-two, motherfucker. You remember five-two?"

Lucy plucked my arm, hoping that it was about Ben. I shook my head, telling her I didn't understand, but the sharp fear of bad memories was already cutting deep.

I gripped the phone with both hands. I needed both to hang on.

"Who is this? What are you talking about?"

"This is payback, you bastard. This is for what you did."

I held the phone even tighter, and heard myself shout.

"What did I do? *What are you talking about?*"

"You know what you did. I have the boy."

The line went dead.

Lucy plucked harder.

"Who was it? What did they say?"

I didn't feel her. I barely heard her. I was caught in a yellowed photo album from my own past, flipping through bright green pictures of another me, a much different me, and of young men with painted faces, hollow eyes, and the damp sour smell of fear.

Lucy pulled harder.

"Stop it! You're scaring me."

"It was a man, I don't know who. He says he took Ben."

Lucy grabbed my arm with both hands.

"Ben was *stolen*? He was *kidnapped*? What did the man say? What does he *want*?"

My mouth was dry. My neck cramped with painful knots.

"He wants to punish me. For something that happened a long time ago."

BOYS BEING BOYS

On the second day of his five-day visit, Ben waited until Elvis Cole was washing his car before sneaking upstairs. Ben had been planning his assault on Elvis Cole's personal belongings for many weeks. Elvis was a private investigator, which was a pretty cool thing to be, and he also had some pretty neat stuff: He had a great videotape and DVD collection of old science fiction and horror movies that Ben could watch any time he wanted and about a hundred superhero magnets stuck all over his refrigerator and a bullet-proof vest hanging in his front entry closet. You didn't see that every day. Elvis even had business cards saying he was "the biggest dick in the business." Ben showed one to his friends at school and everyone had laughed.

Ben was convinced—profoundly supremely certain—that Elvis Cole had a treasure of other cool stuff stashed in his upstairs closet. Ben knew, for instance, that Elvis kept guns up there, but he also knew that the guns and ammunition were locked in a special safe that Ben could not open. Ben didn't know what he would find, but he thought he might luck out with a couple of issues of Playboy or some neat police stuff like handcuffs or a blackjack (what, to his mom's horror, his Uncle René down in St. Charles Parish called a "nigger-knocker").

So when Elvis went outside to wash his car that morning, Ben peeked out the window. When he saw Elvis filling a bucket with soapy water, Ben raced through the house to the stairs.

Elvis Cole and his cat slept upstairs in an open loft that looked down over the living room. The cat didn't like Ben or his mom, but Ben tried not to take it personally. This cat didn't like anyone except for Elvis and his partner, Joe Pike. Every time Ben walked into a room with that cat, the cat would lower its ears and growl. This cat wouldn't run if you tried to

*shoo it, either; it would creep toward you sideways
with its hair standing up. Ben was scared of it.*

Ben worked his way to the head of the stairs, then
peered over the top riser to make sure the cat wasn't
sleeping on the bed.

The coast was clear.

No cat.

The water still ran.

Ben ran to the closet. He had already been in Elvis's closet a couple of times when Elvis showed his
mom the gun safe, so he knew that the little room
contained boxes on high shelves, Tupperware containers filled with mysterious shadows that might be
pictures, stacks of old magazines, and other poten-
tially cool stuff. Ben riffled through the magazines
first, hoping for hot porn like his friend Billy Toman
brought to school, but was disappointed by their
content: mostly boring issues of Newsweek and the
Los Angeles Times Magazine. Ben hoisted himself
up to see what was on top of the gun safe, a huge
steel box as tall as Ben that filled the end of the closet,
but all he found were a few old baseball caps, a clock
where time had stopped, a framed color picture of an
old woman standing on a porch, and a second framed
picture of Elvis and Ben's mom sitting in a restaurant. No handcuffs or nigger-knockers.

A high shelf stretched across the closet. The shelf
was beyond Ben's reach, but he saw boots, some
boxes, a sleeping bag, what looked like a shoe shine
kit, and a black nylon gym bag. Ben thought that the
gym bag might be worth checking out, but he would
need to grow a couple of feet to reach it. Ben considered the safe. If he pushed himself up, then sat on the

safe, he could probably reach the gym bag. He carefully placed his hands on top of the safe, heaved himself straight up, then hooked a knee on top and pushed himself up. He was crushing some of the hats and had knocked over the picture of the old lady, but so far so good. He reached for the gym bag, stretching as far as he could, but couldn't quite reach it. He leaned farther, holding onto the shelf with one hand and reaching for the gym bag with the other, and that's when he lost his balance. Ben tried to catch himself, but it was too late: He tumbled sideways and pulled the gym bag with him. He hit the floor with a rain of shirts and pants.

"Crap!"

When Ben scooped up the clothes, he found the cigar box. It must have been sitting on top of the gym bag, and had fallen when he pulled the bag down. A few faded snapshots, some colorful cloth patches, and five blue plastic cases had spilled from the cigar box. Ben stared. He knew that the blue cases were special. They looked special. Each case was about seven inches long with a gold band running vertically down the left side and raised gold letters in the lower right corner that read UNITED STATES OF AMERICA.

Ben pushed the clothes aside and sat cross-legged to examine his discovery.

The pictures showed soldiers in Army uniforms and helicopters. Some guy sat on a bunk, laughing, with a cigarette dangling from the corner of his mouth. A word was tattooed high on his left arm. Ben had to look close to read it because the photograph was blurry: RANGER. Ben figured it was the man's name. Another picture showed five soldiers standing in front of a helicopter. They looked like hardcore badass dudes: Their faces were painted green and black; they were loaded with rucksacks, ammo packs, hand grenades, and black rifles. The second soldier from the left was holding a little sign with numbers on it. Their features were hard to see because of the paint, but the soldier on the far right looked like Elvis Cole. Wow.

Ben put down the pictures and opened a blue case. A red, white, and blue ribbon about an inch and a half long was pinned to gray felt. Beneath it was a red, white, and blue pin like a smaller version of the ribbon, and below that was a medal. The medallion was a gold five-pointed star hanging from another ribbon, and covered by a clear plastic bubble. In the center of the gold star was a tiny silver star. Ben closed the case, then opened the others. Each of the cases contained another medal.

He put the medals aside, then looked through the rest of the pictures: One showed a bunch of guys in black T-shirts standing around outside of a tent, drinking beer; another showed Elvis Cole sitting on sandbags with a rifle across his knees (he was shirtless and he looked really skinny!); the next picture showed a man with a painted face, a floppy hat, and a gun, standing in leaves so thick it looked like he was stepping out of a green wall. Ben had hit the mother lode! This was exactly the kind of cool stuff he had hoped to find! He concentrated so hard on the pictures that he never heard Elvis approach.

Elvis said, "Busted."

Ben jerked with surprise and felt himself flush.

Elvis stood in the door, thumbs hooked in his pockets, his raised eyebrows saying, What do we have here, sport?

Ben was mortified and ashamed. He thought Elvis would be mad, but Elvis sat on the floor next to him and stared at the pictures and little blue cases thoughtfully. Ben felt his eyes well and thought Elvis would probably hate him forever.

"I'm sorry I snooped in your stuff."

It was all Ben could do not to cry.

Elvis made a little faraway smile and rubbed Ben's head.

"It's okay, bud. I said you could look around while you were here—I just didn't think you'd go climbing in my closet. You don't have to sneak around. If you want to check out my things, all you have to do is ask. Okay?"

It was still hard to look Elvis in the eye, but Ben burned with curiosity. He held out the picture showing the five soldiers by the helicopter.

"Is that you, second from the end?"

Elvis stared at the picture, but did not touch it. Ben showed him the picture of the guy on the bunk.

"Who's this guy, Ranger?"

"His name was Ted Fields, not Ranger. A Ranger is a kind of soldier. Some guys were so proud of being Rangers they got the tattoo. Ted was proud."

"What do Rangers do?"

"Push-ups."

Elvis took the photo from Ben and put it back into the cigar box. Ben grew worried that Elvis would stop answering his questions, so he snatched up one of the blue cases and opened it.

"What's this?"

Elvis took the case, closed it, then put it back into the cigar box.

"They call it a Silver Star. That's why there's a little silver star in the center of the gold star."

"You have two."

"The Army had a sale."

Elvis put away another box. Ben saw that Elvis was uncomfortable with the medals and the pictures, but this was the coolest stuff that Ben had ever seen and he wanted to know about it. He snatched up a third medal case.

"Why is this one purple and shaped like a heart?"

"Let's get this stuff away and finish with the car."

"Is that what you get when you're shot?"

"There are all kinds of ways to be wounded."

Elvis put away the last medal case, then picked up the pictures. Ben realized that he really didn't know much about his mom's boyfriend. Ben knew that Elvis must have done something pretty darned brave to win all these medals, but Elvis never talked about any of that. How could a guy have all this neat stuff and keep it hidden? Ben would wear his medals every day!

"How did you get that Silver Star medal? Were you a hero?"

Elvis kept his eyes down as he put the pictures in the cigar box and closed the lid.

"Not hardly, bud. No one else was around to get them, so they gave them to me."

"I hope I get a Silver Star medal one day."

Elvis suddenly looked as if he was made of steel and thorns, and Ben grew scared. The Elvis that Ben knew didn't seem to be there at all, but his hard eyes softened and Elvis came back to himself. Ben was relieved.

Elvis took one of the Silver Stars from the cigar box and held it out.

"Tell you what, bud—I'd rather you take one of mine."

And just like that, Elvis Cole gave Ben one of his Silver Stars.

Ben held the medal like a treasure. The ribbon was shiny and smooth; the medallion was a lot heavier than it looked. That gold star with its little silver center weighed a lot, and its points were really sharp.

"I can keep it?"

"Sure. They gave it to me, and now I'm giving it to you."

"Wow. Thank you! Could I be a Ranger, too?"

Elvis seemed a lot more relaxed now. He made a big deal out of placing his hand on Ben's head like Ben was being knighted.

"You are officially a U.S. Army Ranger. This is the best way to become a Ranger. Now you don't have to do all those push-ups."

Ben laughed.

Elvis closed the cigar box again and put it back on the high shelf along with the gym bag.

"Anything else you want to see? I have some real smelly boots up here and some old Odor-Eaters."

"Ewww. Gross."

Now they both were smiling, and Ben felt better. All was right with the world.

Elvis gently squeezed the back of Ben's neck and steered him toward the stairs. That was one of the things Ben liked best about Elvis; he didn't treat Ben like a child.

"Okay, m'man, let's finish washing the car, and then we can pick out a movie."

"Can I use the hose?"

"Only after I put on my raincoat."

Elvis made a goofy face, they both laughed, and then Ben followed Elvis downstairs. Ben put the Silver Star in his pocket, but every few minutes he fingered the sharp points through his pants and thought that it was pretty darned cool.

Later that night Ben wanted to see the other medals and the pictures again, but Elvis had acted so upset that Ben didn't want to ask. When Elvis was taking a shower, Ben heaved himself back atop the safe, but the cigar box was gone. Ben didn't find where Elvis had hidden it, and he was too embarrassed to ask.

3
· · ·

The police arrived at twenty minutes after eight that night. It was full-on dark, with a chill in the air that was sharp and smelled of dust. Lucy stood sharply when the doorbell rang.

I said, "I've got it. That's Lou."

Adult missing persons were handled by the Missing Persons Unit out of Parker Center downtown, but missing or abducted children were dealt with on a divisional level by Juvenile Section detectives. If I had called the police like anyone else, I would have had to identify myself and explain about Ben to the complaint operator, then again to whoever answered in the detective bureau, and a third time when the duty detective handed me off to the Juvenile desk. Calling my friend Lou Poitras saved time. Poitras was a Homicide lieutenant at Hollywood Station. He rolled out a Juvie team as soon as we got off the phone, and he rolled out with them.

Poitras was a wide man with a body like an oil drum and a face like boiled ham. His black leather coat was stretched tight across a chest and arms that were swollen from a lifetime of lifting weights. He looked grim as he kissed Lucy's cheek.

"Hey. How you guys doing?"

"Not so good."

Two Juvenile Section detectives got out of a car behind him. The lead detective was an older man with loose skin and freckles. His driver was a younger woman with a long face and smart eyes. Poitras introduced them as they came into the house.

"This is Dave Gittamon. He's been a sergeant on the Juvie desk longer than anyone I know. This is Detective, ah, sorry, I forgot your name."

"Carol Starkey."

Starkey's name sounded familiar but I couldn't place it. She smelled like cigarettes.

Poitras said, "Have you gotten another call since we spoke?"

"No. We had the one call, and that was it. I tried reverse dialing with Star sixty-nine, but they must've called from a blocked cell number. All I got was the phone company computer."

"I'm on it. I'll have a backtrace done through the phone company."

Poitras brought his cell phone into the kitchen.

We took Gittamon and Starkey into the living room. I described the call that we received and how I had searched for Ben. I showed them the Game Freak, telling them that I now believed Ben had dropped it when he was taken. If Ben had been abducted from the slope beneath my house, then the spot where I found the Game Freak was a crime scene. Gittamon glanced at the canyon through the glass doors as he listened. Lights glittered on the ridges and down through the bowl, but it was too dark to see anything.

Starkey said, "If he's still missing in the morning, I'll take a look where you found it."

I was anxious and scared, and didn't want to wait.

"Why don't we go now? We can use flashlights."

Starkey said, "If we were talking about a parking lot, I'd say fine, let's light it up, but we can't light this type of environment well enough at night, what with all the brush and the uneven terrain. We'd as likely destroy any evidence as find it. Better if I look in the morning."

Gittamon nodded agreeably.

"Carol has a lot of experience with that type of thing, Mr. Cole. Besides, let's hold a good thought that Ben's home by then."

Lucy joined us at the glass doors.

"Shouldn't we call the FBI? Doesn't the FBI handle kidnappings?"

Gittamon answered with the gentle voice of a man who had spent years dealing with frightened parents and children.

"We'll call the FBI if it's necessary, but first we need to establish what happened."

"We know what happened: Someone stole my son."

Gittamon turned from the doors and went to the

couch. Starkey sat with him, taking out a small spiral notebook.

"I know that you're frightened, Ms. Chenier, I would be frightened, too. But it's important for us to understand Ben and whatever led up to this."

I said, "Nothing led up to this, Gittamon. Some asshole just grabbed him."

Lucy was good in court and was used to thinking about difficult things during stressful situations. This was infinitely worse, but she did well at keeping herself focused. Probably better than me.

She said, "I understand, Sergeant, but this is my child."

"I know, so the sooner we do this, the sooner you'll have him back."

Gittamon asked Lucy a few general questions that didn't have anything to do with being grabbed off a hill. While they spoke, I wrote down everything the caller had said to me, then went upstairs for a picture of Ben and one of the snapshots Ben had found of me in my Army days. I had not looked at that picture or any of the others for years until Ben found them. I hadn't wanted to see them.

Poitras was sitting on the Eames chair in the corner when I got back.

He said, "PacBell's working on the trace. We'll have the source number in a couple of hours."

I gave the pictures to Gittamon.

"This is Ben. The other picture is me. I wrote down what the man said, and I'm pretty sure I didn't leave anything out."

Gittamon glanced at the pictures, then passed them to Starkey.

"Why the picture of you?"

"The man who called said 'five-two.' You see the man next to me holding the sign with the number? Five-two was our patrol number. I don't know what else this guy could have meant."

Starkey glanced up from the pictures.

"You don't look old enough for Vietnam."

"I wasn't."

Gittamon said, "All right, what else did he say?"

I pointed at the sheet.

"I wrote it down for you word for word. He didn't say much—just the number and that he had Ben, and that he was paying me back for something."

Gittamon glanced over the sheet, then passed it to Starkey, too.

Poitras said, "You recognize his voice?"

"I don't have any idea who he is. I've been racking my brain, but, no, I didn't recognize it."

Gittamon took back the picture from Starkey and frowned at it.

"Do you believe him to be one of the men in this picture?"

"No, that's not possible. A few minutes after this picture was taken, we went out on a mission, and everyone was killed but me. That makes it stand out, the five-two; that's why I remember."

Lucy sighed softly. Starkey's mouth tightened as if she wanted a cigarette. Gittamon squirmed, as if he didn't want to talk about something so uncomfortable. I didn't want to talk about it, either.

"Well, ah, was there some kind of incident?"

"No, not if you're asking if it was my fault. It just went bad. I didn't do anything except survive."

I felt guilty that Ben was missing and embarrassed that he seemed to be missing because of me. Here we were all over again, another nightmare delivered to Lucy's doorstep by yours truly.

I said, "I don't know what else the man on the phone could have meant. That's all it could be."

Starkey shifted toward Gittamon.

"Maybe we should get Ben's description out to patrol."

Poitras nodded, telling her to get on with it. "Talk to the phone company, too. Have them set up a line trap on Elvis's phone."

Starkey took her cell phone into the entry. While Starkey was making the calls, Gittamon asked about my past few days with Ben. When I told him I found Ben looking through my closet, Gittamon raised his eyebrows.

"So Ben knew about this five-two business?"

"Not about the others getting killed, but he saw the pictures."

"And this was when?"

"Earlier in the week. Three days ago, maybe. What does that have to do with anything?"

Gittamon concentrated on the picture, as if he was on the edge of a profound thought. He glanced at Lucy, then looked back at me.

"I'm just trying to see how this fits. The implication is that he took Ms. Chenier's son as revenge for something that you did—not Ms. Chenier, but you. But Ben isn't your son or stepson, and hasn't lived with you except these past few days. I understand that correctly, don't I? You and Ms. Chenier maintain separate residences?"

Lucy unfolded herself on the hearth. Gittamon was obviously considering other possibilities, and Lucy was interested.

"Yes, that's right."

Gittamon nodded, and looked back at me.

"Why would he take Ms. Chenier's son if it's you he hates so much? Why wouldn't he just burn down your house or shoot you or even just sue you? You see what I'm getting at?"

I saw, and didn't much like it.

"Look, that's not it. Ben wouldn't do that. He's only ten."

Lucy glanced from Gittamon to me, then back, not understanding.

"What wouldn't Ben do?"

"Lou, for Christ's sake."

Poitras nodded, agreeing with me.

"Dave, Ben wouldn't do that. I know this kid."

Lucy said, "Are you saying that Ben staged his own abduction?"

Gittamon placed the picture on the coffee table as if he had seen enough.

"No, ma'am, it's too early to say, but I've seen children stage abductions for all manner of reasons, especially when they're feeling insecure. A friend's older brother could have made the call to Mr. Cole."

I was angry and irritated. I went to the doors. A frightened part of me hoped that Ben would be on the deck, watching us, but he wasn't.

I said, "If you don't want to raise false hopes, then stop. I spent the past five days with him. Ben wasn't feeling insecure, and he wouldn't do that."

Lucy's voice snapped behind me.

"Would you rather someone kidnapped him?"

She wanted to believe it so badly that hope glowed in her eyes like hot sparks.

Poitras pushed up from the Eames chair. "Dave? If you have enough to get started, let's roll out of here. I want to knock on a couple of doors. Maybe someone down the hill saw something."

Gittamon gestured to Starkey that she could close her notebook, then stood to join Poitras.

"Ms. Chenier, please, I'm not saying Ben staged his own abduction—I'm really not, Mr. Cole—but it's something we have to consider. I'd like a list of Ben's friends and their phone numbers. It's still early enough to make a few calls."

Lucy stood with them, as intent and focused as I had ever seen her.

"I'll have to get them from home. I can go do that right now."

I said, "Gittamon, you going to ignore the goddamned call?"

"No, Mr. Cole, we're going to treat this as an abduction until we know otherwise. Can you put together a list of the people involved with whatever happened to you in the Army and any other information you have?"

"They're dead."

"Well, their families. We might want to speak with their families. Carol, would you get together with Mr. Cole on that?"

Starkey handed me her card as the four of us went to the door.

Starkey said, "I'll come by tomorrow morning to

see where you found the Game Freak. I can get the names then. What's a good time?"

"Sunrise."

If Starkey heard the anger in my answer she didn't show it. She shrugged.

"Better light around seven."

"Fine."

Gittamon said, "If he calls again, let us know. You can phone any time."

"I will."

That was it. Gittamon told Lucy that he would be expecting her call, and then they left. Lucy and I did not speak as we watched them drive away, but once they were gone Ben's absence was a physical force in the house, as real as a body hanging from my loft. Three of us present, not just two. Lucy picked up her briefcase. It was still where she dropped it.

"I want to get those names for Sergeant Gittamon."

"I know. I'll get my names together, too. Call me when you get home, okay?"

Lucy glanced at the time, then closed her eyes.

"Jesus, I have to call Richard. God, that's going to be awful, telling him about this."

Richard Chenier was Lucy's ex-husband and Ben's father. He lived in New Orleans, and it was only right that she tell him that his son was missing. Richard and Lucy had argued often about me. I guessed they would argue more.

Lucy fumbled with her briefcase and her keys, and all at once she started crying. I cried, too. We held each other tight, the two of us crying, my face in her hair.

I said, "I'm sorry. I don't know what happened or who would do this or why, but I'm sorry."

"Don't."

I didn't know what else to say.

I walked her out to her car, then stood in the street as she drove away. The lights were on in Grace's house, Grace with her two little boys. The cold night air felt good, and the darkness felt good, too. Lucy had been kind. She had not blamed me, but Ben had been with me, and now he was gone. The weight of the moment was mine.

After a while, I went back inside. I brought the Game Freak to the couch and sat with it. I stared at the picture of me with Roy Abbott and the others. Abbott looked like a twelve-year-old. I didn't look much older. I had been eighteen. Eight years older than Ben. I didn't know what had happened to Ben or where he was, but I would bring him home. I stared at the men in the picture.

"I'll find him. I'm going to bring him home. I swear to God I will."

The men in the picture knew I would do it.

Rangers don't leave Rangers behind.

4

· · ·

THE ABDUCTION: PART ONE

The last thing Ben saw was the Queen of Blame gouging the eyes from a Flathead minion. One moment he was with the Queen on the hillside below Elvis Cole's house; the next, unseen hands covered his face and carried him away so quickly that he didn't know what was happening. The hands covered his eyes and mouth. After the initial surprise of being jerked off his feet, Ben thought that Elvis was playing a trick on him, but the trick did not end.

Ben struggled and tried to kick, but someone held him so tightly that he could neither move nor scream for help. He floated soundlessly across the slope and into a waiting vehicle. A heavy door slammed. Tape was pressed over his mouth, then a hood was pushed over his head, covering him with blackness. His arms and legs were taped together. He fought against the taping, but now more than one person held him. They were in a van. Ben smelled gasoline and the pine-scented stuff that his mother used when she cleaned the kitchen.

The vehicle moved. They were driving.

The man who now held him said, "Anyone see you?"

A rough voice answered from the front of the vehicle.

"It couldn't have gone any better. Make sure he's okay."

Ben figured that the second voice belonged to the man who took him and was now driving. The man holding him squeezed Ben's arm.

"Can you breathe? Grunt or nod or something to let me know."

Ben was too scared to do either, but the first man answered as if he had.

"He's fine. Christ, you should feel his heart beating. Hey, you were supposed to leave his shoe. He still has his shoes."

"He was playing one of those Game Boy things. I left the game instead. That's better than a shoe."

They drove downhill, then up. Ben worked his jaws against the tape, but he couldn't open his mouth.

The man patted Ben's leg.

"Take it easy."

They drove for only a few minutes, then they stopped. Ben thought they would get out, but they didn't. He heard what sounded like a power saw in the distance, and then someone else climbed into the van.

The third man, one who Ben hadn't yet heard, said, "Heez owt on heez dek."

Ben had heard Cajun French and French accents for much of his life, and this was familiar, though somehow different. A French man speaking English, but with some other accent under the French. That made three of them; three total strangers had taken him.

The man who had taken him said, "Roger that. I see him."

The man who held him said, "I can't see shit from back here. What's he doing?"

"He's moving down the slope."

Ben realized that they were talking about Elvis. The three men were watching Elvis Cole. Elvis was looking for him.

The man with Ben said, "This is bullshit, sitting back here."

The rough voice said, "He found the kid's toy. He's running back to his house."

"I wish I could see."

"There's nothing to see, Eric. Stop bitching and settle down. Now we wait for the mother."

THE ABDUCTION: PART TWO

When they mentioned his mother, Ben felt an intense jolt of fear, suddenly terrified that they would hurt her. His eyes filled and his nose clogged. He tried to pull his arms free of the tape, but Eric weighed him down like a heavy steel anchor.

"Take it easy. Stop it, goddamnit."

Ben wanted to warn his mom and get the police and kick these men until they cried like babies, but he couldn't do any of that. Eric held tight.

"Jesus, stop flopping around. You're going to hurt yourself."

They waited for what seemed like hours, then the rough voice said, "I'll make the call."

Ben heard the door open and somebody get out. After a minute, the door opened again and whoever it was got back in.

The rough voice said, "That's it."

They drove down out of the hills, then back up again on winding streets. After a while, the van braked. Ben heard the mechanical clatter of a garage door opening. They eased forward, then the engine shut off and the garage door closed behind them.

Eric said, "C'mon, kid."

Eric cut the tape holding Ben's legs, then Ben was jerked by his feet.

"Ow!"

"C'mon, you can walk. I'll tell you where."

The man held tight to Ben's arm.

Ben was in a garage. The hood pushed up enough for him to glimpse the van—white and dirty, with dark blue writing on the side. Eric turned him away before he could read what was written.

"We're coming to a step. Step up. C'mon, lift your goddamned feet!"

Ben felt for the step with his toe.

"Shit, forget it. This is taking too long."

Eric carried Ben into the house like a baby. Being carried made Ben mad. He could have walked! He didn't have to be carried!

Ben glimpsed dim rooms empty of furniture, and then Eric dropped his legs.

"I'm putting you down. Stand up."

Ben stood.

"Okay, I put a chair behind you. Siddown. I've got you. You won't fall."

Ben lowered himself until the chair took his weight. It was hard to sit with his arms taped to his sides; the tape pinched his skin.

"Okay, we're good to go. Is Mike outside?"

Mike. Mike was the man who had taken him. Eric had waited in the van. Now Ben knew two of their names.

The third man said, "I want to see heez face."

Eye-wahnt-tu-see-heez-fehss.

His voice was eerie and soft.

"Mike won't like it."

"Stand behind him if you are afraid."

Stand-beehighnd-heem.

The voice was only inches away.

"Christ. Whatever."

Ben didn't know where he was or what they were doing, but he was suddenly scared again, just like when they talked about his mother. Ben had not yet seen any of the three men, but he knew that he was about to, and the thought of seeing them scared him. He didn't want to see them. He didn't want to see any of this.

The hood was pulled off from behind.

An enormously tall man stood in front of him,

staring down at Ben without expression. The man was so tall that his head seemed to brush the ceiling, and so black that his skin drank the room's dim light and glowed like gold. A row of round purple scars the size of pencil erasers lined the man's forehead above his eyebrows. Three more scars followed the line of his cheeks below each eye, each scar a hard knob like something had been pushed under the skin. The scars terrified Ben; they looked creepy and obscene. Ben tried to twist away, but Eric held tight.

Eric said, "He's an African, kid. He won't eat ya until he cooks you."

The African carefully peeled the tape from Ben's mouth. Ben was so afraid that he trembled. It was dark outside; full-on night.

"I want to go home."

Eric made a soft laugh like he thought that was funny. Eric had short red hair and milky skin. A gap showed between his front teeth like an open gate.

Ben was in an empty living room with a white stone fireplace at one end and sheets hung over the windows. A door opened behind them, and the African stepped away. Eric spoke fast as a third man came into the room.

"Mazi has the African thing goin'. I told him not to."

Mike slapped his palm into Mazi's chest so fast that the African was falling back even before Ben realized that Mike had hit him. Mazi was tall and big, but Mike looked stronger, with thick wrists and gnarled fingers and a black T-shirt that was tight across his chest and biceps. He looked like G.I. Joe.

Mazi caught himself to stay on his feet, but he didn't hit back.

Mazi said, "Ewe ahr dee bawss."

"Roger-fucking-that."

Mike pushed the African farther away, then glanced down at Ben.

"How you doing?"

Ben said, "What did you do to my mother?"

"Nothing. We just waited for her to get back so that I could call. I wanted her to know you're gone."

"I don't want to be gone. I want to go home."

"I know. We'll take care of that as soon as we can. You want something to eat?"

"I want to go home."

"You need to pee?"

"Take me home. I want to see my mom."

Mike patted Ben's head. He had a triangle tattooed on the back of his right hand. It was old, with the ink beginning to blur.

"I'm Mike. He's Mazi. That's Eric. You're going to be with us for a while, so be cool. That's just the way it is."

Mike smiled at Ben, then glanced at Mazi and Eric.

"Put'm in the box."

It happened just as fast as when they plucked him from the hill beneath the walnut trees. They scooped him up again, retaped his legs, and carried him through the house, holding him so tight that he couldn't make a sound. They brought him outside in the cold night air, but they covered his eyes so he couldn't see. Ben kicked and struggled as they pushed him into a large plastic box like a coffin. He tried to sit up, but they pushed him down. A heavy lid slammed closed over him. The box suddenly moved and tipped, then fell away beneath him as if they had dropped him down a well. He hit the ground *hard*.

Ben stopped struggling to listen.

Something hard rained on top of the box with a scratchy roar only inches over his face. Then it happened again.

Ben realized what they were doing with an explosion of horror. He slammed into the sides of his plastic prison, but he couldn't get out. The sounds that rained down on him grew further and further away as the rocks and dirt piled deep and Ben Chenier was buried in the earth.

5
...

Ted Fields, Luis Rodriguez, Cromwell Johnson, and Roy Abbott died three hours after our team picture was taken. Team pictures had been taken before every mission, the five of us suited up alongside the helicopter like a high-school basketball team before the big game. Crom Johnson used to joke that the pictures were taken so the army could identify our bodies. Ted called them "death shots." I turned the picture Ben had found face down so I wouldn't have to see them.

I had taken a couple of hundred snapshots of red dirt, triple-canopy jungles, beaches, rice paddies, water buffalo, and the bicycle-clogged streets and bazaars of Saigon, but when I returned to the United States those images seemed meaningless, and I had thrown them away. The place had lost its importance to me, but the people had mattered. I kept only twelve pictures, and I was in three of them.

I listed the people in the remaining pictures, then tried to remember the names of the other men who had served in my company, but I couldn't. After a while the idea of making a list seemed silly; Fields, Abbott, Johnson, and Rodriguez were dead, and no one else in my company had reason to hate me or steal a ten-year-old boy. No one I had known in Vietnam would.

Lucy called just before eleven. The house was so quiet that the sudden ring was as loud as a gunshot. My pen tore the page.

She said, "I couldn't stand not knowing. Did he call back?"

"No, not yet. I would have called. I'll call you right away."

"God, this is awful. It's a nightmare."

"Yeah. I'm trying to make this list and I'm sick to my stomach. How about you?"

"I just got off the phone with Richard. He's flying out tonight."

"How was he?"

"Furious, accusatory, frightened, belligerent—nothing I didn't expect. He's Richard."

Losing her son wasn't bad enough, so now she had this. Richard hadn't wanted Lucy to move to Los Angeles, and he had never liked me; they fought often about it, and now they would fight even more. I guess she was calling for the moral support.

She said, "He's supposed to call from the plane

with his flight information, but I don't know. Jesus, he was such an asshole."

"You want me to come by tomorrow after Starkey leaves? I can do that."

Richard could shout at me instead of her.

"I don't know. Maybe. I'd better get off the line."

"We can talk as long as you want."

"No, now I'm worried that man will try to call you again about Ben. I'll talk to you tomorrow."

The phone rang a second time almost as soon as I put it down. The second time, I didn't jump, but I let it ring twice, taking the time to ready myself.

Starkey said, "This is Detective Starkey. I hope I didn't wake you."

"Sleep isn't an option, Starkey. I thought you were him."

"Sorry. He hasn't called again, has he?"

"Not yet. It's late; I didn't think you'd still be on the job."

"I waited to hear from the phone company. They show you received a call at six fifty-two this evening. Does that time out about right?"

"Yeah, that's when he called."

"Okay, the call was made from a cell number registered to a Louise Escalante in Diamond Bar."

"I don't know her."

"I figured you wouldn't. She says her purse was stolen this afternoon, along with her phone. She says she doesn't know you or anything about this, and her billing records support that the call to you was out of her pattern of use. I'm sorry, but I think she's a dead end."

"Did you think about calling the number?"

Her voice cooled.

"Yes, Mr. Cole, I did. I've dialed it five times. They've turned off the phone."

Stealing a phone meant the man who took Ben had criminal experience. He had anticipated the line trace, which meant he had planned his action. Smart crooks are harder to catch than stupid crooks. They are also more dangerous.

"Mr. Cole?"

"I'm here. I was thinking."

"You getting those names together for me?"

"I'm doing that now, but I'm thinking about another possibility, too. I've had run-ins with people, Starkey, doing what I do. I've helped put some people in jail or out of business, and they're the kind of people who would hold a grudge. If I make a list, would you be willing to run their names, too?"

"Sure. Not a problem."

"Thanks. I appreciate this."

"I'll see you in the morning. Try to get some sleep."

"Like that could happen."

The darkest part of the night stretched through the hours, but little by little the eastern sky lightened. I barely noticed. By the time Starkey arrived, I had filled twelve legal-sized pages with names and notes. It was six forty-two when I answered the door. She was early.

Starkey held up a cardboard tray with two cups from Starbucks.

"I hope you like mocha. This is how I get my chocolate fix."

"That's nice of you, Starkey. Thanks."

She passed one of the cups to me. Morning light filled the canyon with a soft glow. She seemed to consider it, then glanced at the Game Freak. It was on the dining table with the pages.

"How far down the hill did you find the toy?"

"Fifty, sixty yards, something like that. You want to get going down there now?"

"The sun as low as it is, we'll have indirect light. That's not good. When the sun is higher, we'll get direct light. It'll be easier to see small objects and reconstruct what happened."

"You sound like you know what you're talking about."

"I've worked a few scenes."

She brought her coffee to the table.

"Let's see what you have with the names. Show me the most likely candidates first."

I showed her the list of people from my civilian cases first. The more I had thought about it, the more it seemed likely that one of them was behind what had happened to Ben. We sipped the coffee as we went through their names. Beside each name I had written down the crimes they had committed, whether or not they had been sentenced to prison, and whether or not I had killed anyone close to them.

Starkey said, "Jesus, Cole, it's all gangbangers, mobsters, and murderers. I thought you private guys did nothing but knock down divorce work."

"I pick the wrong cases."

"No shit. You have reason to believe that any of these people are familiar with your military history?"

"So far as I know, none of them know anything about me, but I guess they could find out."

"All right. I'll run them through the system to see if anyone's been released. Now let's talk about these other four men, the guys who died. Could their families blame you for what happened?"

"I didn't do anything for anyone to blame me."

"You know what I mean. Because their kid died and you didn't."

"I know what you meant and I'm telling you no. I wrote to their parents after it happened. Luis Rodriguez's mother and I corresponded until she died. That was six years ago. Teddy Fields's family sends me Christmas cards. When I mustered out, I went to see the Johnsons and Ted's family. Everyone was upset, sure, but no one blamed me. It was mostly just sad."

Starkey watched me as if she was convinced there had to be more, but she couldn't imagine what. I stared back at her, and once more thought she looked familiar.

I said, "Have we met? You looked familiar last night and now you look familiar again, but I can't place you."

Starkey glanced away. She took a foil packet from her jacket and swallowed a white tablet with the coffee.

"Can I smoke in here?"

"You can smoke on the deck. You sure we haven't met?"

"Positive."

"You look like someone."

Starkey studied the deck longingly, then sighed.

"Okay, Cole, here's how you know me: Recent

current events for a thousand. The answer is: *Ka-boom*."

I didn't know what she meant. Starkey spread her hands like I was stupid.

"Don't you watch *Jeopardy*? Bombs. Bombers. The Bomb Squad lost a tech in Silver Lake a couple of months ago."

"That was *you*?"

"I gotta have a smoke. This is killing me."

Starkey pulled a pack of cigarettes from her jacket and broke for the deck. I followed her.

Carol Starkey had bagged a serial cop-killer who murdered bomb technicians. Mr. Red had been head-line news in L.A., but most of the stories were about Starkey. Three years before Mr. Red, Starkey herself had been a bomb tech. She had been trying to de-arm a bomb in a trailer park when an earthquake trig-gered the initiator. Both Starkey and her partner had been killed, but Starkey was resuscitated at the scene. She had literally risen from the dead, which had yoked her with lurid nicknames like the Angel of Death and Demolition Angel.

Maybe she read what I was thinking. She shook her head as she fired up the cigarette, scowling at me.

"Don't even dream about asking, Cole. Don't ask if I saw white lights or pearly gates. I get that out the ass."

"I don't care about that, and I wasn't going to ask. All I care about is finding Ben."

"Good. That's all I care about, too. The bomb squad stuff, that's behind me. Now I do this."

"I'm happy for you, Starkey, but the bomb squad

stuff was only a couple of months ago. Do you know anything about finding a missing boy?"

Starkey blew a geyser of smoke, angry.

"What are you asking, if I'm up to the job?"

I was angry, too. I had been angry since last night and I was getting more angry by the second.

"Yeah, that's exactly what I'm asking."

"I reconstructed bombs and bomb scenes, and traced explosives through the most perverted land-scape you can imagine. I made cases against the ass-holes who built bombs and the dickwads who trade the components those assholes use. *And* I nailed Mr. Red. So you don't have to worry about it, Cole. I know how to detect, and you can bet your private-eye ass that I'm going to find this boy."

The sun was high now. The slope was bright. Star-key snapped her cigarette over the rail. I looked to see where it hit.

"Hey, we have a fire hazard up here."

Starkey faced me like the mountain was already an inferno and couldn't get any worse.

"We got plenty of light. Show me where you found the toy."

TIME MISSING: 15 HOURS, 32 MINUTES

Starkey changed shoes outside at her car, then met me on the side of my house wearing a pair of beat-up Asics cross-trainers with her pants rolled to her knees. Her calves were white. She stared warily down at the slope.

"It's steep."

"Are you scared of heights?"

"Jesus, Cole, I was just saying. The soil here is loose, I see a lot of irregular ground cover, and you've already been tramping around down there. That's going to make it harder. I want you to be careful not to contaminate the scene any more than you already have, which means all you're gonna do is show me where you found the Game Freak, then get the hell out of my way. We clear?"

"Look, maybe I was out of line. I'm good at this, too, Starkey. I can help."

"That remains to be seen. Show me."

When I stepped over the edge, she followed, but she looked awkward and uncomfortable.

Ben played on the hill so much that he had worn narrow paths that flowed with the rise and fall of the earth like trickling water. I led Starkey down the slope by following alongside the paths so that we wouldn't disturb his footprints. The ground was rugged and unbroken where I walked, and I noticed that Starkey was using the path.

"You're walking on his footprints. Walk where I walk."

She stared down at her feet.

"All I see is dirt."

"Just walk where I walk. Come over by me."

Ben's trail was easy to follow until we reached the base of the trees, then the soil grew rocky. It didn't matter; I knew the way from yesterday. We cut across the slope. Starkey slipped twice and cursed both times.

"Put your feet where you see me putting mine. We're almost there."

"I hate the outdoors."

"I can tell."

I pointed out the patch of rosemary where I had found the Game Freak and several of Ben's footprints. Starkey squatted in place as if she was trying to memorize every rock and spike of rosemary. After all the slipping and cursing, she was careful at the scene.

She glanced at my feet.

"You wearing those shoes yesterday?"

"Yeah. New Balance. You can see the prints I left yesterday."

I pointed my prints out to her, then lifted a foot so that she could see the sole of my shoe. The soles were cut with a pattern of raised triangles and a large N in each heel. The triangles and N were obvious in some of my prints. Starkey studied the pattern, then a couple of my footprints, then frowned at me.

"Okay, Cole, I know what I said when we were up at your house, but I'm more your city-type person, you know? My idea of the outdoors is a parking lot. You seem to know what you're doing down here, so I'm going to let you help. Just don't fuck up anything, okay?"

"I'll try not to."

"We just wanna figure out what happened. After that, we'll bring in SID."

Criminalists from LAPD's Scientific Investigation Division would be responsible for identifying and securing any evidence of the crime.

Starkey divided the area into a rough grid of squares which we searched one square at a time. She moved slowly because of the poor footing, but she was methodical and good with the scene. Two of Ben's prints suggested that he had turned around to return to my house, but the impressions were jumbled and could have meant anything; then his prints headed downhill.

She said, "Where are you going?"

"I'm following Ben's trail."

"Jesus, I can barely see the scuffs. You a hunter, or what?"

"I used to do this."

"When you were a kid?"

"In the Army."

Starkey glanced at me as if she wasn't sure what that meant.

Ben's footprints led through the grass for another eight feet, but then I lost his trail. I went back to his last print, then spiraled out in an expanding circle, but found no more prints or any other sign of his passing. It was as if he had sprouted wings and jumped into the air.

Starkey said, "What do you see?"

"If someone grabbed Ben, we should see signs of a struggle or at least the other person's footprints, but I don't see anything."

"You're just missing it, Cole."

"There's nothing to miss. Ben's prints just stop, and the soil here bears none of the scuffs and jumbled prints that you'd expect to find if he struggled."

Starkey crept downhill, concentrating on the ground. She didn't answer for a few minutes, but then her voice was quiet.

"Maybe Gittamon was right about him being involved. Maybe you can't find a struggle because he ran away."

"He didn't run away."

"If he wasn't snatched, then—"

"Look at his prints—they come this far and then they stop. He didn't go back uphill, he didn't go downhill or sidehill; they just stop. He didn't just vanish. If Ben ran away, he would have left prints, but he didn't; he didn't walk away from this point. Someone carried him."

"Then where are the other person's prints?"

I stared at the ground, shaking my head.

"I don't know."

"That's stupid, Cole. We'll find something. Keep looking."

Starkey paralleled my move downhill. She was three or four yards to my side when she stopped to study the ground.

"Hey, is this the boy's shoe or yours?"

I went to see. A faint line marked the heel of a shoe that was too large to be Ben's. The impression was crisp without being weathered, and was free of debris. I compared the crispness of its edge with the edges that marked Ben's shoe prints. They had been made at about the same time. I got behind the print and sighted forward through the center of the heel to see which way the print was headed. It pointed directly to the place where Ben's trail ended.

"It's him, Starkey. You got him."

"We can't know that. One of your neighbors could have been dicking around up here."

"No one was dicking around. Keep looking."

Starkey pushed a stalk of rosemary into the soil to

mark the print's location, and then we widened our circle. I searched the ground between the new print and Ben's, but found nothing more. I worked back in the opposite direction covering the same ground a second time, but still found nothing. Fragments of additional shoe prints should have been salted through Ben's like the overlapping pieces of a puzzle. I should have found scuffs, crushed grass, and the obvious evidence of another human moving across the earth, but all we had was the partial heel print of a single shoe. That couldn't be, but it was, and the more I thought about the lack of evidence, the more frightened I became. Evidence was the physical history of an event, but the absence of a physical history was its own kind of evidence.

I considered the surrounding brush and the flow of the slope, and the trees that surrounded us with their dead winter leaves spread over the ground. A man had worked his way uphill through heavy brush and brittle leaves so quietly that Ben did not hear him approaching. The man would not have been able to see him through the thick brush, which meant that he had located Ben by the sound of the Game Freak. Then, when he found him, he took a healthy ten-year-old boy so quickly that Ben had no chance to call out.

I said, "Starkey."

"There's bugs down here, Cole. I fuckin' hate bugs."

She was examining the ground a few feet away.

"Starkey, forget the names I gave you from my old cases. None of those people are good enough to do this."

She misunderstood.

"Don't worry about it, Cole. I'll have SID come out. They'll be able to tell what happened."

"I already know what happened. Forget the names from my case files. Just run the people who served with me, and forget everything else."

"I thought you said none of those guys would do it."

I stared at the ground, then at the thick brush and broken land, thinking hard about the people I had known and what the best of them could do. The skin on my back prickled. The leaves and branches that surrounded us became the broken pieces of an indistinct puzzle. A man with the right skills could be ten feet away. He could hide within the puzzle and watch us between the pieces and we would never see him even as his finger tightened over a trigger. I lowered my voice without realizing it.

"The man who did this has combat experience, Starkey. You're not seeing it, but I can see it. He's done this before. He was trained to hunt humans and he's good at it."

"You're creeping me out. Take a breath with that, okay? I'll have SID come out."

I glanced at my watch. Ben had been missing for sixteen hours and twelve minutes.

"Is Gittamon with Lucy?"

"Yeah, he's searching Ben's room."

"I'm going to see them. I want to tell them what we're dealing with."

"Look, Cole, don't get spooky with all this. We don't know what we're dealing with, so why don't you wait until SID gets here?"

"Can you find your way back?"

"If you wait two minutes I'll go with you."

I walked back up the hill without waiting. Starkey trailed after me, and called out from time to time for me to slow down, but I never slowed enough for her to catch up. Shadows from a past that should have been buried lined the path back up to my house. The shadows outnumbered me, and I knew I would need help with them. When I reached my house, I went into the kitchen and phoned a gun shop I know in Culver City.

"Let me have Joe."

"He isn't here."

"It's important you find him. Tell him to meet me at Lucy's right away. Tell him that Ben Chenier is missing."

"Okay. Anything else?"

"Tell him I'm scared."

I hung up and went out to my car. I started the engine, but sat with my hands on the steering wheel, trying to stop their shaking.

The man who took Ben had moved well and with silence. He had studied when we came and when we left. He knew my home and canyon, and how Ben went down the slope to play, and he had done it all so well that I did not notice. He had probably stalked us for days. It took special training and skills to hunt humans. I had known men with those skills, and they scared me. I had been one of them.

6

...

Beverly Hills makes people think of mansions and hillbillies, but the flats south of Wilshire are lined with modest stucco homes and sturdy bungalow apartments that would go unnoticed in any American town. Lucy and Ben shared an apartment in a two-story building shaped like a U, with the mouth facing the street and the arms embracing a stairway courtyard filled with birds-of-paradise and two towering palms. It was not a limousine street, but a black Presidential stretch was waiting by the fire hydrant outside her building.

I wedged my car into a parking spot half a block down and walked up the sidewalk. The limo driver was reading a magazine behind the wheel with the windows raised and the engine running. Two men were smoking in a Mercury Marquis parked across the street in front of Gittamon's car. They were thick men in their late forties with ruddy faces, short hair, and the flat expressions of men who were used to being in the wrong place at the wrong time and weren't much bothered by it. They watched me like cops.

I went up the stairs and rang her bell. A man I had never met before answered the door.

"May I help you?"

It was Richard. I put out my hand.

"Elvis Cole. I wish we weren't meeting like this."

Richard's face darkened. He ignored my hand.

"I wish we weren't meeting at all."

Lucy stepped in front of him, looking uncomfortable and irritated. Richard was good at making her angry.

She said, "Don't start."

"I told you this would happen, didn't I? How many times did I tell you, but you wouldn't listen?"

"Richard, just stop, please."

I said, "Yes, now would be the time to stop."

Something sour flickered in Richard's eyes, but then he turned back into her apartment. Richard was Lucy's age, but his hair had thinned badly and he had gained weight since I last saw him. He wore a black knit shirt, khaki slacks that were wrinkled from the plane, and Bruno Magli mocs that cost more than I made in a week. Even wrinkled and sleepless, Richard looked rich. He was a full partner in a law firm specializing in international oil concerns and owned a natural gas company with multi-national holdings.

Lucy lowered her voice as I followed her inside.

"They just got here. I called to tell you that he landed, but I guess you were on your way over."

Richard had joined a solidly built man in a dark business suit in Lucy's living room. The man had steel-gray hair so short that he was nearly bald, and eyes that looked like the wrong end of gun sights. He put out his hand.

"Leland Myers. I run security for Richard's company."

Richard said, "I brought Lee to help find Ben since you people managed to lose him."

As Myers and I shook, Gittamon came out of the hall with Ben's orange iMac. He huffed with the weight as he put it on a little table by her door.

"We'll have his E-mail by the end of the day. You'd be surprised what children tell their friends."

I was annoyed that Gittamon was still chasing the staged abduction theory, but I wanted to be careful with how I described what we found on the slope to Lucy.

"You're not going to find anything in his E-mail, Sergeant. Starkey and I searched the slope this morning. We found a shoe print where Ben dropped his Game Freak. It was probably left by the man who took Ben, and he was likely someone who served with me in Vietnam."

Lucy shook her head.

"I thought the others were dead."

"They are, but now I think that the person who

did this has a certain type of combat experience. I gave Starkey a list of names, and I'll try to remember more. She called SID to try for a cast of the print. Any luck, and we might get a pretty good guess of his height and weight."

Richard and Myers glanced at each other, then Richard crossed his arms, frowning.

Richard said, "Lucy told me the man mentioned Vietnam last night, and that all of this had something to do with you. Were we doubting this before now?"

"People can say anything, Richard. Now I know he's for real."

Myers said, "What do you mean, a certain type of combat experience?"

"You don't learn how to move the way this man moved by hunting deer on the weekends or going through ROTC. This guy spent time in places where he was surrounded by people who would kill him if they found him, so he knows how to move without leaving a trail. Also, we didn't find signs of a struggle, which means Ben never saw him coming."

I told them how Ben's footprints ended abruptly and that we had found only the one other print. Myers took notes while I described the scene, with Richard crossing and recrossing his arms with increasing agitation. By the time I finished he was pacing Lucy's small living room in tight circles.

"This is fucking great, Cole. You're saying some kind of murdering Green Beret commando like Rambo took my son?"

Gittamon checked his pager, looking unhappy with me.

"We don't know that, Mr. Chenier. Once SID reaches the scene, we'll investigate more thoroughly. Mr. Cole might be jumping at conclusions without enough evidence."

I said, "I'm not jumping at anything, Gittamon. I came here because I want you to see for yourself. SID is on the way now."

Richard glanced at Gittamon, then stared at Lucy.

"No, I'm sure that Mr. Cole has it right. I'm sure this man is every bit as dangerous as Cole believes. Cole has a history of drawing people like this. A man named Rossier almost killed my ex-wife back in Louisiana thanks to Mr. Cole."

The corners of Lucy's mouth tightened with pale dots.

"We've been over that enough, Richard."

Richard kept going.

"Then she moved here to Los Angeles so another lunatic named Sobek could stalk our son—how many people did he kill, Lucille? Seven, eight? He was some kind of serial killer or something."

Lucy stepped in front of him, and lowered her voice.

"Stop it, Richard. You don't always have to be an asshole."

Richard's voice grew louder.

"I tried to tell her that associating with Cole puts them in danger, but would she listen? No. She didn't listen because our son's safety wasn't as important as her getting what she wants."

Lucy slapped him with a single hard shot that snapped on his cheek like a firecracker.

"I told you to stop."

Gittamon squirmed as if he wished he were any-where else. Myers touched Richard's arm.

"Richard."

Richard didn't move.

"Richard, we need to get started."

Richard's jaw knotted as if he wanted to say more but was chewing the words to keep them inside. He glanced at Lucy, then averted his eyes as if he sud-denly felt awkward and embarrassed by his outburst. He lowered his voice.

"I promised myself I wouldn't do that, Lucille. I'm sorry."

Lucy didn't answer. Her left nostril pulsed as she breathed. I could hear her breathing from across the room.

Richard wet his lips, the awkwardness giving him the air of a little boy who had been caught doing something naughty and embarrassing. He moved away from her, then shrugged at Gittamon.

"She's right, Sergeant—I'm an asshole, but I love my son and I'm worried about him. I'll do whatever I can to find him. That's why I'm here, and that's why I brought Lee."

Myers cleared his throat.

"We should see this hill Cole described. Debbie's good with a crime scene. He should be in on this."

Gittamon said, "Who's Debbie?"

Richard glanced at Lucy again, then sat on a hard chair in the corner. He rubbed his face with both hands.

"Debbie DeNice; it's short for Debulon or something. He's a retired New Orleans detective. Homicide or something, right, Lee?"

"Homicide. Phenomenal case clearance rate."

Richard pushed to his feet.

"The best in the city. Everyone I brought is the best. I'll find Ben if I have to hire Scotland-fucking-Yard."

Myers glanced at Gittamon, then me.

"I'd like to get my people up to your house, Cole. I'd also like a copy of those names."

"Starkey has the list. We can make a copy."

He glanced at Gittamon.

"If SID is on the way, we'd better get going, but I'd also like a quick brief on what we know and what's being done, Sergeant. Can I count on you for that?"

"Oh, yes, absolutely."

I gave him directions to my house. Myers copied them onto a Palm Pilot, then offered to carry Ben's computer down to Gittamon's car. They left together. Richard followed after them, but hesitated when he reached Lucy. He glanced at me, and his mouth tightened as if he smelled bile.

"Are you coming?"

"In a minute."

Richard looked at Lucy, and the hardness around his mouth softened. He touched her arm.

"I'm staying at the Beverly Hills on Sunset. I shouldn't have said those things, Lucille. I regret them and I apologize, but they're true."

He glanced at me again, then left.

Lucy raised a hand to her forehead.

"This is a nightmare."

TIME MISSING: 18 HOURS, 05 MINUTES

The sun had risen like a mid-morning flare, so intense that it washed the color from the sky and made the palm trees glimmer. Gittamon had gone by the time I reached the street, but Richard was waiting by the black limo with Myers and the two men from the Marquis. They were probably his people from New Orleans.

They stopped talking when I came around the birds-of-paradise, and Richard stepped in front of the others to meet me. He didn't bother hiding his feelings now; his face was angry and intent.

"I've got something to say to you."

"Let me guess: You're not going to ask where I bought the shirt."

"This is your fault. It's only a matter of time before one of them gets killed because of you, and I'm not going to let that happen."

Myers drifted up and touched Richard's arm.

"We don't have time for this."

Richard brushed away his hand.

"I want to say it."

I said, "Take his advice, Richard. Please."

Debbie DeNice and Ray Fontenot moved to Richard's other side. DeNice was a large-boned man with gray eyes the color of soapy dishwater. Fontenot was an ex-NOPD detective like DeNice. He was tall and angular with a bad scar on his neck.

DeNice said, "Take his advice or what?"

It had been a long night. Pressure built in my head until my eyes felt hard. I answered him calmly.

"It's still morning. We're going to see a lot of each other."

Richard said, "Not if I can help it. I don't like you, Cole. I don't trust you. You draw trouble like flies to puke, and I want you to stay away from my family."

I made myself breathe. Further up the street, a middle-aged woman walked a pug. It waddled as it looked for a place to pee. This man was Ben's father and Lucy's former husband. I told myself that if I said or did anything to this man it would hurt them. We didn't have time for this nonsense. We had to find Ben.

"I'll see you up at the house."

I tried to go around them, but DeNice stepped sideways to block my path.

"You don' know whut you dealin' with, podnuh."

Fontenot smiled softly.

"Oh, yeah, you got that right."

Myers said, "Debbie. Ray."

Neither of them moved. Richard stared at Lucy's apartment and wet his lips again as he had upstairs. He seemed more confused than angry.

"She was stupid and selfish to move to Los Angeles. She was stupid to be involved with someone like you, and selfish to take Ben away. I hope she comes to her senses before one of them dies."

DeNice was a wide man with a lurid face that made me think of a homicidal clown. He had small scars on the bridge of his nose. New Orleans was probably a tough beat, but he looked like the kind of man who enjoyed it tough. I could have tried again to step around him, but I didn't.

"Get out of my way."

DeNice opened his sport coat to flash his gun, and I wondered if they were impressed with that down in the Ninth Ward.

DeNice said, "You don't get the picture."

Something flickered at the edges of light; an arm roped with thick veins looped around DeNice's neck; a heavy blue .357 Colt Python appeared under his right arm, the sound as it cocked like breaking knuckles. DeNice floundered off balance as Joe Pike lifted him backwards, Pike's voice a soft hiss.

"Picture this."

Fontenot clawed under his own jacket. Pike snapped the .357 across Fontenot's face. Fontenot staggered. The woman down the street glanced over, but all she saw were six men on the walk with one of them clutching his face.

I said, "Richard, we don't have time for this. We have to find Ben."

Pike wore a sleeveless gray sweatshirt, jeans, and dark glasses that glittered in the sun. The muscles in his arm were bunched like cobblestones around DeNice's neck. The red arrow tattooed across his deltoid was stretched tight with inner tension.

Myers watched Pike the way a lizard watches, not really seeing, more like he was waiting for something that would trigger his own preordained reaction: attack, retreat, fight.

Myers spoke calmly.

"That was stupid, Debbie, stupid and unprofessional. You see, Richard? You can't play with people like this."

Richard seemed to wake, as if he was coming out of a fog. He shook his head.

"Jesus Christ, Lee, what does DeNice think he's doing? I just wanted to talk to Cole. I can't have something like this."

Myers never looked away from Joe. He took DeNice's arm even though Pike still held him.

"I'm sorry, Richard. I'll talk to him."

Myers tugged the arm.

"We're good now. Let go."

Pike's arm tightened.

I said, "Richard, listen. I know you're upset, but I'm upset, too. We have to focus on Ben. Finding Ben comes first. You have to remember that. Now go get into your car. I don't want to have this conversation again."

Richard's jaw popped and flexed, but then he went to his car.

Myers was still watching Pike.

"You going to let go?"

DeNice said, "You better let go, you mother-fucker!"

I said, "It's okay now, Joe. Let him go."

Pike said, "Whatever."

DeNice could have played it smart, but didn't. When Pike released him, DeNice spun and threw a hard straight punch. He moved a lot faster than a thick man should and used his legs with his elbow tight to his body. DeNice had probably surprised a lot of men with his speed, which is why he thought he could do it. Pike slipped the punch, trapped DeNice's arm in a joint lock, and hooked DeNice's legs from under him in the same moment. DeNice hit the side-walk flat on his back. His head bounced on the concrete.

Richard called from the limo.

"Goddamnit, Lee!"

Myers checked DeNice's eyes. They were glassy. He pulled DeNice to his feet and pushed him toward the Marquis. Fontenot was already behind the wheel, holding a bloody handkerchief to his face.

Myers considered Pike for a moment, then me.

"They're just cops."

He joined Richard at the limo, and then both cars drove away.

When I turned to Joe, I saw a dark glimmer at the edge of his lip.

"Hey. What's that?"

I looked more closely. A red pearl colored the corner of his mouth.

"You're bleeding. Did that guy tag you?"

Pike never got tagged. Pike was way too fast ever to get tagged. He touched away the blood, then climbed into my car.

"Tell me about Ben."

BOY MEETS QUEEN

"Help!"

Ben pressed his ear to a tiny hole cut into the top of the box, but all he heard was a faraway *shush* like when you hold a seashell to your ear.

He cupped his mouth to the hole.

"Can anyone hear me?"

No one answered.

A light had appeared over Ben's head that morning, shining like a faraway star. An air hole had been cut into the box. Ben put his eye to the hole, and saw a tiny disk of blue at the end of a tube.

"I'm down here! Help me! Help!"

No one answered.

"HELP!"

Ben had ripped the tape from his wrists and legs, then freaked out during the night: He kicked the walls like a baby having a tantrum, and tried to push off the top by getting on all fours. He thrashed around like a worm on a hot sidewalk because he thought that bugs were eating him alive. Ben was absolutely and completely certain that Mike and Eric and the African had been T-boned by a speeding bus on their way to the In-N-Out Burger. They had been crushed to red goo and bone chips, and now no one knew that he was trapped in this awful box. He would starve to death and die of thirst and end up looking like something on *Buffy the Vampire Slayer*.

Ben lost track of time and drifted at the edges of sleep. He didn't know if he was awake or asleep.

"HELPI'MDOWNHERE!PLEASELETME OUT!"

No one answered.

"MA-MAAAAAAAAA!"

Something kicked his foot and he jumped as if ten thousand volts had amped through his body.

"Jesus, kid! Stop whining!"

The Queen of Blame leaned on her elbow at the far end of the box: a beautiful young woman with silky black hair, long golden legs, and voluptuous breasts spilling out of a tiny halter. She didn't look happy.

Ben shrieked, and the Queen plugged her ears.

"Christ, you're loud."

"You're not real! You're only a game!"

"Then this won't hurt."

She twisted his foot. *Hard*.

"Ow!"

Ben scrambled backwards, slipping and sliding with no place to go. She couldn't be real! He was trapped in a nightmare!

The Queen grinned nastily, then touched him with the toe of a gleaming vinyl boot.

"You don't think I'm real, big guy? Go ahead. Feel it."

"No!"

She arched her eyebrows knowingly and stroked her boot along his leg.

"You know how many boys wanna touch that boot? Feel it. See if I'm real."

Ben reached out with a finger. The boot was as slick as a polished car and as solid as the box around him. Her toes flexed. Ben jerked back his hand.

The Queen laughed.

"You wouldn't last two seconds against Modus!"

"I'm only ten! I'm scared and I want to go home!"

The Queen examined her nails as if she was bored. Each nail was a glistening razor-sharp emerald.

"So go. You can leave any time you want."

"I've been *trying* to go. We're *trapped*!"

The Queen raised her eyebrows again.

"Are we?"

She watched him without expression, tracing her nails over a belly that was as flat as tiles on a floor. Her nails were so sharp that they scratched her skin.

"You can leave any time you want."

Ben thought she was teasing him, and his eyes welled with tears.

"That isn't funny! I've been calling for help all night and no one can hear me!"

The Queen's beautiful face grew fierce. Her eyes blazed like deranged yellow orbs and her hand raked the air like a claw.

"Claw your way out, you idiot! See how SHARP!"

Ben cowered back, terrified.

"Get away from me!"

She leaned closer, fingers weaving like snakes. Her nails were glittering knives.

"FEEL THE SHARP POINTS! FEEL HOW THEY CUT!"

"Go away!"

She lunged at him.

Ben threw his arms over his head. He screamed as the razor-sharp points dug into his leg.

Then he woke up.

Ben found himself curled into a ball, cowering. He blinked into the darkness, listening. The box was silent and empty. He was alone. It had all been a nightmare, except that Ben could still feel the sharp pain of her nails in his thigh.

He rolled onto his side, and the sharp thing bit deeper.

"Ouch!"

He felt to see what was sticking him. Elvis Cole's Silver Star was in his pocket. He took it out, and traced the medal's five points with his fingers. They were hard and sharp, just like a knife. He pressed a point into the plastic overhead, then sawed the medal back and forth. He felt the plastic with his fingers. A thin line was scribed in his sky.

Ben worked the medal back and forth some more, and the line grew deeper. He pushed faster and harder, his arms pumping like pistons. Tiny bits of plastic fell through the darkness like rain.

7
...

THE OPERATOR

Michael Fallon was naked except for faded blue shorts. With the windows covered and the central air off so that the neighbors wouldn't hear it running, the house felt like an oven. Fallon didn't mind. He had been in plenty of Third World shitholes where heat like this was a breath of cool air.

Schilling and Ibo had gone out to steal a car, so Fallon stripped down to exercise. He tried to work out every day, because if your edge wasn't clean the other guy had you, and nobody had Mike Fallon.

He did two hundred push-ups, two hundred crunches, two hundred leg lifts, and two hundred back bends without pausing between sets, repeated the cycle twice more, then triple-timed in place for twenty minutes, bringing his knees high to his chest. Sweat glazed his skin like icing and splattered the floor like rain, but it wasn't much of a workout; Fallon regularly ran ten miles with a sixty-pound ruck.

Fallon was toweling off the sweat when the garage door rumbled open. That would be Schilling and Ibo, but he picked up his .45 just in case.

They came through the kitchen with two bags from Ralphs, Schilling calling like some stiff who was getting home in the 'burbs.

"Mike? Yo, Mike?"

Fallon stepped out behind them. He tapped Schilling with the gun.

Schilling jumped like a bitch.

"Jesus, *fuck*! You scared the shit out of me."

"Pay more attention next time. If I was the wrong guy, you wouldn't have a next time."

"Whatever."

Schilling and Ibo put down the bags, Schilling bitching because Fallon had gotten the drop on him. Ibo tossed a green apple to Fallon, then took a bottle of Orangina for himself. It had to be orange—orange juice, orange soda, Orangina; Ibo wouldn't drink anything else. Fallon needled Schilling about getting the drop, but they both knew that Eric was good. In fact, Eric was excellent. Fallon just happened to be better.

Fallon said, "You get the car okay?"

"Mazi got it. We went down to Inglewood. Half the rides down there are rolling stolen, anyway; the cops won't pay attention even if the owner calls it in."

Ibo said, "Eets good cahr. Nyce seets."

Schilling took two cell phones from a bag and tossed them to Fallon, one, two, a Nokia and a Motorola. They needed the car and the phones for what they had planned.

Fallon watched for a moment as they put out the food, then said, "Listen up."

Schilling and Ibo looked over. They had been planning this for a long time, but now they were getting close to the edge. It would be go or no-go in just a few hours.

"Once we double-cross this guy, there's no going back. Are we all good on this?"

Schilling said, "Hell, yes. I want the money. So does Mazi. Dude, this op is nothing compared to that other shit; fuck what some asshole thinks."

Ibo rapped fists with Schilling, the two of them grinning. Fallon knew how they would answer, but he was glad he had asked. They were in it for the money, like professionals.

"Hoo."

Schilling and Ibo answered, "Hoo."

Fallon dropped to the floor to pull on his socks and shoes. He wanted a shower, but the shower could wait.

"I'm gonna go find an AO. Stow the chow, then check the kid. Make sure he's tight."

The AO was the location they would secure and maintain as the area of operation for the double-cross.

"He's tight. He's under three feet of dirt."

"Check him anyway, Eric. I'll be back after dark, then we can pull him up to make the call. We'll probably have to put him on the phone to convince these guys."

Fallon slipped his gun into his pants, then started for the garage. Schilling called after him.

"Yo. What are we going to do with the kid if we don't get the money?"

Fallon didn't even look back or break stride.

"Put him back in the box and plug up the hole."

8

• • •

Laurence Sobek murdered seven people. Joe Pike was supposed to be the eighth. They were seven innocent human beings, but Sobek blamed them for putting a pedophile named Leonard DeVille into prison for the rape and sodomy of a five-year-old girl named Ramona Ann Escobar. As often happens to men with "short eyes," DeVille was murdered by inmates. All of that had happened fifteen years ago. Joe Pike, who was then with LAPD, had been the arresting officer, and Sobek's seven victims had been witnesses for the prosecution. Sobek shot Pike twice before Pike put him down, and Pike almost died. His recovery had been slow, and sometimes I doubted it. I guess Pike doubted it, too, but with Pike you never know. The Sphinx is a chatterbox compared to Pike.

I told him about Ben and the call as we drove to my house.

Pike said, "The man on the phone didn't make any demands?"

"He told me it was payback. That's all he said. Just that it was payback for what happened in Vietnam."

"You think he's for real?"

"I don't know."

Pike grunted. He knew what happened to me that day in Vietnam. He was the only person I'd told about that day outside of Army personnel and the families of the other four men. Maybe all of us needed to play the Sphinx, time to time.

When we reached my house, a pale blue SID van was parked across my drive, where Starkey was helping a tall, gangly criminalist named John Chen unload his equipment. Gittamon was changing shoes in the backseat of his car. Richard and his people had gathered at the side of my house with their jackets off and sleeves rolled. A nasty purple bruise had risen under Fontenot's eye. DeNice openly glared at us.

Pike and I parked off the road past my house, then walked back to the van. Starkey shot a resentful glance at Gittamon and lowered her voice. She was still smoking.

"You see all these people? Gittamon is letting them come down the hill."

"This is my partner, Joe Pike. He's coming, too."

"Jesus, Cole, this is a fuckin' crime scene, not a safari."

John Chen emerged from the van with a day pack

and an evidence kit like a large metal tackle box. He bobbed his head when he saw us.

"Hey, I know these guys. Hi, Elvis. Hiya, Joe. We worked together on the Sobek thing."

Starkey sucked at her cigarette, then squinted at Pike.

"So you're the one. I heard Sobek put two in your guts and fucked you up pretty bad."

Starkey wasn't long on sensitivity. She blew out a huge bloom of smoke, and Pike moved to stand with Chen. Upwind.

Myers walked over and asked Starkey for the list of names.

She said, "I phoned them in while I was waiting. Any luck, we'll hear back later today."

"Cole said I could have the list. We'll run our own check."

Starkey frowned past her cigarette at me, then took out the list. She gave it to me. I handed it to Myers.

He said, "What are we waiting for?"

Starkey glanced at Gittamon, clearly irritated that he was taking so long, and called out to prod him.

"Any time, Sergeant."

"Almost ready."

He was red-faced from bending over. Myers went back to the others, and Starkey had more of her cigarette.

"Prick."

The black cat who shares the house with me came around the corner. He's old and scruffy and carries his head cocked to the side from when he was shot with a .22. He probably came because he smelled

Pike, but when he saw other people standing in front of the house, he arched his back and growled. Even DeNice looked over.

Starkey said, "What's wrong with that thing?"

"He doesn't like people. Don't take it personally. He doesn't like anyone except for me and Joe."

"Maybe he'll like this."

Starkey flicked her cigarette at him. It hit the ground in a shower of sparks.

I said, "Jesus, Starkey, are you nuts?"

The cat didn't run away like most cats would. Instead, his fur stood like a fright mask and he growled even louder. He stalked toward her sideways.

Starkey said, "Holy Christ, look at that bastard."

Pike went over to the cat and stroked its fur. The cat flopped onto its side and rolled onto its back. That cat worships Joe Pike. Starkey scowled at them like the whole thing was distasteful.

"I hate cats."

Gittamon finished with his shoes and climbed out of his car.

"All right, Carol. Let's see what you found. John, are you ready?"

"Yes, sir."

"Mr. Chenier?"

Starkey said, "Go first, Cole. Take us down."

Pike and I went over the edge first, paralleling Ben's path like I did that morning. Starkey kept up better this time even though she helped Chen with his equipment, but Gittamon and DeNice had trouble with the footing. Myers moved as if he was annoyed with having to wait for the others.

We passed through the walnut trees, then circled

the rise to come out above the area where I found the Game Freak. The sprigs of rosemary that Starkey used to mark the footprints stood in the soil like miniature headstones. I pointed out where Ben's footprints ended, then showed them the partial. I squatted at its heel again, and showed them how it was headed toward Ben. Chen opened his evidence kit, and marked the location with an orange flag. Pike bent next to me to study the partial, then moved downhill without a word.

Starkey said, "Hey, be careful. We don't want to disturb anything."

Gittamon and Richard crowded between Chen and Starkey to see the print, with DeNice and Fontenot behind them. Myers considered the print without expression.

"You haven't found any other evidence?"

Starkey said, "Not yet."

Richard stared at the partial print, so still that he might have been numb. He touched the dry soil beside it, then glanced around at the rosemary and manzanita brush as if to fix the place in his mind.

"Is this where my son was taken, Cole? Is this where you lost him?"

I didn't answer. I stared at the print, and once more followed its line toward Ben. I had searched the ground between the partial and the terminus of Ben's prints at least three times. The distance between them was at least ten feet. The ground between them was soft and dusty, and should have been covered with prints.

I pointed out what I saw, talking more to myself than the others.

"Ben was over there, facing away from us, playing the Game Freak."

Ben Chenier's ghost walked past on the path, its feet leaving Ben's prints. His ghost was hunched over the Game Freak, which was loud with shrieks and the splat of wet blows. A darker ghost stepped through me, moving toward him. Its right foot kissed the impression into the dust in front of me.

"Ben didn't know he was here until he reached this spot. Then maybe Ben heard something or turned for no reason, I don't know which, but the man was scared that Ben would see him and call out."

The dark ghost suddenly accelerated toward Ben, pushing off in the soft soil and leaving the partial print. I watched it happen.

"Ben still didn't know what was happening, not really, or we'd see scuffs in his footprints. Ben had his back turned. He grabbed Ben from behind and lifted him off his feet. He covered Ben's mouth so he couldn't scream."

The dark ghost carried a struggling boy into the brush. When the ghosts faded, I was shaking.

"That's what happened."

Myers was staring at me. So were Starkey and Chen. Myers shook his head, but I couldn't read his expression.

"So where are his other prints?"

"That's how good he was, Myers. He didn't leave other prints. This one was a mistake."

Richard shook his head, disgusted, then got up. Myers got up with him.

Richard said, "I can't believe this is all you have,

one crappy half-assed hole in the dirt, and your only explanation is that Rambo stole my son. Jesus."

DeNice glanced around the hill.

"Maybe they just didn't look hard enough."

Fontenot nodded.

"Bubba, I hear *that*."

Myers nodded at them, and Fontenot and DeNice spread out over the hill.

Gittamon leaned closer to the print.

He said, "Can you make a cast of this, John?"

Chen pinched a bit of soil and let it dribble through his fingers. He didn't like what he saw, and frowned, sourly.

"You see how fine and dry the soil is, like salt? Soil like this won't hold its structure. You got soil like this, you can lose a lot of detail when you make the pour. The weight of the plastic deforms the impression."

Starkey said, "Everything's a drama with you. I've worked fifty blast sites with this guy and it's always the end of the world."

Chen looked defensive.

"I'm just telling you. I can frame the impression to help with the structure, then seal the soil before I pour, but I don't know what I'll get."

Starkey got up.

"You'll get a cast. Stop whining and start working, John. Jesus."

Richard watched DeNice and Fontenot searching through the brush, then shook his head. He checked the time.

"Lee, this is going to take forever at this rate. You

know what to do. Hire more people if we have to and bring in whoever we need. I don't care what it costs."

Starkey watched Gittamon like she was hoping he would say something, and she spoke up when he didn't.

"If more people come out it'll end up like a zoo down here. It's bad enough now."

Richard slipped his hands into his pockets.

"That isn't my problem, Detective. My problem is finding my son. If you want to arrest me for obstruction or some silly thing like that, I'm sure that'll make a good story in the local news."

Gittamon said, "No one's talking about anything like that. We just have to be concerned with preserving the crime scene."

Myers touched Richard's arm. The two of them had a low conversation, then Myers turned back to Gittamon.

"You're right, Sergeant, we need to worry about preserving the evidence and also the case against whoever took Ben. Cole shouldn't be here."

I stared at him, but Myers held the same unreadable expression. Gittamon looked confused.

I said, "I don't get your point, Myers. I've already been here. I was all over this slope searching for Ben."

Richard shifted his shoulders impatiently.

"What's not to understand, Cole? I never practiced criminal law, but I'm enough of a lawyer to know that you'll be a material witness in whatever case arises. You might even be named as a party. Either way, your presence creates a problem."

Starkey said, "Why would he be a party?"

"He was the last person to see my son alive."

The canyon grew hot. Sweat leaked from my pores and blood pushed hard through my arms and legs. Chen was the only one who moved. He tapped a sheet of rigid white plastic into the soil a few inches from the shoe print. He would frame the print like that to support the soil, then spray a thin clear sealant not unlike hair spray to bind the surface. Framing the soil would lend strength. Binding its surface would yield structure. Stability was everything.

I said, "What are you saying, Richard?"

Myers touched Richard's arm again, just as he'd done outside Lucy's apartment.

"He's not accusing you, Cole. It's nothing like that, but it's clear that the man on the phone bears a grudge against you. When everything comes out, maybe it will turn out that you used to know him and didn't like him any more than he likes you."

"I don't know what he's talking about, Myers."

Richard said, "Myers is right. If his lawyer can establish that the grudge goes both ways, he'll argue that you purposefully contaminated the evidence against him. He might even claim that you planted evidence. Look at O.J."

Starkey said, "That's bullshit."

"I used to be a lawyer, Detective. Let me tell you that when you're in court, bullshit sells."

Gittamon squirmed uncomfortably.

"No one is doing anything improper down here."

"Sergeant, I'm on your side—I'm even on Cole's side, as much as it pisses me off to say it, but we have a problem with this. Please. Ask your superiors or someone in the prosecutor's office. See what they think."

Gittamon watched Pike and Richard's detectives moving through the brush. He glanced at Starkey, but all she did was shrug.

He said, "Ah, Mr. Cole, maybe you should wait up at your house."

"What good would it do, Gittamon? I've already been all over this slope, so it won't make any difference if I keep looking."

Gittamon shuffled. He reminded me of the pug, nervous for a place to pee.

"I'll talk to the Hollywood captain. I'll see what he thinks."

Richard and Myers turned away without waiting for more and joined Fontenot and DeNice in the brush. Gittamon hunkered down beside Chen so that he wouldn't have to look at me.

Starkey watched all of them for a moment, then shrugged at me.

"Look, I'll probably hear back on those names in a couple of hours. A regular guy sitting around in Des Moines doesn't just decide to do something like this one day; anyone who would do this is an asshole and assholes have records. If we get a bounce on one of those names you gave us, we'll have something to work with. Just wait upstairs and I'll let you know."

I shook my head.

"You're crazy if you think I'm going to wait."

"We don't have anything else to work with. What else can you do?"

"Think like him."

I waved Pike over, and we climbed the hill to my house.

9

· · ·

When people look at Joe Pike, they see an ex-cop, ex-Marine, the muscles and the ink, dark glasses riding a secret face. Pike grew up at the edge of a small town where he spent his childhood hiding in the woods. He hid from his father, who liked to beat Pike bloody with his fists, then tool up on Pike's mother. Marines weren't frightened of brutal alcoholics, so Pike made himself into a Marine. The Marines saw Pike move well in the woods and the trees, so they taught him other things. Now Pike was the best that I had ever seen at those things and it was all because he once used to be a scared little boy in the woods. When you see someone, all you see is what they let you see.

Pike studied the canyon from my deck. We could hear Starkey and the others below, though we could not see them. The cut of the canyon funneled their voices, and would have funneled Ben's voice, too, if Ben had called out.

I said, "He couldn't know when Ben would leave my house or be alone, so he needed a safe place to watch and wait. He was some other place until he saw Ben going down the slope, then he came here."

Pike nodded at the finger ridge across the canyon.

"Can't see your house from the street below because of the trees and he needed a clear field of view. He had to be across the canyon with a spotting scope or glasses."

"That's the way I see it."

The opposite ridge was a crooked finger of knobby peaks that rose and fell as it stepped down into the basin. Residential streets threaded along its sides, cut by undeveloped wedges where the slopes were too unstable or too steep to hold houses.

Pike said, "Okay, from where he was, he would have been able to see us here on your deck. That means we can see his hiding place."

I went inside for my binoculars and the *Thomas Guide*. I found the page that showed the streets across the canyon, then oriented the map to match the direction of the ridge. There were plenty of places that someone could hide.

I said, "Okay, if it was you, where would you be?"

Pike studied the map, then considered the ridge.

"Forget the streets lined with houses. I'd pick a spot where the locals couldn't see me. That means I'd park where people wouldn't wonder about my car."

"Okay. So you wouldn't leave your car in front of

a house. You'd park on a fire trail or pull off the street into the brush."

"Yeah, but I'd still want fast access to my vehicle. When I saw Ben, I wouldn't have much time to get to my car, drive here, park, then move uphill looking for him."

It was a long way. Ben could easily be back in my house by the time someone got across.

"What about two men? One keeping watch, the other waiting on this side with a cell phone?"

Pike shrugged.

"Either way, someone had to be on the far side, watching. If we're going to find anything, that's where we'll find it."

We picked out obvious reference points like an orange house that looked like a Martian temple and a row of six bearded palms in someone's front yard, and marked their locations on the map. Once we had reference points, we took turns glassing the far hillside for houses being remodeled, clumps of trees on undeveloped land, and other likely places where a man could wait for long hours without being seen. We located them on the map relative to our reference points.

Gittamon came up the hill while we glassed, and nodded at us as he left. I guess he thought we were just killing time. Myers and DeNice came up a little while after and got into the limo. Myers said something to DeNice, and DeNice gave us the finger. Mature. Fontenot trudged up the hill a few minutes later, then DeNice and Fontenot left in the Marquis. Myers went back down the hill to stay with Richard.

We glassed the ridge for almost two hours, then Joe Pike said, "Let's hunt."

Ben had been missing for twenty-one hours.

I thought about telling Starkey what we were doing, but decided that it was better if she didn't know. Richard would bitch and Starkey might feel obligated to remind us that Gittamon had told us not to jeopardize their case. They might have to worry about making a case, but all I cared about was finding a boy.

We snaked our way across the canyon to the opposite ridge; school had not yet let out, adults were still working, and everyone else was hiding behind locked doors. The world gave no sign that a child had been stolen.

Everything looked different from a thousand yards away. Close up, the trees and houses were unrecognizable. We checked and rechecked our map against the landmarks that we had noted and tried to find our way.

The first place we searched was an undeveloped area at the end of a fire road. Unpaved fire roads wrap through the Santa Monica Mountains like veins through a body, mostly so that county work crews can cut brush and eliminate fuel before fire season. We parked between two driveways at the end of the pavement and squeezed around the gate.

Even as we parked, Pike said, "He wasn't here. Parking between these houses is asking to be seen."

We followed the fire road anyway, jogging together to make better time as we searched for a view of my house. The brush and scrub oak were so thick that we never once saw my house or my ridge or anything other than sky. It was like running in a tunnel. We jogged even faster going back to my car.

Seven spots that had seemed likely from my deck were exposed to the neighbors. We scratched them off the map. Four more locations could only be reached by parking in front of houses. We scratched them, too. Every time we saw a home for sale we checked to see if it was occupied. If the house was empty, we went to the door or hopped the side gates to check for a view of my home. Two of the houses could have been used as a blind, but neither showed signs of that kind of use.

Joe Pike has been my friend and my partner for many years; we were used to each other and worked well together, but the sun seemed to sprint across the sky. Finding likely spots took forever; searching them even longer. Traffic picked up as soccer moms and carpools delivered children from school; kids with skateboards and spiky hair watched us from drives. Adults on their way home from work eyed us suspiciously from their SUVs.

I said, "Look at all these people. Somebody saw something. Someone had to."

Pike shrugged.

"Would they see you?"

I looked at the sun and dreaded the coming darkness.

Pike said, "Slow down. I know you're scared, but slow down. We move fast, but we don't hurry. You know the drill."

"I know."

"If you hurry you'll miss something. We'll do what we can, then come back tomorrow."

"I said I know."

Most of the streets were shoehorned belly to butt with contemporary houses built in the sixties for aerospace engineers and set designers, but a few of the streets held stretches that were either too steep or too unstable to carry a foundation. We found three of those stretches with unobstructed views of my home.

The first two were nearly vertical troughs on the inside of sharp curves. You could use them for blinds, but you would need climbing spikes and pitons to hang from the slope. The third was more promising. A shoulder on the point of an outside curve sloped downhill near the foot of the ridge. A house at the beginning of the curve was being remodeled, and more homes sat on the far end, but the point itself was houseless. We pulled off the street and got out of my car. Starkey and Chen were tiny dots of color climbing up to my house. I couldn't tell who was who, but it would have been easy with binoculars.

Pike said, "Good view."

Two small cars and a dusty pickup were parked off the road near us. They probably belonged to the men who worked at the construction site. One more car wouldn't stand out.

I said, "It'll be faster if we split up. You take this side of the shoulder. I'll cross the top, then move down the far side."

Pike set off without a word. I worked my way across the top of the shoulder parallel to the street, trying to find a footprint or scuff mark. I didn't.

Gray knots of brush sprouted over the slope like mold, thinning around stunted oaks and ragged pine trees. I moved downhill in a zigzag pattern, following erosion cuts and natural paths between great stiff balls of sagebrush. Twice I saw marks that might have been made by someone passing, but they were too faint for me to be sure.

The shoulder dropped away. I couldn't see my car or any of the houses on either side of the little point, which meant that the people in those houses couldn't see me. I looked across the canyon. The windows in Grace Gonzalez's house glowed with light. My A-frame hung from the slope with its deck jutting out like a diving board. If I were surveilling my house, this would be a fine place for it.

Pike appeared silently between the brush.

"I went down as far as I could, then the slope dropped away. It's too steep on that side for anyone to use."

"Then help me with this side."

We searched the ground beneath two pines, then worked our way farther down the slope toward a single scrub oak. We moved parallel to each other and ten meters apart, covering more ground that way. Time was everything. Purple shadows pooled around us. The sun kissed the ridge. It would sink faster, racing with the night.

Pike said, "Here."

I stopped as I was about to take a step. Pike knelt. He touched the ground, then lifted his glasses to see better in the dim light.

"What is it?"

"Got a partial here, then another partial. Moving your way."

Dampness prickled my hands. Ben had been missing for twenty-six hours. More than a day. The sun settled even faster, like a sinking heart.

I said, "Do they match with the print we found at my place?"

"I couldn't see that one clearly enough to know."

Pike stepped over the prints. I moved toward the tree. I told myself that these prints could have been made by anyone: neighborhood kids, hikers, a construction worker come looking for a place to piss; but I knew it was the man who had stolen Ben Chenier. I felt it on my skin like too much smog.

I stepped across an erosion cut between two balls of sagebrush and saw a fresh footprint in the dust between two plates of shale. The print pointed uphill, leading up from the tree.

"Joe."

"Got it."

We moved closer to the tree, Pike approaching from the left and me from the right. The tree was withered, with spiky branches that had lost most of their leaves. Thin grass had sprouted in the fractured light under the branches. The grass on the uphill side was flat, as if someone had sat on it.

I did not move closer.

"Joe."

"I see it. I've got footprints in the dirt to the left. Can you see?"

"I see them."

"You want, I can get closer."

Behind us, the sun was swallowed by the ridge. The pooling shadows around us deepened and lights came on in the houses on the far ridge.

"Not now. Let's tell Starkey. Chen can try to match

the prints, and then we have to start knocking on doors. This is it, Joe. He was here. He waited for Ben here."

We backed away, then followed our own footprints up the hill. We drove back to my house to call Starkey. We had seen her leave almost two hours ago, but when we tooled around the curve she was parked outside my front door, no one else, just Starkey, sitting behind the wheel of her Crown Vic, smoking.

We swung into the carport, then hurried out to tell her.

I said, "I think we found where he waited, Starkey. We found prints and crushed grass. We've gotta get Chen out to see if the prints match, and then we have to go door-to-door. The people who live over there might've seen a car or even a tag."

It came out of me in a torrent as if I expected her to cheer, but she didn't. She looked grim, her face dark like a gathering storm.

I said, "I think we have something here, Starkey. What's the matter with you?"

She sucked down the last of her cigarette, then crushed it with her toe.

"He called again."

I knew there was more to it, but I was scared she would tell me that Ben was dead.

Maybe she knew what I was thinking. She shrugged, as if that was an answer to the things I wasn't brave enough to ask.

"He didn't call you. He called your girlfriend."

"What did he say?"

Starkey's eyes were careful, like she was hoping I

would read that part of it, too, so she wouldn't have to explain.

"You can hear it yourself. She hit the Record button on her message machine and got most of the call. C'mon, we want you to see if it's the same man."

I didn't move.

"Did he say something about Ben?"

"Not about Ben. C'mon, everybody's down at the station now. Take your own car. I don't want to drive you back after."

"Starkey, did he hurt Ben? Goddamnit, tell me what he said."

Starkey got into her car and sat quietly for a moment.

"He said you killed twenty-six civilians, then you murdered your buddies to get rid of the witnesses. That's what he said, Cole, you wanted to know. Follow me down. We want you to hear it."

Starkey drove away, and I was swallowed by darkness.

TIME MISSING: 27 HOURS, 31 MINUTES

The Hollywood Division Police Station was a flat red-brick building a block south of Hollywood Boulevard, midway between Paramount Studios and the Hollywood Bowl. The evening streets were choked with traffic going nowhere at a glacial pace. Tour buses cruised the Walk of Fame and lined the curb outside the Chinese Theatre, filled with tourists who had paid thirty-five dollars to sit in traffic. It was full-on dark when I turned into the parking lot behind the station. Richard's limo was parked by a fence. Starkey was waiting by her car with a fresh cigarette.

"Are you carrying a weapon?"

"It's at home."

"You can't bring it inside."

"What, Starkey, you think I want to murder some witnesses?"

Starkey flicked her cigarette hard into the side of a patrol car. A shower of sparks exploded off its fender.

"Don't be so testy. Where's Pike?"

"I dropped him off at Lucy's. If this asshole has her phone number, he probably knows where she lives. You worried this is going to fuck up your case, too?"

She didn't fight me about it.

"That was Gittamon, not me."

We went inside through double glass doors, then along a tile hall into a room marked DETECTIVES. Chest-high partitions cut the room into cubicles, but most of the chairs were empty; either crime was rampant or everyone had gone home. Gittamon and Myers were speaking quietly across the room, Myers with a slim leather briefcase. Gittamon excused himself and came over when he saw us.

"Did Carol explain what happened?"

"She told me about the call. Where's Lucy?"

"We're set up in an interview room. I'm going to warn you that the tape is disturbing. He says some things."

Starkey interrupted him.

"Before we get to that, Cole should tell you what he found. They might have something, Dave."

I described the prints and the crushed grass that Pike and I had found, and what I thought they meant. Gittamon listened like he wasn't sure what to make of it, but Starkey explained.

"Cole's making sense about someone having to be across the canyon. I'll check it out with Chen tomorrow as soon as we have enough light. Maybe we'll get a match on the shoes."

Myers walked over when he saw us talking, and watched me from under his eyebrows like an aborigine staring at the sun.

He said, "You must be a clue magnet, Cole, finding all these things the way you do. Is that just good luck?"

I turned away from him. It was that or hit him in the neck.

"Gittamon, are we going to hear this tape or not?"

They brought me to an interview room where Lucy and Richard were waiting at a clean gray table. The room was painted beige because an LAPD psychologist had determined that beige was soothing, but nobody looked soothed.

Richard said, "Finally. The sonofabitch called Lucy, Cole. He phoned her goddamned house."

He put his hand on her back, but she shrugged it away.

"Richard, you're really pissing me off with the snide remarks."

Richard's jaw knotted, and he looked away. I pulled a chair beside her and lowered my voice.

"How are you?"

She softened for a moment, but then a fierceness came to her face.

"I want to find this sonofabitch myself. I want to undo all this and make sure that Ben is safe and then I want to do things to this man."

"I know. Me, too."

She glanced at me with her fierce eyes, then shook her head and stared at the tape recorder. Gittamon took a seat opposite her, and Starkey and Myers stood in the door.

Gittamon said, "Ms. Chenier, you don't have to hear this again. There's really no need."

"I want to hear it. I'll be hearing it all night."

"All right, then. Mr. Cole, just so you know, Ms. Chenier received the call at five-forty this evening. She was able to record most of the conversation, but not the beginning, so what you're about to hear is an incomplete conversation."

"Starkey told me part of that, yes. Did you trace back to the same number?"

"The phone company is working on it now. This recording you're about to hear is a duplicate, so the sound quality isn't so good. We've sent the original to SID. They might be able to pull something off the background, but it isn't likely."

"All right. I understand that."

Gittamon pressed the Play button. The cheap speaker filled with an audible hiss, then a male voice began in mid-sentence:

THE VOICE: —know you had nothing to do with this, but that fucker's gotta pay for what he did.

LUCY: Please don't hurt him! Let him go!

THE VOICE: Shut up and listen! You listen! Cole

killed them! I know what happened and you don't, so LISTEN!

Gittamon stopped the tape.

"Is this the man who called you last night?"

"Yes, that's him."

Everyone in the room watched me, but Richard and Lucy most of all. Richard was slumped back in his chair with his arms crossed, looking sullen, but Lucy was leaning forward, poised at the edge of the table like a swimmer preparing to race. I had never seen her looking at me that way.

Gittamon noted my answer in his pad.

"All right. Now that you're hearing the voice a second time, does anything about it ring a bell? Do you recognize him?"

"No, nothing. I don't know who it is."

Lucy said, "Are you sure?"

The sinews and tendons stood taut on her hands and her breath labored as if she was holding an enormous weight.

"I don't know him, Luce."

Gittamon touched the button again.

"All right, then. We'll go on."

When he pressed the button, their voices overlapped, each shouting to be heard over the other.

LUCY: Please, I'm begging you—
THE VOICE: I was there, lady, I know!
They slaughtered twenty-six people—
LUCY: Ben is a child! He never hurt anyone! Please!
THE VOICE: They were in the bush, off on their

own, so they figured, what the fuck, no one
will know if we don't tell them, so they swore
each other to secrecy, but Cole didn't trust
them—

LUCY: —tell me what you want! Please, just let
my son go—

THE VOICE: —Abbott, Rodriguez, the
others—he murdered them to get rid of the
witnesses! He fired up his own team!

LUCY: He's a baby—!

THE VOICE: —sorry it had to be your son,
but Cole's gonna pay. This is his fault.

The message stopped.

The tape recorder hissed quietly for several seconds, then Gittamon rewound the tape. Someone
shifted behind me, either Starkey or Myers, then Gittamon cleared his throat.

I said, "Jeez. If he knows all that, I must've let one
get away."

The skin under Lucy's eye flickered.

"How can you joke?"

"I'm joking because it's so absurd. What do you
want me to say to something like this? None of that
happened. He's making it up."

Richard tapped the table.

"How do we know what happened over there or
what you did?"

Lucy snapped an irritated glance at him. She
started to say something but didn't.

Gittamon said, "We're not here to make accusations, Mr. Chenier."

"This asshole on the tape is making the accusations, not me, and to tell you the truth I don't give a rat's ass what Cole did over there. What I care about is Ben, and that *this* sonofabitch—"

He jabbed at the tape recorder.

"—hates Cole so much that he's taking it out on my son."

Lucy said, "Just calm down, Richard. You're making it worse."

Richard squared himself as if he was worn out and tired of talking about it.

"How totally blind about Cole can you be, Lucille? You don't know anything about him."

"I know that I believe him."

"That's perfect. Absolutely perfect. Of course, you would say that."

Richard waved at Myers.

"Lee, let me have that."

Myers passed him the briefcase. Richard took out a manila folder and slapped it on the table.

"FYI, since you know so much: Cole joined the Army because a judge gave him a choice, jail or Vietnam. Did you know that, Lucille? Did he tell you? Jesus Christ, you've exposed yourself and our son to lowlife dangerous trash ever since you've been with this man and you act like it's none of my business. Well, I made it my business because my son is my business."

Lucy stared at the folder without touching it. Richard stared at me, but he was still talking to her.

"I don't care if you're mad, and I don't care if you like it. I had him looked into and there it is: Your boyfriend has been a magnet for trouble ever since he was a kid—assault, assault and battery, grand theft auto. Go on, read it."

A hot wash of blood flooded my face. I felt like a child who had been caught in a lie because the other me was a different me, so far in the past that I had put him away. I tried to remember whether or not I had told Lucy, and knew by the tight expression in her eyes that I hadn't.

"How about my SAT scores, Richard? Did you get that, too?"

Richard talked over me without stopping, and never looked away.

"Did he tell you, Lucille? Did you ask him before you left your son with him? Or were you so caught up in your own self-centered needs that you couldn't be bothered? Wake up, Lucille, Jesus Christ."

Richard stalked around the table without waiting for Lucy or anyone else to speak, and left. Myers stood in the door for a moment, staring at me with his expressionless lizard eyes. I stared back. My pulse throbbed in my ears and I wanted him to say something. I didn't care that I was in the police station. I wanted him to speak, but he didn't. Finally, he turned away and followed Richard out.

Lucy stared at the folder, but I don't think she was looking at it. I wanted to touch her, but I felt too hot to move. Gittamon breathed with a raspy wheeze.

Starkey finally broke the silence.

"I'm sorry, Ms. Chenier. That must have been embarrassing."

Lucy nodded.

"Yes. Very."

I said, "I got into some trouble when I was a sixteen-year-old. What do you want me to say?"

No one looked at me. Gittamon reached across the table to pat Lucy's arm.

"It's hard when a child is missing. It's hard on everyone. Would you like someone to take you home?"

I said, "I'll take her."

"I know this is hard, Mr. Cole, but we'd like to ask you a few more questions."

Lucy stood, still staring at the folder.

"I have the car. I'll be fine."

I touched her arm.

"He made it seem like more than it was. I was a kid."

Lucy nodded. She touched me back, but still didn't look at me.

"I'll be fine. Are we finished here, Sergeant?"

"You are, yes, ma'am. Are you going to be all right tonight? You might want to stay at a hotel or with a friend."

"No, I want to be home if he calls again. Thank you both. I appreciate what you're doing."

"All right, then."

Lucy squeezed around the table, and stopped in the door. She looked at me, but I could see that it was hard for her.

"I'm sorry. That was shameful."

"I'll come by later."

She left without answering. Starkey watched her walk away, then took one of the empty chairs.

"Man, she married a prick."

Gittamon cleared his throat again.

"Why don't we get a little coffee, then keep going.

Mr. Cole, if you'd like the bathroom, I'll show you where it is."

"I'm fine."

Gittamon left for his coffee. Starkey sighed, then gave me one of those weak smiles people make when they feel bad for you.

"Rough, huh?"

I nodded.

Starkey pulled the folder across the table. She read whatever was inside.

"Man, Cole, you were a real fuckup when you were a kid."

I nodded.

Neither of us spoke again until Gittamon returned.

I told them about Abbott, Rodriguez, Johnson, and Fields, and how they came to die. I had not described those events since the day I spoke with their families; not because I was ashamed or because it was painful, but because you have to let go of the dead or the dead will carry you down. Talking about it was like looking down the wrong end of a telescope at someone else's life.

Gittamon said, "All right, this man on the tape, he knows your team number, he knows the names of at least two of these men, and he knows that everyone died except you. Who would know these things?"

"Their families. The guys who served in my company at the time. The Army."

Starkey said, "Cole gave me a list of names earlier. I had Hurwitz run them through NLETS, including the dead guys. We got zip."

"One of them might have a younger brother. One

of them might have a son. He says on the tape, 'He made my life hell.' He's telling us that he suffered."

I said, "He told us that he was there, too, but only five people went out and the other four are dead. Call the Army and ask them. The citation and after-action reports will tell you what happened."

Starkey said, "I already called. I'm gonna read that stuff tonight."

Gittamon nodded, then glanced at his watch. It was late.

"All right. We'll talk to the families tomorrow. We might know more after that. Carol? Anything else?"

I said, "Can I have a copy of the tape? I want to hear it again."

Starkey said, "Go home, Dave. I'll get his tape."

Gittamon thanked me for my time and got up. He hesitated as if he was thinking about taking Richard's folder, then looked at me.

"I want to apologize for that outburst, too. If I had any idea he was going to do that, I wouldn't have allowed it."

"I know. Thanks."

Gittamon glanced at the folder again, then went home. Starkey left with the tape and did not come back. A few minutes later, a detective I had not met brought a copy of the tape, then walked me to the double glass doors and put me outside.

I stood on the sidewalk wishing that I had taken the folder. I wanted to see what Richard knew, but I didn't want to go back inside. The cool night air felt good. The double doors opened again, and a detective who lived up on the hill by me came out. He cupped a cigarette and his lighter flared.

I said, "Hey."

It took him a moment to place me. A few years ago, his house had been damaged in the big earthquake. I didn't know him then or that he was with LAPD, but not long after I jogged past while he was clearing debris and saw that he had a small rat tattooed on his shoulder. The tat marked him as a tunnel rat in Vietnam. I stopped to give him a hand. Maybe because we had that connection.

He said, "Oh, yeah. How ya doin'?"

"I heard you quit."

He frowned at the cigarette, then drew deep before dropping it.

"I did."

"I don't mean the smoking. I heard you left the job."

"That's right. I hadda come around to sign the papers."

It was time to go, but neither of us moved. I wanted to tell him about Abbott and Fields, and how I pretended to be sick after they died because I was scared to go out again. I wanted to tell him that I had not murdered anyone and how the rage in Lucy's eyes scared me and all the other things that I had never been able to talk about because he was older and he had been there and I thought that he might understand, but, instead, I looked at the sky.

He said, "Well, stop around some time. We'll have a beer."

"Okay. You, too."

He walked around the side of the building, and then he was gone. I wondered about the silence that he carried, and then I wondered at my own.

Joe Pike and I once drove down to the tip of the Baja Peninsula with two women we knew. We caught fish in Baja, then camped on the beach at Cortez. That far south, the summer sun heated the Sea of Cortez until it felt like a hot tub. The water was so heavy with salt that if you let yourself dry without first showering, white flakes would rime on your skin. That same heavy water pushed us to its surface, refusing to let us sink. It could lull you, that water. It could make you feel safe even when you weren't.

That first afternoon, the sea was so still that it lay clean as a pond. The four of us swam, but, when the others stroked back to shore, I stayed in the quiet water. I floated on my back without effort. I stared into the cloudless azure sky feeling something like bliss.

I might have dozed. I might have found peace.

I was absolutely still in my world when, in the next instant, a fierce and sudden pressure lifted me without warning as the sea fell away. I tried to kick my legs under me, but the surging force was too great. I tried to right myself, but the swell grew too fast. I knew in a heartbeat that I would live or die or be swept away, and I could change none of it. I had lost myself to an unknown force that I could not resist.

Then the sea settled and once more grew flat.

Pike and the others saw it happen. When I reached shore, they explained: The Sea of Cortez is home to basking sharks. Basking sharks are harmless, but monstrously large, often reaching sixty feet in length and weighing many tons. They cruise at the surface where the water is warm, which is how they earned their name. I had floated into the path of one. It had dipped under me rather than going around. The swell of its tremendous passing had lifted me in its wake.

I had forgotten the feeling of fear when my body and fate were controlled by an unknown power; the feeling of being so purely helpless and alone.

Until this night.

10

. . .

TUNNEL RAT

Sweat pooled in the caverns of Ben's eyes. He ducked his head from side to side, wiping away the sweat onto his shoulders. In the depthless black of the box, he tried to work with his eyes closed, but all of his instincts drove them open as if with an expectation of sight. His clothes were soaked, his shoulders ached, and his hands were cramped into claws, but Ben felt ecstatic: school was out, Christmas was here, he had knocked in the game-winning run. Ben Chenier was approaching the finish line and he was *happy*!

"I'm gonna get out. *I'm getting OUT!*"

A cut opened across his plastic sky like a scar pulling free of its stitches. Ben had worked furiously throughout the night and through the day. The Silver Star bit through the plastic again and again, and loose soil fell like rain.

"Yeah, that's it! *YEAH!*"

He had dulled three of the star's five points, but by the afternoon of the first day the cut had grown into a snaggletoothed leer that stretched across the width of the box. Ben worked his fingers into the gap and pulled as hard as he could. Tiny pebbles bounced around him as dust trickled through the split, but the plastic was strong and did not bend easily.

"SHIT!"

Ben heard a mumble and a thump, and he wondered if he was dreaming again. He wouldn't mind if the Queen of Blame came back; she was hot. Ben stopped working, and listened.

"Answer me, kid. I can hear you down there."

It was Eric! His voice sounded hollow and far away coming down the pipe.

"Answer me, goddamnit."

The light from the pipe was gone; Eric must be so close that he blocked the sun.

Ben held his breath, suddenly more afraid than when they first put him in the box. A few hours ago he had prayed for them to return, but now he was almost out! If they discovered him trying to escape, they would take away the medal, tie his hands, and bury him again—and then he would be trapped forever!

The light returned, and then Eric's voice sounded farther away.

"The little prick won't answer. You think he's okay?"

Ben heard Mazi clearly.

"Eet weel not mahter."

Eric tried once more.

"Kid? You want some water?"

Here in the darkness of the box, Ben hid from them. They wouldn't know if he was alive or dead unless they dug him up, but they wouldn't dig him up during the day. They would wait until dark. No one can see you do bad things in the dark.

"Kid?"

Ben held perfectly still.

"You little shit!"

The light reappeared as Eric moved away. Ben counted to fifty, then grew scared that it wasn't enough. He counted to fifty again, then resumed work. He was in a race with them now; he had to get out before they dug him up. The African's words echoed in the darkness: *Eet weel not mahter.*

Ben felt along the jagged edge of the split until he found a ragged spot near its center, then set to work carving a tiny notch. He worked the Silver Star with small firm moves like a man signing a contract. He didn't need much; just a small tear so that he could get a better grip.

The star cut through the plastic, and the notch grew. He scraped dirt from behind the plastic, then gripped the split again and pulled. A shower of soil fell all at once. Ben sneezed, then brushed dirt from his eyes. The split had opened into a narrow triangular hole.

"YES!"

Ben pushed the soil that had rained down to the end of the box with his feet, then put the Silver Star into his pocket. He pulled his T-shirt over his face like a mask, then scooped out more soil. Ben worked his hand through the split up to his wrist, and finally to his elbow. He dug as far as he could reach, finally creating a large hollow dome. Ben gripped the plastic on either side of the T-shaped hole and hung with all his weight as if he was doing a chin-up. The hole didn't open.

"You dick! You pussy asshole!"

He shouted at the hole.

"You *weenie*!"

He had the door; all he had to do was open it. *OPEN THE DOOR!*

Ben scrunched into a ball, pulling his knees to his chest. He propped a knee onto the left side of the T and gripped the right with both hands. He strained so hard that his body arched from the floor.

The plastic tore like cold taffy slowly pulling apart.

Ben's grip slipped and he fell.

"YES! YESYESYES!"

Ben wiped his hands as best he could, then took another grip. He pulled so hard that his head buzzed, and the roof abruptly split as if the plastic had simply surrendered. A landslide of dirt poured through, but Ben didn't care—the box was open.

Ben pushed the dirt and rocks that had fallen to the end of the box, then peeled open the flap. More dirt piled around him. He worked his arm and then his head up into the hole. The freshly turned soil came easily. He twisted his shoulders through the hole and then he was up to his waist. He clawed dirt down past his sides like a swimmer pulling water, but the more he pulled the more the earth closed around him. Ben grew more frantic with each stroke. He reached higher, clawing for the surface, but the earth pressed in on him from all sides like a cold sea pulling him under.

Ben couldn't breathe!

He was being crushed!

Panic filled him with terror and the absolute certainty that he was going to die—

—then he broke through the surface of soil and cool night air washed his face. A canvas of stars filled the overhead sky. He was free.

The Queen's voice whispered.

"I knew you'd kick its ass."

Ben got his bearings. It was night, and he was in the backyard of a house in the hills. He didn't know which hills, but lights from the city were spread in the distance.

Ben wiggled along the ground until his feet were free. He was in a flower bed at the edge of a patio in the backyard of a really nice house, though the yard was dry and dying. Neighboring houses sat behind walls that were hidden by ivy.

Ben was scared that Mike and the others would hear him, but the house was dark and the windows were covered. He ran to the side of the house, and slipped into the shadows as if they were comfortable old coats.

A walkway ran along the side of the house to the front. Ben crept along the walk, moving so quietly that he could not hear his own footsteps. When he reached a chain-link gate, he wanted to throw it open and run, but he was scared that the men would catch him. He eased the gate open. The hinges made a low squeal, but then the gate swung free. Ben listened, ready to run if he heard them coming, but the house remained silent.

Ben crept through the gate. He was very close to the front of the house. He could see a brightly lit home across the street with cars in its drive. A family would be inside, he thought; a mom and a dad, and grown-ups who would help! All he had to do was sneak across the street and run to the neighbor's door.

Ben reached the end of the house and peeked around the corner. The short, sloping driveway was empty. The garage door was down. The windows were dark.

Ben's face split into a huge toothy grin because he had escaped! He stepped into the drive just as steel hands clamped over his mouth and jerked him backward.

Ben tried to scream, but couldn't. He kicked and fought, but more steel wrapped his arms and legs. They had come from nowhere.

"Stop kicking, ya little prick."

Eric was a harsh whisper in Ben's ear; Mazi an ebony giant at his feet. Tears blurred Ben's eyes. *Don't put me back in the box*, he tried to say; *please don't bury me*! But his words could not get past Eric's iron hand.

Mike stepped out of a shadow and gripped Eric's arm. Ben felt the terrible pressure of his grip in Eric's sudden weakness.

"A ten-year-old kid, and he beat you. I should beat you myself."

"Jesus, we got him. It saves us the trouble of diggin' him up."

Mike ran his hands over Ben's legs, then searched Ben's pockets and came out with the Silver Star. He held it up by the ribbon.

"Did Cole give you this?"

The best Ben could do was nod.

Mike dangled the medal in front of Mazi and Eric.

"He cut his way out with this. See how the points are dull? You fucked up. You should've searched him."

"It's a fuckin' medal, not a knife."

Mike grabbed Eric's throat with such speed that Ben didn't see his hand move. Their faces were only inches apart with Ben sandwiched between them.

"Fuck up again, I'll put you down."

Eric's voice gurgled.

"Yes, sir."

"Keep your shit tight. You're better than this."

Eric tried to answer again, but couldn't. Mike squeezed even harder.

Mazi gripped Mike's arm.

"Ewe ahr keeleeng heem."

Mike let go. He considered the Silver Star again, then pushed it into Ben's pocket.

"You earned it."

Mike turned away into the shadows and Ben caught a glimpse of the house across the street. He saw the family inside. Ben's eyes filled. He had come so close.

Mike turned back to them.

"Bring him inside. It's time to put him on the phone."

Eighty feet away, the Gladstone family enjoyed meat-loaf for dinner as they shared stories about their day. Emile was the father and Susse the mom; Judd and Harley, their sons. Their comfortable home was bright with light, and they laughed often. None of them heard or saw the three men or the boy, and had only a vague sense that minor repair work was being done during the day while the new owners awaited the close of escrow. As far as the Gladstone family knew, the house across the street was empty. No one was home.

PART TWO

· · ·

THE DEVIL
IS ON THE LOOSE

11
...

JOE PIKE

Pike sat unmoving within the stiff branches and leathery leaves of a rubber tree across from Lucy Chenier's apartment. Small gaps between the leaves afforded him a clean view of the stairs leading up to her apartment, and a lesser view of the street and sidewalk. Pike carried a Colt Python .357 Magnum in a clip holster on his right hip, a six-inch SOG fighting knife, a .25-caliber Beretta palm gun strapped to his right ankle, and a leather sap. He rarely needed them. Lucy was safe.

When Cole dropped Pike off earlier that evening, Pike had approached Lucy's apartment on foot from three blocks away. The man who took Ben could have been watching Lucy's apartment, so Pike checked the nearby buildings, roofs, and cars. When he was satisfied that no one was watching, Pike circled the block to come up behind the bungalows across the street. He slipped into the dense trees and shrubs surrounding them, and became a shadow within other shadows. He wondered what was happening at Hollywood Station, but his job was to wait and watch, so that's what he did.

Lucy's white Lexus appeared an hour or so later. She parked at the curb, then hurried upstairs. Pike had not seen her since he left the hospital some months ago; she was smaller than he remembered, and now carried herself with a stiffness that indicated she was upset.

Richard's black limo rolled up ten minutes after Lucy got home and double-parked alongside her Lexus. Richard got out by himself and climbed the stairs. When Lucy opened the door she was framed by gold light. The two of them spoke for a moment, then Richard went in. The door closed.

The Marquis arrived from the opposite direction, Fontenot driving with DeNice along for the ride. They stopped in the street with their engine idling. Myers jumped out of the limo to speak with them. Pike tried to listen, but their voices were low. Myers was angry and slapped the top of the Marquis. "—*this is bullshit! Get your shit together and find that kid!*" Then he trotted for the stairs. DeNice got out of the Marquis and into the limo. Fontenot accelerated away, but swung into a driveway one block up, turned around, and parked in the dark between two trees. Even as Fontenot parked, Richard and Myers hurried down, got into the limo, and sped away. Pike waited for Fontenot to follow them, but Fontenot settled behind the wheel. Now two of them watched Lucy. Well, one and a half.

Pike was good at waiting, which was why he excelled in the Marines and other things. He could wait for days without moving and without being bored because he did not believe in time. Time was what filled your moments, so if your moments were empty, time had no meaning. Emptiness did not flow or pass; it simply was. Letting himself be empty was like putting himself in neutral: Pike was.

Cole's yellow Corvette pulled to the curb. Like always, it needed a wash. Pike kept his own red Jeep Cherokee spotless, as well as his condo, his weapons, his clothes, and his person. Pike found peace in order, and did not understand how Cole could drive a dirty car. Cleanliness was order, and order was control. Pike had spent most of his life trying to maintain control.

ELVIS COLE

The jacaranda trees that lined Lucy's street were lit by lamps that were old and yellow with age. The air was colder than in Hollywood, and rich with the scent of jasmine. Pike was watching, but I could not see him and did not try. Fontenot was easy to make, hunched in a car up the block like Boris Badenov pretending to be Sam Spade. I guess Richard wanted someone watching out for Lucy, too.

I climbed the stairs and knocked twice at her door,

soft. I could have used my key, but that seemed more confident than I felt.

"It's me."

The deadbolt turned with a quiet slap.

Lucy answered in a white terry robe. Her hair was damp and combed back. She always looked good that way, even with her face closed and unsmiling.

She said, "They kept you a long time."

"We had a lot to talk about."

She stepped back to let me in, then closed and locked the door. She was holding her cordless phone. The television was running something about vegetarians with brittle bones. She turned it off, then went to the dining room table, all without looking at me, just as she hadn't looked at me when she left Gittamon's office.

I said, "I want to talk to you about this."

"I know. Would you like some coffee? It's not fresh, but I have hot water and Taster's Choice."

"No, I'm okay."

She put the phone on the table, but kept her hand on it. She looked at the phone.

"I've been sitting here with this phone. Ever since I got home I've been scared to put it down. They set up one of those trap things on my phone in case he calls again, but I don't know. They said I could make calls like normal, and not to worry about it. Ha. Like normal."

I guess staring at the phone was easier than looking at me. I covered her hand with mine.

"Luce, what he said, those things aren't true. Nothing like that happened, none of it."

"The man on the tape or Richard? You don't have

to say this. I know you couldn't do anything like that."

"We didn't murder people. We weren't criminals."

"I know. I know that."

"What Richard said—"

"*Shh.*"

Her eyes flashed hard, and the *shh* was a command.

"I don't want you to explain. I've never asked before, and you've never told me, so don't tell me now."

"Lucy—"

"Don't. I don't care."

"Luce—"

"I've heard you and Joe talk. I've seen what you keep in that cigar box. Those are your things to know, not mine, I understand that, like old lovers and the stupid things we do when we're kids—"

"I wasn't hiding anything."

"—I thought, he'll tell me if he needs to, but now it all seems so much more important than that—"

"I wasn't keeping secrets. Some things are better left behind, that's all, you move past and go on. That's what I've tried to do, and not just about the war."

She slipped her hand from under mine, and sat back.

"What Richard did tonight, that was unforgivable, having you investigated. I apologize. The way he dropped that folder on the table—"

"I got into some trouble when I was a kid. It wasn't horrendous. I wasn't hiding it from you."

She shook her head to quiet me and lifted the phone in both hands as if it was an object of study.

"I've been holding onto this goddamned phone so tight that I can't feel my hand, wondering whether I'll ever see my baby again, and I thought if only I could force myself into the mouthpiece through these little holes and come out on the other end of the line—"

She stiffened with a tension that made her seem brittle. I leaned toward her, wanting to touch her, but she drew back.

"—to get my baby; I saw myself doing it the way you see yourself in a dream, and when I squeezed out of the phone at the other end, Ben was in a nice warm bed, safe and sleeping, this beautiful peaceful ten-year-old face, so peaceful that I didn't want to wake him. I watched his beautiful face and tried to imagine what you looked like when you were his age—"

She looked up with a sadness that seemed painful.

"—but I couldn't. I've never seen a childhood picture of you. You never mention your family, or where you're from, or any of that except for the jokes you'll make. You know, I tease you about Joe, how he never talks, Mr. Stoneface, but you don't say any more than him, not about the things that matter, and I find that so strange. I guess you moved on."

"My family wasn't exactly normal, Luce—"

"I don't want you to tell me."

"—my grandpa raised me, mostly, my grandfather and my aunt, and sometimes I didn't have any-one—"

"Your secrets are your own."

"They're not *secrets*. When I was with my mother, we moved a lot. I needed rules, and there weren't any rules. I wanted friends, but I didn't have any because

of the goofy way we lived, so I made some bad choices
and got in with bad kids—"

"Shh. Shh."

"I needed someone to be there, and they were
what I had. They came around with a stolen car, and
I went along for a ride. How dumb is that?"

She touched my lips.

"I mean it. You keep your life inside like little secret creatures. All of us do, I guess, but it's different
now, we're different, what it means to me is different."

She touched my chest over my heart.

"How many secret creatures do you keep?"

"I'll find Ben, Luce. I swear to God I'll find him
and bring him home."

She shook her head so gently that I almost did not
see.

"No."

"Yes, I will. I'll find him. I'm going to bring him
home."

Her sadness grew to an ache so clear that it broke
my heart.

"I don't blame you for this happening, but that
doesn't matter. All that matters is that Ben is gone,
and I should have known it would happen."

"What are you talking about? How could you
know?"

"Richard is right, Elvis. I shouldn't be with you. I
shouldn't have let my child stay with you."

My belly cramped with a sour heat. I wanted her
to stop.

"Luce—"

"I really and truly don't blame you, but things like

this—like what happened in Louisiana and last year with Laurence Sobek—I can't have those things in my life."

"Lucy. Please."

"My son had a normal childhood before I knew you. I had a normal life. I let my love for you blind me, and now my son is gone."

Tears gathered on her lashes, then fell along her cheeks. She didn't blame me; she blamed herself.

"Luce, don't talk like that."

"I don't care what that man said on the tape, but I could hear his hatred for you. He hates you, and he has my son. He hates you so much that you can only make it worse. Leave it to the police."

"I can't walk away; I have to find him."

She gripped my arm and her nails cut into my skin.

"You're not the only person who can find him. It doesn't have to be you."

"I can't leave him. Don't you see?"

"You'll get him killed! You're not the only one who can do this, Elvis; you're not the last detective in Los Angeles. Let the others find him. Promise me."

I wanted to help her stop hurting. I wanted to pull her close and hold her and feel her hold me, but my own eyes filled and I shook my head.

"I'm going to bring him home, Luce. I can't do anything else."

She let go of my arms, then wiped her eyes. Her face was as dark and hard as a death mask.

"Get out."

"You and Ben are my family."

"No. We're not your family."

I felt impossibly heavy, like I was made of lead and stone.

"You're my family."

"GET OUT!"

"I'll find him."

"YOU'LL GET HIM KILLED!"

I left her like that and went down to my car. I couldn't feel the chill anymore. The sweet scent of the jasmine was gone.

JOE PIKE

Elvis got into his car, but sat without moving. Pike touched a leaf out of the way, better to see. When Cole's cheek caught the light, he saw that Cole was crying. Pike took a deep breath. He worked hard to keep his moments empty, but that wasn't always easy.

After Cole drove away, Pike left the rubber tree and slipped through the shadows alongside the bungalow and into the adjoining yard. He worked his way up an alley until he was a block behind Fontenot, then crossed to Lucy's side of the street. He moved in the shadows and passed within fifteen feet of Fontenot's car, but Fontenot did not see him. Pike slipped behind the birds-of-paradise, then up to Lucy's door. Fontenot was out of the picture. The building blocked his view.

Pike stood well back from the peephole. Lucy had been uneasy with him since the Sobek business, so he wanted her to see him before she opened the door. He knocked. Soft.

The door opened.

Pike said, "I'm sorry about Ben."

She was a strong, good-looking woman, even wrung out the way she was. Before Lucy and Ben moved from Louisiana and before the Sobek thing, Pike had joined her and Elvis at a tennis court. Neither Pike nor Elvis knew much about tennis, but they played her just to see, the two of them on one side against Lucy on the other. She was quick and skillful; her balls snapped low across the net just out of reach. She laughed easily and with confidence as she cut them to pieces. Now, she looked uncertain.

"Where's Elvis?"

"Gone."

Lucy glanced past him at the street.

She said, "When did you get back from Alaska?"

"A few weeks ago. May I come in?"

She let him enter. After she closed the door, she waited with her hand on the knob. Pike saw that she was uncomfortable. He wouldn't be staying.

"I'm across the street. I thought you should know that."

"Richard has someone outside."

"I know about him. He doesn't, about me."

She closed her eyes and leaned against the door as if she wanted to sleep until this was over. Pike thought he understood. It must be terrible for her with Ben missing. His own mother took the punches meant for him. Every night.

Pike wasn't clear why he had come or what he wanted to say. It was good to be clear. He was unclear about too many things these days.

Pike said, "I saw Elvis leave."

She shook her head, still with her eyes closed, still leaning into the door.

"I don't want either of you involved. You'll only make things worse for Ben."

"He hurts."

"Jesus, I hurt, too, and it's not your business. I know he's hurt. I know that. I'm sorry."

Pike tried to find the words.

"I want to tell you something."

The weight of his silence made her open her eyes.

"What?"

He didn't know how to say it.

"I want to tell you."

She grew irritated and stood away from the door.

"Jesus, Joe, you never say anything but here you are. If you want to say something, say it."

"He loves you."

"Oh, that's too perfect. God knows what's happening to Ben, but it's all about him to you."

Pike considered her.

"You don't like me."

"I don't like the way violence follows you; you and him. I've known police officers all my life, and none of them live like this. I know federal and state prosecutors who've spent *years* building cases against murderers and mob bosses, and none of them have their children stolen—in *New Orleans*, for God's sake, and none of them draw violence like you! I was out of my mind to get involved in this."

Pike considered her, then shrugged.

"I haven't heard the tape. All I know is what Starkey told us. Do you believe it?"

"No. Of course not. I told him so. Jesus, do I have to have that conversation again?"

She blinked, then crossed her arms, holding tight.

"*Goddamn*it, I hate to cry."

Pike said, "Me, too."

She rubbed hard at her face.

"I can't tell if that's a joke. I never can tell if you're joking."

"If you don't believe those things, then trust him."

She shouted now.

"It's about *Ben*. It's not about me or him or you. I have to protect myself and my son. I cannot have this insanity in my life. I am *normal*! I want to be *normal*! Are you so perverted that you think this is normal? It isn't! It is insane!"

She raised her fists as if she wanted to pound his chest. He would have let her, but she only stood with her hands in the air, crying.

Pike didn't know what else to say. He watched her for a time, then turned off the lights.

"Turn them on after I'm gone."

He let himself out. He slipped down the stairs and through the shrubs, thinking about what she had said until he was alongside the Marquis. The windows were down. Fontenot was hunched low behind the wheel like a ferret peering over a log. Here was Pike, ten feet away, and Fontenot didn't know. Pike hated him for it. Fontenot had seen Elvis come out of Lucy's apartment, and Pike hated him for having seen his friend in such pain. The empty moments that swirled around Pike filled with rage. Their growing weight became a tide. Pike could have killed Fontenot ten minutes ago, and thought about killing him now.

Pike moved closer to the Marquis. He touched the rear door. Fontenot didn't know. Pike slapped the roof, the sound as loud as a gunshot. Fontenot made a startled grunt as he jumped, and scrambled under his jacket for his gun.

Pike aimed at Fontenot's head. Fontenot went completely still when he saw Pike's gun. He relaxed a bit when he recognized Pike, but he was too scared to move.

"Jesus Christ, what are you doing?"

"Watching you."

Fontenot's face floated at the end of Pike's gun like a target balloon. Pike tried to speak, but the wave of heavy moments drowned his voice into a whisper and threatened to carry him away.

"I want to tell you something."

Fontenot glanced up and down the sidewalk like he expected to see someone else.

"You scared the shit out of me, you motherfucker. Where'd you come from? What in hell are you doin'?"

Pike emptied the moments as they washed over him. He fought the wave back.

"I want to tell you."

"What?"

The moments emptied. Pike had control. He lowered the gun.

Fontenot said, "What is it you wanna say, god-damnit?"

Pike didn't answer.

He melted into the darkness. A few minutes later he was once more in the rubber tree, and Fontenot still didn't know.

Pike thought about Lucy and Elvis. Cole had

never told him very much, either, but you didn't need to ask if you looked closely. The worlds that people build for themselves are an open book to their lives— people build what they never had, but always wanted. Everyone was the same that way.

Pike waited. Pike watched. Pike was.

The empty moments rolled past.

12
...

FAMILY MAN

His name was Philip James Cole until he was six years old. Then his mother announced, smiling at him as if she were giving him the most wonderful gift in the world, "I'm going to change your name to Elvis. That's a much more special name than Philip and James, don't you think? From now on, you're Elvis."

Jimmie Cole, six years old, didn't know if his mother was playing a game. Maybe it was the uncertainty that made him so scared.

"I'm Jimmie."

"No, now you're Elvis. Elvis is just the finest name, don't you think, just the finest name in the

world? I would've named you Elvis when you were born but I hadn't heard of it yet. Go ahead and say it. Elvis. Elvis."

His mother smiled expectantly. Jimmie shook his head.

"I don't like this game."

"Say it, Elvis. That's your new name. Isn't it exciting? We'll tell everyone tomorrow."

Jimmie started crying.

"I'm Jimmie."

She smiled at him with all the love in the world, cupped his face in her hands, and kissed his forehead with warm, sweet lips.

"No, you're Elvis. I'm going to call you Elvis from now on and so is everyone else."

She had been gone for twelve days. She did that sometimes, just up and left without saying a word because that was the way she was, a free spirit she called it, a crazy head case he had heard his grandfather say. She would vanish and her son would wake to find their apartment or trailer or wherever they were living that month empty. The boy would find his way to a neighbor where someone would call his grandfather or his mother's older sister and one of them would take him in until she returned. Every time she left he was angry with himself for having driven her away. Every day while she was gone he promised God he would be a better boy if only she'd come back.

"You'll be happy being an Elvis, Elvis, just wait and see."

That night, his grandfather, an older man with

pallid skin who smelled like mothballs, waved his newspaper in frustration.

"You can't change the boy's name. He's six years old, for Christ's sake. He has a name."

"Of course I can change his name," his mother said brightly. "I'm his mother."

His grandfather stood, then sat again in a wide tattered chair. His grandfather was always angry and impatient.

"That's crazy, girl. What's wrong with you?"

His mother pulled and twisted her fingers.

"There is NOTHING wrong with me! Don't say that!"

His grandfather's hand flapped.

"What kind of mother runs off like you, gone for days without a word? Where do you come up with this crazy stuff like with this name? The boy has a name! You should get a job, for Christ's sake, I'm tired of paying your bills. You should go back to school."

His mother twisted her fingers so desperately that Jimmie thought she would pull them off.

"There is NOTHING NOTHING NOTHING wrong with me! Something's wrong with YOU!"

She ran out of the tiny house and Jimmie ran after her, terrified that he would never see her again. Later, at their apartment, she spent the evening working with a small oil paint kit she had bought at the TG&Y, painting a picture of a red bird.

Jimmie wanted her to be happy, so he said, "That's pretty, Mama."

"The colors aren't right. I can never make the colors right. Isn't that sad?"

Jimmie didn't sleep that night, fearful that she would leave.

The next day she acted as if nothing had happened. She brought Jimmie to school, marched him to the head of his first-grade class, and made the announcement.

"We want everyone to know that Jimmie has a new name. I want all of you to call him Elvis. Isn't that a really special name? Everyone, I want you to meet Elvis Cole."

Mrs. Pine, a kindly woman who was Jimmie's teacher, stared at Jimmie's mother with a strange expression. Some of the kids laughed. Carla Weedle, who was stupid, did exactly what she was told. "Hello, Elvis." All of the kids laughed. Jimmie bit his tongue so he would not cry.

His teacher said, "Mrs. Cole, may I speak with you, please?"

During lunch that day, a second-grader named Mark Toomis, who had a head shaped like a potato and four older brothers, made fun of him.

"What do you think you are, a rock and roll greaser? I think you're queer."

Mark Toomis pushed him down and everyone laughed.

Three months earlier, his mother disappeared in the middle of summer. Like every other time she went away, Jimmie woke to find her gone. Like all the other times, she did not leave a note or tell him that she was going; she just went. They were living in a converted garage apartment behind a big house then, but Jimmie was scared to ask the old people who lived in the house if they knew where his mother was; he had heard them yelling at her about the rent. Jimmie waited all day, hoping that his mom hadn't really left, but by dark he ran crying to the house.

That night, his Aunt Lynn, who spent a lot of time on the phone whispering to his grandfather, fed him peach pie, let him watch television, and snuggled him on the couch. She worked at a department store downtown and dated a man named Charles.

His Aunt Lynn said, "She loves you, Jimmie. She just has her problems."

"I try to be good."

"You are a good boy, Jimmie! This isn't about you."

"Then why does she leave?"

His Aunt Lynn hugged him. Her breasts made him feel safe.

"I don't know. She just does. You know what I think?"

"Uh-uh."

"I think she's trying to find your father. Wouldn't that be great, if she found your daddy?"

Jimmie felt better after that, and even kind of excited. Jimmie had never met his father or even seen a picture of him. No one talked about him, not even his mom, and no one knew his name. Jimmie once asked if his grandfather knew his dad, but the old man had only stared at him.

"Your stupid mother probably doesn't even know."

Jimmie's mom stayed gone five days that time, then, like always, returned without explanation.

Now, all these months later, that evening after her twelve-day absence and the announcement of Jim-

mie's new name, Jimmie and his mom were eating hamburgers at the tiny table in their kitchen.

He said, "Mommy?"

"What is it, Elvis?"

"Why did you change my name?"

"I gave you a special name because you're such a special little boy. I like that name so much I might change my own name, too. Then we would both be Elvis."

Jimmie had spent most of the past twelve days thinking about what his Aunt Lynn told him that summer—that his mom was searching for his daddy when she went away. He wanted it to be true. He wanted her to find him and make him come home so that they could be a family like everyone else. Then she wouldn't go away anymore. He worked up his courage to ask.

"Were you trying to find my daddy? Is that where you went?"

His mother stopped with the hamburger halfway to her mouth. She stared at him for the longest time with a harsh cast to her eye, then put down her hamburger.

"Of course not, Elvis. Why ever would I do something like that?"

"Who's my daddy?"

She leaned back, her face playful.

"You know I can't tell you that. Your daddy's name is a secret. I can't ever tell anyone your daddy's name and I won't."

"Was his name Elvis?"

His mother laughed again.

"No, you silly."

"Was it Jimmie?"

"No, and it wasn't Philip, either, and if you ask me every other name that ever was I'll tell you no, no, no. But I will tell you one special thing."

Jimmie grew scared. She had never told him anything about his father, and he suddenly wasn't sure he wanted to know. But she was smiling. Kinda.

"What?"

She slapped the table with both hands, her face as bright as an electric bulb. She leaned close, her face playful and gleaming.

"Do you really want to know?"

"Yes!"

His mother seemed alive with an energy that she could not contain. Her hands kneaded the edge of the table.

"This is my gift to you. My one special gift, a gift that no one else can give to you, only me."

"Please tell me, Mama. Please."

"I'm the only one who knows. I'm the only one who can give you this special thing, do you understand?"

"I understand!"

"Will you be good if I tell you? Will you be extra-special good, and keep it a secret just between us?"

"I'll be good!"

His mother sighed deeply, then touched his face with a love so gentle he would remember it for years.

"All right, then, I'll tell you, an extra-special secret for an extra-special boy, just between us, forever and always."

"Between us. Tell me, Mama, please!"

"Your father is a human cannonball."

Jimmie stared at her.

"What's a human cannonball?"

"A man so brave that he fires himself from a cannon just so he can fly through the air. Think about that, Elvis—flying through the air, all by himself up above everyone else, all those people wishing they could be up there with him, so brave and so free. That's your father, Elvis, and he loves us both very much."

Jimmie didn't know what to say. His mother's eyes danced with light as if she had waited her entire life to tell him.

"Why does he have to be a secret? Why can't we tell everyone about him?"

Her eyes grew sad, and she touched his face again in the soft and gentle way.

"He's our secret because he's so special, Elvis, which is both a blessing and a curse. People want you to be ordinary. They don't like it when people are different. They don't like it when a man soars over their heads while they stand in the dirt. People hate you when you're special; it reminds them of everything that they aren't, Elvis, so we'll keep him as our little secret to save ourselves that heartache. You just remember that he loves you and that I love you, too. You remember that always, no matter where I go or how long I'm away or how bad times get. Will you remember that?"

"Yes, Mama."

"All right, then. Now let's go to bed."

Her crying woke him later that night. He crept to her door where he watched his mother thrash be-

*neath her sheets, speaking in voices he did not under-
stand.*

Elvis Cole said, "I love you, too, Mama."

Four days later she vanished again.

*His Aunt Lynn brought Elvis to his grandfather,
who took the newspaper outside so that he could
read in peace. That night, the old man made them
potted meat sandwiches with lots of mayonnaise
and sweet pickles, and served them on paper towels.
The old man had been distant all afternoon, so Elvis
was scared to say anything, but he wanted to tell
someone about his father so badly that he thought he
would choke.*

Elvis said, "I asked her about my daddy."

*The old man chewed his sandwich. A dab of
white mayonnaise was glopped on his chin.*

"He's a human cannonball."

"Is that what she told you?"

*"He gets shot out of a gun so that he can fly
through the air. He loves me very much. He loves
Mommy, too. He loves us both."*

*The old man stared at Elvis as he finished eating
his sandwich. Elvis thought he looked sad. When the
sandwich was gone, the old man balled his paper
towel and threw it away.*

"She made that up. She's out of her fucking mind."

*The next day, his grandfather called the Child
Welfare Division of the Department of Social Services. They came for Elvis that afternoon.*

13

· · ·

I brought the tape home, and played it without stopping to think or feel. The SID would digitize the tape, then push it through a computer in an attempt to determine the caller's location by identifying background sounds. They would map the caller's vocal characteristics for comparison with suspects at a later time. I already knew that I didn't and wouldn't recognize the voice, so I listened to get a sense of the man.

"They slaughtered twenty-six people, fuckin' innocent people! I'm not sure how it got started—!"

He had no accent, which meant he probably wasn't from the South or New England. Rodriguez had been from Brownsville, Texas, and Crom Johnson from Alabama; they both had thick accents, so their childhood friends and families probably had accents, too. Roy Abbott had been from upstate New York and Teddy Fields from Michigan. Neither had accents that I could remember, though Abbott spoke with the careful pronunciation of a Yankee farmer and used expressions like "golly."

"They were in the bush, off on their own—"

The man on the tape sounded younger than me; not a kid, but too young to have been in Vietnam. Crom Johnson and Luis Rodriguez both had younger brothers, but I had spoken with them when I got back to the world. I didn't believe that they would be involved. Abbott had sisters, and Fields was an only.

"—they swore each other to secrecy, but Cole didn't trust them—"

His language was arch and melodramatic, as if he had chosen his words to amp the drama in minimal time.

"—Abbott, Rodriguez, the others—he murdered them to get rid of the witnesses! He fired up his own friends!"

The events he described had the feel of a straight-to-video movie. Forced.

"—I was there, lady, I know!"

But he wasn't. Only five of us were in the jungle that day, and the other four died. Crom Johnson's body was never recovered, but his head had come apart in my hands.

I played it again.

"I know what happened and you don't, so LISTEN!"

He sounded angry, but the anger rode the top of his voice. His words should have hummed with rage the way a power line sings from the energy burning through it, but he seemed to be saying the words without truly feeling them.

I made a fresh cup of coffee, then listened to the tape again. The false quality in his tone convinced me that he did not know me or the others—he was faking. I had spent all evening unsuccessfully trying to figure out who he was, but maybe the answer was to figure out how he knew what he knew. If he hadn't served with me, then how did he know about Rodriguez and Abbott? How did he know our team number, and that I was the only one who survived?

The house creaked like a beast shifting in its sleep. The stairs to my loft grew threatening; the hall to Ben's room ended in darkness. The man on the tape had watched me and my house, so he had known when we were home and when we weren't. I went upstairs for the cigar box, and sat with it on the floor.

When a soldier mustered out of the Army, he or she was given what was known as a Form 214. The 214 showed the soldier's dates of service, the units in which he served, his training, and a list of any citations he received; kind of a one-line version of his career. Details were few. But whenever a soldier was awarded a medal or commendation, he or she was also given a copy of orders accompanying the medal, and those orders described why the Army saw fit to make its presentation. Rod, Teddy, and the others had died, and I had been given a five-pointed star with a red, white, and blue ribbon. I had never worn it, but I kept the orders. I reread them. The description of the events that day were slight, and included the name of only one other man involved, Roy Abbott. None of the others were mentioned. The man who took Ben could have gotten some of his information from my house, but not all of it.

It was ten minutes after five when I folded the papers and put them aside. Ben had been missing for over thirty-six hours. I hadn't slept in almost fifty. I brushed my teeth, took a shower, then put on fresh clothes. At exactly six A.M., I called the Army's Department of Personnel in St. Louis. It was eight A.M. in St. Louis; the Army was open for business.

I asked to speak with someone in the records department. An older man picked up the call.

"Records. This is Stivic."

I identified myself as a veteran, then gave him my date of separation and social security number.

I said, "I want to find out if anyone has requested my 201 file. Would you guys have a record of that?"

Where the 214 was the skeleton of a military record, a soldier's 201 file contained the detailed history of his career. Maybe my 201 showed the other names. Maybe the man on the tape had been able to get a copy, and that's how he knew about Rodriguez and Johnson.

"We'd have a record if it was sent."

"How can I find out?"

"You'd know. Anyone can get your 214, but your 201 is private. We don't give out the 201 without written permission unless it's by court order."

I said, "What if someone pretended to be me?"

"You mean, like you could be someone else pretending to be you right now?"

"Yeah. Like that."

Now Stivic sounded pissed off.

"What kind of bullshit is this, a joke?"

"My house was robbed. Someone stole my 214, and I think he might've gotten my 201 for nefarious purposes."

I probably shouldn't have used "nefarious"; it sounded like bad television.

Stivic said, "Okay, look: The 201 doesn't work that way. If you wanted a copy of your 201, you'd have to file the request in writing, along with your thumb print. If someone else wanted your 201, say, for a job application or something like that, you'd still have to give your permission. Like I already told you, the only way someone gets that 201 without you knowing about it is by court order. So unless this guy stole your thumb, you don't have to sweat it."

"I still want to know if someone requested it, and I don't have eight weeks to wait for the answer."

"We have thirty-two people in our department. We ship two thousand pieces of mail every day. You want me to holler if anyone remembers your name?"

I said, "Were you a Marine?"

"Master Sergeant, retired. If you want to know who requested what, gimme your fax number and I'll see what I can do. If not, it's been nice talkin' to ya."

I gave him my fax number just to keep him going.

"I have one more question, Master Sergeant."

"Shoot."

"My 201, can you pull it up there on your computer?"

"Forget it. I'm not telling you anything that's on anyone's 201."

"I just want to know if it contains an account of a certain action. I don't want you to give me the information, just whether or not the account contains two names. If it does, I'll request the file, and you can have all the thumb prints you want. If not, then I'm wasting both our time."

He hesitated.

"Is this a combat action?"

"Yes, sir."

He hesitated again, thinking about it.

"What's that name?"

I heard him punching keys as I told him, then the soft whistle of his breath.

"Are the names Cromwell Johnson and Luis Rodriguez in the report?"

His voice came back hoarse.

"Yes, they are. Ah, you still want to know if anyone requested this file?"

"I do, Master Sergeant."

"Gimme your phone number and I'll walk it through myself. It might take a few days, but I'll do that much for you."

"Thanks, Master Sergeant. I really appreciate this."

I gave him my phone number, then started to hang up. He stopped me.

"Mr. Cole, ah, listen . . . you would've made a good Marine. I woulda been proud to serve with ya."

"They made it sound better than it was."

His voice grew soft.

"No. No, they don't do that. I spent thirty-two years in the Marine Corps, and now I'm on this phone 'cause I lost my foot in the Gulf. I know how they make it sound. I know what's what. So I'll walk this through for you, Mr. Cole, that's the goddamned least I can do."

He hung up before I could thank him again. These old Marines are amazing.

It was not quite six-thirty, which made it almost nine-thirty in Middletown, New York. If the man on the tape didn't or couldn't scam a copy of my 201, then the only other name he had to work with was Roy Abbott. The day would be half over for a family of dairy farmers. I had written to the Abbotts about Roy's death, and spoken with them once. I didn't remember Mr. Abbott's first name, but the New York Information operator showed only seven Abbotts in Middletown, and she was happy to run through the list. I remembered his name when I heard it. She read off the number, then I hung up. I thought about what I would say and how I would say it. *Hi, this is Elvis Cole, does anyone in your family want to kill me?* Nothing seemed right and everything seemed awkward. *Remember the day Roy came home in a box?* I made another cup of coffee, then forced myself back to the phone. I called.

An older woman answered.

"Mrs. Abbott?"

"Yes, who is this?"

"My name is Elvis Cole. I served with Roy. I spoke with you a long time ago. Do you remember?"

My hands shook. Probably from the coffee.

She spoke to someone in the background, and Mr. Abbott came on the line.

"This is Dale Abbott. Who is this, please?"

He sounded the way Roy described him; plain-spoken and honest, with the nasal twang of an up-state farmer.

"Elvis Cole. I was with Roy in Vietnam. I wrote to you about what happened a long time ago, and then we spoke."

"Oh, sure, I remember. Mama, this is that Ranger, the one who knew Roy. Yes, how are you, son? We still have that letter of yours. That meant a lot to us."

I said, "Mr. Abbott, has anyone called recently, asking about Roy and what happened?"

"No. No, let me ask Mama. Has anyone called about Roy?"

He didn't cover the phone. He spoke to her as clearly as to me, as if the two conversations were one. Her voice was muffled in the background.

He said, "No, she says no, no one called. Should they have?"

When I dialed their number I didn't know what I would say. I hadn't wanted to tell them why I was calling or about Ben, but I found myself telling him all of it. Maybe it was my history with Roy, maybe the honest clarity in Dale Abbott's voice, but the words poured out of me as if I were giving confession, that I had lost a child named Ben Chenier to a man on the phone, that I was scared I would not be able to find Ben, or save him.

Dale Abbott was quiet and encouraging. We spoke for the better part of an hour about Ben and Roy and many things: Roy's four younger sisters were married with families, three to farmers and one to a man who sold John Deere tractors. Three of the four had sons named after Roy, and one a son named after me. I had never known that. I had no idea.

At one point, Mr. Abbott put on Roy's mom, and, while she spoke with me, he found the letter that I had written and came back on the line.

He said, "I've got your letter right here, that one you wrote. We made copies for all the girls, you know. They wanted copies."

"No, sir. I didn't know that."

"I want to read something you wrote. I don't know if you'll remember, but this meant a lot to me. This is you, now; this is you, writing: *I don't have a family, so I liked hearing about Roy's. I told him that he was lucky to come from people like you and he agreed. I want you to know that he fought to the end. He was a Ranger all the way, and he did not quit. I am so sorry that I could not bring him home to you. I am so sorry I failed.*"

Mr. Abbott's voice grew thick and he stopped reading.

"You didn't fail, son. You brought Roy home. You brought our boy home."

My eyes burned.

"I tried, Mr. Abbott. I tried so hard."

"You *did*! You brought my boy back to us, and you did not fail. Now you go find this other little boy, and you bring him home, too. No one here blames you, son. Do you understand that? No one here blames you, and never did."

I tried to say something, but couldn't.

Mr. Abbott cleared his throat, and then his voice was strong.

"I only have one more thing to say. What you wrote in your letter, that part about you not having a family, that's the only part that wasn't true. You've been part of our family since the day Mama opened the mail. We don't blame you. Son, we love you. That's what a family does, doesn't it, love you no matter what? Up there in Heaven, Roy loves you, too."

I told Mr. Abbott that I had to go. I put down the phone, then brought the coffee out onto my deck. The lights in the canyon faded as the eastern sky grew bright.

The cat crouched at the edge of my deck, his legs tucked tight underneath as he stared at something in the murky light below. I sat by him with my own legs dangling off the deck. I touched his back.

"What do you see, buddy?"

His great black eyes were intent. His fur was cool in the early-morning chill, but his heart beat strong in the warmth beneath.

I bought this house not so many years after I came back from the war. That first week after escrow closed, I stripped the floors, spackled the walls, and began the process of making someone else's home into mine. I decided to rebuild the rail around the deck so I could sit with my feet dangling in space, so I was outside one day, working away, when the cat hopped onto the corner of my deck. He didn't look happy to see me. Here was this cat with his ears down and his head cocked, staring at me like I was yesterday's bad surprise. The side of his face was swollen with a dripping red wound. I remember saying, "Hey, buddy, what happened to you?" He growled and his hair stood, but he didn't seem scared; he was cranky because he didn't like finding a stranger in his house. I brought out a cup of water, then went back to work. He ignored the cup at first, but after a while he drank. Drinking looked hard for him, so eating was probably worse. He was skanky and thin, and probably hadn't eaten in days. I took apart the tuna sandwich I was saving for lunch, and made a paste with the tuna and mayonnaise and a little water. He arched his back when I put the tuna paste near the cup. I sat against the house. The two of us watched each other for almost an hour. After a while, he edged toward the fish, then lapped at it without taking his eyes from me. The hole in the side of his head was yellow with infection, and appeared to be a bullet wound. I held out my hand. He growled. I did not move. The muscles in my shoulder and arm burned, but I knew that if I drew back we would lose the bond we were building. He sniffed, then crept closer. My scent had been mixed with the tuna, and the tuna was still on my fingers. He growled softly. I did not move. The choice was his. He tasted my finger with a tiny cat kiss, then turned to show me his side. That's a big step for cats. I touched the soft fur. He allowed it. We have been friends ever since, and he has been the most constant living creature in my life since that day on the deck. Even now, he still was; this cat and Joe Pike.

I stroked his back.

"I am so sorry I lost him. I won't lose him again."

The cat head-bumped my arm, then peered at me with his black mirror eyes. Seeing me, he purred.

Forgiveness is everything.

A BAD DAY AT THE OFFICE

The five members of team 5-2 sat on the steel floor in the bay of the helicopter, the wind ripping up clouds of red dust. Cole grinned at the cherry, Abbott, a short, sturdy kid from Middletown, New York, waiting for Abbott's lurp hat to fly off.

Cole nudged Abbott's leg.

"Your hat."

"What?"

They leaned close to each other and shouted over the roar of the turbine engine. They were still on the lift pad at Fire Base Ranger, the big rotor overhead spooling up as the pilots readied to launch.

Cole touched his own faded, floppy lurp hat currently shoved under the right cheek of his ass.

"Your hat's going to blow off."

Abbott saw that none of the Rangers except him were wearing their hats so he snatched his off. Their sergeant, a twenty-year-old from Brownsville, Texas, named Luis Rodriguez, winked at Cole. Rodriguez was one week into his second tour.

"You think he's nervous?"

Abbott's face tightened.

"I'm not nervous."

Cole thought that Abbott looked like he was about to puke. Abbott was new meat. He had been in the bush on three training missions, but those were close to the Fire Base and held little chance of contact with the enemy. This was Abbott's first true Long Range Patrol mission.

Cole patted Abbott's leg and grinned at Rodriquez.

"No way, Sergeant. This is Clark Kent with a Ranger scroll. He drinks danger for breakfast and wants more for lunch; he catches bullets in his teeth and juggles hand grenades for fun; he doesn't need this helicopter to fly to the fight, he just likes our company—"

Ted Fields, also eighteen and from East Lansing, Michigan, encouraged Cole's rap.

"Hoo!"

Rodriguez and Cromwell Johnson, the radio operator, the nineteen-year-old son of a sharecropper from Mobile, Alabama, automatically echoed the grunt.

"Hoo!"

It was a Ranger thing. Hoo-Ah. Hoo for short.

They were all grinning at Abbott now, the whites of their eyes brilliant against the mottled paint that covered their faces. Here they were, the five of them—four with serious bush time plus the cherry— five young men wearing camouflage fatigues, their arms and hands and faces painted to match the jungle, packing M16s, as much ammo, hand grenades, and claymore mines as they could carry, and the bare minimum of gear necessary to survive a one-week reconnaissance patrol in the heart of Indian Country.

Cole and the others were trying to take the edge off the new guy's fear.

The Huey's crew chief tapped Rodriguez on the head, gave him a thumbs-up, and then the helicopter tilted forward and they were off.

Cole leaned close to Abbott's ear, and cupped his mouth so that his voice wouldn't blow away.

"You're going to be fine. Stay calm and stay silent."

Abbott nodded, serious.

Cole said, "Hoo."

"Hoo."

Roy Abbott had come into the Ranger company three weeks earlier and had been assigned a bunk in Cole's hootch. Cole liked Abbott as soon as he saw the pictures. Abbott didn't talk out his ass the way some new guys did, he paid attention to what the older guys told him, and he kept his shit Ranger-ready, but it was the pictures that did it. First thing the new guy did was pin up pictures; not fast cars or Playmates, but pictures of his mom and dad and four younger sisters: The old man ruddy-faced in a lime-green leisure suit; Abbott's mother heavy and plain; and the four little girls, each one a sandy-haired clone of their mother, all neat and normal with tucked skirts and pimples.

Cole, stretched out on his bunk with his hands behind his head, looked on in fascination. He watched the pictures go up and asked about them.

Abbott eyed Cole suspiciously, as if one sharpy too many had made fun of him. Cole would have bet ten dollars that Abbott said Grace before meals.

"You really wanna know?"

"Yeah, else I wouldn't've asked."

Abbott described how everyone worked the farm and lived in the same little community where their aunts and uncles and cousins and grandparents had lived for almost two hundred years, working that same land, attending those same schools, worshipping the same God, and pulling for the Buffalo Bills football team. Abbott's father, a deacon in their church, had served in Europe during World War II. Now Abbott was following in his footsteps.

When Abbott was done with his own history, he asked Cole, "How about your family?"

"It's not the same thing."

"What do you mean?"

"My mother's crazy."

Abbott finally asked another question because he didn't know what else to say.

"Was your dad in the Army, too?"

"Never met him. I don't know who he is."

"Oh."

Abbott grew quiet after that. He finished putting away his gear, then went off to find the latrine.

Cole swung out of his bunk to look more closely at the pictures. Mrs. Abbott probably baked biscuits. Mr. Abbott probably took his son deer hunting on opening day. Their family probably ate dinner together at a great long table. That's the way it was in real families. That's the way Cole had always imagined it.

Cole spent the rest of the afternoon sharpening his Randall knife and wishing that Roy Abbott's family was his.

The helicopter banked hard over a ridge, dove for a shabby overgrown clearing, flared as if it was landing, then bounced into the sky.

Abbott clutched his M16, eyes wide in surprise as the slick climbed above the ridgeline.

"Why didn't we land? Was it gooks?"

"We'll make two or three false inserts before we un-ass. That way Charlie doesn't know where we get off."

Abbott craned forward to see out of the banking slick.

Rodriguez, who was the Team Leader, shouted at Cole.

"Don't let this asshole fall out!"

Cole grabbed Abbott's rucksack and held on. Since the day with the pictures, Cole had taken Abbott under his wing. Cole taught him what to strip from his field kit to lighten his load, how to tape down his gear so nothing rattled, and had gone out on two of Abbott's training missions to make sure he got his shit together. Cole liked to hear about Abbott's family. Johnson and Rodriguez came from big families, too, but Rod's father was a drunkard who beat his kids.

The weather briefing that morning told them to expect showers and limited visibility, but Cole didn't like the heavy clouds stacked over the mountains. Bad weather could be a lurp's best friend, but really bad weather could kill you; when lurps got into deep shit they radioed for gun ships, medevacs, and extraction, but the birds couldn't fly if they couldn't see. It was a long way to walk home when you were outnumbered two hundred to one.

The slick made two more false insertions. The next insert would be for real.

"Lock and load."

All five Rangers charged their rifles and set the safeties. Cole figured that Abbott would be scared, so he leaned close again.

"Keep your eye on Rodriguez. He's gonna run for the tree line as soon as we un-ass. You watch the trees, but don't shoot unless one of us shoots first. You got that?"

"Yeah."

"Rangers lead the way."

"Hoo."

The helicopter pulled a tight bank into the wind, nosed over, then cut power and flared two feet off a dry creek in the bottom of a ravine. Cole pulled Abbott's arm to make sure he jumped, and the five of them thudded into the grass. The slick pulled pitch and powered away even as they hit the ground, leaving them behind. They ran for the trees, Rodriguez first, Cole at the rear. As soon as the jungle swallowed them, team 5-2 flopped to the ground in a five-pointed star, their feet at its center, the Rangers facing out. This way they could see and fight in a 360-degree perimeter. No one spoke. They waited, watching for movement.

Five minutes.

Ten minutes.

The jungle came to life. Birds chittered. Monkeys barked. Rain tapped at the ground around them, dripping inexorably through the triple canopy overhead to soak their uniforms.

Cole heard the low rumble of an air strike far to the west, then realized it was thunder. A storm was coming.

Rodriguez took a knee, then eased to his feet. Cole tapped Abbott's leg. Time to get up. They stood. No one spoke. Noise discipline was everything.

They set off up the hill. Cole knew the mission

profile inside and out: They would crest the ridge to their north, then follow a well-worn NVA trail, looking for a bunker complex where Army spooks believed a battalion of North Vietnamese Army regulars was massing. A battalion was one thousand people. The five members of team 5-2 were sneaking into an area where the odds would be two hundred to one.

Rodriguez walked point. Ted Fields walked slack behind him, meaning that as Rod looked down to pick a quiet path, Fields would pick up his slack by watching the jungle ahead for Charlie. Johnson carried the radio. Abbott followed Johnson, and Cole followed Abbott, covering their rear. Cole walked point on some missions, with Rod walking slack and Fields walking cover, but Rod wanted Cole on the cherry.

They stretched into a thin line, three or four meters apart, and moved quietly uphill. Cole watched Abbott, cringing every time the new guy caught a vine on his gear, but overall he thought the kid was a pretty good woodsman.

Thunder rolled over the ridge, and the air grew misty. They climbed into a cloud.

It took thirty minutes of hard work to crest the hill, then Rodriguez gave them a rest. Darkness had fallen with the weather, cloaking them in twilight. Rod made eye contact with each man in turn, glancing at the sky, his expression saying that the crappy weather was screwing them. If they needed air cover, they wouldn't get it.

They slipped a few meters down the opposite side of the ridge, then Rod suddenly raised a closed fist.

All five of them automatically dropped to a knee, rifles out, leftside/rightside to cover both flanks. Rod signaled Cole, the last man. He made a V sign, like a peace sign, then cupped his fingers into a C. He pointed at the ground, then opened and closed his fist three times—five, ten, fifteen. Rod was estimating fifteen Vietcong soldiers.

Rod moved out, and, one by one, the rest of them followed. Cole saw a narrow trail pocked with overlapping footprints. The prints were made by sandals cut from old tires and were still crisp, telling Cole that they had been made only ten or fifteen minutes ago. The VC were near.

Abbott glanced back at Cole. His face was streaked with rain, and his eyes were wide. Cole was scared, too, but he forced a smile. Mr. Confidence. Keep it tight, troop; you can do this.

Team 5-2 had been in the jungle for fifty-six minutes. They had less than twelve minutes left to live.

They continued along the ridge for less than a hundred meters when they found the main trail. It was laced by VC and NVA prints, and a lot of the traffic was fresh. Rod made a circle with his upraised hand, telling the others that the enemy was all around them. Cole's mouth was dry even with the rain.

Exactly three seconds later, all hell would break loose.

Rod stepped alongside a tall banyan tree just as a gnarled finger of lightning arced down the tree, jumped to Rod's ruck, and detonated the claymore mine strapped to the top of his pack. The top half of Ted Fields vaporized in a red mist. Meat and blood blew back over Johnson, Abbott, and Cole as the backblast from the mine kicked Rodriguez into the tree. The concussion hit Cole like a hypersonic tidal wave and knocked him down. Cole's ears rang and a great writhing snake of light twisted wherever he looked. The lightning's flash had blinded him.

Johnson screamed into his radio.

"Contact! We have contact!"

Cole scrambled forward. He climbed over Abbott and covered Johnson's mouth.

"Be quiet! Chuck's all around us, Johnson, stop shouting! That was lightning."

"Fuck lightning, that was mortars! I didn't come ten thousand miles to get hit by lightning!"

"It was lightning! It set off Rod's claymore."

What could be the odds? A million to one? Ten billion to one? Here they were on the side of a mountain surrounded by Chuck and a lightning bolt fired them up.

Johnson said, "I can't see. I'm fuckin' blind."

"You hit?"

"I can't see. All I see is squiggly shit."

"That's the afterburn, man, like a flashbulb. I got that, too. Just take it easy. Fields and Rod are down."

Cole's vision slowly cleared, and he saw that Johnson's head was bleeding. He twisted around to see Abbott.

"Abbott?"

"I'm good."

Cole pushed the radio phone into Johnson's hands again.

"Get the base. Tell'm to get us the hell out of here."

"I got it."

Cole crawled past Johnson to check Fields. Fields was a red lace of blood and shredded cloth. Rodriguez was alive, but one side of his head was gone, exposing his brain.

"Sergeant? Rod?"

Rodriguez did not respond.

Cole knew that Charlie would arrive soon to investigate the explosion. They had to leave immediately if they wanted to survive. Cole went back to Johnson.

"Tell'm we have one KIA and one head wound. We're going to have to drag back over the ridge to where we came in."

Johnson repeated Cole's report in a low murmur, then pulled out a plastic-covered map to read off their coordinates. Cole motioned Abbott forward.

"Watch the trail."

Abbott didn't move. He stared at what was left of Ted Fields, opening and closing his mouth like a fish trying to breathe. Cole grabbed Abbott's harness and jerked him.

"Goddamnit, Abbott, watch for Chuck! We don't have time for this."

Abbott finally lifted his rifle.

Cole wrapped a pressure bandage around Rodriguez's head, working as fast as he could. Rod thrashed and tried to push him away. Cole lay on him to pin him down, then wrapped his head with a second bandage. The rain pounded down, washing away the blood. Thunder made the forest shudder.

Johnson crawled up beside him.

"Fuckin' thunderstorm has'm grounded, man. I knew that shit would happen. Fuckin' weather ass-

holes, sendin' us out in this shit. Ain't even seen Charlie, and we're fucked by a buncha goddamned lightnin'. Fucked, an' the slicks can't get in. We're on our own out here."

Cole finished tying off Rodriguez, then pulled out two Syrettes of morphine. Morphine could kill someone with a head wound, but they had to carry Rod and they had to move fast; if Charlie caught them, then everyone would die. Cole popped both Syrettes into Rodriguez's thigh.

"You think the three of us can carry Rod and Fields?"

"Fuck, no, are you crazy? Fields ain't nothing but hamburger."

"Rangers don't leave Rangers behind."

"Didn't you hear what I just tol' you? They can't get the slick in here. The thunderhead's gotta move out before anybody's goin' anywhere."

Ted Fields's leg was still twitching, but Cole willed himself not to look at it. Maybe Johnson was right about Fields; they could come back for him later, but right now they had to evacuate the area before Charlie found them, and it would take two of them to carry Rodriguez.

"Okay, we'll leave Teddy here. Abbott, you're gonna help me carry Rodriguez. Crom, get the rear and tell'm what we're doing."

"I'm on it."

Johnson transmitted their intentions as Cole and Abbott lifted Rodriguez between them. That's when a bright red geyser erupted from Abbott, followed by the chunking snap of an AK-47.

Johnson screamed, "Gooks!" and sprayed the jungle with bullets.

Abbott dropped Rodriguez and fell.

The jungle erupted in noise and flashes of light.

Cole fired past Johnson even though he couldn't see the enemy. He swung his M16 in a tight arc, emptying his magazine in two short bursts.

"Where are they?!"

"I got Charlie! I got you, you motherfuckers!!"

Johnson jammed in a fresh magazine and rattled off shorter bursts, four- and five-shot groups. Cole reloaded and fired indiscriminately. He still didn't see the enemy, but bullets snapped past him and kicked up leaves and dirt all around him. The noise was deafening, but Cole barely heard it. It was that way in every firefight; the adrenaline rush amped out sounds and numbed you.

He emptied a second magazine, ejected it, then rammed home a third. He fired into the trees, then crawled over Rodriguez to check Abbott. Abbott was pressing on his stomach to cover his wound.

"I've been shot. I think I was shot!"

Cole pulled Abbott's hand away to check the wound, and saw a gray coil of intestine. He pushed Abbott's hand back on the wound.

"Press on it! Press hard!"

Cole fired at shadows, and shouted at Johnson.

"Where are they?! I don't see them!"

Johnson didn't answer. He reloaded and fired with mechanical determination—brrp, brrp, brrp!

Cole watched Johnson's bullets chew up a heavy thatch of jungle, then saw muzzle flashes to the right. Cole drained his magazine into the flashes, reloaded, *then tore a hand grenade from his harness. He shouted to warn Johnson, then threw the grenade. It went off with a loud CRACK that rippled through the trees. Cole threw a second grenade. CRACK! Johnson lobbed a grenade of his own—CRACK!*

"Fall back! Johnson, let's go!"

Johnson scuttled backward, firing as he withdrew. Cole shook Abbott.

"Can you get to your feet? We gotta get out of here, Ranger! Can you stand?"

Abbott rolled over and pushed to his knees. He kept his left hand pressed hard to his stomach, and moaned with the effort.

Cole fired into the trees, then threw another grenade. Johnson didn't need to be told what to do; he knew. Fields might be dead, but Rodriguez was alive. They would carry him out.

Johnson and Cole fired short bursts behind them, then got on either side of Rodriguez and lifted him by his harness.

Cole shouted, "Go, Abbott. Go! Uphill the way we came."

Abbott stumbled away.

Cole and Johnson dragged Rodriguez away, firing awkwardly with their free hands. The shooting died down when they threw the grenades, but now it built steadily again; Charlie shouted to each other through the green.

"Minh dang duoi bao nhieu dua?"

"Chung dang chay ve phia bo song!"

Cole felt bullets snap past. Johnson grunted and stumbled, then caught himself.

"I'm okay."

Johnson had been hit in the calf.

Then Cole felt two hard thuds shudder through Rodriguez and knew that their team leader had been hit again.

Johnson said, "Motherfuckers!"

"Keep running!"

Rodriguez belched a huge gout of blood and his body convulsed.

"Jesus Christ!"

"Fucker's dead! Motherfucker's dead!"

They put Rodriguez down behind a tree. Johnson fired down the hill, chewing up two magazines as Cole checked Rodriguez for a pulse. There was none.

Cole's eyes burned hot and angry; first Fields, now Rodriguez. Cole emptied his magazine, then pulled the grenades from Rod's harness. He threw one, then another—CRACK! CRACK! Johnson stripped Rod's ammo, and they fell back, Cole firing as Johnson ran, then Johnson firing to cover Cole. Cole had still not seen a single enemy soldier.

They caught up with Abbott at the top of the hill and took cover behind a fallen tree. The rain fell even harder now, draping them in a gray caul.

"Johnson, get on the radio. Tell'm we've got to get out of here."

Cole stripped off Abbott's gear, then pulled open his shirt.

"Don't look, cherry! Keep your eyes on the trees. You watch for Charlie, okay? Watch for Charlie."

Abbott was crying.

"It burns! It hurts like the dickens. It really hurts!"

Cole loved Roy Abbott in that moment, loved him and hated him both, loved him for his innocence and fear, and hated him for taking a round that now slowed them down and might get them killed.

Johnson held Abbott's hand.

"You're not gonna die, goddamnit. We don't let cherries die on their first mission. You gotta earn your death out here."

Cole said, "Rangers lead the way. Say it, Roy. Rangers lead the way."

Abbott struggled to echo, fighting back tears.

"Rangers lead the way."

Abbott's intestines had burst through his abdominal wall like a mass of snakes. Cole pushed them back into his body, then wrapped Abbott with pressure bandages. The bandages soaked through with red even before Cole finished wrapping him, a sure sign of arterial bleeding. Cole wanted to run away, leaving Abbott and the blood and Charlie behind, but he fumbled a morphine Syrette out of his med kit and pushed it into Abbott's thigh.

"Wrap him again, Johnson. Pull it tight, then hook him up."

Rangers saw such heavy combat that each man carried cans of serum albumin blood expander strapped to their web gear. Cole threw the empty Syrette aside and snatched up the radio as Johnson hooked up Abbott's serum can.

"Five-two, five-two, five-two. We have heavy contact. We have two KIA and one critical wounded, over."

The tinny voice of their company commander, Captain William "Zeke" Zekowski, came back scratchy in his ear. The thunderstorm was ruining their communication.

"*Say again, five-two.*"

Cole wanted to smash the phone, but instead he carefully repeated himself. *Panic kills. Keep it tight. Rangers lead.*

"*Understand, five-two. We've got a slick and two gunships in orbit three miles out, but they can't get in with that weather, son. It's blowing through fast, so you hang on.*"

"*We are pulling back. Do you copy?*"

The crackle of static was his only answer. The rain beat at them so hard that it was like standing in a shower.

"Does anyone hear me?"

Static.

"*Sonofabitch!*"

No radio. No extraction. Nothing. They were on their own.

When Johnson finished taping the serum IV to Abbott's forearm, they helped him to his feet. Now the rain was their friend; the heavy curtain of water would hide them and wash away their signs and make it hard for Charlie to follow. They would be safe until the others came to save them.

Johnson stepped out front to take the point when a shot cracked dully under the rain and his head blew apart. Johnson collapsed at their feet.

Abbott screamed.

Cole spun around and fired blindly. He dumped his magazine, then picked up Johnson's rifle and emptied that magazine, too.

"Shoot, Abbott! Fire your weapon!"

Abbott fired blindly, too.

Cole shot at everything. He fired because something was trying to kill him and he had to kill it first. He threw his last hand grenade, CRACK!, then stripped a grenade from Johnson's harness. CRACK! He stripped off Johnson's ammo packs, then stripped off the radio. Johnson's head came apart like a rotten melon.

"*Run, goddamnit! RUN!*"

He pushed Abbott down the hill, then fired another magazine into the rain. He reloaded, fired, then hoisted the radio. Bullets slammed into the deadfall in front of him, sending up a spray of splinters and wood chips.

Cole ran. He caught up to Abbott, hooked an arm under his shoulders, and pulled him forward.

"RUN!"

They tumbled down the side of the mountain, stumbling through glistening green leaves as thick as leather. Vines ripped at their legs and clawed at their rifles. The pop of gunfire stayed close at their heels.

Cole led them down a steep incline into a drainage overflowing with a torrent of rain. He stayed in the water so that they wouldn't leave tracks, pulling Abbott along the rushing stream and out into the wider ravine. Charlie shouted behind them.

"Rang chan phia duoi chung!"

"Toi nghe thay chung no o phia duoi!"

Somewhere to their left, an AK ripped on full automatic.

Abbott plowed headlong into a tree and crashed into the weeds, tearing the IV needle from his arm. Cole pulled Abbott to his knees, hissing for him to get to his feet.

Abbott's face was white where the grease paint had washed away.

"I'm gonna vomit."

"Get up, Ranger. Keep going."

"My stomach hurts."

The entire front of his uniform and the thighs of his pants were saturated with blood.

"Get up."

Cole pulled Abbott onto his shoulders in a fireman's carry. He staggered under the weight; between Abbott and his gear, he carried almost three hundred pounds. The jungle thinned. They were getting close to the clearing where the slick had dropped them.

Cole wrestled free the radio as he stumbled along the creek.

"Five-two, five-two, five-two, over."

The captain's broken voice came back.

"Copy, five-two."

"Johnson's dead. They're all dead."

"Settle down, son."

"Three KIA, one wounded critical. Charlie's on our ass. You hear me? Charlie's right behind us."

"Stand by."

"Don't tell me to stand by! We're dying out here."

Cole was crying. He sucked breath like a steam engine, and he was so scared that his heart seemed in flames.

The captain's voice came back.

"Cole, is that you?"

"Everyone is gone. Abbott's bleeding to death."

"A First Cav slick thinks he can get to you from the south. He's low on fuel, but he wants to try."

More shouts came from behind Cole, and then an

AK opened up. Cole didn't know if the VC saw him or not, but he didn't have the strength to look around. He staggered on. Abbott began screaming.

"I'm almost at the clearing."

"He's flying up the ravine under the clouds. You have to pop a smoke for him, son. We cannot vector to your position, over."

"Roger smoke."

"This goddamned storm is rolling right at our gunships. They cannot reach you for support."

"I understand."

"You're on your own."

Cole broke out of the jungle into the clearing. The dry creek was now filled with rushing water. Cole sloshed in up to his waist and waded across, fighting the current. His arms and legs felt dead, but then he was out of the water and on the other side. He rolled Abbott onto the high grass and looked for the helicopter. He thought he saw it, a black speck blurred by the rain. Cole pulled a smoke marker. Bright purple smoke swirled behind him.

The black speck tilted on its side and grew.

Cole sobbed.

They were coming to save him.

He dropped to his knees beside Abbott.

"Hang on, Roy; they're coming."

Abbott opened his mouth and spit up blood.

Something flashed past Cole with a sharp whip-crack as the rattling hammer of an AK sounded in the tree line. Cole fell to his belly. Muzzle flashes danced in the green wall like fireflies. Mud splashed into his face.

Cole emptied his magazine at the flashes, jammed in another, and fired some more.

"Abbott!"

Abbott slowly rolled onto his belly. He dragged his weapon into the firing position and fired a single round.

The jungle sparkled. More and more flashes joined the first until the jungle was lit by twinkling lights. Mud hopped and jumped, and the tall stringy grass fell around Cole as if it were being mowed by invisible blades. He burned through his magazine in a single burst, packed in another, and burned through that one. His rifle's barrel was hot enough to sear flesh.

"Fire your weapon, Abbott! FIRE!"

Abbott fired once more.

Cole heard the blurring thump of the helicopter now.

He reloaded and fired. He was down to his last four-pack of magazines, but the trees were alive with enemy soldiers.

"Shoot, damnit!"

Abbott rolled onto his side. His voice was soft.

"I didn't think it would be like this."

The helicopter was suddenly loud and the grass around them swirled. Cole shot at the flashes. Overhead, the 60-gunner opened up. His big .30-caliber weapon chewed at the jungle.

Cole rolled over as the heavy slick wobbled to the earth. It was pocked with bullet holes and trailing smoke. First Cavalry troops jammed the cargo bay like refugees. They added their fire to the 60-gun. The slick had been shot to hell, but still the pilot was *bringing his ship through a thunderstorm and into a wall of gunfire. Slick pilots had steel balls.*

"C'mon, Roy, let's go."

Abbott did not move.

"Let's go!"

Cole slung his rifle, lifted Abbott, and lurched to his feet. Something hot ripped through his pants and then he felt a loud spang! *A bullet shattered the radio. Cole stumbled to the helicopter and heaved Abbott into the bay. Cav troopers piled atop each other to make room.*

Cole clambered aboard.

AK fire popped and pinged into the bulkhead.

The crew chief screamed at him.

"They told us it was only one guy!"

Cole's ears rang so loudly that he could not hear.

"What?"

"They told us there was just one man. We're too heavy. We can't take off!"

The turbine howled as the pilot tried to climb. The helicopter wallowed like a whale.

The crew chief grabbed Abbott's harness.

"Push him off! We can't fly!"

Cole leveled his M16 at the center of the crew chief's chest. The crew chief let go.

"He's dead, Ranger, push him off! You're going to get us killed!"

"He's coming with me."

"We're too heavy! We can't fly!"

The turbine spooled louder. Oily smoke swirled through the door.

"Push him out!"

Cole wrapped his finger over the trigger. Rod and

Fields and Johnson were gone, but Abbott was going home. Families take care of their own.

"He's coming with me."

The Cav troops knew that Cole would pull the trigger. Rage and fear burned off the young Ranger like steam. He would do anything and kill anyone to complete his mission. The Cav troops understood. They pushed off ammo cans and rucksacks, anything they could shed to lighten the load.

The turbine shrieked. The rotor found hold in the thick humid air, and the helicopter lumbered into the sky. Cole lowered his weapon across Abbott's chest and protected his brother until they were home.

The thunderhead passed from the mountains four hours later. A reaction force comprised of Rangers from Cole's company assaulted the area to reclaim the bodies of their comrades. Specialist Fourth Class Elvis Cole was among them.

The bodies of Sgt. Luis Rodriguez and Sp4c Ted Fields were recovered. The body of Sp4c Cromwell Johnson was missing and presumed carried away by the enemy.

For his actions that day, Sp4c Elvis Cole was awarded the nation's third-highest decoration for bravery and valor, the Silver Star.

It was Cole's first decoration.

He would earn more.

Rangers don't leave Rangers behind.

14
· · ·

After I spoke with the Abbotts, I phoned the other families to let them know that the police would be calling, and why. Between Master Sergeant Stivic and the families, I was on the phone for almost three hours.

Starkey rang my bell at eight forty-five. When I opened the door, John Chen was waiting behind her in his van.

I said, "I spoke with the families this morning. None of them had anything to do with this or know anyone who would. You get any hits on the other names I gave you?"

Starkey squinted at me. Her eyes were puffy, and her morning voice was thick with smoke.

She said, "Are you drunk?"

"I've been up all night. I spoke with the families. I listened to that damned tape a dozen times. Did you get any hits or not?"

"I told you last night, Cole. We ran the names and got nothing. You don't remember I said that?"

I felt irritated with myself for forgetting. She had told me when I was with them at the Hollywood station. I grabbed my keys and stepped outside past her.

"C'mon. I'll show you what we found. Maybe John can match the prints."

"Lay off the coffee. You look like a meth freak about to implode."

"You're no beauty yourself."

"Fuck yourself, Cole. That might be because Gittamon and I got our asses reamed at six this morning by the Bureau commander, wanting to know why we're letting you fuck up our evidence."

"Did Richard complain?"

"Rich assholes *always* complain. Here's the order of the day: You're gonna take us over to whatever this is you've found, then you're gonna stay out of our business. Never mind that you seem to be the only guy around here besides me who knows how to detect. You're out."

"If I didn't know better, I'd think you just paid me a compliment."

"Don't let it go to your head. It turns out Richard was right, you being a material witness. It just feels like kicking a guy when he's down, is all, shutting you out like this, and I don't like it."

I felt bad for snapping at her.

She said, "I guess you didn't suddenly recognize

the voice on the tape or remember something that would help?"

I wanted to tell her my take on what the caller had said, but I figured that it would sound self-justifying.

"No. I've never heard his voice in my life. I played it over the phone to the families, and they didn't recognize it, either."

Starkey cocked her head as if she were surprised.

"That was a good idea, Cole, playing the tape for them like that. I hope none of them lied to you."

"Why'd you have Hurwitz bring me the tape last night instead of doing it yourself?"

Starkey went to her car without answering.

"Drive yourself. You'll need to get back on your own."

I locked the house, then led them across the canyon to the shoulder where Pike and I had parked the day before. It took about twelve minutes. Starkey changed into her running shoes while Chen unloaded his evidence kit. The shoulder had been empty yesterday, but now a line of small trucks and cars spilled around the curve from the nearby construction site. Starkey and Chen followed me across the hump and down through the brush. We passed the twin pines, then followed the erosion cut toward the lone scrub oak. As we got closer to the prints, I felt both anxious and afraid. Being here was like being closer to Ben, but not if the shoe prints didn't match. If they didn't match, we had nothing.

We reached the first print, a clean clear sole pressed into the dust between shale plates.

"This one's pretty clear. We'll see more below."

Chen got down on his hands and knees for a closer

look. I stood so close that I was almost on top of him.

Starkey said, "Stop crowding him, Cole. Get back."

Chen glanced up and grinned.

"It's the same shoe, Starkey. I can see it even without the cast. Size eleven Rockports showing the same pebbled sole and traction lines."

My heart thudded hard in my chest, and the dark ghost moved past me again. Starkey punched my arm.

"You fuck."

Starkey could sweet-talk with the best of them.

Chen flagged eight more prints, and then we reached the tree. The heartier weeds had sprung up with the morning dew, but the depression behind the tree was still clear.

"That's it, just this side of the oak at its base. See where the grass is crushed?"

Starkey touched my arm.

"You wait here."

Starkey moved closer. She stooped to look at my house from under the oak's limbs, then considered the surrounding hillside.

"All right, Cole. You made a good call. I don't know how you found this place, but this is okay. You figured this bastard good. John, I want a full area map."

"I'll need help. We've got a lot more physicals than yesterday."

Starkey squatted at the edge of the crushed grass, then bent to look close at something in the dirt.

She said, "John, gimme the tweezers."

Chen handed her a Ziploc bag and tweezers from his evidence kit. Starkey picked up a small brown ball with the tweezers, eyeballed it, then put it into the bag. She looked up into the tree, then at the ground again.

I said, "What is it?"

"They look like mouse turds, but they're not. They're all over the place."

Starkey picked one from a broad leaf of grass and put it onto her palm. Chen looked horrified.

"Don't touch it with your bare skin!"

I moved closer to see, and this time she didn't tell me to step back. A dozen dark brown wads the size of a BB stood out clearly on the hardpack. More brown flecks clung to the grass. I knew what they were as soon as I saw them because I had seen things like this when I was in the Army.

"It's tobacco."

Chen said, "How do you know?"

"A smoker on patrol chews tobacco to get his fix. You chew, there's no smoke to give you away. That's what this guy did. He chewed, then spit out the bits of the tobacco when they were used up."

Starkey glanced at me, and I knew what she was thinking. Another connection to Vietnam. She handed the bag to Chen. She dry-swallowed another white pill, then studied me for a moment with a deep vertical line between her eyebrows.

"I want to try out something on you."

"What?"

"Over by your house, this guy doesn't leave anything, one measly little partial that we could barely see. Here, he leaves crap all over the place."

"He felt safe here."

"Yeah. He had a good spot down here where no one could see him, so he didn't give a shit. I'm thinking that if he got careless down here, maybe he got careless up at the street, too. There aren't many houses on this stretch, and we got that construction site right here around the curve. I've gotta call Gittamon and have patrol pull the door-to-door to this side of the canyon, but there aren't that many people to talk to. By the time Gittamon and the uniforms get out here, you and I could have it done."

"I thought I wasn't supposed to be involved."

"I didn't ask for a lot of conversation. You want to do it or you want to waste time?"

"Of course I want to do it."

Starkey glanced at Chen.

"You tell anyone, I'll kick your ass."

We left Chen calling SID for another criminalist, and walked back along the curve to the construction site. A single-story contemporary had been ripped apart to expand the ground floor and add a second story. A long blue Dumpster sat in the street in front of the house, already half-filled with trimmed lumber and other debris. A framing crew was roughing in the second floor while electricians pulled wire through the first-floor conduit. Here it was late fall, but the workmen were shirtless and in shorts.

An older man with baggy pants was bent over a set of plans in the garage, explaining something to a sleepy young guy wearing electrician's tools. The drywall inside the garage and the house had been pulled down, leaving the studs exposed like human ribs.

Starkey didn't wait for them to notice us or excuse the interruption. She badged the older guy.

"LAPD. I'm Starkey, he's Cole. Are you the boss here?"

The older man identified himself as Darryl Cauley, the general contractor. His face closed with suspicion.

"Is this an INS thing? If someone's sneaking under the wire, I got a signed bond from every sub saying these people are legal."

The younger guy started away, but Starkey stopped him.

"Yo, stay put. We want to talk to everyone."

Cauley darkened even more.

"What is this?"

Talking to people wasn't one of Starkey's strengths, so I answered before he decided to call his attorney.

"We believe that a kidnapper was in the area, Mr. Cauley. He parked or drove on this street every day for the past week or so. We want to know if you noticed any vehicles or people who seemed out of place."

The electrician hooked his thumbs on his tools and perked up.

"No shit? Was someone kidnapped?"

Starkey said, "A ten-year-old boy. It happened the day before yesterday."

"Wow."

Mr. Cauley tried to be helpful, but explained that he divided his time between three different job sites; he rarely stayed at this house more than a couple of hours each day.

"I don't know what to tell you. I got subs coming and going, I got the different crews. Do you have a picture, what do they call it, a mug shot?"

"No, sir. We don't know who he is or what he looks like. We don't know what he was driving, either, but we believe he spent a lot of time around the curve where your crew is parked."

The electrician glanced toward the curve.

"Oh, man, that is so creepy."

Cauley said, "I'd like to help, but I don't know. These guys here, their friends drop by, their girlfriends. I got another site over in Beachwood, last month a limo pulls up with all these suits from Capitol Records. They signed one of the carpenters to a record deal for three million dollars. You never know, is what I'm saying."

Starkey said, "Can we talk to your crew?"

"Yeah, sure. James, you wanna call your guys? Tell Frederico and the framers to come down."

Between the framers and the electricians, Cauley had nine men working that day. Two of the framers had trouble with English, but Cauley helped with the Spanish. Everyone cooperated when they heard that a child was missing, but no one remembered anyone out of the ordinary. The day felt half over by the time we finished even though it was not yet noon.

Starkey fired up a cigarette when we reached the Dumpster.

"Okay. Let's do the houses."

"He wouldn't have parked more than five or six houses on either side of the curve. The farther he had to walk, the bigger the risk that someone would see him."

"Okay. And?"

"Let's split up. I'll take the houses on the far side and you take the houses on this side. It'll be faster."

Starkey agreed. I left her with the cigarette and trotted back past our cars to the houses on the far side of the curve. An Ecuadorean housekeeper answered at the first house, but she hadn't seen anyone or anything, and wasn't able to help. No one answered at the next house, but an elderly man wearing a thin robe and slippers answered at the third. He was so frail with osteoporosis that he drooped like a dying flower. I explained about the man on the slope and asked if he had seen anyone. The old man's toothless mouth hung open. I told him that a boy was missing. He didn't answer. I slipped my card into his pocket, told him to call if he remembered something, then pulled the door closed. I spoke with another housekeeper, a young woman with three small children, then reached another house where no one was home. It was a weekday and people were working.

I thought about trying the houses farther up the street but Starkey was leaning against her Crown Vic when I got back to our cars.

I said, "You get anything?"

"C'mon, Cole, do I look like it? I've talked to so many people who haven't seen anything that I asked one broad if she ever went outside."

"People skills aren't your strong point, are they?"

"Look, I've gotta call Gittamon to get some help out here. I want to run down the garbage men, the mailman, the private security cars that work this street, and anyone else who might've seen something, but you and I have taken it as far as we can. You gotta split."

"C'mon, Starkey, there's plenty to do and I can help do it. I can't walk away now."

She spoke carefully, with a soft voice.

"It's scut work, Cole. You need to get some rest. I'll call you if we get something."

"I can call the security companies from my house."

My voice sounded desperate even to me. She shook her head.

"You know that movie they make you watch before the plane takes off, when they're telling you what to do in an emergency?"

My head was filled with a faraway buzz as if I were drunk and hungry at the same time.

"What does that have to do with anything?"

"They tell you that if the plane loses pressure, you're supposed to put on your own oxygen mask before you put on your kid's. The first time I saw that I thought, bullshit, if I had a kid I'd sure as shit put on her mask first. It's natural, you know? You want to save your child. But the more I thought about it, the more it made sense. You have to save yourself first because if you're not alive, you sure as hell can't help your child. That's you, Cole. You have to put on your mask if you want to help Ben. Go home. I'll call you if something pops."

She walked away from me then and joined Chen at his van.

I climbed into my car. I didn't know if I would go home, or not. I didn't know if I would sleep, or could. I left. I drove around the curve and saw a pale yellow catering van parked by the Dumpster because that's the way it works. You lay the bricks until you get a break.

The van had just arrived.

Maybe if I hadn't been so tired I would have thought of it sooner: Construction crews have to eat, and catering vans feed them, twice a day every day, breakfast and lunch. It was eleven-fifty. Ben had been missing for almost forty-four hours.

I left my car in the street and ran to a narrow door at the back of the van that had been propped open for the heat. Inside, two young men in white T-shirts were bent over a grill. A short round woman barked orders at them in a mix of Spanish and English as they dished up grilled chicken sandwiches and paper plates spilling over with tacos and salsa *verde* to the line at the window. The woman glanced over and nodded toward the open wall of the van.

"You got to stand in line over here."

"A little boy has been kidnapped. We think the man who took him spent a lot of time on this street. You might have seen his car."

She came to the door, wiping her hands on a pink terry towel.

"Wha' you mean, a little boy? You the police?"

The electrician from earlier was in line at the window.

He said, "Yeah, he's with the cops. Some guy stole a kid, can ya believe that, right around here? They're trying to find him."

The woman stepped out of the van to join me in the street. Her name was Marisol Luna, and she owned the catering business. I described the scene on

the other side of the curve, and asked if she had noticed any vehicles parked in that area during the past
two weeks or anyone who didn't seem to fit.

"I don' think so."

"What about when no one else was parked there?
One vehicle by itself."

She rubbed her hands through the towel as if it
helped worry up her memories.

"I see the plumber. We finish the breakfast here
and we goin' that way—"

She pointed toward the curve, and the buzzing in
my head grew worse.

"—an' I see the plumber go down the hill."

I glanced toward the work crew, searching for
Cauley. Marisol Luna was the first person I found
who had seen anything.

"How do you know he was the plumber? Was he
working here at this house?"

"It say on the truck. Emilio's Plumbing. I remember 'cause my husband, his name is Emilio. That's
why I remember the truck. I smile when I see the
name, an' I tell my husband that night, but he no
look like my Emilio. He black. He have things on his
face like bumps."

I called out to the construction workers.

"Where's Cauley? Can someone get Cauley?"

Then I turned back to Mrs. Luna.

"The man who went down the hill was black?"

"No. The man in the truck, he black. The man on
the hill, he Anglo."

"Two men?"

The buzzing in my head grew more frantic, like

riding a caffeine rush. The electrician came around the end of the truck with Mr. Cauley.

He said, "You guys have any luck?"

"Have you had a plumber or plumbing contractor working here named Emilio or Emilio's Plumbing, anything like that?"

Cauley shook his head.

"Nope, never. I use the same sub over and over, all my jobs, a man named Donnelly."

Mrs. Luna said, "The truck, it say Emilio's Plumbing."

The electrician said, "Hey, I've seen that truck."

The buzz in my head suddenly vanished and my body stopped aching. Blood tingled under my skin. I felt light and alive with a clarity that was perfect. It was the same feeling I had when we were hidden along a VC trail and I heard the VC approaching and waited for Rod to fire and knew either I would have them or they would have me, but either way the whole bloody thing was about to go down.

I said, "I need you to come with me, Mrs. Luna. I need you to talk to the police right now. They're just around the curve."

Marisol Luna got into my car without complaint or objection. I didn't take the time to turn around. We drove to Starkey in reverse.

TIME MISSING: 43 HOURS, 50 MINUTES

The sun glared angrily from low in the southern sky, heating the great bowl of air in the canyon until it came to a boil. Rising air pulled a soft breeze up from the city that smelled of sulfur. Starkey held her hand to shield her eyes from the sun.

"Okay, Mrs. Luna, tell me what you saw."

Marisol Luna, Starkey, and I stood in the street at the top of the curve. Mrs. Luna pointed back toward the construction site, telling us how she remembered it.

"We come aroun' the curve there, and the plumber truck is right here."

She indicated that the plumber's van had been pretty much where we were standing, not on the shoulder but in the street. It could not have been seen from the construction site or the surrounding houses.

"My truck is big, you know? Very wide. I say to Ramón, look at this, this guy is taking up all of the street."

I said, "Ramón is one of the guys who works for her."

"Let her tell it, Cole."

Mrs. Luna continued.

"I have to stop because I cannot get around the van unless he move. Then I see the name, and it make me smile like I tell Mr. Cole. I tell my husband that night, I say, hey, I saw you today."

Starkey said, "When did this happen?"

"That would be three days. I see it three days ago."

The day before Ben was stolen. Starkey took out her notebook.

Mrs. Luna described the van as white and dirty, but she couldn't recall anything else except that the name on its side was Emilio's Plumbing. As Starkey continued questioning her, I called Information on

my cell phone and asked if they had a listing for
Emilio's Plumbing. No such listing existed either in
Los Angeles or in the Valley. I had them check the
Santa Monica and Beverly Hills listings as well, under
plumbing, plumbers, plumbing supplies, and plumbing contractors, but by then I didn't expect anything—
these guys could have stolen the van in Arizona or
painted the name themselves.

Mrs. Luna said, "It say Emilio's. I am sure."

Starkey said, "So tell me about the two men. You
came around the curve here and their van was blocking the road. Which way was it facing?"

"This way, facing me. I see in the windshield, you
know? The black man was driving. The Anglo man
was on the other side, standing there. They were
talking through the window."

Mrs. Luna stepped onto the shoulder and turned,
showing us their positions.

"They look when they see us, you know? The
black man, he have these things on his face. I think he
sick. They look like sores."

She touched her cheeks, and wrinkled her nose.

"He big, too. He a really big man."

Starkey said, "Did he get out of the van?"

"No, he inside driving."

"Then how do you know he was big?"

Mrs. Luna raised her arms high and wide over her
head.

"He fill the windshield like thees. He jus' big."

Starkey was frowning, but I got the picture and
wanted to move on.

"What about the white guy? Anything you remember about him? Tattoos? Glasses?"

"I didn't look at him."

"Was his hair long or short? You remember what color?"

"I sorry, no. I lookin' at the black man and the truck. We tryin' to get by, you see? I off the road tryin' to get aroun' him, an' I get over too much. I had to back up. The other man, he step back 'cause his frien' have to make room for us, it so narrow here. I watchin' the truck go away 'cause I tellin' Ramón, you see that stuff on his face? Ramón lookin', too. He say they warts."

Starkey said, "What's Ramón's last name?"

"Sanchez."

"Is he back at your truck now?"

"Yes, Mrs."

Starkey made note of that.

"Okay, we'll want to talk to him, too."

I put us back on track.

"So the black man drove away and the other guy went down the hill, or the black guy waited for the other guy to come back?"

"No, no, he go. The other one make that sign when he go. You know, that nasty one."

Mrs. Luna looked embarrassed.

Starkey showed her middle finger.

"The white guy flipped him off? Like this?"

"Yeah. Ramón, he laugh. I backin' up my truck 'cause I too close to the rocks so I got to watch out for that, but I see him make the sign an' go down the hill. I think he should go back to the house, but he go down the hill instead, an' I say, that funny, why he goin' down the hill? Then I think he must wanna go to the bathroom."

"Did you see where he went down there or see him come back?"

"No. We left. We had another breakfast to serve before we get ready for lunch."

Starkey took down Mrs. Luna's name, address, and phone number, then gave her a card. Starkey's pager went off again, but she ignored it.

She said, "This has been a big help, Mrs. Luna. I'll probably want to talk to you some more this evening or tomorrow. Would that be okay?"

"I happy to help."

"If you remember anything else, don't wait to hear from me. Talking the way we have might bring up a memory. You might remember something about the truck or the men that could help us. It might seem small, but I'll tell you something—nothing's too small. Whatever you remember could help us."

Starkey took out her phone and went to the edge of the shoulder, calling her office to start a wants-and-warrants search and BOLO on the van. The uniformed commander at Hollywood station would relay the information along to Central Dispatch at Parker Center, advising every Adam car in the city to be on the lookout for a van with Emilio's Plumbing written on its side.

I told Mrs. Luna that I would drive her back, but she didn't respond. She watched Starkey with her brow furrowed, as if she were seeing more than Starkey at the edge of the slope.

"She right about the memory. I remembering now. He have a cigar. He was standing like that—like the lady—and he take out a cigar."

The tobacco.

"That's right. He have a cigar. He didn't smoke it, but he chewed it. He bite off little pieces, then spit them out."

I tried to encourage her. I wanted the memories to come and the picture to build. We walked out to join Starkey at the edge. I touched Starkey's arm, the touch saying *listen*.

Mrs. Luna stared out at the canyon, then turned back toward the street as if she could see her catering truck pinched against the hill and the plumber's van driving away.

"I got the truck away from the rocks an' I put it in gear. I look back at him, you know? He was looking down. He was doing something with his hands, and make me think, what? I wanted to get going 'cause we late, but I watch him to see. He unwrap the cigar and put it in his mouth and then he went down there."

She pointed downhill.

"That's when I think he must be going to the bathroom. He have dark hair. It was short. He wear a green T-shirt. I remember that now. It dark green and look dirty."

Starkey glanced at me.

"He unwrapped the cigar?"

Mrs. Luna put her fingers together below her belly.

"He do something with it, something down here, then he put it in his mouth. I don't know what he was doing, but what else?"

I realized what Starkey was asking.

I said, "The wrapper. If he tossed the wrapper, we might get a print."

I started searching the edge of the shoulder, but Starkey shouted at me.

"*Stop it,* Cole! Get back! Do not disturb this scene!"

"We might be able to find it."

"You're gonna step on it or kick dirt over it or push it under a leaf, so get the hell back! I know what I'm doing! Stand in the street."

Starkey took Mrs. Luna's arm. She was so focused now that I might not have been with them.

"Don't think too hard, Mrs. Luna. Just let it come. Show me where he was when he did that. Where was he standing?"

Mrs. Luna crossed the street to where her truck had been, then looked back at us. She moved one way and then the other, trying hard to remember. She pointed.

"Go right a little bit. A little more. He was there."

Starkey looked down at the surrounding ground, then squatted to look more closely.

Mrs. Luna said, "I sure he right there."

Starkey touched the ground for balance, and eyeballed a widening area.

I spoke quietly to Mrs. Luna.

"What time were you here, eight, nine?"

"After nine. I think nine-thirty, maybe. We got to get the truck ready for lunch."

By nine-thirty the heat would have been climbing, and, with it, the air. A breeze would have been coming up the canyon just as it was now.

"Starkey, look to your left. The breeze would have been blowing uphill to your left."

Starkey looked to her left. She crept forward a

step, and then to her left. She touched aside rosemary sprigs and weeds, and then she crept again. Her movements were so slow that she might have been wading through honey. She dribbled a handful of dirt through her fingers and watched the dust float on the breeze. She followed its trail, more to the left and farther out on the shoulder, and then she slowly stood.

I said, "What?"

Mrs. Luna and I both hurried over. A clear plastic cigar wrapper was hooked in dead weeds. It was dusty and yellow with a red and gold band inside. It could have blown here from anywhere. It might have been here before him or come after, but maybe he left it behind.

We didn't touch it or even go close. We stood over the wrapper as if even the weight of light might make it vanish, and then we shouted for John Chen.

TIME MISSING: 43 HOURS, 56 MINUTES

JOHN CHEN'S ADVICE TO THE LOVELORN

First thing Chen did was flag the shoe prints, the crushed bed of grass behind the oak tree, and the heavier concentrations of spitwad tobacco balls. Chen didn't think twice about some guy working up tobacco balls; two years before, Chen worked a series of burglaries by a jewel thief dubbed the Fred Astaire Burglar: Fred hot-prowled mansions in Hancock Park while wearing a top hat, spats, and tails. Hidden surveillance cameras in two of the houses showed Fred literally cutting the rug with the ol' soft shoe as he flitted from room to room. Fred was so colorful that the *Times* made him out to be a dashing cat burglar in the Cary Grant/*It Takes a Thief* tradition, but, in truth, Fred left calling cards that the *Times* neglected to report: In every house, Fred dropped trou and crapped on the floor. Hardly dashing. Hardly debonair. Chen had dutifully bagged, tagged, graphed, and analyzed Fred's fecal material at fourteen different crime scenes, so what were a few spitballs compared with cat-burglar shit?

When the flags were set, Chen measured and graphed the scene. Each piece of evidence was assigned its own evidence number, then each number was located on the graph so that Chen, the police, and the prosecutors would have an accurate record of where each item was found. Everything had to be measured and the measurements recorded. It was tedious work, and Chen resented having to do it by himself. SID was sending out another criminalist— that skanky bitch Lorna Bronstein who thought she was better than everyone else—but it might be hours before she arrived.

Starkey had been helping until Cole dragged her back up the hill. Starkey was okay. Chen had known her since her days on the Bomb Squad, and kinda liked her even though she was skinny and had a face like a horse.

Chen was thinking about asking her out.

John Chen thought about sex a lot, and not just with Starkey. In fact, he thought about it at home, at the labs, and while driving; he rated every woman he saw as to sexual desirability, immediately dismissing any who fell below his admittedly diminishing standards (beggars can't be choosers) as "hogs." Didn't matter where he was, either: He thought about sex at homicides, suicides, shootings, stabbings, assaults, vehicular manslaughter investigations, and in the morgue; he woke every morning obsessing about sex, then added his log to the fire (so to speak) by watching that hot little number Katie Couric flashing her business on the *Today* show. Then he'd head off to work where armies of man-killer love muffins fanned the flames. The city was *filled* with them: Hard-bodied housewives and nymphomaniac actresses cruised the freeways in a never-ending search for man meat, and John Chen was the ONE guy in L.A. who missed out! Sure, his silver Boxster drew looks (he had bought it for just that reason and dubbed it his 'tangmobile), but every time some hottie looked past the sleek German lines of his Black Forest Love Rocket and saw *his* six foot three, hundred-thirty pound, four-eyed geeky ass, she quickly looked away. It was enough to give a guy issues.

John spent so much time fantasizing about sex that he sometimes thought that he should see a shrink, but, you know, it was better than thinking about death.

Starkey wasn't exactly in his top ten "Must Do" list, but she wasn't a hog. He once asked if she wanted to go for a ride in his Porsche, but Starkey said only if she could drive. Like that would ever happen.

John was having second thoughts. Maybe letting her drive wouldn't be so bad.

Chen was giving it serious consideration when Starkey shouted for him to haul his ass up right away.

"Hurry," she shouted. "C'mon, John, get up here!"

Bitch. Always in the driver's seat.

When Chen reached them, he found Starkey and Cole hovering over a clump of weeds like a couple of kids over buried treasure. A short squat Latina who had to be pushing retirement was with them. Chen immediately dismissed her. Hog.

"What are you screaming about? I got a lot to do."

Starkey said, "Stop with the tone and look at this."

Cole squatted to show him something in the weeds.

"Starkey found a cigar wrapper. We think it's his."

Chen took off his glasses for a closer inspection. Humiliating, but necessary: Chen looked like a world-class geek with his nose only inches from the ground, but he wanted to see the wrapper clearly. It appeared to have been folded twice, and still contained a red and gold cigar band. The plastic evidenced slight weathering, but the band had not yet lost its brilliance, indicating that it had been here no more than a few days; red dyes faded fast. The plastic appeared to be smudged under a light layer of dust.

As Chen considered the smudges, Starkey related that Mrs. Luna had seen the suspect manipulate a cigar, though she had not seen him remove the wrapper or toss it away.

Chen pretended to listen, but mostly he fumed at how Starkey kept smiling at Cole and punching him on the shoulder.

Chen grumbled in his best sullen voice.

"Okay, I'll log it. Lemme get the kit."

"Log it, yeah, but we're bringing this straight to Glendale. I want you to check it for prints."

Chen wondered if she was drinking again.

"Now?"

"Yeah, right now."

"Bronstein's on her way."

"I don't want to wait for fuckin' Bronstein. We've got something here, John. Let's run it to Glendale and fish for a hit!"

Chen glanced at Cole for help, but Cole had the frayed eyes of a psychokiller. Maybe both of them were drunk.

"You know we can't leave the scene. C'mon, Starkey—if we leave, we break the chain of custody with all the evidence down below. It won't be good in court."

"I'll take that chance."

"It's not worth taking. I mean, if she *saw* the guy drop a wrapper that might be one thing, but we don't even know this is his. It could belong to anyone."

Starkey pulled Chen aside so that Mrs. Luna couldn't hear. Cole tagged along like Starkey's lapdog. They were probably already doing each other.

Starkey lowered her voice.

"We won't know that until we run the prints."

"We might not find prints. All I see are smudges. Smudges aren't the same as prints."

Chen hated that he sounded so whiny, but she wouldn't let it go. Leaving the scene unattended was a direct violation of SID and LAPD policy.

She said, "Nothing down that hill even comes close to this. It might not be his, John; maybe it isn't. But even if all you find is a few points, we might be able to name him, and that puts us closer to finding the boy."

"It puts me closer to getting fired, is what it does."

Chen was worried. Starkey had done her damnedest to destroy herself and her career after she was blown up in the trailer park; she had been dumped by the Bomb Squad and then by CCS, so now she was stuck in a dead-end Juvenile desk. Maybe she was trying to kill herself again. Maybe she wanted to be fired. Chen edged closer to sniff her breath. Starkey pushed him back.

"Goddamnit, I'm not drinking."

Cole said, "John."

Chen scowled—here it came: Cole would probably threaten to kick his ass, him and his partner, Pike. Chen was certain that Cole was fucking her. Pike was probably fucking her, too.

Chen said, "I'm not doing it."

Cole said, "If the wrapper helps us, we'll tell them that you found it."

Starkey glanced at Cole, then nodded.

"Sure, if John wants the credit, it's his. This could be the breakthrough moment, man; guaranteed face-time on the evening news."

Chen thought about it. He had done pretty well with tips from Pike and Cole in the past. He had gotten a promotion and the 'tangmobile out of it, and had almost gotten laid. Almost. Chen glanced at Mrs. Luna to see if she could hear any of this, but she was safely away.

He said, "You cool with losing the evidence down below?"

Starkey's pager buzzed, but she ignored it.

"All I care about is finding this boy. Nothing down there matters if it helps us too late."

Cole stared at her for the longest time, then turned back to Chen.

He said, "Help us, John."

Chen thought it through: Yeah, it was a long shot, but nothing under the oak tree would or could give them an immediate ID on the perp, and this might. The odds weren't likely, but hope lived in possibilities. John, for instance, hoped to make the evening news. Helping to find the kid wouldn't be so bad, either.

Starkey's pager buzzed again. She turned it off.

Chen made up his mind.

"I'll get my stuff."

Starkey smiled wider than Chen had ever seen, then put her hand on Cole's shoulder. She left it. Chen hurried down the hill for his evidence kit, thinking that if Starkey drooled on Cole any more, she'd drown him with spit.

15

. . .

When they brought Ben inside after they caught him on the side of the house the night before, Mike took a cell phone from a green duffel bag, then went into another part of the house. Eric and Mazi made Ben sit on the floor in the living room. When Mike came back, he held the phone a few inches from Ben's mouth. Ben sensed that someone was probably on the other end of the line, listening.

Mike said, "Say your name and address."

Ben shouted as loud as he could.

"HELP! HELP ME—!"

Eric clamped a hand over his mouth. Ben was terrified that they would hurt him because he had called for help, but Mike only turned off the phone and laughed.

"Man, that was perfect."

Eric squeezed Ben's face hard. Eric was still pissed off because Ben got him in trouble by almost getting away, so his face was flushed as red as his hair.

"Stop shouting or I'll cut off your fucking head."

Mike said, "You with the heads. He did great, yelling for help like that. Stop squeezing his face."

"You want the fuckin' neighbors to hear?"

Mike tucked the phone back into the duffel, then took out a cigar. He peeled off the wrapper as he considered Ben.

"He won't yell anymore, will you, Ben?"

Ben stopped squirming. He was scared, but he shook his head, no. Eric let go.

Ben said, "Who was that on the phone?"

Mike glanced at Eric, ignoring him.

"Put him in the room. If he starts screaming, put him back in the box."

Ben said, "I won't scream. Who was that? Was that my mama?"

Mike didn't tell him or answer any of his other questions. Eric locked him in an empty bedroom with giant sheets of plywood nailed over the windows, and told him to get some sleep, but Ben couldn't. He tried to pull the plywood off the windows, but it was nailed too tight. He spent the rest of the night huddled at the door, trying to hear them through the crack. Sometime during the middle of the night he heard Eric and Mazi laughing. He listened harder, hoping to find out what they were going to do with him, but they never once mentioned him.

They talked about Africa and Afghanistan, and how they had chopped off some guy's legs. Ben stopped listening and hid in the closet the rest of the night.

Late the next morning, Eric opened the door.

"Let's go. We're bringing you home."

Just like that, they were letting him go. Ben didn't trust that Eric was telling the truth, but he wanted to go home so badly that he pretended it was real. Eric made him go to the bathroom, then marched him through the house to the garage. Eric was wearing a baggy plaid shirt with its tail hanging out. When he reached to open the door to the garage, his shirt pulled tight and Ben saw a pistol outlined at the small of his back. Eric hadn't been wearing the gun yesterday.

The garage was heavy with the smell of paint. They had painted the van brown and covered the writing on its sides. Mazi was waiting behind the wheel. Mike was already gone. Eric led Ben to the rear of the van.

Eric said, "Me and you are gonna ride in back. Here's the deal on that: I won't tie you up if you sit still and keep your mouth shut. If we stop at a red light or somethin' and you start screaming, I'll shut you up good, then it's the bag. We clear on that?"

"Yes, sir."

"I'm not fuckin' with you. Somethin' happens like we get pulled over by the cops, you smile and pretend like you're having a great time. You come through on that, we'll bring you home. Got it?"

"Yes, sir."

Ben would have said anything; he just wanted to go home.

Eric lifted him into the back of the van, then pulled the door. The garage door clambered open as Mazi started the engine. Eric spoke into a cell phone.

"We're go."

They backed out into the street, then drove down the hill. The van was a big windowless cavern with two seats up front and nothing in back except a spare tire, a roll of duct tape, and some rags. Eric sat on the tire with the phone in his lap, and made Ben sit next to him. Ben could see the street past Mazi and Eric, but not much else. Ben wondered if what they had said last night was true, about cutting off legs.

"Where are we going?"

"We're taking you home. We gotta see a man, first, but then you'll go home."

Ben sensed that Eric was telling him that he was going home so that he would behave. Ben glanced at the van's doors, deciding that he would run if he got the chance. When he turned forward again, Mazi was watching him through the mirror. Mazi's eyes went to Eric.

"He go-eeng tu run."

"Fuckit. He's cool."

"Ewe fuhk up ah-gain, Mike weel keel ewe."

"These D-boys take everything too serious. Everything's a fuckin' opera. The kid's cool. Kid, you cool?"

Ben wondered what a D-boy was and if Eric was talking about Mike.

"Uh-huh."

Mazi's eyes lingered on Ben a moment longer, then returned to the road.

They wound their way out of the hills along a residential street that Ben didn't recognize, then climbed onto the freeway. It was a bright clear day and the traffic moved well. Ben saw the Capitol Records Building and then the Hollywood Sign.

"This isn't the way to my house."

"Told you. We gotta see someone first."

Ben snuck another glance at the doors. Handles were set into each door, but Ben didn't see anything that looked like a lock. Ben checked to see if Mazi was watching him, but now Mazi was watching the road.

The downtown skyscrapers grew in the windshield like giraffes huddled together on an African plain. Mazi lifted his hand with the fingers spread wide. Eric picked up the phone.

"Five out."

They left the freeway, slowing as they curved down the ramp. Ben looked at the doors again. They would probably stop at a traffic light or stop sign at the bottom of the ramp. If Ben made it out of the van, the people in the other cars would see him. He didn't think that Eric would shoot him. Eric would chase him, but even if Eric caught him, the other people would call the police. Ben was scared, but he told himself to do it. All he had to do was pull the handle and shove open the door.

The van slowed as it reached the bottom of the ramp. Ben edged toward the door.

Eric said, "Easy."

Eric and Mazi were watching him. Eric took Ben's arm.

"We're not stupid, kid. That African up there, he can read your mind."

Mazi looked back at the road.

They turned between a row of faded warehouses, then over a little bridge along more buildings with lots of spray-paint art and chain-link fences. Ben couldn't see much past Mazi, but the buildings looked abandoned and empty. The van stopped.

Eric spoke into the phone.

"The Eagle has landed."

Eric listened for a moment, then put away the phone. He pulled Ben toward the doors.

"I'm gonna open the doors, but we're not getting out, so don't go nuts."

"You said I was going home."

Eric's grip tightened.

"You are, but first we're gonna do this. When I open the doors, you're gonna see a couple of cars. Mike's here with another guy. Don't start screaming or trying to get out, 'cause I'll fuckin' knock you out. The other guy just wants to see you're okay. If you're cool, we'll give you to him and he'll take you home. You good with that?"

"Yes! I wanna go home!"

"Okay, here we go."

Eric pushed open the door.

Ben squinted at the suddenly bright light, but he stayed quiet and didn't move. Mike was with a large thick man that Ben didn't know in front of two parked cars less than ten feet away. The man looked into Ben's eyes, and nodded, the nod saying, you're going to be okay. Mike was talking to someone else on his phone.

Mike said, "Okay, here he is."

Mike held the phone to the other man's ear so that the other man could talk while Mike still held the phone.

The other man said, "I see him. He's upright and alert. He looks okay."

Mike took back the phone.

"You heard that?"

Mike listened, then spoke into the phone again.

"Now I want you to hear something else."

Mike moved so quickly that Ben didn't understand what was happening even as Mike put a gun to the big man's head and fired one time. Ben jumped at the unexpected explosion. The big man crumpled sideways onto the car, then tumbled off. Mike held the phone near the gun and shot him a second time. Ben moaned from a terrible pressure in his chest, and Eric held him close.

Mike spoke into the phone again.

"You hear that, too? That was me killing the asshole you sent. No negotiations, no second chances—the clock is running."

Mike turned off his phone and slipped it into his pocket. He came to the van. Ben tried to twist away, but Eric held tight.

"He cool?"

"He's cool. Fuck, dude, that was harsh. You mean business."

"They understand that now."

Mike stroked Ben's head with an unexpected kindness. Ben stared at the body as it sank in a growing red pool.

Mike said, "You're okay, son."

Mike pulled off Ben's left shoe. Eric carried Ben out of the van past the body and put him into Mike's backseat. Eric got in with him. Mazi was already behind the wheel. They drove away, leaving Mike with the body.

PART THREE

. . .

RUN THROUGH
THE JUNGLE

16

· · ·

We got our second break when we took Mrs. Luna back to her catering truck. Though Ramón Sanchez was unable to add to what she had already told us, her grill cook, a teenager named Hector Delarossa, remembered the make and model of the van.

"Oh, yeah, it was a sixty-seven Ford four-door factory panel Econoline with the original trim. Crack in the left front windshield and spot rust on the lamps, no caps."

No hubcaps.

I asked him to describe the two men, but he didn't remember either.

I said, "You saw the van had rust spots around the headlights, but you can't describe the men?"

"It's a classic, yo? Me and my bro, Jésus, we're

Econoheads, yo? We're rebuilding a sixty-six. We even got a website, yo? You should check it out."

Starkey called in the make and model to be included in the BOLO, and then I followed her to Glendale. Chen had gone ahead of us.

The Los Angeles Police Department's Scientific Investigations Division shares its space with LAPD's Bomb Squad in a sprawling facility north of the freeway. The low-slung buildings and spacious parking lot made me think of a high school in the 'burbs, only high-school parking lots don't usually sport Bomb Squad Suburbans and cops in black fatigues. Not usually.

We parked beside each other in the parking lot, then Starkey led me to the white building that belonged to SID. Chen's van was outside, side by side with several others. Starkey waved our way past the reception desk, then brought me to a laboratory where four or five workstations were grouped together but separated by glass walls. Criminalists and lab techs were perched on stools or swivel chairs, one in each glass space. Something sharp in the air stung my eyes like ammonia.

Starkey swaggered in like she owned the place.

"Homie in the house! Look what the bomb blew in!"

The techs smiled and called back when they saw her. Starkey gibed with them like a long-lost sorority sister working the home crowd, and seemed more relaxed and comfortable than any time since I had met her.

Chen had put on a white lab coat and vinyl gloves,

and was working near a large glass chamber. He hunched when he saw us as if he were trying to hide inside the coat, and waved at Starkey to keep it down.

"Jesus, paint a target on me with all that noise! Everybody's going to know we're back."

"The walls are glass, John; they already know. Let's see what you have."

Chen had split the wrapper along its length and pinned it flat to a white sheet of paper. Jars of colored powder lined the back of his bench, along with eye droppers and vials, rolls of clear tape, and three of the fluffy brushes that women use to apply makeup. One end of the wrapper was smudged with white powder and little brown stains. The outline of a fingerprint was obvious, but the architecture of the pattern was blurred and indistinct. It looked pretty good to me, but Starkey made a face when she saw it.

"This looks like shit. Are you working here, John, or are you too busy hiding inside your jacket?"

Chen hunched even lower. If he hunched any more he would be under the bench.

"I've only been at it fifteen minutes. I wanted to see if I could get anything with the powder or ninhydrin."

The white smear was aluminum powder. The brown stains were a chemical called ninhydrin, which reacted with the amino acids left whenever you touch something.

Starkey bent for a closer inspection, then frowned at him as if he was stupid.

"This thing's been in the sun for days. It's too old to pick up latents with powder."

"It's also the fastest way to get an image into the system. I figured it was worth the shot."

Starkey grunted. She was okay with whatever might be faster.

"The nin doesn't look much better."

"Too much dust, and the sunlight probably broke down the aminos. I was hoping we'd get lucky with that, but I'm gonna have to glue it."

"Shit. How long?"

I said, "What does that mean, you have to glue it?"

Now Chen looked at me as if I was the one who was stupid. We had a food chain for stupidity going, and I was at the bottom.

"Don't you know what a fingerprint is?"

Starkey said, "He doesn't need a lecture. Just glue the damned thing."

Chen went pissy, like he didn't want to miss out on the chance to show off. He explained while he worked: Every time you touched something, you left an invisible deposit of sweat. Sweat was mostly water, but also contained amino acids, glucose, lactic acid, and peptides—what Chen called the organics. As long as moisture remained in the organics, techniques like dusting worked because the powder would stick to the water, revealing the swirls and patterns of the fingerprint. But when the water evaporated, all you had left was an organic residue.

Chen unpinned the wrapper, then used forceps to place it on a glass dish with the outside surface facing up. He put the dish into the glass chamber.

"We boil a little superglue in the chamber so the

fumes saturate the sample. The fumes react with the organics and leave a sticky white residue along the ridges of the print."

Starkey said, "The fumes are poisonous as hell. That's why he's gotta do it in the box."

I didn't care what he did or how he did it, so long as we got results.

I said, "How long is this going to take?"

"It's slow. I normally use a heater to boil it, but it's faster when you force the boil with a little sodium hydroxide."

Chen filled a beaker with water, then put the water into the chamber close to the wrapper. He poured something labeled methylcyanoacrylate into a small dish, then put the dish into the chamber. He selected one of the bottles from his bench. The liquid inside was clear, like water.

Starkey said, "How long, John?"

Chen ignored us. He dribbled the sodium hydroxide over the superglue, then sealed the chamber. The sodium hydroxide and superglue fizzed, but nothing flashed or burst into flames. Chen turned on a small fan inside the chamber, then stepped back.

"How long?"

"Maybe an hour. Maybe more. I've gotta watch it. So much reactant will build up that you can ruin the prints."

We had nothing to do but wait, and we weren't even sure if anything would be found. I bought a Diet Coke from a machine in the reception area, and Starkey bought a Mountain Dew. We brought our drinks outside so that she could smoke. It was quiet and still in Glendale, with the low wall of the Verdugo Mountains above us and the tip of the Santa Monicas below. We were in the Narrows, that tight place between the mountains where the L.A. River squeezed into the city.

Starkey sat on the curb. I sat beside her. I tried to conjure a picture of Ben alive and safe, but all I saw were flashes of shadow and terrified eyes.

"Did you call Gittamon?"

"And tell him what, that I bailed on a crime scene to come over here with a guy that I was specifically ordered to keep off the case? That would be you, by the way."

Starkey flicked ash from her cigarette.

"I'll call him when we know what John finds. He's been paging me, but I'll wait."

I said, "Listen. I want to thank you."

"You don't have to thank me. I'm doing my job."

"A lot of people have the job, but not everyone busts their ass to get it done. I owe you. However this plays out, I owe you."

Starkey had more of her cigarette, then grinned out over the cars in the parking lot.

"That sounds pretty good, Cole. Now what kind of ass-busting did you have in mind?"

"I didn't mean it that way."

"My loss."

Starkey ate another white tablet. I decided to change the subject. I decided to be clever.

I said, "Starkey, are those breath mints or are you a drug addict?"

"It's an antacid. I have stomach problems from

when I was hurt, so I gotta take the antacid. It messed me up pretty bad inside."

Hurt. Being blown apart and killed in a trailer park was "hurt." I felt like a turd.

"I'm sorry. That wasn't my business."

She shrugged, then flicked her cigarette into the parking lot.

"This morning you asked why I didn't bring you the tape."

"It's not important. I just wondered why the other guy brought it instead of you. You said you'd be back."

"Your 201 and 214 were waiting in the fax machine. I started reading while I was waiting for the tape. I saw that you were wounded."

"Not when I was out with five-two. That was another time."

I should have gone to Canada. Then none of this would be happening.

"Yeah, I know. I saw you got hit by mortar fire. I was just curious about that, is all, what happened to you. You don't have to tell me if you don't want. I know it doesn't have anything to do with this case."

She struck up a fresh cigarette to hide behind the movement, as if she was suddenly embarrassed that I knew why she was asking. A mortar shell was a bomb. In a way, bombs had gotten both of us.

"It wasn't anything like with you, Starkey, not even close. Something exploded behind me and then I woke up under some leaves. I got a few stitches, that's all."

"The report says they took twenty-six pieces of frag out of your back and you almost bled to death."

I wiggled my eyebrows up and down like Groucho Marx.

"Wanna see the scars, little girl?"

Starkey laughed.

"Your Groucho sucks."

"My Bogart's even worse. Want to hear that?"

"You want to talk scars? I could show you scars. I got scars that'd make you shit blue."

"What a pleasant use of language."

We smiled at each other, then both of us felt awkward at the same time. It wasn't banter anymore and it somehow felt wrong. I guess my expression changed. Now both of us looked away.

She said, "I can't have kids."

"I'm sorry."

"Jesus, I can't believe I told you that."

Now neither of us was smiling. We sat in the parking lot, drinking our caffeine as Starkey smoked. Three men and a woman came out of the Bomb Squad and crossed the parking lot to a brick warehouse. Bomb techs. They wore black fatigues and jump boots like elite commandos, but they goofed with each other like regular people. They probably had families and friends like regular people, too, but during their shift they de-armed devices that could tear them apart while everyone else hid behind walls, just them, all alone, with a monster held tight in a can. I wondered what kind of person could do that.

I glanced at Starkey. She was watching them.

I said, "Is that why you're on the Juvenile desk?"

She nodded.

Neither of us said very much after that until John Chen came out. He had the prints.

TIME MISSING: 47 HOURS, 04 MINUTES

White concentric circles covered the wrapper in over-lapping smudges. People don't touch anything with a clean, singular grip; they handle the things they touch—pencils, coffee cups, steering wheels, telephones, cigar wrappers—their fingers shuffle and slide; they adjust and readjust their grip, laying fingerprint on top of fingerprint in confused and inseparable layers.

Chen inspected the wrapper through a magnifying glass attached to a flexible arm.

"Most of this stuff is garbage, but we've got a couple of clean patterns we can work with."

I said, "Is it going to be enough?"

"Depends on how many typica I can identify and what's in the computer. It'll be easier to see when I add a little color."

Chen brushed dark blue powder on two sections of the wrapper, then used a can of pressurized air to blow off the excess. Two dark blue fingerprint patterns now stood in sharp contrast to the white smudges on the wrapper. Chen hunched more closely over the magnifying glass. He grunted.

"Got a nice double-loop core here. Got a clean tentarch on this one. Couple of isles."

He nodded at Starkey.

"Plenty. If he's in the system, we can find him."

Starkey laid her hand on Chen's back and squeezed his shoulder.

"Excellent, John."

I think he purred.

Chen pressed a piece of clear tape on the blue fingerprints to lift them from the wrapper, then fixed the tape onto a clear plastic backing. He set each print onto a light box, then photographed them with a high-resolution digital camera. He fed the digital images into his computer, then used a graphics program to enlarge them and orient them. Chen filled out an FBI Fingerprint Identification Form that was basically a checklist description of the two fingerprints with their characteristics identified by type and location—what Chen called "characteristic points": Every time a ridge line stopped or started it was called a typica; when a ridge split into a Y it was a bifurcation; a short line between two longer lines was an isle; a line that split but immediately came together again was an eye.

The FBI's National Crime Information Center and the National Law Enforcement Telecommunication System don't compare pictures to identify a fingerprint; they compare lists of characteristic points. The accuracy and depth of the list determines the success of the search. If a recognizable match is even in the system.

Chen spent almost twenty minutes logging the architecture of the two prints into the appropriate forms, then hit the Send button and leaned back.

I said, "What now?"

"We wait."

"How long does it take?"

"It's computers, man. It's fast."

Starkey's pager buzzed again. She glanced at it, then slipped it into her pocket.

"Gittamon."

"He wants you bad."

"Fuck him. I gotta have a cigarette."

Starkey was turning away when Chen's computer chimed with an incoming E-mail.

Chen said, "Let's see."

The file downloaded automatically when Chen opened the E-mail. An NCIC/Interpol logo flashed over a set of booking photos showing a man with deep-set eyes and a strong neck. His name was Michael Fallon.

Chen touched a line of numbers along the bottom of the file.

"We've got a ninety-nine point nine-nine percent positive match on all twelve characteristic points. It's his cigar wrapper."

Starkey nudged me.

"So? Do you know him?"

"I've never seen him before in my life."

Chen scrolled the file so that we could read Fallon's personal data; brown, brown, six, one-ninety. His last known residence was in Amsterdam, but his current whereabouts were unknown. Michael Fallon was wanted for two unrelated murders in Colombia, South America, two more in El Salvador, and had been indicted under the International War Crimes Act by the United Nations for participating in mass murder, genocide, and torture in Sierra Leone. Interpol cautioned that he was to be considered armed and extremely dangerous.

Starkey said, "Jesus Christ. He's one of those people with a fucked-up brain."

Chen nodded.

"Lesions. They always find lesions in people like this."

Fallon had extensive military experience. He had served in the United States Army for nine years, first as a paratrooper, then as a Ranger. He had served an additional four years, but whatever he had done during those years was described only as "classified."

Starkey said, "What the fuck does that mean?"

I knew what it meant, and felt a sharp tightness in my chest that was more than fear. I knew how he had come by the skills to watch and move and leave no sign when he stole Ben. I had been a soldier, and I had been good at it. Mike Fallon was better.

"He was in Delta Force."

Chen said, "The terrorist guys?"

Starkey stared at his picture.

"No shit."

Delta. D-boys. The Operators. Delta trained for hard, hot insertions against terrorist targets, and membership was by invitation only. They were the best killers in the business.

Starkey said, "All this Army stuff, maybe he got a hard-on for you while he was in the service."

"He doesn't know me. He's too young for Vietnam."

"Then why?"

I didn't know.

We kept reading. After Fallon left the service, he had used his skills to work as a professional soldier in Nicaragua, Lebanon, Somalia, Afghanistan, Colombia, El Salvador, Bosnia, and Sierra Leone. Michael Fallon was a mercenary. Lucy's words came to me:

This isn't normal. Things like this don't happen to normal people.

Starkey said, "This is just great, Cole. You couldn't have a garden-variety lunatic after you. You gotta have a professional killer."

"I don't know him, Starkey. I've never heard of him. I've never known anyone named Fallon, let alone someone like this."

"*Someone* knows him, buddy, and he sure as hell knows you. John, can we get a hard copy of this?"

"Sure. I can print the file."

I said, "Print one for me, too. I want to show Lucy, then talk to the people in her neighborhood. After that, we can go back to the construction site. It's easier when you show people a picture. One memory leads to another."

Starkey smiled at me.

"We? Are we partners now?"

Somewhere in the minutes between the parking lot and our waiting for the file, it had become "we." As if she wasn't on LAPD and I wasn't a man desperate to find a lost boy. As if we were a team.

"You know what I meant. We finally have something to work with. We can build on it. We can keep going."

Starkey smiled wider, then patted my back.

"Relax, Cole. We're going to do all that stuff. Play your cards right, and I might let you tag along. I'm gonna put this on the BOLO."

Starkey put it on the BOLO, then phoned a request for information about Fallon to the L.A. offices of the FBI, the U.S. Secret Service, and the Sheriffs. After that, we rolled back to Lucy's. We.

The street outside Lucy's apartment was jammed with Richard's limo, Gittamon's black and white, and a second black and white with MISSING PERSONS UNIT emblazoned on the side. Gittamon answered the door when we knocked. He seemed surprised to see us, then angry. He glanced back inside, then lowered his voice. He kept the door pulled like he was hiding.

"Where have you been? I've been calling you all morning."

Starkey said, "I was working. We found something, Dave. We know who took the boy."

"You should have told me. You should have answered my calls."

"What's going on? Why is Missing Persons here?"

Gittamon glanced back inside, then opened the door.

"They fired us, Carol. Missing Persons is taking the case."

TIME MISSING: 47 HOURS, 38 MINUTES

Richard rubbed his hand nervously through his hair. His clothes were wrinkled worse than yesterday, as if he had slept in them. Lucy sat cross-legged on the couch, and Myers was leaning against the far wall. He was the only one of them who looked rested and fresh. They were listening to an immaculately groomed woman in a dark business suit and her male clone, who were seated on chairs that had been pulled from the dining room. Lucy had been looking at them, but now she stared at me. She didn't want me involved, yet here I was. Making it worse.

Gittamon cleared his throat to interrupt. He stood at the edge of the living room like a child who had been reprimanded before the class.

"Ah, Lieutenant, excuse me. This is Detective Starkey and Mr. Cole. Carol, this is Detective-Lieutenant Nora Lucas and Detective-Sergeant Ray Alvarez, from the Missing Persons Unit."

Lucas had one of those shrunken, porcelain faces with absolutely no lines; probably because she never smiled. Alvarez held my hand too long when we shook so that he could make a point with Gittamon.

"I thought we understood that Mr. Cole wasn't going to be involved, Sergeant."

I said, "Let go of my hand, Alvarez, or you'll see how involved I can be."

Alvarez hung onto my hand for a moment longer just to show me that he could.

"These are interesting allegations against you on that tape. We'll talk about them as we review the case."

Richard ran his hand through his hair again as he paced to the window. He seemed irritated. He looked at Lucas and Alvarez.

"What can you people do that's any different from what's already being done?"

Myers said, "More horsepower."

Lucas nodded.

"That's right. We'll bring the full weight and authority of the Missing Persons Unit to finding your son, not to mention our experience. Finding people is what we do."

Alvarez leaned forward on his elbows.

"We're the A-team, Mr. Chenier. We'll get the

case organized, review what's been done, and find your son. We'll also cooperate with you and Mr. Myers in your own efforts."

Richard turned impatiently from the window and motioned for Myers to peel himself away from the wall.

"Good. That's great. Now I want to get back to finding my son instead of just talking about it. Come on, Lee."

I said, "We know who took him."

Everyone looked at me as if they weren't sure what I had said or why I had said it. Lucy opened her mouth, then stood.

"What did you say?"

"We know who took Ben. We have a description on the vehicle and two men, and an ID on one of them."

Myers peeled himself from the wall.

"You're full of shit, Cole."

Starkey held out her copy of the Interpol file so that Lucy could see Fallon's picture.

"Look at this man, Ms. Chenier. Try to remember if you've seen him before. Maybe at a park when you were with Ben, or after school or when you were at work."

Lucy studied Fallon as if she was falling into his picture. Richard hurried across the room so that he could see.

"Who is that? What did you find out?"

I ignored Richard and the rest of them. I was totally focused on Lucy.

"Think hard, Luce—maybe you had one of those feelings like you were being followed; maybe you got a weird vibe from someone you saw, and this was him."

"I don't know. I don't think so."

Lucas said, "Who is that?"

Starkey glanced at Lucas and Alvarez, then handed the sheet to Gittamon.

"His name is Michael Fallon. I've already put it out on a BOLO, along with a description of the vehicle they used. At least one other man was involved—a black male with distinctive marks on his face, but we don't have an ID for him yet. Probably because we're not the A-team."

Richard stared at Fallon's picture. He breathed hard and rubbed his hair again. He shoved the picture at Myers.

"You see this? You see what they have? They've got a fucking suspect."

Myers nodded with little roach eyes.

"I can see that, Richard."

The roach eyes came to me.

"How do you know it's him?"

"We found a cigar wrapper on the ridge opposite my house. We found it near footprints that match the footprint where Ben was taken."

Richard's eyes were bright.

"That footprint we saw? The one you showed us yesterday?"

Starkey said, "Yeah. We got an NCIC hit on fingerprints from the wrapper on twelve out of twelve points. It doesn't get more positive than that."

Both Lucas and Alvarez got up so they could see the picture, too. Lucas glanced at Gittamon.

"You didn't tell me about this."

Gittamon shook his head as if he were on the spot.

"I didn't know. I called her, but she didn't call back."

Starkey said, "We found the wrapper this morning. We only got the ID a few minutes ago. That's what Cole and I were doing while you people were figuring out how to steal our case."

"Take it easy, Detective."

"Read his goddamned warrants. Fallon is a professional killer, for Christ's sake. He's got a war-crimes indictment in Africa. He's murdered people all over the world."

Lucas said, "*Detective*!"

She glanced at Lucy as she said it, and her voice snapped across Starkey like a slap.

This guy is a professional killer. He's murdered people all over the world.

And now he has your son.

Starkey flushed deep when she realized what she had done.

"I'm sorry, Ms. Chenier. That was insensitive."

Richard went to the door, anxious to leave.

"Let's get on this, Lee. We can't waste any more time with this."

Myers didn't move.

He said, "I'm not wasting time. I'm investigating how Cole knows this man. Everything I've heard so far fits with the tape. Cole and Fallon have a lot in common. How do you know each other, Cole? What does this guy want from you?"

"He doesn't want anything from me. I don't know

him, never met him, and don't have any idea why he's doing this."

"That isn't what he says on the tape."

"Fuck yourself, Myers."

Lucy's forehead was lined in concentration.

"This doesn't make sense. He has to have some connection with you."

"He doesn't. There isn't."

Lucas whispered to Alvarez, then spoke loudly to interrupt.

"Let's not get sidetracked. This is a good start, Detective. Ray, call SID to confirm the identification, then have Central distribute the picture."

Lucas had assumed command of the case, and she wanted everyone to know that she was still running the show.

"Mr. Chenier, Ms. Chenier—what we want to do now is bring the elements of the investigation together. This won't take long, then we can get on with developing this lead."

Starkey said, "It's already developed. We just have to find the sonofabitch."

Gittamon touched her arm.

"Carol. Please."

Richard muttered something, then opened the door.

"You people can do what you want, but I'm going to find my son. Lee, goddamnit, let's go. Do you need a copy of that?"

"I have what I need."

"Then let's get the hell out of here."

They left.

Alvarez turned toward Gittamon.

"Sergeant, you and Starkey wait outside. We'll review what you've done so far when we're finished with Ms. Chenier."

Starkey said, "Have you people been asleep? We made a major breakthrough here. We don't need to have a meeting about it."

Alvarez raised his voice.

"Wait outside until we're finished. You, too, Gittamon. Stop wasting time and get on with it."

Starkey stalked out, and Gittamon followed, so humiliated that he shuffled.

Alvarez said, "You stick around, too, Cole. We want to know why this guy has it in for you."

"No, I'm not wasting more time with that. I'm going to find Ben."

I looked at Lucy.

"I know you don't want me involved, but I'm not going to leave it alone. I'm going to find him, Luce. I'm going to bring him back to you."

"You'd better be downstairs, Cole. I'm not asking; I'm telling."

Alvarez said something else, but I had already shut the door. Starkey and Gittamon were on the sidewalk by his car, arguing. I ignored them.

I went to my car. I could get in, I could drive, but I didn't know where to go or what to do. I looked at Michael Fallon's picture and tried to figure out what to do.

This doesn't make sense. He has to have some connection with you.

All investigations run the same course: You follow the trail of a person's life to see where it crosses with another. Fallon and I had both been in the Army, but we had been in the Army at different times, and, so far as I knew, our lives had never crossed. So far as I knew, his life had never crossed the life of any man with whom I served, and I didn't see how it would. A Delta-trained killer. A professional mercenary. A man wanted for murder in El Salvador and war crimes in Africa who had come to Los Angeles to steal Ben Chenier and make up a lie. Current whereabouts unknown.

I glanced up and down the street to see if I could spot Joe. He would be here, watching, and I needed him.

"*Joe!*"

Men like Michael Fallon lived and worked in a shadow world that I knew nothing about; they paid cash and were paid in cash, lived under other names, and moved in circles so clannish that they were known in their true lives by very few others.

"*Joe!*"

Pike touched my shoulder. He might have stepped out of a tight thatch of plants at the corner of the building. His dark glasses gleamed like polished armor in the sun. My hands shook when I gave him the file.

"This man took Ben. He's lived all over the world. He's fought and done things everywhere. I don't have any idea how to find him."

Pike had lived and worked in dark places, too. He read through the file without speaking until he had finished. Then he put the pages away.

"Men like this don't fight for free. People hire him, so somebody somewhere knows how to reach him. All we have to do is find that person."

"I want to talk to them."

Pike's mouth twitched, then he shook his head.

"They won't talk to you, Elvis. People like this won't even let you get close."

Pike stared, but he didn't seem to be staring at me. I wondered what he was thinking.

"I can't go home. I can't just wait."

"It's out of your hands."

Pike disappeared between the buildings with the same distant look on his face, but I was too worried about Ben to notice.

17
. . .

PIKE

Pike thought that Cole's eyes looked like tunnels the color of bruises. Pike had seen the same purple eyes on cops cruising the edge of a burnout and combat soldiers with too much trigger time. Cole was in The Zone; amped up, wrung out, and driving forward like the Terminator with mission lock. You get in The Zone, Pike knew, and your thinking grew fuzzy. You could get yourself killed.

Pike ran the three blocks to his Jeep, feeling awkward in the way he moved. His back was tight from having been still for so long and his shoulder was numb. The jogging hurt his shoulder, but Pike ran anyway.

Mercenaries didn't simply show up in a war zone and get hired to kill people or train foreign troops; they were recruited by private military corporations, security firms with international contracts, and "consultants." The talent pool was small. The same people hired the same people over and over, just like software engineers jumping from job to job in Silicon Valley. Only with shorter life expectancies.

Pike once knew a few consultants, but he didn't know if they were still in the business. He didn't know if any of them would be willing to help, or, if so, what they would want or how long it would take. He didn't even know if they were alive. Pike had been out of that life for a long time, else he would have called from his car. He no longer remembered their numbers.

Pike drove to his condo in Culver City. When he reached home, he pulled off his sweatshirt, then drank a bottle of water with a handful of Aleve and aspirin. The phone numbers for the men he had known were in a safe he kept in his bedroom. They weren't written as digits, but as a coded list of words. He got them, then made the calls.

The first four numbers were no longer in use. A young woman with a bubbly voice answered the fifth number, which had clearly been recycled into the system. The sixth number was another disconnect, and the seventh a dentist's office. War was a business with a high casualty rate. Pike scored on the eighth.

"Yeah?"

Pike recognized the voice as soon as he heard it. As if they had spoken only that morning.

"This is Joe Pike. Remember?"

"Hell, yeah. How ya been?"

"I'm trying to find a professional named Michael Fallon."

The man hesitated, and the easy familiarity was gone.

"I thought you left the game."

"That's right. I'm out."

Pike sensed that the man was suspicious. They had not spoken for almost ten years, and now the man was wondering if Pike was working with the Feds. The government took a dim view of its citizens hiring themselves to foreign governments or paramilitary groups, and had laws against it.

The man spoke carefully.

"I don't know what you got in mind, Pike, but I'm a security consultant. I run background checks and offer references in a variety of military specialties, but I don't do business with terrorists, drug dealers, or dictators, or associate with anyone who does. That shit's illegal."

He was saying all that for the Feds, but Pike happened to know that it was also true.

"I understand. That's not why I'm calling."

"Okay. So what you want is a consultation, right?"

"That's right. His name is Fallon. He was with Delta, but then he went freelance. Two years ago, he lived in Amsterdam. Today, he's in Los Angeles."

"Delta, huh?"

"Yes."

"Those boys bring top dollar."

"I want to see him face-to-face. That's the important part, seeing him face-to-face."

"Uh-huh. Tell me something that might ring a bell."

Pike read from the NLETS report, citing the countries where Fallon was known to have worked; Sierra Leone, Colombia, El Salvador, the others.

The man said, "Shit, he's been around. I know some people who worked in those places. You really out of the game?"

"Yes."

"That's a shame, man. What's in this for me?"

Pike had known that the man would want something, and Pike was prepared to pay. People like this never did anything for free. Pike had not mentioned that part to Elvis, and wouldn't.

"A thousand dollars."

The man laughed.

"I'd rather book you into a job. I still get offers, you know. Your thing, you'd get top dollar, too. They need people like you in the Middle East."

"Two thousand."

"I can probably find someone who knows this guy, but I might have to call all over the goddamned world. I'm not wasting my time for a few bucks. I'm going to have costs."

"Five thousand."

It was an outrageous amount, but Pike already knew that the man wanted more than money. Pike hoped that the figure would be persuasive.

"Pike, I wouldn't be Fallon on a bet, you and your face-to-face. I don't care if he's Delta or not. But you have to see it from my side—if something happens to this guy, your Fed buddies will use this little transaction between us to hammer me as an accessory before the fact or maybe even a co-conspirator. I got no friends over there."

"No one is listening."

"Yeah, right."

Pike didn't respond. Pike had learned that if he didn't say anything, people often told themselves what they wanted to hear.

"Tell you what, I'll ask around, but you gotta let me book a job for you. I don't know what or when, but one day I'll call. That's it. That's my price. If I find someone who can help you with the face-to-face, you gotta go. Yes, no, I don't give a shit. That's what it costs."

Pike regretted calling this number. He wished that it had been disconnected like the others. He considered trying to find someone else, but the first seven numbers had given him nothing. Ben was waiting. Elvis was waiting. The weight of their need kept him on the phone.

"C'mon, Pike, it isn't just the calls. I haven't heard from you in ten years. If I find somebody who's dealt with him, I'll have to vouch for you."

A Zen fountain sat on a polished black table in the corner of Pike's living room. It was a small bowl filled with water and stones. The water burbled between the stones with the gentle sounds of a forest stream. Pike listened to the burble. It sounded like peace.

"You knew it was coming, Pike. That's why you called. I'm jamming you up with this, but that's what you wanted. You're looking for something, and it isn't just Fallon. We both know what you want."

Pike watched the water move in the little fountain. He wondered if the man was right.

"All right."

"Give me your number. I'll call back when I have something."

Pike gave the man his cell phone number, then stripped off his clothes. He brought the phone into his bathroom so he could hear it from the shower. He let hot water beat into his back and shoulder, and tried his best to think about nothing.

Forty-six minutes later, the phone rang. The man gave him a name and an address, and told him that it had been arranged.

18
· · ·

Two messages were waiting on my answering machine when I got home. I hoped that Joe or Starkey or maybe even Ben had called, but one was Grace Gonzalez from next door, asking if she could do anything to help, and the other was Crom Johnson's mother, returning my call. I didn't feel strong enough to talk to either.

From my deck I could see that Chen's van was back on the ridge across from my house, along with a second SID van and a Hollywood Division radio car. Several of the construction workers stood by the vans, watching downhill as Chen and the others worked.

Normal people bring in their mail after they get home from work, so that's what I did. Normal people have a glass of milk, take a shower, then change into fresh clothes. I did that, too. It felt like pretending.

I was eating a turkey sandwich in front of the television when my phone rang. I grabbed it, thinking that it was Joe, but it wasn't.

"This is Bill Stivic from the Army's Department of Personnel in St. Louis. I'm calling for Elvis Cole, please."

Master Sergeant Bill Stivic, USMC, retired. It felt like weeks since I had spoken with him. It had only been that morning.

I glanced at the time. It was past business hours for a government office in St. Louis. He was calling on his own dime.

"Hi, Master Sergeant. Thanks for getting back to me."

"No problem. It seemed pretty important to you."

"It is."

"Okay, well, here's what we have—first, like I told you this morning, anyone can have the 214, but we never send the 201 to anyone except you unless it's by court order or we get a request from a law enforcement agency, you remember?"

"I remember."

"The records here show that we telefaxed your file to a police detective named Carol Starkey out where you live in Los Angeles. That was yesterday."

"That's right. I spoke with Starkey today."

"Okay, the only other request we've had for your files was eleven weeks ago. We were served with a State court order by a judge named Rulon Lester in New Orleans."

"A judge in New Orleans."

"That would be it. Both your 201 and 214 were sent to his office at the State Superior Court Building in New Orleans."

Another dead end. I thought of Richard waving the manila folder. The bastard had gone all out to check up on me.

"Those are the only two times my files have been sent? You're sure they couldn't have been sent to anyone else?"

"That's it, just the two. The records section keeps track for eight years."

"You have a phone number for the judge, Master Sergeant?"

"They don't keep a copy of the order, just that your files were sent and why, along with the court's filing number. You want that?"

"Yes, sir. Let me get a pen."

He read it off along with the date of the order and the date that my file had been sent. I thanked him for the help, then put down the phone. New Orleans was in the central time zone like St. Louis, so the courts would be closed, but their offices might still be open. I called the Information operator in New Orleans and got numbers for the State Superior Court and Judge Lester's office. The coincidence between Richard living in New Orleans and a judge there ordering my files was obvious, but I wanted to be sure.

A woman with a clipped Southern accent answered on the first ring.

"Judge Lester's office."

I hung up. Lester would have had no legitimate reason for writing a court order to force the Army to release my files. He would have done so only as a favor to Richard or because Richard had paid him, either of which was an abuse of his office. He almost certainly wouldn't talk to me about it.

I thought it through, then dialed the number again.

"Judge Lester's office."

I tried to sound older and Southern.

"This is Bill Stivic with the Army's Department of Personnel in St. Louis. I'm trying to track down a file we sent to the judge in response to an order he issued."

"The judge has left for the day."

"Then I'm in a world of hurt, sugar. I pulled a whammy of a mistake when I sent the file down to y'all. I sent the original, and that was our only copy."

Sounding desperate was easy.

"I'm not sure I can help you, Mr. Stivic. If the file is admitted evidence or case documentation, it can't be returned."

"I don't want it returned. I should've made a copy before I sent it, I know, but, well, I don't know what I was thinking. So if you could find it, maybe I could get you to overnight a copy to me up here. I'd pay for it out of my own pocket."

Sounding pathetic was easy, too.

She said, "Well, let me take a look."

"You're a lifesaver, you truly are."

I gave her the date and the file number from Lester's court order, then held on while she went to look. She came back on the line a few minutes later.

"I'm sorry, Mr. Stivic, but we don't have those records any longer. The judge sent them on to a Mr.

Leland Myers as part of the requested action. Perhaps you could get a copy from his office?"

I let her give me Myers's number, and then I hung up. I thought about the folder that Richard slapped on the table when we were listening to the tape. Myers had probably handled the investigation. It felt like a dead end, and left me deflated. Fallon could have gotten most of what he knew by breaking into my house, and could have learned the rest a thousand other ways. All I had learned from Stivic was what I already knew—Richard hated my guts.

I went back to the turkey sandwich that I had left in front of the television, but threw it away. I no longer wanted it. My body ached and my eyes burned from the lack of sleep. The past two days were catching up with me like a freight train bearing down on a man caught on the tracks. I wanted to stretch out on the floor, but I thought that I might not be able to get up. The phone rang again when I was standing in the kitchen, but I wanted to let it ring. I wanted to stand there in the kitchen and never move again. I answered. It was Starkey.

"Cole! We got the van! An Adam car found the van downtown! They just called it in!"

She shouted out the location, but her voice was strained with something ugly as if the news she shared wasn't good. The aches were suddenly gone, as if they had never been.

"Did they find Ben?"

"I don't know. I'm on my way now. The others are on the way, too. Get down there, Cole. You won't be that far behind me, where you are. Get down there right away."

The tone in her voice was awful.

"Goddamnit, Starkey, what is it?"

"They found a body."

The phone fell out of my hands. It floated end over end, taking forever to fall. By the time it hit the floor I was gone.

TIME MISSING: 48 HOURS, 25 MINUTES

The Los Angeles River is small, but mean. People who don't know the truth of it make fun of our river; all they see is a tortured trickle that snakes along a concrete gutter like some junkie's vein. They don't know that we put that river in concrete to save ourselves; they don't know the river is small because it's sleeping, and that every year and sometimes more it wakes. Before we put the river in that silly trough centered on a concrete plain at the bottom of those tall concrete walls, it flashed to life with the rain to wash away trees and houses and bridges, and cut its banks to breed new channels almost as if it was looking for people to kill. It found what it looked for too many times. Now, when it wakes, the river climbs those concrete walls so high that wet claws rake the freeways and bridges as it tries to pull down a passing car or someone caught out in the storm. Chain-link fences and barbed wire spine along the top of the walls to keep out people, but the walls keep in the river. The concrete is a prison. The prison works, most of the time.

The van had been left under an overpass in the river's channel between the train yards and the L.A.

County Jail. Starkey was waiting in her car at a chain-link gate, and rolled when she saw me coming. We squealed down a ramp into the channel and parked behind three radio cars and two D-rides from Parker Center. The patrol officers were in the shade at the base of the overpass with two kids. The detectives had just arrived; two were with the kids and a third was peering into the van.

Starkey said, "Cole, you wait until I see what's what."

"Don't be stupid."

The van had been painted to change its appearance, but it was a four-door '67 Econoline with a cracked windshield and rust around the headlights. The new paint was thin, letting the *Em* from *Emilio's* show through like a shadow. The driver's door and the left rear door were open. A bald detective with a shiny head was staring into the back end. Starkey trotted ahead of me, and badged him.

"Carol Starkey. I put out the BOLO. We heard you got a vic."

The detective said, "Oh, man, this one's nasty."

I moved past him to see inside, and Starkey grabbed my arm, trying to stop me. I was holding my breath.

"Cole, please let me look. Stop."

I shook her off, and there it was: a thick-bodied Caucasian man in a sport coat and slacks spread on his stomach with both arms down along his sides and one leg crossed over the other as if he had been dumped or rolled into the back of the van. His clothes and the floor around him were heavy with blood. His head had been cut from his body at the top of his neck. It was tipped against a spare tire just behind the front seat. Like that, his face was hidden. Fat desert flies covered the body like bees in a blood garden. Ben was not in the van.

Starkey said, "Jesus Christ, they cut off his fucking head."

The detective nodded.

"Yeah. The things some people will do."

"You get an ID?"

"Uh-uh, not yet. I'm Tims, out of Robbery-Homicide. We just got here, so we haven't been cleared. The CI's on the way."

They wouldn't disturb the victim until the Coroner Investigator examined the scene. The CI was responsible for determining the cause and time of death, so the police weren't supposed to do anything but preserve the evidence until the CI cleared the scene.

I said, "We're looking for a boy."

"What you see is what we got—one corpse and no blood trails. Why'd you ask about a boy?"

"Two men driving this van kidnapped a ten-year-old boy two days ago. He's missing."

"No shit. Well, if you have suspects here, I want their names."

Starkey gave him Fallon's name and description, along with a description of the black guy. While he was writing it down, I asked him who opened the van. He nodded toward the kids with the uniforms.

"Them. They came down here to ride on the ramps—you know, go up and down? They saw the blood dripping and opened it up. Way the blood's still leaking out the side panel over there, I'd say this couldn't have happened more than three or four hours ago."

Starkey said, "Did you check them for his wallet?"

"Didn't have to. See on his butt where the sport coat's pushed up? You can see the bulge. Wallet's still in his pocket."

I said, "Starkey."

"I know. Tims, listen, if we can put this van to a location or get a line on Fallon, we'll be closer to finding the boy. The vic might have had a hand in it. We need an ID."

Tims shook his head. He knew what she was asking.

"You know better than that. The CI's on his way. It won't be long."

I glanced at Starkey, then went to the driver's door.

Tims said, "Don't touch anything."

Blood had pooled around the driver's seat. I could see part of the body, but I couldn't see his face. I looked under and around the seats as best I could without touching the van, but all I saw was blood and the grime that builds up in old vehicles.

Tims and Starkey were still at the rear. The other two detectives and the uniforms were with the kids. I climbed up into the front seat and squeezed between the seats into the van's bay. It smelled like a butcher shop on a warm summer day.

When Tims saw me, he lurched toward the rear doors as if he was going to jump in with me. He didn't.

"Hey! Get outta there! Starkey, get your partner outta there!"

Starkey stepped in front of Tims and braced her

arms across the door as if she was peering inside at me. She was also blocking the door to keep him from pulling me out. One of the detectives and two of the uniforms ran over to see why Tims was shouting.

"Cole. Would you please do this fast?"

Flies swarmed around me in an angry cloud, pissed off that I had disturbed them. The blood on the floorboards was as slick as hot grease. I took the dead man's wallet, then went through his pockets. I found a set of keys, a handkerchief, two quarters, and a card key from the Baitland Swift Hotel in Santa Monica. An empty shoulder holster was strapped under his arm. I tossed the wallet and other things onto the front seat, then turned back to the head. The skin was purple and streaked with grime. The cervical vertebra showed openly in the flesh like a white marble knob and the hair was jellied with blood clots; it was obscene and awful, and I didn't want to touch it. I didn't want to be here with the flies and the blood. Tims was shouting, but his voice receded until it was just another fly buzzing in the heat. I balled the handkerchief and used it to upright the head. When I tipped the head, I saw that it had been placed on a black K-Swiss cross-training shoe. A boy's shoe.

"Cole, who is it? What?"

"It's DeNice. Starkey, they left Ben's shoe. Ben's shoe is in here."

"Did they leave a note? Is there anything else?"

"I don't see anything. Just the shoe."

The Missing Persons car rolled down the ramp with its blue dash lights popping, and Richard's limo brought up the rear.

Starkey said, "Get out of there. Bring his things with you. We might find something that tells us how he found them. Don't touch your face."

"What?"

"You have blood all over yourself. Don't get it in your eyes or your mouth."

"It's Ben's shoe."

I wasn't able to say anything else.

Starkey trotted away to intercept Lucas and Alvarez. I climbed out of the van and put everything on the ground. My hands were gloved in blood. The wallet and Ben's shoe and the other things were smeared with it. One of the uniforms stepped back like I was radioactive.

He said, "Dude, you're a mess."

Lucas stepped around Starkey and steamed to the van. She looked inside, then staggered backwards as if she had been slapped.

She said, "Oh, my God."

DeNice's wallet contained sixty-two dollars, a Louisiana driver's license for one Debulon R. DeNice, credit cards, a Fraternal Order of Police membership card, a Louisiana hunting license, and photographs of two teenaged girls, but nothing that indicated how he had found Fallon or had come to be dead in the van. I had also found a set of keys, a handkerchief, and two quarters, but that didn't help me, either.

Richard and Myers pushed past Alvarez, and Richard turned white when he saw the blood.

Lucas said, "Mr. Chenier, wait at your car. Ray, they shouldn't be here. Jesus Christ."

Richard said, "What's in there? Is it—? Is—?"

"It's DeNice. They left his head in Ben's shoe."

Richard and Myers looked into the van before Alvarez could stop them, and Richard made a deep
gasping sound as if something were caught in his
chest.

"Holy God!"

Richard grabbed Myers to steady himself, then
turned away, but Myers stared into the van. His jaw
flexed and knotted, but the rest of him was still. One
of the big flies lit on his cheek, but he didn't seem to
feel it.

I said, "They left Ben's shoe. Ben's shoe was in
that."

Richard raked his hands through his hair and
turned in a frantic circle. I thought about what Pike
had said about men like Fallon doing whatever they
did for money. I thought about DeNice in the van
with the blood and the gore and Ben's lonely shoe,
and I knew that they hadn't done this for me. They
had done it for Richard.

"They didn't just kill him, Richard—*THEY CUT
OFF HIS HEAD!*"

Richard threw up. Starkey looked worried, but
maybe because I was screaming.

"Take it easy, Cole. You're shaking. Breathe deep."

Richard was bent over and heaving. He looked
frantic and sick.

I said, "They hit you for ransom, didn't they?
They're jamming you for ransom and you got cute
with DeNice."

Starkey and Lucas looked at me. Richard straightened up, then hunched again.

"You don't know what you're talking about! None
of that's true!"

Myers said, "You're talking out your ass, Cole. We're doing everything we can to find these bastards."

"These guys are using DeNice to scare somebody and they weren't trying to scare me."

Richard's face blotched with fury.

"FUCK YOU!"

Lucas said, "How can you say that?"

"Fallon's a mercenary. He doesn't do anything unless he's going to make money and Richard has money. They're working the ransom."

Richard lurched forward like he was going to hit me, but Myers took his arm. Richard trembled as if he was coming apart.

"This is all your fault, you bastard. I'm not going to stand here listening to this while my son is missing. We have to find my boy and you're talking bullshit!"

Richard stumbled to his limo. He leaned against the side of it and threw up again. Myers watched him, but his eyes didn't look so flat anymore.

I said, "What's going on, Myers?"

Myers walked away and joined Richard at his car.

I said, "He's lying. They're both lying."

Starkey watched Myers and Richard, then considered the van.

"We're talking about the man's son here, Cole. If these guys were grinding him for ransom, why wouldn't he tell us?"

"I don't know. He's scared. Look what they did to DeNice."

"Then why all that stuff with you?"

"I don't know. Maybe it started with me about

something else but when Richard got here they saw the money."

Starkey didn't look convinced.

"And maybe DeNice just got too close to them."

"DeNice wasn't good enough to find them. They arranged some kind of meet because they're hitting up Richard for ransom, and they used DeNice to make sure he pays."

It was the only way the pieces fit.

Lucas wet her lips, as if the notion of it disturbed her.

"I'd better speak with Mr. Chenier. I'll speak with Mr. Myers, too."

Starkey said, "Maybe we can backtrace DeNice's moves from last night to see how he got here. We can talk to that other guy, too, Fontenot. Maybe he knows something."

Lucas nodded absently, then looked back at the van as if it held secrets we might never know.

"This isn't a simple missing person case anymore."

Starkey said, "No. If it ever was."

Lucas looked back at Ben's shoe, then considered me.

"I have some Handi Wipes and alcohol in my car. You need to take care of yourself."

Starkey stayed with Lucas and Alvarez to question Richard and Myers about what they knew. I took the Handi Wipes and alcohol to my car. I took off my shirt and shoes, then poured the alcohol over my arms and hands. I got off as much of the blood as I could with the Handi Wipes, poured on more alcohol, then used even more Handi Wipes. I put on a

T-shirt and an old pair of running shoes that I kept behind my front seat, then sat in my car watching the cops. Lucas, Alvarez, and the Parker Center detectives were bunched around Richard and Myers. Richard shouted that they didn't know what they were talking about. Richard was freaking out, but Myers was as calm as a spider waiting at the edge of its web. I stared at the van and saw what they had left in it even though I was a hundred feet away. I would always see it. I would never be able to stop seeing it. They had cut off his head, and the men who did it had Ben.

My cell phone rang. I looked at the caller ID. It was Pike. I told him about DeNice. I told him about going inside the van. My voice sounded strange, as if it was muted by fog and wind. I kept talking until I heard him telling me to shut up.

He said, "I found someone who can help."

I started my car and left.

19

· · ·

BEN

Eric and Mazi treated Ben differently after Mike shot the man. They stopped to pick up In-N-Out burgers on the way back to the house (double meat, double cheese, and an order of onion rings and fries for everybody). When they reached the house, they didn't lock Ben in the room or tie him; they let him sit with them in the empty living room while they ate and played cards, and gave him an Orangina. They were a lot more relaxed. Even Mazi laughed. It was as if killing that man had freed them.

After they finished the burgers, Eric made a face.

"Man, I shoulda passed on the onions."

Mazi said, "Yes?"

Eric broke wind loudly.

Mazi said, "Ewe body is rotteen."

They sat in a circle on the floor. Ben snuck glances at the gun that bulged under Eric's shirt, trying to think of a way to get it. All he thought about for most of the afternoon was getting the gun, shooting them, then running to the house across the street. When Mike came back, he would shoot him, too.

When Ben looked up from the gun, he saw Mazi staring at him again. It creeped Ben out, the way he did that.

Mazi said, "He theenkeeng about ewe gun."

"Big fuckin' deal. He did all right out there. He's a natural-born killer."

Ben said, "I can shoot."

Eric raised his eyebrows, glancing up from his cards.

"That's right, you're a coonass. You people hunt before you can walk. What kinda shooting you do?"

"I have a twenty-gauge shotgun and a .22. I've been duck hunting with my uncles and my grandpa. I've shot my mom's pistol."

"Well, there you go."

Mazi said, "Waht meenz koonahz?"

"A coonass is a Frenchman from Louisiana."

Eric liked it that they were talking about guns. He reached under his shirt, and took out the gun. It was big and black, with a checked grip and worn engraving on its side.

"You wanna hold it?"

Mazi said, "Stop eet. Put ewe gun ah-way."

"Fuck off. What could it hurt?"

Eric turned the pistol from side to side so Ben could see.

"This is a Colt forty-five Model nineteen-eleven. It used to be the standard-issue combat sidearm until the Army went pussy with this nine millimeter shit. A nine holds more bullets, but a nine ain't shit; you don't need more bullets if you hit your target with this."

Eric waved the gun toward Mazi.

"Take a big nigger like Mazi here, he's strong as a cape buffalo and ten times as mean. You can shoot him all day with a nine and he'll keep comin', but you put one of these in him, you'll knock him flat on his ass. This gun's a stopper."

Eric waved the pistol back to Ben.

"You wanna hold it?"

Ben said, "Yeah."

Eric pressed something on the gun and the magazine fell out. He pulled the slide. The gun coughed up a bullet and Eric caught it in the air. He handed the gun to Ben.

Mazi said, "Mike see thees, he keek ewe ass."

"Mike's off havin' all the fun while we do this, so fuck'm."

Ben took the gun. It was heavy, and too big for his hands. Eric set the magazine on the floor, showed Ben how to work the safety and the slide, then handed back the gun so that Ben could do it himself. The slide was hard to pull.

Ben held the gun tightly. He pulled back the slide and locked it in place. All he had to do was shove in the magazine, release the slide, and it would be loaded and cocked. The magazine was right by his knee.

Eric took back the gun.

"That's enough."

Eric jammed in the magazine, jacked the slide, then returned the loose bullet to the magazine. He set the safety, then put the gun on the floor in front of him.

"Fuck all that shit about no round in the chamber. You gotta keep one in the box and good to go. If you need it, you won't have time to dick around."

They played cards all afternoon as if they did this kind of thing every day. Ben sat close to Eric, thinking about the gun being loaded and cocked with one in the box. All he had to do was release the safety. He rehearsed doing it in his mind. If he got his chance, he wouldn't have time to dick around.

Eric went to the bathroom, but brought the gun with him. When he returned, the gun was back in his pants, but now Eric had clipped it onto his far side. Ben told them that he had to go to the bathroom, too. Mazi brought him. When they came back to the cards, Ben sat on Eric's side near the gun.

Mike didn't return until almost dark.

When he walked in, he said, "Okay, we're set."

"Ewe find dee plaze?"

"It's Delta, man. Everything's rigged and ready to rock. They won't see it coming."

Eric said, "Fuck all that, I wanna know if we're getting the money."

"After they see what's in the van, I'd say yes."

Eric laughed.

"This is so sweet."

"I'm gonna grab a shower. Get your shit together. Once we leave here, we won't come back."

Ben stayed close to Eric. If they worked it the same as before, Mike would leave by himself, and Ben would go with Eric and Mazi. Ben planned to sit as close to Eric's gun as possible. He could make himself throw up so that Eric would turn away, or drop something so that Eric would have to pick it up. *Hey, buddy, your shoe's untied!* A chance would appear, and Ben wouldn't have time to dick around. He would stay with Eric like a second skin.

Ben's mom had told him about something called visualization, which all the best tennis players do to help their game. You imagine yourself smashing a perfect service ace or a killer passing shot, and you see yourself winning. It's a mental rehearsal that helps you do the real thing.

Ben imagined every possible scenario for grabbing Eric's gun: Eric getting into the car ahead of him, Eric getting out, Eric bending over to pick up a quarter, Eric chasing a bug—Ben only needed one brief moment when Eric's back was turned, and Ben would do this: He would lift Eric's shirt with his left hand and grab the gun with his right; he would jump backwards hard as Eric turned, and release the safety; he wouldn't yell *Stop or I'll shoot!* or anything stupid like that; he would pull the trigger. He would keep pulling the trigger until they were dead. Ben visualized himself doing it just like that— POWPOWPOWPOWPOW. It's a stopper.

Suddenly, it was time. Mike came from the back of the house with a short pump-action shotgun and a pair of binoculars.

Mike said, "This is it, ladies. Showtime."

Eric shoved up from the floor like it couldn't come too soon, pulling Ben with him.

"Fuckin' A. Let's get it on."

They slung their duffel bags and trooped through the house. Ben was so scared that his ears buzzed, but he stayed close to Eric. A battered blue compact that Ben hadn't seen before was waiting in the garage next to the sedan. Eric steered him toward the compact.

Eric said, "Okay, troop, step lively."

Behind them, Mike said, "Hang on."

They stopped.

"The kid's coming with me."

Mike took Ben's arm and turned him toward the sedan. Eric climbed into Mazi's car. Ben pulled back from Mike.

"I don't want to go with you. I want to go with Eric."

"Fuck what you want. Get in the car."

Mike pushed him into the passenger side, then got in behind the wheel with his shotgun. The garage door opened, and Mazi and Eric drove away. Ben watched Eric's pistol go with them, cocked, good to go, with one in the box. It was like seeing a life preserver drift out of reach while he drowned.

Mike started the engine.

"You just sit still and be cool like before, and everything will work out all right."

Mike put the shotgun on the floor so that it rested between his legs. Ben looked at it. He had a twenty-gauge Ithaca shotgun at home and had once killed a mallard.

Ben stared hard at the shotgun, and then stared at Mike.

"I know how to shoot."

Mike said, "So do I."

They backed out of the garage.

20

· · ·

Pike was waiting for me at one of those flat anonymous office buildings that were clustered all through Downey and the City of Industry, just south of LAX; cheap buildings thrown up by aerospace companies during the defense boom in the sixties, surrounded then as now by parking lots jammed with midsized American cars driven to work by men wearing ill-fitting dark suits.

When I got out of my car, Pike studied me in that motionless way he has.

I said, "What?"

"They have a bathroom in here."

He brought me into the lobby. I went into the men's room, turned on the hot water, and let it run until steam fogged the mirror. DeNice's blood was still speckled around my nails and in the creases of my skin. I washed my hands and arms with green soap, then put them under the running hot water. My hands turned bright red again, almost as red as the blood, but I kept them in the water trying to burn them clean. I washed them twice, then took off my shirt and washed my face and neck. I cupped my hands and drank, then looked at myself in the mirror but I was hidden by fog. I went back to the lobby.

We walked up three flights of stairs and into a waiting room that smelled like new carpet. Polished steel letters on the wall identified the company: THE RESNICK RESOURCE GROUP—*Problem Resolution and Consultation.*

Problem resolution.

A young woman smiled at us from a desk built into the wall.

"May I help you?"

She had an English accent.

Pike said, "Joe Pike for Mr. Resnick. This is Elvis Cole."

"Ah, yes. We're expecting you."

A young man in a three-piece suit came out of a door behind the receptionist and held it for us. He was carrying a black leather bag.

"Afternoon, gentlemen. You can come with me."

Pike and I stepped past him into a hall. As soon as we were out of the waiting room, the young man opened the bag. He was fit, with the pleasant professional expression of a mid-level executive on the way up. He wore an Annapolis class ring on his right hand.

"I'm Dale Rudolph, Mr. Resnick's assistant. The

weapons go in here and will be returned when you leave."

I said, "I'm not armed."

"That's fine."

Pike put his .357, a .25, the sap, and a double-edge SOG knife into the bag. Rudolph's expression never changed, as if men de-arming themselves was an everyday occurrence. Welcome to life in the Other World.

"Is that everything?"

Pike said, "Yes."

"All right. Stand erect and lift your arms. Both of you, please."

Polite. They taught manners at Annapolis.

Rudolph passed a security wand over us, then put the wand into the bag.

"Okey-doke. We're good to go."

Rudolph led us into a bright airy office that could have belonged to someone who sold life insurance except for the pictures that showed mobile rocket batteries, Soviet gunships, and armored vehicles. A man in his late fifties with crewcut gray hair and coarse skin came around his desk to introduce himself. He was probably a retired admiral or general with connections to the Pentagon; most of these guys were.

"John Resnick. That's all, Dale. Please wait outside."

"Aye, sir."

Resnick sat on the edge of his desk, but didn't offer us a seat.

"Which one's Pike?"

Pike said, "Me."

Resnick looked at him.

"Our mutual friend speaks well of you. The only reason I agreed to see you is because he vouched for you."

Pike nodded.

"He didn't mention anyone else."

I wanted to identify myself as the sidekick, but sometimes I'm smart. I let Pike handle it.

Pike said, "If our mutual friend spoke well of me, then that should cover it. Either I'm good or I'm not."

Resnick seemed to like that answer.

"Fair enough. Perhaps you'll have the chance to show me just how good, but we can discuss that another time."

Resnick knew what we wanted and got to the point.

"I used to work with a PMC in London. We used Fallon once, but I would never use him again. If you're trying to hire him, I would recommend against it."

I said, "We don't want to hire him, we want to find him. Fallon and at least one accomplice abducted my girlfriend's son."

Resnick's left eye flickered with an unexpected tension. He studied me as if he were deciding whether or not I knew what I was saying, then he sat a bit taller.

"Mike Fallon is in Los Angeles?"

I told him again.

"Yes. He took my girlfriend's son."

Resnick's left eye flickered harder and the tension spread through him. But then he shrugged.

"Fallon is a dangerous man. I can't believe that he's in Los Angeles or anyplace else in the country, but if he is and he did what you said, you should go to the police."

"We've been with the police. The police are trying to find him, too."

Pike said, "Without my resources. You know him. The thought is that you know how to reach him, or know someone who does."

Resnick considered Pike, then slid off his desk and went to his seat. The sun was beginning to lower and bounced off the cars. Jets arced out of LAX heading west over the sea. Resnick watched them.

"That was years ago. Michael Fallon is under a war-crimes indictment for atrocities he committed in Sierra Leone. Last I heard, he was living in South America, Brazil, I think, or maybe Colombia. If I knew how to find him, I would have told the Justice Department. Jesus, I can't believe he had the balls to come back to the States."

Resnick glanced at Pike again.

"If you find him, will you kill him?"

He asked it as simply as if he wanted to know whether or not Pike enjoyed football.

Pike didn't answer, so I answered for him.

"Yes. If that's your price for helping us, then yes."

Pike touched my arm. He shook his head once, telling me to stop.

I said, "If you want him dead, he's dead. Not, then not. All I care about is the boy. I'll do anything to get the boy."

Pike touched me again.

Resnick said, "I believe in rules, Mr. Cole. In a

business like mine, rules are all we have to keep us from becoming animals."

Resnick went back to the jets. He watched them wistfully, as if a jet could take him away from something that he could not escape.

"When I was in London, we hired Mike Fallon. We sent him to Sierra Leone. He was supposed to guard the diamond mines under a contract we had with the government, but he went over to the rebels. I still don't know why—the money, I guess. They did things you can't imagine. You would think I'm making it up."

I told him what I saw in the van at the edge of the Los Angeles River. Resnick turned back from the jets as I described it. I guess it sounded familiar. He shook his head.

"A fucking animal. He can't work as a mercenary anymore, not with the indictments. No one will hire him. You think he kidnapped this child for ransom?"

"I think so, yes. The boy's father has money."

"I don't know what to tell you. Like I said, the last I heard he was in Rio but I'm not even sure of that. There must be a lot of money at stake for him to come back."

Pike said, "He has an accomplice. A large black man with sores or warts on his face."

Resnick swiveled toward us and touched his own face.

"On his forehead and cheeks?"

"That's right."

He leaned forward with his forearms on the desk. It was clear that he recognized the description.

"Those are tribal scars. One of the men Fallon

used in Sierra was a Benté fighter named Mazi Ibo.
He had scars like that."

Resnick grew excited.

"Is a third man involved?"

"We don't know. It's possible."

"All right, listen, now L.A. is starting to make
sense. Ibo was tight with another merc named Eric
Schilling. I guess it was a year ago, something like
that, Schilling contacted us looking for security
work. He's local, from here in L.A, so Ibo might have
contacted him. We might have kept something."

Resnick went to work on his computer, punching
keys to bring up a database.

I said, "Was he involved in Sierra Leone?"

"Probably, but he wasn't listed in the indictments.
That's why he can still work. He was one of Fallon's
people. That's why it stood out when he contacted
us. I won't hire any of Fallon's people even if they
weren't involved. Yeah, here it is."

Resnick copied an address from his computer,
then handed it to me.

"He had a mail drop in San Gabriel under the
name Gene Jeanie. They always use these fake names.
I don't know if it's still good, but it's what I have."

"Do you have a phone for him?"

"They never give a phone. It's like the mail drop
and the fake names. It's a way to stay insulated."

I glanced at the address, then passed it to Pike. I
stood, but my legs felt wobbly. Resnick came around
his desk.

He said, "We're talking about very dangerous
people right now. Don't mistake these men for your
basic shit-eating criminals. Fallon was as good as it

gets, and he trained these people. No one is better at killing."

Pike said, "Bears."

Resnick and I both glanced at him, but Pike was staring at the address. Resnick gripped my hand and held it. He looked into my eyes as if he was searching for something.

"Do you believe in God, Mr. Cole?"

"When I'm scared."

"I pray every night. I pray because I sent Mike Fallon to Sierra Leone, so I've always felt that part of his sin must be mine. I hope you find him. I hope the little boy is safe."

I saw the desperate darkness in Resnick's face, and recognized it as my own. A moth probably saw the same thing when it looked into a flame. I should not have asked, but I could not help myself.

I said, "What happened over there? What did Fallon do?"

Resnick stared at me for the longest time, then confessed.

SIERRA LEONE
AFRICA
1995

THE ROCK GARDEN

Ahbeba Danku heard the gunfire that morning only moments before the screaming boy fled down the road from the mine to her village. Ahbeba was a pretty girl, twelve years old this past summer, with long feet and hands, and the graceful neck of a prin-

cess. Ahbeba's mother claimed that Ahbeba was, in fact, a royal princess of the Mende tribe, and prayed every night for a prince to take her eldest daughter as his bride. The family could claim as many as six goats for their dowry, her mother predicted, and would be so rich that they could escape the endless war that the rebels of the Revolutionary United Front waged against the government for control of the diamond mines.

Ahbeba thought her mother crazy from smoking too much of the majijo plant. It was far more likely that Ahbeba would marry one of the young South African mercenaries who protected the mine and village from the rebels. They were strong handsome boys with guns and cigarettes who grinned brazenly at the girls who, in turn, flirted with the young men shamelessly.

Ahbeba spent most days with her mother, sisters, and the other village women tending a rock-strewn subsistence farm near the Pampana River. The women cared for a small goat herd and grew sweet potatoes and a hard pea known as a kaiya while their men (including Ahbeba's father) mined the slopes of the gravel pit for diamonds. As diggers and washers, the men were paid eighty cents per day plus two bowls of rice flavored with pepper and mint and a small commission on any diamond they found. It was hard, dirty work, shoveling gravel out of the steep slopes by hand, then pumping it into small washing plants where it was sorted by size, sluiced for gold, and picked through for diamonds. The men worked in shorts or underwear for twelve hours a day with only the dust that caked their skin as pro-

tection from the sun and the South Africans to protect them from the rebels. Princes were in short
supply. Even more rare than diamonds.

That morning, Ahbeba Danku had been left to
grind kaiya into meal while her sisters tended the
crops. Ahbeba didn't mind; working in the village
gave her plenty of time to gossip with her best friend,
Ramal Momoh (who was two years older and had
breasts the size of water bladders), and flirt with the
guards. Both girls were blue with pea meal as they
snuck glances at the guard who stood at the edge of
the village. The young South African, who was tall
and slender and as pretty as a woman, winked at
them and beckoned them to join him. Ahbeba and
Ramal giggled. Each was daring the other to do it,
saying you, no, you, when a string of faraway pops
crackled down the hill.

Poppoppop . . . pop . . . pop . . . poppoppop.

The guard jerked toward the sound like a street
puppet in the Freetown bazaar. Ramal jumped up so
quickly that the grinding stone tipped over.

"They're shooting at the mine."

Ahbeba had heard the guards shoot rats before,
but it was nothing like this. Older women stepped
from their huts and younger children paused in their
play. The young South African called across the village to another guard, then unslung his rifle. His eyes
were bright with fear.

Bursts of automatic-weapon fire layered over
each other in a furious overlapping rage that ended
as quickly as it began. Then the valley was silent.

"Why were the guards shooting? What is happening?"

"That wasn't the guards. Listen! Do you hear?"

A boy's scream reached the village, and then the thin figure of a child raced between the huts. Ahbeba recognized eight-year-old Julius Saibu Bio, who lived at the northern edge of their village.

"That's Julius!"

The boy pulled to a halt, sobbing, flapping his hands as if he was shaking off something hot.

"The rebels are killing the guards! They killed my father!"

The South African guard ran several steps toward Julius, then turned back toward the trees just as a white man with hair the color of flames stepped from the leaves and shot the South African twice in the face.

The village exploded in chaos. Women scooped children and infants into their arms and ran to the bush. Children burst into tears. Ramal ran.

"Ramal! What's happening? What do we do?"

"Run! Run NOW!"

Two more South African guards burst from between the huts. The flame-haired man dropped to a knee and fired again—bapbap, bapbap—so fast that the shots sounded as one. Both South Africans fell.

Ramal disappeared into the jungle.

Ahbeba started for her family's hut, then ran back for Julius. She took him by the arm.

"Come with me, Julius! We have to hide!"

A flatbed truck crowded with men roared into the village, horn blowing. Men jumped off the truck in twos and threes as it raced between the huts. The flame-haired man shouted orders at them in Krio, the

English-based Creole that was spoken by almost everyone in Sierra Leone.

The rebels fired into the air and beat the running women and children with the butts of their rifles. Ahbeba picked up Julius to run, but more rebels jumped from the truck behind her. A skinny teenager with a rifle as big as himself dragged Ramal from the bush, pushed her down, then kicked her in the back. A man wearing nothing but shorts and a fluorescent pink vest shot at the village dogs, laughing every time a dog screamed and spun in a circle.

Julius shrieked.

"Make them stop! Make them stop!"

The flatbed truck skidded to a stop in the center of the village. As quickly as the gunfire had come and gone from the mine, the village was captured. The South Africans were dead. No one was left to protect them. Ahbeba sank to the ground, and tried to pull herself and Julius into the earth. This could not be happening to a princess waiting for a prince.

A muscular man in wraparound sunglasses and a ragged Tupac T-shirt clambered up onto the truck's bed to glare at the villagers. He wore a bone necklace that clattered against the ammo belts slung from his neck. Other men stood beside him, one wearing a headband made of bullets; another, a net shirt sewn with small pouches made from the scrotums of warthogs. They were fierce and terrible warriors, and Ahbeba was very afraid.

The man with the bone necklace waved a sleek black rifle.

"I am Commander Blood! You will know this name and fear it! We are freedom fighters of the Revolutionary United Front, and you *are* traitors to the people of Sierra Leone! You dig our diamonds for outsiders who control the puppet government in Freetown! For this, you will die! We will kill everyone here!"

Commander Blood fired his rifle over the heads of the villagers and ordered his men to line everyone up to be shot.

The flame-haired man and another white man came around the side of the truck. The second man was taller and older than the first, wearing olive-green pants and a black T-shirt. His pale skin was burned from the sun.

He said, "No one's killing anyone. There's a better way to do this."

He spoke Krio like the flame-haired man.

The two white men were on the ground; Commander Blood stood on the truck's bed. The commander charged like a lion to the edge of the bed so that he towered over the men. He fired his weapon angrily.

"I have given the order! We will kill these traitors so that word will spread throughout the diamond fields! The miners must fear us! Line them up! Now!"

The man in the black shirt swung his arm as if throwing a punch and hooked Commander Blood's legs out from beneath him. The commander landed flat on his back. The man jerked him from the truck to the ground and stomped his head. Three fierce warriors jumped from the truck to help their commander. Ahbeba had never seen men fight so fiercely nor in such strange ways—the man and his flame-haired friend twisted the warriors to the ground so *quickly the fight ended in a heartbeat, with the two men defeating four. One of the warriors was left screaming in pain; two others were unconscious or dead.*

Ramal edged close to her and whispered.

"They are demons. Look, he wears the mark of the damned!"

As the black-shirted man held Commander Blood by the neck, Ahbeba saw a triangle tattooed on the back of his hand. Ahbeba grew even more fearful. Ramal was wise and knew of such things.

The demon pulled Commander Blood to his feet, then ordered the others to bring the dead South African guards to the well at the center of the village. The commander was dazed and submissive; he did not object. The flame-haired man spoke into a small radio.

Ahbeba waited anxiously to see what would happen. She held Julius close and tried to calm him, fearing that his sobbing might draw the rebels' attention. Twice she saw brief chances to escape, but she could not leave the boy. Ahbeba told herself that there was safety in numbers; that she and Julius would be safe within the crowd.

As the rebels stacked the dead South Africans by the well, a second truck rumbled into the village. This truck was battered and misshapen and cowled with black dust. Great winged fenders hooded the tires like a sorcerer's cloak, and broken headlamps stared crookedly over a grill like a hyena's snaggle-toothed grin; the rust on its teeth was the color of dried blood. A dozen young men with glassy unblinking eyes squatted in the truck. Many had bloody bandages wrapped tightly around their upper arms. Those without bandages showed jagged scars cut into these same places.

Ramal, who had been to Freetown and knew of such things, said, "You see their arms? Their skin has been split so that cocaine and amphetamines can be packed into the wounds. They do this to make themselves crazy."

"Why?"

"It makes them better fighters. Like this, they feel no pain."

A tall warrior jumped down from the new truck and joined the two white men. He wore a sackcloth tunic and baggy trousers, but that is not what drew Ahbeba's eye; his face was as cut and planed as a finished diamond. His upper arms bore the same scars as his men, but, unlike the others, his face was also marked: three round scars were set like eyes along each cheek and a row of smaller scars lined his forehead. His eyes were fired with a heat that Ahbeba did not understand, but he was breathtakingly beautiful, as beautiful and as princely as any man that Ahbeba had ever seen. He held himself like a king.

The black-shirted man twisted Commander Blood toward the stack of South African corpses.

He said, "This is how you create fear."

He glanced at the tall African warrior, who motioned his men from the truck. They jumped to the ground, howling and hooting as if possessed. They were not armed with rifles and shotguns like the first group of rebels; they carried rusty machetes and axes.

They swarmed over the dead South African

guards. The machetes rose and fell as the crazy-eyed rebels hacked off their heads. They threw the heads into the well.

Ahbeba sobbed and Ramal hid her eyes. All around them, women and children and old men wailed. Ishina Kotay, a strong young woman with two babies, as fast as any boy in the village when she was a girl, jumped to her feet and bolted for the jungle. The flame-haired man shot her in the back.

Ahbeba felt light-headed, as if she had smoked the majijo plant. She lost track of what was happening, and vomited. The world grew hazy and small with empty spaces between moments of brilliant clarity. The day had begun with cakes for breakfast as the first kiss of light brushed the ridges above her village. Her mother had spoken of princes.

Commander Blood fired his rifle into the air and jumped up and down, howling like his men. The rest of the rebels jumped up and down, too, caught up in the frenzy.

"Now you know the wrath of the RUF! This is the price you pay for defying us! We will fill the well with your heads!"

The white demon and the tall scarred warrior turned toward the huddled villagers. Ahbeba felt their gaze sweep over her as if their eyes held weight.

The white demon shook his head.

"Stop jumping around like a baboon. If you kill these people, then no one will know what happened here. Only the living can fear you. Do you understand that?"

Commander Blood stopped bouncing.

"Then we must leave living proof."

"That's right. Proof that will scare the shit out of the other miners. Proof that your enemies can't deny."

Commander Blood walked over to the headless bodies of the South African guards.

"What could be more terrible than what we have done?"

"This."

The white demon spoke to the scarred warrior in a language that Ahbeba did not understand, and then the drug-crazed rebels ran forward with their axes and machetes, and hacked off the hands of every man, woman, and child in the village.

Ahbeba Danku and the others were left alive to tell their story, and did.

PART FOUR

. . .

THE
LAST DETECTIVE

21

...

I called Starkey from the parking lot while Pike phoned the San Gabriel Information operator. Starkey answered her cell on the sixth ring.

I said, "I have two more names for the BOLO. Are you still at the river?"

"We're gonna be here all night with this mess. Hang on while I grab my pen."

"The man Mrs. Luna saw with Fallon is named Mazi Ibo, m-a-z-i, i-b-o. He worked for Fallon in Africa."

"Hang on, Cole, slow down. How do you know that?"

"Pike found someone who recognized the description. You'll be able to get his picture off the NLETS for a positive with Mrs. Luna. Did Richard cop to the ransom?"

"He still denies it. They tore outta here an hour ago, but I think you're onto it, Cole. That poor bastard was shitting bullets."

Pike lowered his phone and shook his head. Schilling wasn't listed.

"Okay, here's the other name. I don't know whether he's involved, but he might be in contact."

I gave her Schilling's name and told her how he was connected to Ibo and Fallon.

She said, "Hang on. I gotta get to my radio. I want to put this stuff out on the BOLO."

"He keeps a mail drop in San Gabriel. We just checked with Information, but they don't show a listing. Can you get it?"

"Yeah. Stand by."

Pike watched me as I waited, then shook his head again.

"He won't be listed under any name we know."

"We don't know that. We might get lucky."

Pike studied the mail drop address, then flicked it with his finger, thinking. He looked up as Starkey came back on the line.

She said, "They got squat for Eric Schilling. What's that address?"

I gestured for the address, but Pike slipped it into his pocket. He took my phone and turned it off.

I said, "What are you doing?"

"They'll have a rental agreement, but she'll have to get a warrant. This place, it'll be closed by the time everyone gets there. They'll have to find the owner, wait for him to come down, it'll take forever. We can get it faster."

I understood what Pike meant and agreed to it without hesitation, as if the rightness of it was obvious and beyond debate. I was beyond hesitation or even consideration. I had become forward movement. I had become finding Ben.

Pike went to his Jeep and I went to my car, my head filled with the atrocities that Resnick had described. I still heard the flies buzzing inside the van and felt them bumping my face as they swirled up from the blood. I realized that I didn't have my gun. It was locked in my gun safe because Ben had been staying with me, and was still there. I suddenly wanted a weapon badly.

I said, "Joe. My gun's at the house."

Pike opened his passenger door and reached under the dash. He found a black shape and walked over with the shape palmed flat against his thigh so that bystanders wouldn't see. He passed it to me, then went back to his Jeep. It was a Sig Sauer 9mm in a black clip holster. I clipped it onto my right hip under my shirt. I thought it would make me feel safer, but it didn't.

The I-10 freeway stretched across the width of Los Angeles like a rubber band pulled to its breaking point, running from the sea to the desert, then beyond. Traffic was building and heavy, but we drove hard on our horns, as much on the shoulder as not.

Eric Schilling's mail drop was a private postal service called Stars & Stripes Mail Boxes in a strip mall in a part of San Gabriel where most of the people were of Chinese descent. The mall held three Chinese restaurants, a pharmacy, a pet store, and the postal business. The parking lot was crowded with families on their way to dinner at the restaurants, or lingering outside the pet store. Pike and I parked on the side street, then walked back to the mail drop. It was closed.

Stars & Stripes was a storefront business in full view of the mall, with the pet store on one side and the pharmacy on the other. An alarm strip ran along its glass front and door. Inside, mailboxes were set into the walls in the front part of the store, divided from the back office by a sales counter. The owner had pulled a heavy steel fence across the counter to divide the store into a front and back. Customers could let themselves into the front after hours to get their mail, but not steal the stamps and packages that were kept in the office. The curtain looked strong enough to cage a rhino.

Schilling's box number was or had been 205. We wouldn't know if the box still belonged to Schilling until we were inside. I could see box 205, but I couldn't tell whether it held any mail. For all I knew, Fallon had sent him a treasure map leading to Ben Chenier.

Pike said, "The rental agreements will be in the office. It might be easier to get in through the back."

We walked around the side of the mall to the alley that ran behind it. More cars lined the alley, along with Dumpsters and service doors for the shops. Two men in white aprons sat on crates in the open door of one of the restaurants. They peeled potatoes and carrots into a large metal bowl.

The name of each business was painted on its ser-

vice door, along with NO ENTRANCE and PARKING FOR
DELIVERY ONLY. We found the door for Stars & Stripes
Mail Boxes. It was faced with steel and set with two
industrial-strength deadbolt locks. The hinges were
heavy-grade, too. You would need a truck and chains
to pull them out of the wall.

Pike said, "Can you pick the locks?"

"Yeah, but not fast. These locks are made to resist
picks, and we have these guys over here."

Pike and I looked at the men, who were doing
their best to ignore us. It would be faster to go
through the front.

We walked back to the parking lot. A Chinese
family with three little boys was standing outside the
pet store, watching the puppies and kittens inside.
The father held his smallest son in his arms, pointing
at one of the puppies.

He said, "How about that one? You see how he
plays? The one with the spot on his nose."

Their mother smiled at me as we passed and I
smiled back, everything so civil and peaceful, everything so fine.

Pike and I went to the glass door. We could wait
for someone to come for their mail and walk in with
them, but hanging around for a couple of hours was
not an option. Starkey could have arranged a warrant
and roused the owner to open the place if we wanted
to wait until midnight.

I said, "When we break the door, the alarm is
going to ring here in the store. It might also ring at a
security station, and they'll call the police. We have
to pop the face off his mailbox, get past the curtain,
then go through the office. All these people here in

the parking lot will see us, and someone will call the police. We won't have much time. Then we have to get out of here. They'll probably get our license numbers."

"Are you trying to talk me out of this?"

The evening sky had darkened to a rich blue and was growing darker, but the street lights had not yet flicked on. Families walked along the narrow walk, coming out of the restaurants or waiting for their names to be called. An old man hobbled out of the pharmacy. Cars crept through the little parking lot, hoping for a space. Here we were, about to break into some honest citizen's place of business. We would destroy property, and that property would have to be paid for. We would violate their rights, and that was something you couldn't pay for, and we would scare the hell out of all these people who would end up witnesses against us if and when we were brought to trial.

"Yes, I guess I am. Let me do this part by myself. Why don't you wait in your car?"

Pike said, "Anyone can wait in the car. That isn't me."

"No, I guess not. Let's put our cars in the alley. We'll go in the front here, but leave through the back."

We put our cars outside the service door, then walked back around to the front again. Pike brought a crowbar. I brought a flathead screwdriver and my jack handle.

The family from the pet store was standing directly in front of Stars & Stripes Mail Boxes. The man and the woman were trying to decide which restaurant would seat them faster with the kids.

I said, "You're too close to the door. Please step aside."

The woman said, "I'm sorry. What?"

I pointed at the door with my jack handle.

"There's going to be glass. You need to move."

Pike stepped close to her husband like a towering shadow.

"*Go.*"

They suddenly understood what was going to happen and pulled their children away, speaking fast in Chinese.

I hit the door with my jack handle and shattered the glass. The alarm went off with a loud steady buzz that echoed through the parking lot and across the intersection like an air-raid siren. The people in the parking lot and on the sidewalks looked toward the sound. I knocked the remaining glass out of the door frame, and then I went in. Something sharp raked my back. More glass fell, and Pike came in after me.

Pike went for the curtain and I went for the mailbox. The boxes were built sturdy, with bronze metal doors set flush to a metal frame. Each door had a small glass window so you could see whether you had mail and a reinforced lock. Schilling's box was packed with mail.

I worked the screwdriver's blade under the door, then hammered it open with the jack handle. None of the mail was addressed to Eric Schilling or Gene Jeanie; it was addressed to Eric Shear.

"It's him. He's using the name Eric Shear."

The alarm was so loud that I shouted.

I shoved the letters into my pockets, then ran to help Pike.

The metal curtain ran along tracks in the floor and ceiling so that you couldn't climb over or under, and was stretched between two metal pipes anchored into the walls. We used the crowbar and the jack handle to break away pieces of the wall from under one of the pipes, then pried the pipe from the wall. It bent at a crazy angle and we pushed it aside.

Outside, someone shouted, "Hey, look at that!"

People were gathering in the parking lot. They crouched behind cars or stood in small groups, pointing at the shop and craning their heads to try to see what we were doing. Two men gawked through what was left of the front door, then hurried away. I didn't know how long Pike and I had been inside, but it couldn't have been long: forty seconds; a minute. The alarm clouded the little store with noise. It was so loud that it would cover the sound of approaching sirens.

We shoved through the collapsing curtain and into the office. Towering stacks of packages crowded the floor and an enormous bag of Styrofoam packing peanuts hung from the ceiling. A file cabinet stood in the corner beside a small desk cluttered with what looked like unsorted mail and UPS receipts. Pike checked the service door as I went to the files.

Pike shouted over the alarm that the way was clear.

"We're good. The deadbolts open with levers."

I opened the top file drawer expecting to see folders filled with paperwork, but the drawer contained office supplies. I pulled the next two drawers, but they only held more supplies. Pike peeked out the back door to see if anyone was coming. Our time was running out.

"Faster."

"I'm looking."

I scattered papers, magazines, and envelopes from the desk, then opened its drawer. It was the only drawer left. The drawer had to contain rental agreements for the customers who rented the boxes, but all I found were ordering records for the services and supplies that Stars & Stripes needed to conduct its business; nothing referred to the boxes or the clients who rented them.

Pike tapped my back, and looked toward the parking lot.

"We got a problem."

An overweight man in a yellow knit shirt was surrounded by people in the parking lot, all of them pointing our way. The shirt was too tight, so his belly bulged over his belt like a Baggie filled with jelly. The word SECURITY was stenciled on the shirt over his heart like a badge, and he wore a pistol in a black nylon holster clipped to his right hip. So much flab spilled from his pants that the pistol was almost hidden. He crept forward with his hand on his gun. He looked scared.

I said, "Jesus Christ, where'd he come from?"

"Keep looking."

Pike slipped past me with his pistol out. I caught his arm.

"Joe, don't."

"I'm not going to hurt him. Keep looking."

The guard knelt behind a car and peered over the

trunk. Pike moved into the door so that the guard saw him. That was enough. The guard threw himself to the ground and curled up behind the tire. At least he didn't start shooting. Discretion is the better part of valor when all you get is minimum wage.

Pike and I heard the sirens at the same time. He glanced back at me, and I waved him back. We had run out of time.

"Let's go."

"Did you find it?"

"No."

Pike fell back past the counter to the service door. "Keep looking. We have a few seconds."

"We can't find him from jail."

"Keep looking."

That's when I saw the brown cardboard box under the desk. It was just the right size and shape for storing file folders. I pulled it out from under the desk, and pushed off the top. It was filled with folders that were numbered from one to six hundred, and I knew that each number corresponded to a box. I pulled the folder marked 205.

"We're out. Go!"

Pike jerked open the door. Outside, the air was cool and the alarm wasn't so loud. The two men with their potatoes shouted into their kitchen when they saw us, and others came out as we left. We turned our cars onto a service street behind a Cineplex theater eight blocks away, and looked through the file. It contained a rental agreement for Eric Shear. The rental agreement had a phone number and his address.

Eric Shear lived in a four-story apartment building on the western edge of San Gabriel called the Casitas Arms, less than ten minutes from the mail drop. It was a large building, the kind that packed a hundred apartments around a central atrium and billed itself as "secure luxury living." Places like that are easy to enter.

We parked in a red zone across the street, then Pike got into my car. When I turned on my phone I found three messages from Starkey, but I ignored them. What would I tell her, that the next BOLO she received would be about me? I dialed Schilling's number. An answering machine picked up on the second ring with a male voice.

"Leave it at the beep."

I hung up and told Pike that it was a machine.

He said, "Let's go see."

Pike brought the crowbar. We walked along the side of the building until we found an outside stairwell that residents could use instead of the lobby elevators. The stair was enclosed in a cagelike door that required a key, but Pike wedged the crowbar into the gate and popped the lock. We let ourselves in, then climbed to the third floor. Eric Shear's apartment number was listed as 313. The building was laid out around a central atrium with long halls that T'd into shorter halls. Three-thirteen was on the opposite side of the building.

It was early evening, just after dark. Cooking smells and music came from the apartments along

with an occasional voice. I heard a woman laugh.
Here were these people living their lives and none of
them knew that Eric Shear was really Eric Schilling.
They probably smiled at him in the elevator or nodded in the garage, and never guessed at what he did
for a living, or had done. *Hey, how are ya? Have a
nice day.*

We followed the hall past a set of elevators until
we reached a T. Arrows on the facing wall showed the
apartment numbers to the left and right. Three-
thirteen was to our left.

I said, "Hang on."

I edged to the corner and peeked into the adjoining hall. Three-thirteen was at the end of the hall opposite an exit door that probably led to a set of stairs
like the one we had climbed. Two folded sheets of
paper were wedged into Schilling's door a few inches
above the knob.

Pike and I eased around the corner and went to
either side of the door. We listened. Schilling's apartment was silent. The papers wedged into the jamb
were notices reminding all tenants that rent was due
on the first of the month and that the building's water
would be turned off for two hours last Thursday.

Pike said, "He hasn't been home in a while."

If they had been put in the door on the dates that
were shown, then no one had been into or out of
Schilling's apartment in more than six days.

I put my finger over the peephole, and knocked.
No one answered. I knocked again, then took out the
gun and held it down along my leg.

I said, "Open it."

Pike wedged the crowbar between the door and

the jamb, and pushed. The frame splintered with a loud crack and I shoved through the door into a large living room with the gun up and out. A kitchen and dining area were across the living room. A hall opened to our left, showing three doorways. The only light came from a single ceiling fixture that hung in the entry. Pike crossed fast to the kitchen, then followed me down the hall, guns first through each door to make sure that the apartment was empty.

"Joe?"

"Clear."

We went back to the entry to shut the door, then turned on more lights. The living room had almost no furniture, just a leather couch, a card table, and an enormous Sony television in the corner opposite the couch. The apartment was so spare that its impermanence was obvious, as if Schilling was prepared to walk away at a moment's notice and leave nothing behind. It was more like a camp than a home. A small cordless phone sat on the counter that divided the kitchen from the living room, but there was no answering machine. It was the first thing I looked for, thinking we might find a message.

I said, "His answering machine must be in back."

Pike moved back to the hall.

"Saw it when I cleared the bedroom. I'll take the bedroom, you check out here."

So many Corona and Orangina bottles cluttered the kitchen counters that one man couldn't have drunk them all. Dirty dishes were piled in the sink, and take-out food containers spilled out of a wastebasket. The food had been there so long it smelled sour. I emptied the wastebasket onto the floor and looked for the take-out receipts. The most recent date on the receipts was six days ago. The orders were large, way too much for a man living alone and easily enough for three.

I said, "They were here, Joe."

He called back.

"I know. Come see this."

I moved back to the bedroom.

Pike was kneeling by a rumpled futon, which was all that passed for furniture in the room. The closet door was open, revealing that the closet was virtually empty. A few shirts and some dirty underwear were piled on the floor. Like the rest of the apartment, Schilling's bedroom held a feeling of emptiness, as if it was more a hiding place than a home. A radio/alarm clock sat on the floor by the futon, along with a second cordless digital phone with a message machine built into its base.

"Did you hear something on his machine?"

"No messages. He has some mail here, but I called you for this."

Pike turned toward a row of snapshots that had been push-pinned to the wall above the futon. They were pictures of dead people. The dead were various races. Some wore the tattered remains of a uniform while others wore nothing at all. They had been shot or blown apart, mostly, though one was horribly burned. A red-haired man who grinned like an All-American boy gone mad posed with the bodies in several of the pictures. At his side in two of the pictures was a tall black man with marks on his face.

Pike tapped a picture.

"Ibo. The red hair would be Schilling. These pictures aren't just from Sierra Leone, either. Look at the vics. This could be Central America. This one could be in Bosnia."

One of the pictures showed the red-haired man holding a human arm by the pinkie as if it were a trophy bass. I felt sick to my stomach.

"They lost their minds."

Pike nodded.

"It's what Resnick said, they abandoned the rules. They became something else."

"I don't see anyone who looks like Fallon."

"Fallon was Delta. Even insane he would be too smart to let his picture be taken."

I turned away.

"Let's see his mail."

Pike had found a stack of mail held together by a rubber band. They were all addressed to Eric Shear at the mail drop and contained bank statements showing a checking account balance of $6123.18, canceled checks, and his phone bills for the past two months. Almost all of his calls were to area codes around Los Angeles, but six calls stood out from the others like a beacon. Three weeks ago, Eric Schilling had phoned an international number in San Miguel, El Salvador, six times over a four-day period.

I glanced at Pike.

"You think it's Fallon? Resnick thought South America."

"Dial it and see."

I studied Schilling's phone, then pressed the Re-dial button. A number rang, but a perky young woman's voice answered with the name of a local pizza restaurant. I hung up, then studied the phone some more. Digital phones will sometimes store outgoing and incoming calls, but Schilling's did not. I dialed the El Salvador number from Schilling's bill. The international connection made a faraway hiss as it bounced off the satellite, then I got a ring. The El Salvador number rang twice, then was answered by a recording.

"You know the drill. Talk to me."

I felt the same cold prickle I had felt that first day on the slope, but now anger boiled around it like mist. I hung up. It was the same man who had called me the night Ben was stolen and was recorded on Lucy's tape.

"It has to be him. I recognize his voice."

Pike's mouth twitched.

"Starkey's going to love this. She's going to bag a war criminal."

I studied the pictures again. I had never met Schilling or Fallon or anyone else shown in the pictures—these people had no history with me; they had no reason to be in Los Angeles or to know anything about me. Thousands of children came from families with more money than Richard, but they had kidnapped Ben. They had tried to make it seem as if their motive was vengeance against me, and now they were almost certainly holding up Richard for ransom money; yet he was denying it. All kidnappers tell their victims not to go to the police, and I could understand Richard was scared, but that was the only part that made sense. The pieces of the puzzle did not fit together, as if each piece was from a different puzzle and no matter how I tried to arrange them the picture they built made no sense.

We overturned the futon and looked through the sheets, but found nothing more. I went into the bathroom. Magazines were stacked beside the toilet. The wastebasket overflowed with wads of tissue, Q-tips, and cardboard toilet paper tubes, but several white pages jutted up through the trash. I upended the basket. A photocopy of my 201 Form fell to the floor.

I said, "Joe. Schilling has my file."

Pike stepped into the door behind me. I flipped through the files with a slow sense of numbness, then handed the pages to Joe.

"The only two people who had copies of this were Starkey and Myers. Myers had a judge in New Orleans get a copy of my file for Richard. No one else could have had it."

The pieces of the puzzle came together like leaves settling to the bottom of a pool. The picture they built was hazy, but began to take shape.

Pike stared at the pages.

"Myers had this?"

"Yeah. Myers and Starkey."

Pike cocked his head. His face grew dark.

"How would Myers know them?"

"Myers handles security for Richard's company. Resnick said that Schilling called him for security work. Maybe Myers hired him. If he knew Schilling, then Schilling could have brought in the others."

Pike glanced at the pages again, then shook his head, still trying to see it.

"But why would Myers give them your file?"

"Maybe it was Myers's idea to steal Ben."

Pike said, "Jesus."

"Myers had an open window into Richard's life.

He knew about me and Lucy, he knew that Lucy and Ben were out here, and he knew that Richard was worried about them. Fallon and Schilling couldn't have known anything about that, but Myers would have known all of it. Richard probably did nothing but bitch about how much danger they were in because of me, so maybe Myers started thinking he could use Richard's paranoia to get some of Richard's money."

"Set up a kidnapping, then control the play from inside for the payoff."

"Yeah."

Pike shook his head.

"It's thin."

"How else could they get my file? Why target Ben as the victim and try to make me look like the reason it's happening?"

"You going to call Starkey?"

"What would I tell her and what could she do? Myers isn't going to admit it unless we have proof."

We went back to the bedroom and looked through Schilling's phone bills again to see if Schilling had phoned Louisiana, but his bills showed no calls outside the Los Angeles area except for the calls to El Salvador. We went through the entire apartment again. We searched every place we could think of to find something that would connect Schilling to Myers or Myers to Schilling until we ran out of places to search, and still we had nothing. Then I thought of another place we could look.

I said, "We have to get inside Myers's office. Come on."

I ran to the door, but Pike did not follow. He stared at me as if I had lost my mind.

"What's wrong with you? Myers's office is in New Orleans."

"Lucy can do it. Lucy can search his office from here."

I explained as we ran to our cars.

22

· · ·

Lucy stared at me past the edge of the door as if she were hiding. Her face was masked in a darkness that went beyond the absence of light; as soon as I saw her I knew they had told her about DeNice.

She said, "One of Richard's detectives—"

"I know. Joe's downstairs. Let me come in, Luce, I need to talk to you."

I eased the door open and stepped in without waiting for her to ask. She was holding her phone. I doubt that she had put it down since last night.

She seemed dazed, like the weight of the nightmare had drained all her strength. She sleepwalked to the couch as if she were numb.

"They decapitated him. A detective from downtown, he said they left Ben's shoe in the blood."

"We're going to get him, Luce. We're going to find him. Did you speak with Lucas or Starkey?"

"They were here a little while ago. The two of them and a detective from downtown."

"Tims."

"They told me about the van. They said it was going to be on the news, and they didn't want me to see it like that. They asked me about Fallon again, and two other men, an African man and someone named Schilling. They had pictures."

"How about Richard? Did they mention Richard?"

"Why would they mention Richard?"

"Did you speak with him this evening?"

"I've called him, but he hasn't returned my calls."

She frowned at me, and looked even more concerned.

"Why would they mention Richard? Did something happen to Richard, too?"

"We think that Fallon might have contacted Richard to ask for ransom money. That's probably why Fallon did what he did to DeNice, to scare Richard into paying."

"They didn't say that."

She frowned deeper and shook her head.

"Richard didn't say anything about that."

"If Fallon scared him badly enough, he wouldn't, and I think that Fallon scared him plenty. Fallon scared all of us. Lucy, listen, I think that Myers is involved. That's why they took Ben, and that's how they knew about me. Through Myers."

"Why would—"

I put the copy of my 201 in her hands. She looked at it without understanding.

"This is my military record. It's private. You can't get it from the Army unless I request it or you have a court order. The Army sent out only two copies of this thing, Luce, one to Starkey because of this investigation, and one to a judge in New Orleans three months ago. That judge sent it to Leland Myers."

Lucy looked at the pages. I knew from the way she darkened that she was remembering Richard in the interview room.

"Richard had you investigated."

"Myers is his head of security, so Myers would have handled that. Myers also handles security at Richard's overseas facilities. I talked to a man today who says that Schilling was looking for security work in Central America."

"Richard has holdings in El Salvador."

She glanced up again, and now she didn't seem so hazy. Her anger showed in the way she held her head.

"The judge in New Orleans, who was he?"

"Rulon Lester. Do you know him?"

She thought about it, trying to place the name, then shook her head.

"No, I don't think so."

"I spoke with his assistant. He sent my file to Myers, so Myers had one of only two copies that the Army released. Joe and I found this copy in an apartment in San Gabriel that belongs to Eric Schilling. He made at least six phone calls to a number in San Miguel, El Salvador, that belongs to Michael Fallon. It's Fallon on your tape, Lucy. I called the number. I recognized his voice."

I opened Schilling's phone bills and pointed out the calls to El Salvador. She stared at the number, then dialed it into her phone. I watched her as it rang. I watched as she listened. Her face darkened as she listened to his voice, and then she jabbed hard at the phone to end the call. She smashed the phone down onto the arm of the couch. I didn't stop her. I waited.

"The only way they could have gotten my 201 file is through Myers. Myers probably set up the entire thing and brought them in on it. They nabbed Ben with me as the smoke screen because Richard would buy into that. Myers probably even talked him into coming out here with people of his own to find Ben. That way, Myers could ride it from the inside and control how Richard reacted. He was Richard's point man in the investigation. He could feed Richard the ransom demand and encourage him to go along."

Lucy stood hard.

"Richard's at the Beverly Hills Hotel. Let's go see him."

I didn't move.

"And tell him what? We have the file, but we can't prove Myers knows them. If we don't have something definite, he'll deny everything and then we're stuck. He'll know that we know, and then the only thing left for him is to get rid of the evidence."

Get rid of Ben.

Lucy lowered herself onto the couch and stared at me.

"You said you need my help. You already know how you want me to help, and it's something you can't do or you would be doing it."

"If Myers hired these people before he started

thinking about this, then he probably hired them straight up. Richard's company would have a record of it. We have Fallon's phone number in El Salvador and Schilling's number in San Gabriel. If Myers called either of them at any time and for any reason from a company phone, those records will exist."

"But we don't want to ask Richard because Richard might lose it with Myers."

"Myers can't know."

Lucy slumped back, thinking. She glanced at her watch.

"It's almost ten in Louisiana. Everyone from the office should be home."

She went into her bedroom, then returned with a battered leather address book, and flipped through the pages.

"I had friends at Richard's company before we were divorced. I was close to some of these people. Everyone knew he was an asshole, especially the people who knew him the best."

She settled back with her phone and pulled her legs up so that she was sitting cross-legged and dialed a number.

"Hello, Sondra? It's Lucy. Yeah, here in L.A. How are you?"

Sondra Burkhardt had been Richard's comptroller for sixteen years. She oversaw an accounting department which was responsible for paying the company's bills, collecting monies, and tracking cash flow. Most of her job was done by computer, but she told the computer what to do. Sondra had played tennis with Lucy at LSU, and Lucy had gotten her the job. Sondra also had three children, the youngest of whom was six, and Lucy was her godmother.

"Sondra, I need a favor that's going to sound strange and I don't have time to—"

Lucy paused, listening, then nodded.

"Thanks, babe. Okay, I'm going to give you three names, and I need to know whether or not they were ever on the payroll. Can you do that from home?"

I interrupted.

"Central America. Any time in the past year."

Lucy nodded.

"They would have been foreign hires, probably in Central America sometime in the past year. Myers would have been the one to hire them. No, I don't have Social Security numbers, just the names. I understand, that makes it harder. I know."

Lucy gave her the names, then asked if we could get a list of all the calls that Myers had made to Los Angeles and El Salvador. Lucy frowned as she listened to the answer, then asked Sondra to hang on and covered the phone. She looked at me.

"If we can't tell her when he made the calls, she might have to check through thousands of calls. They make hundreds of international calls every day."

"See if she can check for the specific numbers."

Lucy asked her, then covered the phone again.

"Yeah, she can do that, but she'll have to do it by billing period. I guess that's the way the database is set up."

I checked the phone bills for the dates of the four-day period when Schilling had called El Salvador. Myers would have been involved in the planning.

"Have her check whatever billing period includes

these four days. If we don't get anything, she can
check the prior period."

Lucy gave her Schilling's phone number, Fallon's
number in San Miguel, and the dates. After that,
Lucy settled back with the phone to her ear and
waited.

"She's looking."

"Okay."

We stared at each other. Lucy made a very small
smile, and I smiled back. It felt as if the awkwardness
between us had somehow vanished in the mutual effort of searching for Ben, as if we were one again and
not two, and in that moment my heart seemed to
quiet. But then her brow knotted and Lucy tightened
in a way that brought her forward.

She said, "I'm sorry, Sondra, say that again."

I said, "What?"

She held up her hand to silence me. Her brow furrowed as she concentrated. Lucy shook her head as if
she didn't understand what she was hearing, but then
I realized that she was resisting what she was hearing.

I said, "What is it?"

"She found eleven calls to the San Miguel number,
none to L.A., but eleven to San Miguel. Myers only
made four of the calls. Richard made the other
seven."

"That can't be right. It had to be Myers. Myers
must have used his phone."

Lucy shook her head as if she were numb.

"They weren't made from Richard's office. The
company pays for the phones at his house, too. Richard called San Miguel from home."

"Can she print out the call list?"

Lucy asked in a monotone robotic voice.

"Yes."

"Have her make a hard copy."

Lucy asked for a hard copy.

"Have her fax it to us."

Lucy gave her fax number, then asked Sondra to send it. Lucy's voice was distant, like a little girl lost in the woods.

The list of calls printed out of Lucy's fax a few minutes later. We stood over the fax as if it were a crystal ball and we were waiting to see the future.

Lucy read the list, holding my hand so tightly that her nails cut into my skin. She saw for herself. She repeated Richard's home number aloud.

"What did he do? Oh, my God, what did he do?"

I had been wrong about everything. Richard had been so frightened that something bad would happen to Ben and Lucy because of me that he had decided to make it happen himself. He arranged for the fake kidnapping of his own son so that he could blame it on me. He wanted Lucy to come to her senses. He wanted to drive us apart to save her, so he had hired people who were willing to do anything—Fallon and Schilling and Ibo. He probably hadn't known who they were or what they had done until Starkey and I pulled the Interpol file. I guess Myers had helped him put it together. But once Fallon had Ben, Fallon had double-crossed him and now Richard was caught.

"*Oh my God, what did he do?*"

Richard had lost Ben.

I took the fax and the other things, and then I took Lucy's hand.

"Now it's time to see Richard. I'll bring him home to you, Luce. I'm going to get Ben."

We went down the stairs together, then drove to Richard's hotel.

TIME MISSING: 52 HOURS, 21 MINUTES

The Beverly Hills Hotel was a great pink beast that sprawled along Sunset Boulevard where Benedict Canyon emptied into Beverly Hills. That part of Beverly Hills was home to some of the wealthiest people in the world, and the Pink Palace fit well, resting on a little rise like a Mission Revival crown jewel. Movie stars and Middle-Eastern oil sheiks felt comfortable staying behind the manicured walls; I guess Richard felt comfortable there, too. He was in a bungalow that cost two thousand dollars a night.

Lucy knew which room was his, and was the only one of the three of us who looked like she belonged at the hotel. I looked like a maniac, and Pike just looked like Pike.

We crossed the lobby, then followed a winding path through verdant grounds that smelled of night-blooming jasmine. Ben could be anywhere, but Richard was home; Myers had answered his phone. That meant Fallon still had Ben, and Richard was still trying to buy him back.

Pike said, "How do you want to play this?"

"You know how I'm going to play it."

"In front of Lucy?"

She said, "You don't have a choice."

The bungalows that dotted the path were expensive because they were private; each little bungalow separate from the others, and hidden by landscaping. It was like walking through a tailored jungle.

Ahead of us, we saw Fontenot standing outside a door at a fork in the path. He was smoking, and bouncing from foot to foot. Nervous. Myers came out of a room, spoke to him, then went up the path. Fontenot went into the room that Myers had left.

"Is that Richard's?"

"No, Myers is staying in that one. It's not a full bungalow; it's just a room. Richard has the bungalow across."

"Wait here."

"You're out of your mind if you think I'm waiting."

"Wait. I want to get Fontenot first, then we'll see Richard. Fontenot might know something that will help us, and it'll be faster if you wait."

Pike said, "Fontenot will help. I promise."

Lucy looked at Joe, and nodded. She knew he meant it, and that speed was everything.

Lucy stayed on the path in the shadows while Joe and I went to the door. We didn't bother with knocking or pretending to be room service or anything cute like that; we hit the door so hard that the doorknob caught in the wall. That made three busted doors in one day, but who's counting?

Fontenot was watching television with his feet up on the bed. A pistol sat on the floor beside him, but Pike and I were inside and on him before he could reach it. He hesitated, seeing our guns, then wet his lips.

I said, "Did you see DeNice? Did you see what they did to him?"

Fontenot was shaky getting to his feet. He had the twitchy eyes of someone who had been nervous for most of the day and was even more nervous now. The room smelled of bourbon.

"What the fuck? What are you doing?"

I kicked his gun under the bed.

"Is Richard in his room?"

"I don't know where Richard is. Get out of here. You got no business being here."

Pike snapped his pistol across Fontenot's face like before. Fontenot fell sideways onto the bed. Pike cocked his pistol and pressed the muzzle into Fontenot's ear.

I said, "We know. We know that Richard hired them. We know this was all about fucking me over, but it turned upside down. Is Richard in contact with these people? Has he made a deal for Ben?"

Fontenot closed his eyes.

"Is Ben still alive?"

Fontenot tried to say something, but his lower lip trembled. He closed his eyes tighter, like he was trying not to see.

"They cut off Debbie's head."

I shouted into his face.

"IS BEN STILL ALIVE?"

"Richard doesn't have enough money. They want it in cash, and he can't get enough. They only gave him a few hours. We got some of it, but not all. That's why Debbie went to see them, and look what they did. We been trying to put this together all day, but look what they did."

Something moved behind me. Lucy had come to the door.

She said, "How much do they want for my son?"

"Five million. They want five million in cash, but Richard couldn't put it together. He's been trying all day, but that was all he could get."

Fontenot waved at the closet, and cried even more.

A large Tumi duffel was in the closet. It was heavy with packs of hundred-dollar bills, but it wasn't heavy enough.

TIME MISSING: 52 HOURS, 29 MINUTES

When Myers opened the door, I pushed Fontenot hard into the room. Richard was haggard, with his hair sticking out as if he'd been running his hands over his head all afternoon. Even Myers looked beaten. Richard was holding his cell phone with both hands, like a bible.

"Get out. Get them out of here, Lee."

Pike heaved the bag into the middle of the floor.

"Look familiar?"

A smile flickered at the corner of Myers's mouth. He was probably relieved.

"I'd say they have the money and they know what we're doing."

Lucy came in behind Joe. Richard's eyes widened and he raked his hand across his head as if it had become a nervous tick.

"They don't know anything. Keep your mouth shut."

Myers stared at him.

"Richard, stop. It's time to stop before this mess gets worse. The wheels are coming off, Richard. Jesus Christ, wake up."

Lucy was as rigid as a statue. Her legs were tight together, her face closed. Her eyebrows were knitted so deeply that her eyes were hidden.

"You self-absorbed sonofabitch. Where is my son?"

Richard's eyes fluttered like two trapped moths. His mouth hung loose, as if he had aged a thousand years since yesterday. I didn't feel so angry anymore; I felt empty, and worried for Ben.

Richard was so scared that I turned to Myers.

"What's Fallon doing, Myers? How are they playing this?"

Richard screamed.

"Shut up!"

Myers moved faster than I thought he could; he grabbed Richard by the shirt and bent him backwards toward the bed.

"They know. Get your head around it, Richard—*they know*. Now let's get back to business. Your son is waiting."

Myers shoved him away, then turned back to the black Tumi bag.

"That's three-point-two million, but they want five. We tried to tell them, but, you know, no one ever believes you with something like this. DeNice was their answer."

Myers stepped around the money, then looked at me.

"Fallon knows what he's doing, Cole. He's been jamming us all day, pushing it forward to keep us off balance. We didn't even know it was happening until this morning. That's how fast it's been, just this one day. All of it started this morning."

"Where are you with it?"

"He gave us today to get the money, that's it. Just the one business day. Richard has to call them by nine. That's in eight minutes. Fallon told us not to bother calling after that. You know what he'll do after that."

Pike said, "You should have told the police."

Myers glanced at Richard, then shrugged.

Richard said, "They were supposed to take him away for a few days. He was supposed to watch videos and eat pizza until we came out, that's all it was supposed to be."

Lucy took a step toward him.

"You had him *stolen*, you asshole! You had your son *kidnapped*! And you didn't even love him enough to admit it or ask for help."

"I'm sorry. It wasn't supposed to be this way. I'm sorry."

Lucy slapped him, then hit him with her fist. He didn't move, and he didn't try to protect himself. She hit Richard over and over again, grunting loudly with each effort—*unh, unh, unh*—like when she played tennis.

"Luce."

I caught her arms gently and eased her away.

Richard blubbered like a baby with snot running from his nose. Lucy had broken it. He slumped onto the edge of the bed, and sat there shaking his head.

"I don't have the money. I can't get it in time. It wasn't supposed to be like this. It wasn't."

Myers said, "We have four minutes."

Fontenot shook his head.

"He wants the money this bad, he'll wait. We can tell him it'll just be another hour, that the money is on the way. He'll go for it."

Pike spoke softly.

"No, he won't. He's pressing because that's how he controls the situation. He wants to keep you off balance. He won't give you time to think. He wants the money, but he also wants to survive the mission, and that means he will not let you stall. He planned the operation, and now he's working the plan. He'll do what he said he would do, and then he'll disappear."

Fontenot said, "Jesus Christ, you make it sound like he's in a war."

Richard rubbed his face. His fingers went through his hair. He seemed calmer now, but still nervous.

"I don't know what to do. I don't have the money."

I looked at Myers again.

"What's supposed to happen if you had the money?"

"He would tell us where to meet them, then we'd trade the money for Ben."

I looked at the Tumi bag. It was a big bag because three million dollars took up a lot of room, but five million would take up almost twice as much.

I went over to the bed and sat beside Richard. We stared at each other for a moment, and then he glanced away.

I said, "Do you love him?"

Richard nodded.

"I love him, too."

Richard blinked a bit, and his eyes filled with sorrow. His voice was hoarse.

"You can't know how much I hate you."

"I know, but now we're going to save Ben together."

"Haven't you been listening? I already offered them the three million, but they wouldn't take it. They want five. They said it's five or nothing, and I don't have that much. I can't get it. I don't know what to tell them."

I put the hotel phone into his hands.

"Do what you do best, Richard. Lie. Tell them that you have all five million and that you're ready to trade for your son."

Richard stared at the phone, and then he dialed.

23

. . .

Richard made the call at exactly nine P.M. and he was convincing. Myers and I listened on the extension. Fallon told Richard to bring the money to the west end of Santa Monica Airport. He told Richard to bring it alone.

Myers and I both shook our heads.

Richard's voice shook when he answered.

"No goddamned way. Myers is coming. It'll be just us, and you'd better have Ben. If Ben's not there, I'll call the police. I should call the police anyway."

"Is Myers listening?"

"I'm here, you prick."

"It's the west end of the airport on the south side. Drive past the hangars and stop. Get out of your car but stay next to it, and wait."

Myers said, "No boy, no money. You won't even get close to the money unless we see the boy."

"I just want the money. Stop, get out of your car, and you'll see me when I want you to see me. I won't be close to you, but you'll see me. When you see me, call this number again. Do you understand?"

"I'll call you when I see you."

"Guess what happens if I see anyone else?"

"I don't have to guess."

"That's right. You don't. Fifteen minutes."

Fallon hung up.

Richard put down his phone and looked at me.

"What do we do?"

"Exactly what he told you to do. We'll do the rest."

Pike and I left at a dead run. We knew that Fallon was probably already at the airport and would be set up so that he could see Richard approach and watch for the police. Speed was everything. We had to get to the airport before Richard, we had to stay out of sight, and we had to come at Fallon in a way he didn't expect.

I drove fast, and so did Pike, the two of us rat-racing across the city.

Sunset Boulevard glowed with violet-blue light that rippled and shimmered on the hood of my Corvette. The cars we raced past were frozen in place, their taillights stretched in front of us like liquid red streaks. I couldn't shift hard enough, I couldn't drive fast enough. We screamed across Westwood into Brentwood, and then toward the sea.

Santa Monica Airport was a nice little place, one lonely airstrip built during a time when inland Santa

Monica was mostly clover fields and cows, north of LAX and west of the 405. The city grew up around it, and now the airfield was surrounded by homeowners and businesses who hated the noise and lived in fear of a crash. You could get a good hamburger there, and sit on benches across from the tower to watch the airplanes take off and land. Ben and I had done that more than once.

The north side of the airfield was mostly corporate offices and the Museum of Flying; old hangars and parking ramps lined the south. Many of the hangars on the south had been converted into offices or businesses, but many were empty; I guess they were cheaper to abandon than repair.

I called Myers's cell as we got close.

"We're almost there, Myers. Where are you?"

"We just left the hotel. I'd say twelve or fifteen minutes. We're cutting it close."

"You're driving?"

"Yeah. Richard's in back."

"When you reach the airport, slow down. Drive slow so that Pike and I have enough time."

"We can't be too late, Cole."

"They'll see your limo turn into the airport. They'll know you're here. That's what matters. They know you're from out of town, so just drive like you're confused."

"Shit, man, I'm doing that now."

I had to smile, even then.

"I'll call you back when we're there."

I leaned on the horn all the way down Bundy, slowing for red lights but never once stopping, and twice Joe Pike pulled ahead. I straddled the curb to get around slower cars and hung on their bumpers, then downshifted hard into the oncoming lanes. I hit a trash can on Olympic Boulevard, and raked a street sign as we blew under the freeway. My right headlight went out.

All four tires smoked as I turned toward the sea.

I picked up the phone.

"Myers?"

"I'm here."

"Two minutes."

We blew west two blocks north of the airport past a long row of offices and charter jet hangars. The tower stood silently in the distance, asleep for the night, its only sign of life a throbbing green and white light.

Pike stopped at the embankment by the end of the runway, but I kept going. The office buildings gave way to a soccer field, and then to residential streets. I left my car a block away and ran on foot to the dark hangars that lined the south side of the field like overgrown shadows.

Fallon would probably have a man on the roof and maybe another on the little service road that Richard would be using. A few cars were parked along the service road, but I couldn't see if anyone was in them and I didn't have time to go from car to car. The rooflines were clean.

I edged past the last hangar, then peeked around the corner. A few small airplanes were tied down on the ramp with a row of fuel trucks parked by them. The trucks were all by themselves at the edge of nothing.

I whispered into the phone.

"Myers?"

"We're at the east side."

"I can't see you."

"I don't care if you can see me; do you see *them*?"

"Not yet. Go slow. I'm moving."

Pike was working his way toward the ramp from the north. I couldn't see him and didn't try; if I saw him, then they could see him, and either way would be bad. A trailer set up as a temporary office jutted out between the hangars. I slipped out to its end for a better view. I scanned the rooflines again, then the shadows along the base of the hangars, and then the trucks. Nothing moved. I listened as hard as I could. Nothing moved. I looked for shadows and shapes that were out of place, but everything seemed normal. No other cars were present. The hangar doors were closed. Fallon was probably waiting nearby if he was waiting anywhere at all.

I whispered into the phone again.

"I don't see anything, Myers."

"They'll hold in place until we get there, but they'll have to move. You'll see them."

I told him where I was hiding.

"Okay, I'm at the drive where he said to turn. I'm making the turn."

Light swept between two hangars, and then the limousine emerged and turned toward me. They were fifty yards away. Maybe sixty.

The limousine stopped.

I said, "I'm right in front of you."

"Copy. We're getting out. We have to call him now."

"Don't hurry. Wait."

The limousine sat with its engine running and lights on. From the end of the trailer I saw all of the ramp and the taxiway and most of the service road that ran along the south side of the airport. Everything was quiet.

"We're getting out. I'm putting in my earpiece so I can hear you. You see something, you tell me, goddamnit."

The passenger door opened, and Myers stepped out. He stood by himself alongside the car.

I checked the roofline and service road again, looking for the telltale bump of a human head or the bulge of a shoulder, but saw nothing. I watched the shadows at the base of the ramp, and saw still more nothing.

The third fuel truck from the end of the row flicked its lights.

I said, "Myers."

His voice came back low.

"I got it. Richard's calling the number."

I strained hard to see inside the truck but it was dark with shadows and too far away. I took out my gun and trained it on the truck's grill. The grip was slippery. I would put down the phone as soon as I saw Ben. My aim was better with both hands.

I said, "Tell him to get out with Ben. Make him show Ben."

Pike would have moved up on the far side. He would be closer than me and have a better position. He was a better shot.

Myers's soft voice came through again.

"Richard's talking to him. Richard's getting out to show the money. He wants to see the bags."

"Don't do that, Myers. Make him show Ben."

"Richard's scared."

"Myers, make him show Ben. I don't see Ben."

"Ben's on the phone."

"That's not good enough. You have to see him."

"Keep your eyes on that fucking truck. Richard's flashing the money."

The limo's back door opened. Myers helped Richard out with the two bags, and then they looked at the truck. Three million dollars is heavy, and five had to look still heavier.

I heard Myers whisper, "C'mon, you fucker."

The truck lights flicked again. All of us waited. All of us stared at the truck.

Twenty feet behind Richard and Myers, a shadow moved between the oil drums that were stacked at the mouth of the hangar. I caught the movement as Myers turned. Schilling and Mazi surged out of the shadows with their pistols up and ready. I had stared at those oil drums again and again, but I had seen nothing.

I yelled, "MYERS!"

Their hands exploded like tiny suns, flashbulbing their faces with red light. Myers went down. They kept shooting him until they reached the money, and then they fired at Richard. He fell backwards into the car.

I fired two fast shots, then turned for the fuel truck, screaming. I expected the truck to rumble to life or shots to come from the darkness, but none of that happened. I sprinted as hard as I could, shouting Ben's name.

Behind me, Schilling and Mazi heaved the money into the limo and got in with it.

Pike ran onto the ramp from the far side of the trucks and fired as the limo squealed away. All of us had thought that they would approach and leave in their own vehicle, but they didn't; the limo was their getaway, just as they'd planned.

I ran low and hard all the way to the truck, but I knew before I reached it that the truck was empty and always had been. Fallon had rigged the lights with a remote. He was someplace else, and Ben was still with him.

I spun back around, but the limo was gone.

PIKE

Pike thought, they're beating us. These people are so damned good that they're beating us.

Schilling and Ibo stepped out from between the oil drums as if they had come through an invisible door, one moment impossible to see, the next their hands flashing fire, with the absolute efficiency of a striking snake. Pike had studied those drums, but seen nothing. They struck so fast that he could not warn Myers. It happened so quickly, and Pike was so far away, that he was nothing more than a witness to the execution.

They were as good as anyone Joe Pike had ever seen.

Pike ran forward, trying to get into range, as Cole shouted. Pike and Cole fired at almost the same instant, but Pike knew they were too late; the limo's left headlight shattered and a bullet careened off its hood. The limo ripped away as Cole raced toward the truck. Pike didn't bother because he knew what Cole would find.

Pike twisted around, searching for movement; someone had controlled the truck's lights, and that would be Fallon, somewhere nearby with a line of sight on the scene; now that Schilling and Ibo had the money, Fallon would also run, and might give himself away.

Then a heavy shot boomed to the north, and Pike spun toward the sound. Not a handgun shot, but something loud and heavy. Light flashed in one of the parked cars, followed fast by a second boom.

Pike saw shadows in the car. A man and a boy.

Pike shouted at Cole as the car pulled away, then ran hard down the hill for his Jeep, his shoulder sending sharp lightning through his arm as he ran.

Pike thought, I'm scared.

BEN

Mike wasn't like Eric or Mazi. Mike didn't bullshit or play the radio and leer at the hot chicks they passed on San Vicente Boulevard. Mike spoke only to give commands. He looked at Ben only to make sure Ben got the point. That was it.

They turned into a parking lot at the airport, then sat with the engine running. Mike never turned off the engine. Like he was scared that it wouldn't start when he needed it. After a while, Mike had lifted the binoculars to watch something across the field. Ben couldn't tell what was happening because it was so far away.

The shotgun rested with the muzzle on the floor and the stock leaning against Mike's knee. It wasn't a regular shotgun like the 20-gauge Ithaca that Ben's grandpa had given him for Christmas; this shotgun was really short, with a black stock, but Ben saw a little button in the trigger guard that he knew was the safety. His own shotgun had the same kind of safety. The safety was off. Ben thought, I'll bet he's got one in the box and good to go just like Eric.

Ben glanced up at Mike again, but Mike was still focused across the field.

Mike scared him. Eric and Mazi were scared of Mike, too. If it had been Eric sitting here concentrating on something across the field, Ben thought he would go for the gun. All he had to do was grab the trigger and the gun would go off. But that was Eric and this was Mike. Mike reminded him of a sleeping cobra, all coiled up and good to go. You might think it was sleeping but you never knew.

Mike lowered the binoculars just long enough to find what looked like a small walkie-talkie from the dashboard, then raised the binoculars again. He keyed the walkie-talkie, and lights flickered across the runway. Mike spoke on his cell phone, and then put the phone to Ben's ear.

"It's your dad. Say something."

Ben grabbed the phone.

"Daddy?"

His father sobbed, and just like that Ben cried like a baby, gushing tears and hiccuping.

"I wanna go home."

Mike took back the phone. Ben grabbed for it, but Mike held him at arm's length. Ben clawed and bit and punched, but Mike's arm was an iron rod. Mike squeezed Ben's shoulder so hard that his shoulder felt crushed.

Mike said, "You going to stop?"

Ben shrank away from Mike as far as possible, embarrassed and ashamed. He cried even harder.

Mike dropped the phone, then peered through the binoculars again. He keyed the walkie-talkie once more, and now the far lights flashed and stayed on.

Overlapping erratic pops came from the far side of the airport then, and Mike straightened, focused so completely on whatever was happening that Ben thought: *Now!*

Ben lunged across the seat. His fingers wrapped around the trigger guard just as Mike grabbed his arm, but Ben had it by then. The shotgun went off like a bomb, and kicked hard into the steering wheel. Ben jerked the trigger again as fast as he could, and the shotgun thundered again, blowing a second hole in the floorboard.

Mike pulled Ben's hand off the gun as easy as tearing paper, and shoved Ben back into his seat. Ben threw his arms over his head, certain that Mike would beat him or kill him, but Mike put the shotgun back in its place, and started maneuvering out of the parking lot.

Once they were going, Mike glanced over at him.

"You're a tough little bastard."

Ben thought, too bad I missed.

24

. . .

Fallon's car moved in the north parking lot, speeding toward the exit. He would have to drive past the soccer field and the Museum of Flying, then between the office buildings before he came out onto Ocean Boulevard. Once he reached Ocean, he would be gone.

My hands shook so badly that they felt like clubs, but I punched Pike's number on speed dial.

"C'mon, Joe—answer. *C'mon.*"

Fallon's car turned past the soccer field and picked up speed. White midsize coupe, looked like two doors. He would be on his way to meet Schilling and Ibo. The limo was big and obvious, and now it was missing a headlight. They would abandon it soon.

Pike suddenly answered.

"I'm moving."

"Eastbound at the end of the soccer field, white two-door coupe. He's at the museum. He'll come out on Ocean. I lost him."

I broke and ran for my car. I ran as hard as I could, phone in one hand, gun in the other, past the hangars and the houses. Pike would be racing north toward Ocean Boulevard, and then he would turn east. He would either spot Fallon's car coming out of the airport or he wouldn't.

A woman was walking a small orange dog in the middle of the street. She saw me running toward her with the gun. She didn't try to get away or go to a house; instead, she hopped from foot to foot, screaming *aiee, aiee, aiee*, and the dog spun in circles. Here was this woman out for a walk, and I thought that if she tried to stop me I would shoot her and her little dog, too. That wasn't me. That wasn't anything like me. Welcome to madness.

I hit the car running and jammed away from the curb so hard that the car fishtailed and the tachometer needle was swallowed in red.

"Joe?"

"East on Ocean."

"*Where is he?*"

"Stop screaming. He's eastbound on Ocean, wait, turning south on Centinela. I have him. Six cars ahead."

Centinela was behind me. I jerked the hand brake to lock the back end and spun the car, smoking the tires out of a one-eighty. Horns all around me blew, but they sounded far away.

I still screamed into the phone.

"Myers is dead. They shot Richard, too. They

shot him, and he fell back into the limo. I don't know whether they killed him or not."

"Just take it easy. We're still southbound. Fallon doesn't know we're still in the game."

Fallon drove with a low profile so he wouldn't get stopped by a passing cop, but all I cared about was catching him. I hit eighty on the side streets, turned parallel to Centinela, then jammed it to a hundred.

"Where is he? Gimme cross streets!"

My car bounced off a dip in the street, but I went even faster. Pike called out the cross streets they were passing. I passed the same cross streets running parallel. I caught up to them one street at a time, and then I pulled ahead. I turned toward Centinela with all four tires sliding and blew a valve coming out of the turn. Smoke poured out behind me, and my engine clattered.

Pike said, "We're picking up speed."

I was close to Centinela and getting closer, three blocks away and then two. I snapped off my lights and jerked to the curb just as Fallon's car rolled through the intersection and turned toward the freeway. Ben sat in the passenger seat. He stared out the window.

"I'm on him, Joe. I see him."

Pike said, "Fall in behind after I make the turn."

Fallon didn't go far, but he wouldn't. He had thought it through well. They would change cars, and then they would get rid of Ben, and Richard if he was still alive. No kidnapping ends any other way.

Pike said, "He's slowing."

Fallon's car slipped under the freeway, then turned.

Pike didn't follow. His lights went off and he pulled to the curb at the corner, watching. I did the same. After a bit, Pike's Jeep crept forward and turned. We eased past building-supply outlets and a veterinarian's clinic to a row of small houses. A dog howled in the clinic. It sounded in pain.

Pike eased into a parking lot and got out. I followed him. We closed our doors just enough for them to catch, and Pike nodded toward a small house across the street with a For Sale sign in its front yard.

"That one."

The limo was mostly hidden behind the house and the white car was as far up the drive as it could go. A dark blue sedan was parked in the front yard. The sedan would probably be their escape vehicle. Lights moved in the house. Fallon and Ben hadn't been there more than two minutes, the limo no more than three. I wondered if Richard was dead in the back. I wondered if they had finished him on the way. The dog howled again.

I started across the street, but Pike stopped me.

"You have a plan or you just going to kick down the door?"

"You know what's going to happen. We don't have any time."

Pike stared at me; he was as still as a glade in a sleeping forest, but with a thunderhead riding the trees.

I pulled away from him, but Pike stepped closer. He grabbed the back of my neck and pulled me eye to eye.

"Don't die on me."

"Ben's inside."

Pike held on.

"They were right in front of us at the airport, and we didn't see them. They beat us. You know what happens if they beat us now."

I took a deep breath. Pike was right. Pike was almost always right. Shadows moved across the windows. The dog howled even louder.

I said, "Check the windows on the far side. I'll go down the drive. We'll meet at the back. They probably entered the house through the back door. They're in a hurry, so maybe they left it unlocked."

Pike said, "Just keep it tight. Maybe we can get shots through the windows, but if we have to go in, we go in together."

"I know. I know what to do."

"Then let's do it."

We split apart as we crossed the street. Pike went to the far side of the house as I moved down the drive. Sheer drapes covered the windows, but they didn't stop me from seeing. The first two windows showed a dark living room, but the hall beyond it was bright. The next windows showed an empty dining room, and then I reached the last two windows on my side of the house. They were brightly lit. I moved away from the house so their glow wouldn't illuminate me, and looked in the windows from the dark shadow of a bush in the neighbor's yard. Mazi Ibo and Eric Schilling were in the kitchen. Ibo walked into another part of the house, but Schilling came out the back door. He had two large duffel bags slung over his shoulders.

An old saying is that no battle plan survives first contact with the enemy.

Schilling stopped by the limo, letting his eyes adjust to the dark. He was less than twenty feet away from me. I didn't move. I held myself absolutely still. My heart hammered, but I didn't let myself breathe.

Schilling took a step, then stopped again as if sensing something. He cocked his head. The dog howled.

Schilling hitched the duffels, then stepped past the white car into the driveway and went toward the front, bringing the money to the blue sedan. I moved softly at first but picked up speed. He heard me when he was halfway down the drive. He dropped low into a crouch and turned fast, but it was too late by then. I hit him hard between the eyes with my pistol, then grabbed him to keep him from falling and hit him twice more.

I eased Schilling down, found his gun, and tucked it in my pants. I hurried to the back door. It was open and the kitchen was empty. Nothing moved in the house, and the silence was awful. Ibo and Fallon might come back at any moment with more bags of money, but the stillness in the house frightened me far more than that. Maybe they heard. Maybe Fallon and Ibo were already tending to business. All kidnappings end the same way for the victim.

I should have waited for Pike, but I stepped into the kitchen and moved toward the hall. My head was buzzing and my heart beat loud. Maybe that was why I didn't hear Fallon behind me until it was way too late.

BEN

Mike turned into a narrow drive that ran alongside a small dark house.

Ben said, "Where are we?"

"End of the line."

Mike pulled him across the seat and into the house. Eric was waiting for them in a dingy pink kitchen with smudged walls and a big empty hole where a refrigerator once stood. Two green duffel bags were heaped on the floor. Dust bunnies the size of Pekinese dogs cowered in the corners.

"We got a problem back here. Look."

"With the money?"

"No, the dickhead."

They followed Eric out of the kitchen and into a small bedroom. Ben saw Mazi shoving money into two more green duffels, but then he saw his father. Richard Chenier was sprawled on the floor against the wall, holding his stomach with blood all over his pants and arm.

Ben shouted, "DADDY!"

Ben ran to his father and none of them stopped him. His father groaned when Ben hugged him, and Ben started crying again. He felt the wet blood and cried harder.

"Hey, pal. Hey."

His dad stroked the side of his face, and started crying, too. Ben was terrified that his father would die.

"I'm so sorry, bud. I am so sorry. This is all my fault."

"Are you going to be all right? Daddy, are you okay?"

His daddy's eyes were so sad that Ben sobbed even louder, and it was hard to breathe.

His father said, "I love you so much. You know that, don't you? I love you."

Ben's words choked in his chest.

Mike and Eric were talking, but Ben didn't hear. Then Mike squatted next to them and examined his father's wound.

"Let me see. Looks like you got one in the liver. It's not sucking. Can you breathe okay?"

Ben's father said, "You bastard. You rotten son-ofabitch."

"You're breathing fine."

Eric came over and stood behind Mike.

"He fell back into the car. What was I going to do? We had to get out of there, but this asshole's in the backseat."

Mike stood, then glanced at the money.

"Don't worry about that right now. Let's keep the ball rolling. Get the money repacked and put it in the car. They're okay right now. We'll take care of it before we leave."

"Someone else was at the airport."

"Forget it. That was Cole. He's still back there, beating off."

Mike and Eric left Mazi packing the money and went into another part of the house.

Ben snuggled close to his father, and whispered.

"Elvis will save us."

His dad pushed himself up to sit a little straighter,

wincing with the pain. Mazi glanced over, then went back to the money.

His dad stared at the blood on his hand as if it was green ketchup, and then he searched Ben's eyes.

"This is my fault. Everything that's happened, getting mixed up with these animals, what happened to you, it's my fault. I'm the stupidest man in the world."

Ben didn't understand. He didn't know why his father was saying these things, but hearing them scared him, and he cried even more.

"No, you're not. You're not stupid."

His father touched his head again.

"I just wanted you back."

"Don't die."

"You're never going to understand and neither is anyone else, but I want you to remember that I loved you."

"Don't die!"

"I'm not. And neither are you."

His father glanced at Mazi, then looked back at Ben. He stroked Ben's head, then pulled Ben's face close and kissed him on the cheek.

His father whispered in Ben's ear.

"I love you, boy. Now you run. Run, and don't stop."

The sadness in his father's voice terrified him. Ben hugged his father and held on tight.

His dad's breath was soft in his ear.

"I'm sorry."

His father kissed him again just as something heavy thumped in another room. Mazi jerked erect with his hands still filled with money, and then Mike pushed Elvis Cole through the door. Elvis fell to one knee, and his eyes fluttered vaguely. His head was bleeding. Mike pressed the shotgun into Elvis's neck.

Mike looked at Mazi.

"Put him in the bathtub and use your knife. The shotgun's too noisy. Then take care of them."

A long slim knife the color of oil on water appeared in Mazi's hand.

Ben's dad said it again, one final time, and this time his voice was strong.

"Run."

Then Richard Chenier pushed himself up from the floor and charged toward Mazi Ibo with a fury that Ben had never seen in his dad. His father caught Ibo in the back and slammed him full-tilt boogie into Elvis and Mike even as Mike Fallon's shotgun erupted and thunder echoed through the house.

Ben ran.

PIKE

Pike crept through the shrubs alongside the house as quietly as air. He reached an empty bedroom first, dark except for an open doorway framed in light. He heard the low voices of men deeper inside the house, but couldn't tell who was speaking or what they were saying.

Schilling appeared in the hall beyond the bedroom, carrying two duffels toward the rear, and then Schilling was gone. Pike cocked the .357.

The next two windows glowed with light. Pike eased closer, but kept out of their glow. Ibo was with

Richard and Ben, but Fallon and Schilling were missing. Pike was surprised to find Richard and Ben still alive, but Fallon was probably keeping them to use as hostages until the very last moment. In a perfect world, Fallon, Schilling, and Ibo would have been in the room together. Pike would have shot them through the window to end this mess. Now, if Pike shot Ibo, he would lose the advantage of surprise with Fallon and Schilling.

Pike knew that Cole was probably at the back of the house, but he decided to wait. Schilling and Fallon might step back into the room at any moment, and then Pike could finish it. Pike didn't want Cole to face these guys, not the way he was, and it would be safest for Ben and Richard. Pike braced his gun against an acacia tree to steady his aim. He settled in to wait.

Then Fallon pushed Cole into the room, and Pike couldn't wait any longer. He ran toward the back, searching for a way into the house.

25

. . .

The dingy kitchen tilted steeply and the back of my head pulsed where Fallon hit me. I tried to stay on my feet, but the room tilted the opposite way and I hit the floor hard. I tried to get up, but my arms and legs bobbed on a greasy vinyl ocean.

Ben.

A faraway voice said, "Come on, asshole."

The kitchen blurred, and then I fell again, thinking that my gun was in my hand, but when I looked down it wasn't. When I looked up, I wasn't in the kitchen anymore. A dark tower swayed over me and two blurs huddled against the far wall. I tipped forward, but caught myself with my hand as the world focused. I think I smiled, but maybe it only seemed that way.

"I found you."

Ben was ten feet in front of me.

Behind me, Fallon tossed two pistols into the pile of money, then spoke to Ibo.

"He had Eric's gun. I've gotta go see what happened."

Ibo stared at me.

"He keel Eric?"

"I don't know. Put him in the bathtub and use your knife. The shotgun's too noisy. Then take care of them."

Ibo pulled out a long curved knife as voices screamed within me. Roy Abbott shouted at me to suck it up. Crom Johnson yelled for me to Ranger on. My mother called my name. Nothing but Ben mattered. I would bring him home even if I was dead.

Ibo took one step toward me, just as Richard Chenier looked into my eyes as if he were seeing me for the first and only time that he would ever see me, and then he heaved up from the floor. Richard did not move fast or well, but he charged across the tiny room with the commitment of a father desperate to save his child. The shotgun exploded over my head. Richard hit Ibo from behind as the first shot punched into his side. He drove Ibo into me and me into Fallon as the second blast wrecked his thigh. I reared up into the shotgun as Ibo spun toward Richard with the knife. The shotgun exploded into the ceiling as Ben ran for the door.

I threw an elbow, but Fallon pushed my arm past and snapped the shotgun down across my face. I hooked my arm over the barrel, and jerked the shotgun close, but Fallon hung on. We bounced off the wall, locked together with the shotgun in a furious demon dance. I butted him, and his nose shattered. He snorted red. Fallon pulled hard on the shotgun, then suddenly let go, and I lost my balance. I fell backwards with the shotgun as Fallon grabbed Schilling's pistol from the money. All of it happened in milliseconds; maybe even faster. Ben screamed.

PIKE

Pike swung around the corner of the house with his gun in a two-hand combat grip, cocked and ready to fire. The backyard was clear. Pike slipped to the back door and glanced into the kitchen. He expected to see Schilling, but the kitchen was empty. Pike didn't like not knowing Schilling's position, but Fallon would kill Cole in a matter of moments.

Pike stepped inside and moved toward the hall, gun up and ready, though his shoulder burned and his grip on his pistol was not firm. The floor popped with his weight, but Pike didn't dare stop. He glanced at the back door to check for Schilling just as Fallon's shotgun went off twice—BOOM BOOM—so loud and heavy that the shots rattled the house.

Pike moved even faster, crossing the hall to enter the bedroom, all reaction now because thinking would slow him down. Fallon and Cole twisted together in a tight embrace, then Cole tumbled backwards with the shotgun. Pike drew down on Fallon in that same moment, finger tightening to drop the hammer, owning Fallon with a dead-on head shot even as Ibo screamed—

"*Eye havh dee boy.*"

Ibo held Ben in front of his head as a shield, with a knife to Ben's throat.

Pike jerked the .357 around at Ibo, but the shot wasn't clean and his hand wasn't steady. Fallon saw Pike in that same heartbeat and brought up his own handgun, inhumanly fast, as fast as Pike had ever seen, and Pike swung his .357 back onto Fallon, knowing in that hyperfast moment that Fallon had him cold, but Fallon hesitated because Cole brought up the shotgun, Cole screaming to pull Fallon's attention, and then all of them were caught in that instant between beats when the human heart is still.

SCHILLING

The gunfire and screams jolted Schilling with the certainty that he was about to die. He woke in Africa. He thought government troops were shooting his men in their sleep. He grabbed for his rifle and tried to roll into the bush, but his rifle wasn't next to him and he was on a driveway in Los Angeles. He crawled into the shrubbery beside the adjoining house.

Schilling thought, *fuck*. Then he puked.

His head cleared, but he felt drunk and woozy. He realized that Ibo, Fallon, and Cole were shouting. He wasn't in Africa; he was in L.A. They were in the house with the money.

Schilling felt the ground for his weapon, but couldn't find it. Fuckit. He crawled toward the house.

COLE

The three guns weaved like snakes poised to strike. I covered Fallon, then swung back to Ibo. Fallon's gun jumped from Pike to me, then back to Pike, and Pike shifted between Fallon and Ibo. Ibo held Ben high to protect his head and chest. If anyone shot, everyone would shoot, and all of us would be consumed by gunfire.

Ibo shouted again, making himself small behind Ben's dangling body.

"EYE HAVH DEE BOY!"

Richard groaned.

Ben struggled to break free. He was oblivious to the knife or maybe past caring. His eyes were on Richard.

I aimed at Ibo's legs. I could cut off his leg with Fallon's shotgun, but that wouldn't stop the knife. I edged to the side, looking for a better angle. Ibo backed into the corner, holding Ben higher, a seven-foot nightmare peeking past Ben's ear.

"Eye keel heem!"

Pike and Fallon were locked on each other, holding their pistols with two-hand grips, arms tight.

Fallon said, "Look at the knife. Shoot me, and he'll bleed out the kid."

Pike said, "He won't see it happen. Neither will you."

I said, "Joe?"

"I'm good."

"Eye do eet!"

"Can you get him, Joe?"

"Not yet."

I swung the shotgun to Fallon, then back to Ibo. The little room was humid with sweat, and close as a crypt. I shouted at Ibo.

"Put him down. Put him down and walk out."

Fallon edged toward the money, and Pike moved closer to Ibo. Pike was on one wall, me on the other; Ibo between us where the walls met. Ben struggled harder, and seemed to be reaching toward his pocket.

Fallon said, "We want the money, you want the kid. We can both walk out."

I swung the shotgun back toward Fallon.

"Sure, Fallon, good, let's do that. You and Ibo put down your weapons, then we'll put down ours."

Fallon smiled tightly, and shifted his aim back to Pike.

"You should drop yours first."

Richard tried to pull his legs under him but he slid in his own blood. I didn't know how much longer he would last.

Ben screamed then, his scream wailing and strange.

"Daddy!"

I edged closer to Ibo.

"Stay bahk!"

Ben struggled harder, and his hand slipped from his pocket. I saw what he held, and knew what he was planning to do.

Fallon shifted his aim from Pike to me. Sweat dripped from his hair to splash on the floor.

"He'll do it. We'll both do it. Give us the god-damned money and we'll give you the kid!"

"You'd kill him anyway."

All of it happened in milliseconds, or maybe even faster. They had us and we had them, but Ben was caught in the middle.

I said, "Ben?"

Ben's eyes were white with fear.

"I'm taking you home. You hear me, buddy? I'm going to bring you home. Joe. You on Fallon?"

"Yo."

I lowered the shotgun.

Fallon shifted his gun back to Joe, then came to me again. He didn't know what I was doing, and the not knowing scared him.

"Mazi!"

"I keel heem!"

I held the shotgun with the muzzle up, showing them that I wasn't going to shoot, and placed it on the floor. I straightened, watching Mazi, then took one step toward him. Fallon shifted his gun again.

Fallon shouted, "We'll kill him, Cole! We'll fuckin' kill you, too!"

I moved closer to Ben.

Ibo screamed, *"I do eet!"*

"I know. You and Fallon would both do it. You're animals."

My voice was quiet and conversational, like I was making an everyday observation about which brand of coffee they preferred. I stopped an arm's length from Ben. Fallon was behind me with the gun, so I couldn't see him, but Pike was behind me, too. I smiled quietly at Ben, the smile telling him that just as I trusted Joe, he needed to trust me; that he would be fine because I had come to bring him home, and would.

I said, "Any time you're ready, bud. Let's go home."

Giving him permission. Saying, do the thing you're thinking, and I will back your play.

Ben Chenier brought the Silver Star up like a claw and raked the medal into Ibo's eyes. Ibo was focused on me, and Ben caught him off guard. Ibo flinched, ducking his head, and that's when I moved. I jammed my fingers behind the blade and twisted the knife from Ben's throat as gunshots exploded behind me. The knife cut deep into my fingers, but I held tight and rolled Ibo's hand backwards over his wrist, turning the knife toward him. Ben tumbled free. Another shot rang out, then another. I didn't know what was happening across the room. I couldn't look.

PIKE

When Cole put down the shotgun and started toward Ibo, Fallon had the advantage. Pike wouldn't shoot so long as Ben was in danger; if he shot Fallon, Ibo would kill Ben; if Pike shot Ibo, Fallon would kill him in that same instant, then swing for Cole. Pike decided that if he got a clean cortical shot on Ibo, he would take it even though Fallon would kill him. Fallon would shoot Pike, then swing for Cole, but Cole might be fast enough to scoop up the shotgun before Fallon got turned around. But Ibo wasn't stupid, and seemed to sense what Pike was thinking; Ibo kept Ben high like a shield with Ben's head protecting his own. Pike had no target. He shifted his aim back to Fallon.

Pike watched Fallon's eyes flick back and forth as

Fallon weighed his own options: He could wait to see what Cole did, or shoot Pike, then take his chances with Cole. The first way, Fallon would be reactive; but if Fallon shot first, he would drive the event and have a measure of control. Cole's face was bloody and his eyes were dazed. Fallon would be thinking about that. He would be thinking that with Cole hurt he had a free shot to put down Pike, then he could still beat Cole. Pike wondered if Fallon knew about the damage to his arm. Fallon was Delta. He would use whatever weakness he found.

Pike thought, *He's going to shoot first.*

Fallon's forehead floated above the tip of Pike's gun. Pike's gun wobbled. His heart pounded, and sweat leaked down the sides of his face. Fallon had his gun up, too, aimed at Pike as Pike was aimed at him, but Fallon's gun was steady. Fallon could easily see Pike's gun wobble. Pike sensed an awareness in the man. Fallon saw his weakness. Their guns were only inches apart.

Fallon's gun came up another half-inch. Fallon had decided that he could win. He was setting himself to fire.

The boar snapped its jaws. It was setting itself to charge.

Pike glanced at Elvis. He glanced at Ben. The pistol's wood grip felt slippery, and his breath came fast, but this wasn't about the bear, and never had been. *His mother crawled under the kitchen table, crying and bloody as his father kicked her, eight-year-old Joe helpless to act; the old man chased down his defenseless son, broke the boy's nose, then used his belt;*

that's how it was, night after night. It was about protecting the people he loved no matter the cost: nothing was worse than doing nothing; not even death. The bear might beat you, but you still had to stand. Joe Pike would stand.

He braced himself for Fallon's bullet, then glanced again at Ibo, hoping for a shot, but Ibo still hid behind Ben. He glanced back at Fallon. The rock-steady gun.

Pike thought, *I'll kill you before I die.*

Then Ibo grunted in a way that neither man expected. Pike glimpsed a sudden movement as Cole and Ibo grappled. Fallon glanced to see, and Pike had his chance. He squeezed the trigger just as Eric Schilling charged out of the hall. Schilling slammed into Pike's back, driving Pike into Fallon. Hot pain flashed through Pike's shoulder, and the .357 boomed harmlessly past Fallon's ear. Fallon moved inhumanly fast. He rolled Pike's gun to the side, trapped Pike's gun arm, then whipped his pistol toward Pike's head. Pike slipped to the side, but Schilling punched him hard in the neck, then hooked Pike's bad arm. More pain flashed in Pike's shoulder and made him gasp. He dropped to his knees to slip Schilling's grip, wrapped Schilling's legs with his bad arm, and lifted. His arm screamed again, but Schilling upended. In the same moment, Fallon cracked his pistol down hard on Pike's face, then pushed the gun into Pike's shoulder. Fallon was fast, but Pike was fast, too. He trapped Fallon's wrist as the gun fired. Pike held on. He had Fallon's wrist, but his bad arm was weak. Fallon was slipping away. Fallon butted Pike hard on the cheek, then kneed him in the groin. Pike took the pain. Across the room, Cole and Ibo were locked in a motionless death struggle, but Ben had gone to his father. Schilling heaved to his knees, then scrambled for a gun that was lying in the money. Fallon kneed Pike again, but this time Pike caught his leg, held it, then swept Fallon's remaining leg out from under him and pushed him over. They crashed to the floor. Fallon's gun flew free with the impact. Two feet away, Schilling came up with the pistol and wheeled toward Pike. Pike rolled off Fallon, came up with his gun, and fired from the floor. He shot Eric Schilling twice in the chest. Schilling screamed, and fired wildly into the wall. Pike fired again, and blew out the side of Schilling's head. Pike rolled back toward Fallon, but Fallon caught the pistol in both hands. Both of them had the gun, and the gun was between them. Fallon's two good arms against Pike's one. Sweat and blood ran from their faces as both men tried to turn the gun. The burning in Pike's arm grew as his shoulder slowly failed. Fallon grunted with his effort, his grunts like a wild boar rooting in the dirt, *uhn, uhn, uhn*. Pike strained harder, but the gun slowly came toward his chest.

Pike thought that if he was going to die, he might as well die here, and he might as well die doing this.

But not yet.

Pike went into the deepest part of himself, a green leafy world of quiet and peace. It was the only place where Pike could truly be free, safe in his aloneness, and at peace with himself. Pike went to that place now, and he drew strength.

Pike stared into Fallon's animal eyes. Fallon sensed

that something had changed. Fear played over his face.

Pike's mouth twitched.

The gun moved toward Fallon.

COLE

The scars on Ibo's face glowed violet as he tried to turn the knife. He was a large, strong man, and he wanted to live, but I pushed so hard that the room darkened around me and filled with starburst speckles. Ibo's arm broke with a wet crack and his wrist folded. He moaned. More shots rang out behind me, but they seemed a part of someone else's world and not mine.

The knife touched the hollow at the base of Ibo's throat. Ibo tried to swing me away, but I held tight to his broken arm and pushed. He hissed as the knife went in. I pushed. The knife slid deep. Ibo's eyes grew wider. His mouth opened and closed. I pushed until the knife wouldn't go farther, then Ibo made a long sigh and his eyes lost focus.

I let go and watched him fall. He slumped like a great tall tree and took forever to hit the floor.

I turned, barely able to stand. Eric Schilling was crumpled in a heap on the money. Ben was with Richard. Pike and Fallon were locked together on the floor, struggling. I picked up the shotgun and staggered over to them. I pointed the shotgun at Fallon's head.

I said, "That's it."

Fallon looked up.

"That's it, you sonofabitch. It's over."

Fallon studied the end of the shotgun, then stared at me. They had a pistol between them. They were fighting for it.

I shouldered the shotgun.

"Let go of it, Fallon. Let go."

Fallon glanced at Pike, then nodded.

The pistol between them fired one loud time—BOOM!—and I thought Joe had been shot, but Fallon slumped back against the wall. Pike rolled away fast and came up with the pistol, ready in case Fallon made a move, but Fallon only blinked down at the hole in his chest. He seemed surprised to see it even though he had made it himself. He looked up at us. Then he was dead.

I said, "Ben?"

I staggered sideways, and fell to a knee. It hurt. My hand was bleeding badly. It hurt, too.

"Ben?"

Ben was trying to make Richard stand up. Richard moaned, so I guessed he was still hanging on. Pike kept me from falling onto my face, and pushed a handkerchief into my hand.

"Wrap your hand and see about Ben. I'll get an ambulance."

I tried to stand again, but couldn't, so I crawled to Ben Chenier. I put my arms around him.

"I found you, Ben. I have you. I'm going to bring you home."

Ben shuddered like he was freezing, and sobbed words that I did not understand. Pike called for an ambulance, then eased us aside. He tied off Richard's leg with his belt to stop the bleeding, then used Schilling's shirt as a compress on the belly wound. I held Ben tight through it all, and never once let go.

"I have you," I said. "I have you."

The sirens came as Ben's tears soaked my chest.

PART FIVE

· · ·

FOUND

26
. . .

The ambulance arrived before the first of the radio cars. Ben wanted to go with his father to the hospital, but the paramedics, correctly and like always, would not allow it. More sirens were coming. That would be the police.

Pike said, "I'll wait. You take Ben."

Ben and I crossed the street to my car. The one dog still howled, making me wonder if it was alone. People from the neighboring houses milled in their front yards, watching the ambulance. Living here wouldn't be the same anymore.

I held Ben until the first radio car arrived. They didn't scream to a screeching stop like you see on TV; they cruised slowly up the street because they didn't know what they would find. We got into my car.

I said, "Let's call your mom."

When Lucy realized it was me, she said, "Is Ben all right? Please God tell me he's all right."

Her voice shook.

"He's as right as he could be. It was bad, Luce. It was awful."

"Oh, thank God. Jesus God, thank you. What about Richard?"

Ben sat quietly while I told Lucy what happened. I was careful in what I said; I didn't know if Ben knew about Richard's involvement, and I didn't want him to hear it from me. Lucy and Richard could tell him, or maybe they wouldn't tell him at all. If she wanted me to pretend that none of this happened, I would. If she wanted me to keep it from Ben, I would. If she wanted me to lie to the police and in court to cover for Ben's father, I would do that, too.

I told her where they were bringing Richard, and offered either to take Ben home or meet her at the hospital. She said she would meet us, then asked if she could speak with her son.

I gave the phone to Ben.

"Your mom."

Ben didn't say anything as we drove to the hospital, but he held onto my arm, and, when I wasn't shifting or steering, I held onto him.

We reached the hospital first. We sat on a long bench in the ER waiting room while the doctors did their work. We sat close, with my arm around his shoulders. Before it was done, Richard Chenier would have been in surgery for eighteen hours. That's a long time under the knife.

Two West L.A. detectives arrived along with a

uniformed sergeant-supervisor. They asked the ad-
mitting nurse about the gunshot victim, then the
older detective walked over. He had short blond hair
and glasses.

He said, "Excuse me. Are you with the man who
was shot?"

"No."

"What's that on your pants?"

"Barbeque sauce."

He moved on to ask the next person.

Ben said, "Why'd you say no?"

"Your mom's going to be here soon. We don't
want to be stuck in a room with those guys."

He seemed to understand that.

I watched the cops until they returned to the ad-
mitting desk, then I leaned toward Ben. Here was this
little ten-year-old boy. He looked so small. He looked
so young.

I said, "How're you doing?"

"I'm okay."

"You saw some awful stuff today. You had some
really bad things happen. It's okay to be scared. It's
okay to talk about it."

"I wasn't scared."

"I was scared. I was really, really scared. I'm really
scared right now."

Ben looked at me, and then frowned.

"Maybe I was a little scared."

"You want a Coke or something?"

"Yeah. Let's see if they have Mountain Dew."

We were looking for the soft-drink machine when
Lucy came through the sliding doors. Her strides

were so fast that she might have been running. We spotted her first.

I called to her.

"Lucy!"

Ben took off running.

"Mommy!"

Lucy crumbled into tears. She hugged Ben so tight that she might have been trying to crush him into her body. She covered him with kisses and smeared him with tears, but that was all right. Every boy wants that from his mother whether he admits it or not. Especially on days like this. I'm sure of it. I know that for a fact.

I walked over. I stood near. If the detectives thought anything of it, they were kind enough not to intrude.

Lucy opened her eyes and saw me. She cried harder, and then she opened her arms.

I said, "I brought him home."

"Yes. Yes, you did."

I held them as hard as I could, but even that wasn't enough.

27
· · ·

Sixteen days later, Lucy came to my house to tell me good-bye. It was a bright, crisp afternoon. No hawks floated overhead, no coyotes had sung for as long as I could remember, but the owl had come back to the pine tree. The night before, he called me.

Lucy and Ben had given up their apartment in Beverly Hills. Lucy had left her job. They were moving back to Baton Rouge, Louisiana. Ben was already there with his grandparents. I understood; really, I did. These things don't happen to normal people, and shouldn't.

They weren't going back for Richard.

Lucy said, "After all that happened to him, Ben needs to be with familiar people and places. He needs to feel safe and secure. I've got a house in our old neighborhood. He'll have his old friends."

We stood on the deck, side by side at the rail. We had spoken often these past sixteen days. We had talked over what she would do, and why, but she was still uneasy and awkward. Here we were, saying good-bye. Here she was, leaving. She would be seeing me soon enough. Richard had been indicted.

The two of us didn't say very much that afternoon, but most of it had already been said. Being with her still felt good to me. We had been way too good and way too special to end it on awkward moments or bad feelings. I didn't want that.

I gave her my best smile, the Studly Do-Right Eye-Wiggle Special, and bumped her hip. Mr. Playful. Mr. Brave.

"Luce, you've only said that eight hundred times. You don't have to say it again. I understand. I think it's right for Ben."

She nodded, but still looked awkward. Maybe it had to be awkward.

I said, "I'm going to miss you. I'm going to miss Ben. I miss you guys already."

Lucy blinked hard and stared at the canyon. She leaned far out on the rail, maybe hoping that I wouldn't notice, or maybe trying to see something that she hadn't yet seen.

She said, "God, I hate this part."

"You're doing this for Ben and for you. It's right for you. I'm good with that."

She pushed in from the rail and came close to me. It was all I could do not to cry.

My voice was a whisper.

"Don't say it. Please don't say it."

"So long as you know."

Lucy Chenier turned and ran into my house. The front door shut. Her car started, then pulled away.

I said, "Good-bye."

28
. . .

My phone rang two days after Lucy left. It was Star-key.

She said, "You gotta be the luckiest asshole I know."

"Who is this?"

"Very funny. Ha ha."

"What's up?"

Joe Pike and I were painting my deck. After the deck, we were going to paint my house. I might even wash my car.

I said, "No offense, but I'm expecting my lawyer to call. We have this little matter of felony burglary."

Pike looked over from the end of the deck. His hands and arms were gray from sanding dried filler and spackle. The postal service that we destroyed was owned by a man named Fadhim Gerella. We had repaid Mr. Gerella for the damage we had done to his business, as well as additional money for lost business during the time he was closed. Mr. Gerella was happy with that, and had refused to press charges, though the San Gabriel District Attorney was being tough about it.

Starkey said, "Your lawyer's going to call, all right, but I'm going to tell you first."

"Tell me what?"

Pike glanced over.

"I just got off the phone with my guy down at Parker about that. You're in the clear, Cole. You and Mr. Sunglasses. The governments of Sierra Leone, Angola, and El Salvador—three fucking *governments,* Cole—interceded in your behalf. You bozos aced three turds up for *genocide,* dude. They'll probably give you a fuckin' medal."

I sat on the deck.

"I don't hear anything, Cole. You still with me?"

"Hang on."

I cupped the phone and told Pike. He never looked up from the sanding.

Starkey said, "Does this call for a celebration or what? How about I buy you some sushi and eight or ten drinks? Better yet, how about you pay? I'm a cheap date—I don't drink."

"You want to take us out?"

"Not Pike, moron. Just you."

"Starkey, are you asking me out?"

"Don't be so full of yourself."

I wiped the sweat and the dust from my eyes, and stared out over the canyon.

"Cole? Did you faint from the excitement?"

"Don't take this wrong, Starkey. I like it that you asked, but this isn't a good time for me."

"Okay. I get that."

"It's been kinda hard."

"I understand, Cole. Forget it. Listen, I'll call you another time."

Starkey hung up. I put down my phone, and stared at the canyon. A dark speck floated over the ridge. Soon, it was joined by another. I went to the rail and watched them. I smiled. The hawks were back.

Pike said, "Call her."

I took the phone inside, and, after a while, I did.

I have the dream often now, almost every night, some nights more than once: The sky darkens; the tortured oaks sway heavy with moss; the night's soft breeze stirs with anger and fear. I am once more in that nameless place of graves and monuments. I stare down at the hard black rectangle, burning to know who lies within the earth, but no name marks this resting place. I have spent my whole life searching for the secrets I do not know.

The earth calls my name.

I stoop. I place my palms on the marble, and gasp at the cold. Ice crawls up my arms like ants beneath my skin. I lurch to my feet and try to run, but my legs will not answer. The wind rises, bending the trees.

Shadows flicker at the edge of light, and voices whisper.

My mother appears in the mist. She is young, the way she was, and fragile as a baby's breath.

"Mama! Mama, help me!"

She floats against the wind like a spirit.

"Please, you have to help me!"

I reach for her, praying she will take my hand, but she hovers without response as if she does not see. I want her to save me from the secrets here. I want her to protect me from the truth.

"I'm scared. I don't want to be here, but I don't know how to leave. I don't know what to do."

I hunger for her warmth. I need the safety of her arms. I try to go to her, but my feet are rooted deeply.

"I can't move. Help me, Mama."

She sees me. I know she sees me because her eyes fill with sorrow. I reach for her until my shoulders scream but she is too far away. I am furious. I hate her and love her in the same awful moment.

"Goddamnit, I don't want to be alone anymore. I never wanted to be alone."

The winds rise to a howl; a bit of her blows away like smoke.

"Mama, please! Don't leave me again!"

Cracks scribe over her as if she were a puzzle. A piece of her blows away. Then another.

"Mama!"

The pieces that were my mother blow away. Not even a shadow remains. Not even a shadow.

She is gone. She has left me.

I stare at the grave with a broken heart. In the

strange way of this life, a shovel appears in my hands. If I dig, I will find; if I find, I will know.

The black earth opens.

The casket is revealed.

A voice that is not my own pleads for me to stop, to look away, to save myself from what lies here, but I no longer care. I am alone. I want the truth.

I push my hands into the cold earth and pry my fingers beneath the lid. Splinters pierce my flesh. The casket opens with a scream.

I stare at the small body, and I am looking at myself.

The child is me.

He opens his eyes. He sobs with joy as I lift him from the crypt, and throws his arms around me. We hold each other tight.

"It's all right," I say. "I found you, and I will never leave."

The wind rages. Leaves tumble across the tombs and the damp mist cuts through my clothes, but all that matters is that I have found him.

His laughter is a chime in the darkness. So is mine.

"You're not alone," I say. "You will never again be alone."

Please turn the page for
Robert Crais's latest
Elvis Cole and Joe Pike novel,

A DANGEROUS MAN

1.

Isabel Roland

Three tellers were working the morning Isabel Roland was kidnapped. Clark Davos, a sweet guy whose third baby had just been born; Dana Chin, who was funny and wore fabulous shoes; and Isabel, the youngest teller on duty. Isabel began working at the bank a little over a year ago, three months before her mother died. Five customers were in line, but more customers entered the bank every few seconds.

Mr. Ahbuti wanted bills in exchange for sixteen rolls of nickels, twelve rolls of dimes, and a bag filled with quarters. As Isabel ran coins through a counter, her cell phone buzzed with a text from her gardener. Sprinkler problems. Isabel felt sick. The little house she inherited from her mother was driving her crazy. The sprinklers, a leaky roof over the porch, roots in the pipes because of a stupid pepper tree, the ancient range that made scary popping noises every time she turned on the left front burner. Always a new problem, and problems cost money. Isabel had grown up in the house, and loved the old place, but her modest salary wasn't enough to keep it.

Isabel closed her eyes.

Why did you have to die?

Abigail George touched her arm, startling her. Abigail was the assistant branch manager.

"I need you to take an early lunch. Break at eleven, okay?"

Isabel had punched in at nine. It was now only ten forty-one, and Izzy had eaten an Egg McMuffin and hash browns on her way into work. She felt like a bloated whale.

"But it's almost eleven now. I just ate."

Abigail smiled at Mr. Ahbuti, and lowered her voice.

"Clark has to leave early. The baby again."

They both glanced at Clark. His baby had come early, and his wife wasn't doing so well.

Abigail shrugged apologetically.

"I'm sorry. Eleven, okay? *Please?*"

Abigail squeezed her arm, and hurried away.

Isabel gave Mr. Ahbuti his cash, and called for the next customer when Dana hissed from the adjoining station.

"*Iz.*"

Dana tipped her head toward the door and mouthed the words.

"*It's him.*"

Ms. Kleinman reached Izzy's window as the man

joined the line. He was tall and dark, with ropey arms, a strong neck, and lean cheeks. Every time he came in, Dana went into heat.

"*Iz.*"

Dana finished with her customer, and whispered again.

"Studburger."

"Stop."

"Double meat. Extra sauce."

"Shh!"

Ms. Kleinman made a one-hundred-dollar cash withdrawal.

As Izzy processed the transaction, she snuck glances at the man. Gray sweatshirt with the sleeves cut off, faded jeans tight on his thighs, and dark glasses masking his eyes. Isabel stared at the bright red arrows tattooed high on his arms. She wanted to touch them.

Dana whispered.

"Manmeat on a stick."

Isabel counted out twenties.

As Ms. Kleinman walked away, Dana whispered again.

"Finger lickin' good."

Izzy cut her off by calling the next customer.

"Next, please."

The man was now third in line. Dana called for a customer, and the man was now second. Clark called, and the man was hers.

"*Iz.*"

Dana.

"Ask him out."

"Sh!"

"You know you want to. Do it!"

Izzy said, "Next, please."

Dana hissed, "Do it!"

When he reached her window, Izzy smiled brightly.

"Good morning. How may I help you?"

He laid out three checks and a deposit slip. Two of the checks were made payable to Joe Pike, and the third to cash. They totaled a considerable amount.

Joe Pike said, "For deposit."

"You're Mr. Pike?"

She knew his name, and he probably knew she knew. He came in every three or four weeks.

"I've helped you before."

He nodded, but offered no other response. He didn't seem friendly or unfriendly. He didn't seem interested or uninterested. She couldn't read his expression.

Isabel fed the checks through a scanner. She wanted to say something clever, but felt stupid and awkward.

"And how's your day so far?"

"Good."

"It's such a pretty day, and here I am stuck in the bank."

Pike nodded.

"You're so tan, I'll bet you're outside a lot."

"Some."

Nods and one-word answers. He clearly wasn't interested. Isabel entered the transaction into her terminal, and gave him the deposit receipt.

The man said, "Thank you."

He walked away, and Isabel felt embarrassed, as if his lack of interest proved she was worthless.

"*Iz!*"

Dana leered across the divider.

"I saw you talking!"

"He thanked me. Saying thanks isn't talking."

"He never talks. He thinks you're *hot*."

"He didn't even see me."

"Shut *up*! He *wants* you!"

If only.

Isabel wondered if she could scrape together two hundred dollars for a new garden timer.

She glanced at her watch. Ten fifty-two. Eight minutes from a lunch she didn't want, and an event that would change her life.

2.

Karbo and Bender

Karbo and Bender missed her at home by ten minutes. Materials found inside gave them her place of employment, so now they waited at a meter six blocks from a bank near the Miracle Mile.

Karbo slumped in the passenger seat, sipping a café mocha.

"Ever kidnap anyone?"

Bender glanced away. Bender was the driver. Karbo was the smile. They had worked for Hicks before, but never together. Karbo and Bender met for the first time at four that morning outside a strip mall in Burbank. They would part in approximately two hours, and never meet again.

Karbo said, "Sorry. My mistake."

No questions allowed. They knew what they were

supposed to do, how they were supposed to do it, and what was expected. Hicks prepped his people.

Bender gestured behind them.

"Here he comes."

Karbo lowered his window.

Hicks was a hard, pale dude in his forties. Nice-looking, not a giant, but broader than average. Nonthreatening, if you didn't look close. A nasty edge lurked in his eyes, but he hid it well. Karbo and Bender were nice-looking, nonthreatening guys, too. Especially Karbo.

Hicks had come from the bank.

"She's a teller. Figure on making the grab at lunch."

Bender arched his eyebrows.

"Why lunch?"

"People eat lunch. Employees park in back, but with all these little cafés, no way she'll drive. She'll probably exit the front, and give you a shot. You get the shot, take it."

Bender's eyebrows kissed in a frown.

"Wouldn't it make sense to wait at her house, grab her when she gets home?"

Hicks glanced left and right, relaxed, just looking around.

"Time is an issue. You want out, say so, and I'll get someone else."

Karbo changed the subject. He didn't want out. He wanted the money.

"I have a question. What if she goes out the back?"

"If she exits the rear, you're out of the play. If she isn't alone, say she comes out with a friend, you're out of the play. Maybe she won't even come out.

Maybe she brought a sandwich. No way to know, right? You have one job, and only the one."

Karbo said, "The front."

People would be watching the rear, for sure, but this was how Hicks operated. Compartmentalization. Minimum information. If an element got popped, they had nothing to give. Karbo admired the tough, precise way Hicks did business.

Hicks rested his hand on the door.

"Picture."

Hicks had given them a five-by-seven photograph of a twenty-two-year-old woman. Having changed the play, he didn't want the picture in their possession. The picture was evidence.

Bender returned the picture, and Hicks offered a final look.

"Burn her face into your brains. We can't have a mistake."

A high school photo printed off the internet showed a young woman with short dark hair, glasses, and a smile with a crooked incisor.

Karbo said, "Burned."

Bender cleared his throat. Karbo sensed the man thought they were moving too fast, but the money was huge, and their involvement would end in minutes.

Bender said, "What's she wearing?"

"Pink shirt. Kinda dull, not bright. A pink shirt over a tan skirt. I couldn't see her shoes."

Hicks tucked the picture into his jacket.

"She'll be easy to spot, but if anything looks weird, drive away. Anyone with her, drive away. Am I clear?"

Karbo and Bender nodded.

"Clear."

"Go."

Hicks walked away and Bender eased from the curb.

Their ride was a dark gray Buick SUV owned by a leasing company in La Verne, California. Late model, low miles, the full option package. They had picked up the Buick at 4:22 that morning, specifically for use in the crime. After they delivered the girl, they would hand off the Buick, pick up their cars and money, and go their separate ways.

Karbo thought Bender was having second thoughts, but Bender surprised him.

"Beautiful day, isn't it? Lovely, lovely day."

Karbo studied the man for a moment. "Yeah."

"Gorgeous. A perfect day."

Bender hadn't said ten words all morning, even when they were searching the woman's house. Karbo figured he was nervous.

"I know we're not supposed to ask, but you've worked gigs before?"

Bender tapped the blinker and changed lanes. "Three or four."

"This will be easy. Hicks's gigs are always easy."

"Snatching a person in front of a bank in broad daylight can't make the top of the Easy list."

"You didn't have to say yes. You should've backed out."

"Right."

"I don't want to work with someone I can't trust."

"I'm concerned, is all. He's making this up on the fly."

"A lot of these gigs, this is what happens."

"You're not concerned? You don't see the risk here?"

Karbo saw the risk. He also saw the reward.

"Look at this face."

Karbo grinned and fingered his dimples.

"I'll have her in the car in ten seconds tops. No big scene, I promise. Five minutes later, she's out of our lives. What could be easier?"

"You may be a moron."

Karbo shrugged.

"True, but you get to stay in the car. I'm the guy who gets out."

Bender finally nodded.

"You're right. And if anything looks weird, we drive away."

"Damned right we do. Fast."

Bender seemed to relax, and found a spot at a meter with an eyes-forward view of the bank.

Karbo liked the location. A commercial street lined with single-story storefronts two blocks south of Olympic. A straight shot to the freeway if needed. The girl would turn toward or away from them when she left the bank, and either was fine. A lot of people were out and about, but this shouldn't matter if Karbo did his job quickly and well.

Karbo said, "You were right."

"About?"

"The day. It's a beautiful day in the neighborhood."

"You're a moron. A perfect day doesn't make this any less risky."

They watched the bank. They didn't pay attention

to the people who went into the bank, or the men who came out. They watched for a twenty-two-year-old woman wearing a pink shirt over a tan skirt.

They paid no attention to the man wearing a sleeveless gray sweatshirt. They did not see the red arrows tattooed high on his arms, and barely noticed when he entered the bank. They paid even less attention when he emerged a few minutes later.

This was their mistake.

Their perfect day was about to turn bad.

3.

Isabel

Ten fifty-three.

Isabel helped her last customer, logged out of her terminal, and closed her station. She wasn't hungry, so she wondered if she had time to run home and catch the gardener.

Dana said, "Iz?"

Dana leered, and lowered her voice.

"We can look up his number. You can call, and tell him there was a problem with the transaction."

Isabel rolled her eyes, and left the bank at eleven-oh-two.

She didn't feel up to dealing with the gardener, so she decided to get a smoothie. She was debating between chocolate and chocolate-caramel when a shiny new SUV pulled to the curb ahead of her. A good-looking guy climbed out, opened the rear passenger door, and looked around as if he was confused. He saw her, and offered a tentative smile.

"Oh, hey, excuse me?"

Izzy returned his smile.

"Yes?"

He approached and touched her arm, exactly as Abigail had touched her arm moments before. His smile and manner were halfway between embarrassed and little-boy-charming.

"I'm supposed to return this gift, and I can't find the darned address. I'm totally lost."

He touched her toward the open door, his fingers a polite invitation to help with his problem.

Isabel went with him, and saw nothing inside but a clean backseat in the clean car beneath a clean blue sky. Another man sat at the wheel, and never looked at her.

Isabel didn't have time to turn, or ask which address he couldn't find. He shoved her hard, shoulder and hip, and drove her into the car. She grabbed at the edge of the roof, trying to save herself, but her grip broke free.

"Stop, what are you—stop!"

He dove in on top of her. The door slammed.

Isabel screamed, but his hand covered her mouth. She screamed as hard as she could, but her scream could not escape.

4.

Joe Pike

Upscale mid-city area: boutiques and pastry shops, a Tesla filling a loading zone, an older gentleman walking twin beagles, a homeless man splayed in the shade from a shopping cart heavy with plastic bags. Pike wasn't looking to save someone's life on the day he left the bank.

Pike's red Jeep Cherokee was parked across the street. He departed the bank at 10:54, and slid behind the wheel. He tucked the deposit receipt into the console, removed his .357 Magnum from beneath the front seat, and considered the two female tellers.

Dana and Isabel. Pike had noticed the expressive glances and whispered comments they traded. Their infatuation might have been welcome if they worked at a coffee shop or fitness center, but not at a job where they had access to his banking information. Pike's current business interests included a partnership in a detective agency, a custom gun shop in Culver City, and several rental properties. His former employers included the United States Marine Corps, the Los Angeles Police Department, and various private military contractors. During his contract years, his fees were paid by foreign governments approved by the United States, shell companies controlled by the CIA and NSA, and multinational corporations. This employment had been legal, but the transfer of funds from his employers had left a digital trail that a curious bank employee might question. Pike had maintained accounts at this particular bank for almost two years, and wondered if it was time to move on.

Pike was pondering this when Isabel's pink shirt caught his attention. She stepped from the bank, paused to put on a pair of sunglasses, and set off along the sidewalk. A dark gray SUV eased to the curb ahead of her. The driver's head turned as the vehicle passed, and something about the way he tracked her felt off.

Pike noticed details. The Marines had trained him to maintain situational awareness. Multiple tours in hot spots from Central America to Afghanistan had baked in his skills. The driver wasn't simply looking at Isabel; he seemed to be locked on a target.

A nice-looking man got out of the passenger seat, and opened the backseat door. Pike saw the man's head and shoulders across the roof. He turned, and Isabel smiled. They appeared to know each other, but Pike read a question in her body language.

The man touched her arm, and gestured toward the vehicle. Isabel went with him as the older gentleman with the beagles passed behind them. The older gentleman paid no attention.

Isabel and the man looked in the SUV, and disappeared so quickly the SUV might have swallowed them. In the instant she vanished, Pike saw a flash of shock in her eyes. Her fingers clutched the roof, and then she was gone. The blinker came on, and the SUV eased into traffic.

Pike wasn't sure what had happened. He watched the departing vehicle, and clocked the surroundings. The gentleman urged his beagles along, but a woman in a bright floral dress stood frozen. She gaped at the SUV as if she had seen something monstrous, but didn't know what to make of it. No one else stopped, or stared, or shouted for help.

The SUV put on its blinker, and turned at the next corner.

But the skin across Pike's back tingled as it had in the deserts and jungles. He started his Jeep, and followed.